Also by Harriette Simpson Arnow

THE FLOWERING OF THE CUMBERLAND
(1963)

SEEDTIME ON THE CUMBERLAND
(1960)

THE DOLLMAKER
(1954)

HUNTER'S HORN
(1949)

MOUNTAIN PATH
(1936)
(as Harriette Simpson)

The
Weedkiller's
Daughter

THE
WEEDKILLER'S
DAUGHTER

Harriette Simpson Arnow

Alfred A. Knopf

NEW YORK · 1970

This Is a Borzoi Book
Published by Alfred A. Knopf, Inc.

Copyright © 1969 by Harriette Simpson Arnow
All rights reserved under International
and Pan-American Copyright Conventions.
Published in the United States
by Alfred A. Knopf, Inc., New York,
and simultaneously in Canada
by Random House of Canada Limited, Toronto.
Distributed by Random House, Inc., New York.
Library of Congress Catalog Card Number: 68–23960
Acknowledgment is extended to Folkways Records
for permission to quote from
"Les Trois Beaux Canards," sung by Jacques Labrecque."
Manufactured in the United States of America
First Edition

The Weedkiller's Daughter

1

"Stand right here," they had said. "It's the safest spot. The place looks deserted, but there's a cook in the kitchen. The back door is open; if someone tries to bother you, scream and run in."

And so she stood among the garbage cans in the shadows behind the drive-in and watched the couple she called Uncle Jeff and Aunt Margaret as they rushed on tiptoe back to their car; soundless as thieves they were trying to be. She could still feel their kisses on each cheek, and hear their whispered good-byes along with all those silly warnings.

Would she be that way, afraid, when she was as old as they —somewhere around fifty? One of the biggest nights of her life, yet they worried over the time. "So late," they had said. "Your parents will get suspicious. And that sack of party favors and things under your *rebozo* makes it bulge. Try to keep your arms over it—just in case."

They had acted as if the warmish rainy night were a wild, girl-hungry beast; and Detroit, even away up here past the northern edge, was for her a jungle of rioters and holdup men. The silliest thing was the way they had worried over that boy waiting on the other side of the drive-in to take her home. His driving? His character? His way with girls?

She had tried to soothe them. "He's no more interested in me than I am in him. I think he's some kind of big-wheel senior at

3

school. I've heard him talk in Assembly. Anyway, this is more business than a real date. He has a perfect reputation. So polite; he somehow makes me think of a plastic gardenia. He's kind of—."

"Priggish?" Uncle Jeff had finished for her; and both had smiled as if she were still five years old. Now, they planned to follow his car: "—just to make certain you get safely home."

She watched the dim shapes disappear into the car parked near the end of the exit on the empty side of the drive-in parking lot, unlighted because when the night grew old, as now, few customers came. The taillights went on; and the car moved slowly, almost soundlessly, into a side street, where it stopped at the spot from which "we can see you safely into that boy's car."

She loved them, but—. She'd better get to the corner of the building; there, she'd peep, then dash for the car; mustn't let him know her "protectors" were following him. She staggered after the first step as her foot came hard down against damp cement, her big toe plowing into a gucky softness. She had unknowingly worked a foot out of the miserable high-heeled thing her mother had bought for what she thought was to be a high-school party. Careful not to loosen her arms from the bulging shawl, she picked up the shoe, and, not wanting to put that dirty big toe back into it, carried it to the corner.

She stopped to study the drive-in lot, deserted save for the boy's car, empty. Back to her, he paced restlessly up and down as he watched the street. If she ran tiptoe, she might make it into the car without his seeing that she wore only one shoe. And she had better hurry. The click of his heels on the cement said he was already annoyed by the long wait.

The stillness of the sleeping city let him hear the small sounds she made. He also saw that lopsided run in one shoe, she thought. Hard to say; the long wait had got him, and he didn't mind showing it. He answered her apologies for being late with an angry:

"*You're* sorry! One hour and forty minutes I waited in that cruddy joint. I had to tip the carhop extra to let me stay. —Please buckle your seat belt."

She sat stiff and straight, arms clutched about the great

4

black shawl wrapped around head, shoulders, and breast. They were on the expressway before she had with quick but cautious movements of her hands, fastened the belt. "You chose the drive-in," she reminded him. " 'Respectable and inconspicuous,' you said. Add the extra tip to your time-and-a-half for overtime."

"But who can pay for the static your old man's going to throw out when I bring his fifteen year—."

"Pardon me, but I'll be sixteen in April."

"This is September. —home at three o'clock in the morning. And stewed. I saw you staggering up to the car."

The secret of where she had been would cool him down. She couldn't tell that. Yet she should try to talk. And how did one talk to an angry boy who was nothing more than a familiar stranger? "I wish you wouldn't imagine things," she got out at last. "I was at a lovely place. *Warm* is the only word I can think of, no chills from saying the wrong thing, or disapproving stares."

"Who doesn't need a place to take the chill away? But if I knew the name of any night spot that lets a young girl like you drink until she's the picture of a little floozy, I'd report it."

"Thank you. Do you charge extra for this lecture or does it come in a package deal like the how-to lesson with the new sailboat?"

He ignored her question. She looked behind, and saw, keeping at a discreet distance, the familiar lights of Uncle Jeff's car. There was little else to watch. The tired time of night had come; she would have been lonesome, had not the warm feeling from the party been wrapped about her like the shawl. Everything perfect and beautiful—except for one big lack.

Uncle Lans, her godfather, could not come. He'd telephoned apologies and sent gifts, but no gift could take the place of his actual self. And she hadn't seen him in so long, so long. A good while ago his wife had died, and left him to manage his children, see to the servants, plus his man's work in business; it wasn't his fault he couldn't get to the party or have the time for her he'd used to have when she was little. —Think of the nice things you've had this evening; big ones, little ones—like getting there, for example.

5

Plane trips were almost always nice, but this one, swooping through the twilight, north and east into Canada, had been—if she could write a poem—but no poor poem by Susan Schnitzer could say what the clouds had said. If she could paint a picture. Two pictures: earth below in the smudgy twilight, lights of the heavy traffic glinting through spatters of rain; the ugliness of summer's dying before autumn came alive; more ugliness in the hard, too-shiny airport corridors, always dead-seeming, no matter how loud the people.

At last, a seat by a porthole as you sailed into the cloudlands, then higher and into the sunset on the valleys and mountains of cloud below, a pearly white world touched here and there with rosy light from the setting sun. Times, you could think a ship's captain had invited you to the bridge to watch some wild, wild sea, breaking-wave mountains and flying foam caught one microinstant in stillness. As you flew farther from the sunset, the valleys filled with twilight, and—.

"You smell like The Primitive's basement at wine-bottling time. I can't take you home like this. Try a cigarette—or something. I don't smoke."

The disgust and anger in his voice brought her down from the cloud world, but the words were only senseless sounds until at last *wine* penetrated. The smell of wine was bugging him. She shrugged. Supposing her parents were home? They wouldn't smell the wine and that wonderful champagne on her breath because of the liquor on their own. "Do you know," she asked, "there are places in the world where it's no sin for even children to have wine?"

He nodded. "But Eden Hills is not one of those places."

She sighed. "I know." She studied the humps and bulges under the shawl; nodded after a moment, then began a careful loosening. In spite of her care, the shawl slipped from her head to let two large silver clasps slide down so that hair fell across her face until only the tip of her nose was visible. Searching under the shawl with one hand, she found at last a party favor—a small box of mints. She opened the dainty box after one annoyed glance at the boy; she had intended the little gift as a keepsake to remain unopened forever; but anything to cool this

6

piece of crossness by her side. She offered him one; he declined, but she ate two, slowly, as if the candies were pills to be chewed. They may have helped her breath, but the mint smell seemed to do nothing for the boy.

He started another lecture on "such places," that ended with: "If I had known what you were up to, I'd never have helped you. And no name-dropping about my help."

She tossed back her hair. "Do you really think Robert Thomas Hedrick III—that is your name isn't it?—has weight enough to fall?"

He was good at ignoring insults; never heard that one; smoothly old-mannish as he said: "And don't tell Iggy. Poor kid would feel guilty. He somehow managed to give me the idea you were some kind of pitiful custody case."

She gave him a quick speculative glance, then turned back to road-watching. It would be nice to cool him down with the truth, but never could she say: "Yes, I am a kind of custody case. You see there was in my family a kind of civil war; ended now for years—or so my parents think. I lost; the winning side got me. Yes, I drank wine; mostly champagne to celebrate my grandmother's sixty-second birthday." She glanced around to find him looking at her instead of the road.

"Now, will you get into your other shoe, and fix that hair? We'll be there soon."

"Don't worry. Remember? We danced so hard my hairdo crumbled. Anyway there'll be nobody home to see. —Oh, I just remembered, *I've* danced, but not my shoes."

She searched again under the shawl until she found a square of sandpaper. "Ah, the dance for the shoes; I've found it." She chanted softly to herself as with quick, light raspings she roughened the slipper's sole: "You're too pretty to scruff, hateful though you may be, but I must, I must. Just enough to show the floor was crowded; all the football boys, the cheer-leading girls, and the marching bandsmen, all come out for the first big high-school formal of the year, the Opening-Our-Football-Season Prom. My escort was a marvelous dancer, and oh so surefooted, so only a bit of scuffing over heels and toes."

The sandpapering quickened as she kept time to the jump-

7

ing syllables: *"Lev' ton pied, légèr' bergère / Lev' ton pied légèrement,—."* Still singing, she cleaned her dirtied toe with a handkerchief, then put on the slippers. She was fishing on the floor for the hair-clasps when she felt fingers give the small of her bare back one quick investigative touch. She jerked away, and sat pressed against the door, her glance on the boy frightened as well as embarrassed.

"Pardon me," he said, his voice pure ice, "but I couldn't believe my eyes. Can't you fasten your dress?"

"I'll try," she said, and sat as straight as possible, stomach sucked in, as she reached behind and tugged several times. She gave up, explaining: "The zipper won't go any higher." All at once it had been late, too late for anything but a quick change; no time to bother with a girdle, a chore anyway, after all that food and drink. "There's a little button at the neck. If I can fasten that, would you be satisfied?"

"You'd really have to work hard to make things worse."

She found the fastening, and after a short struggle, said: "There, I hope you're happy."

"I have been happier. Suppose your parents should see? What would I tell them? The truth?"

"You don't know the truth," she pointed out.

"I do know that instead of the school dance, I drove you to the Hotel Pontchartrain where you disappeared while I was buying a paper you asked me to get; and that about eight hours later you walked into the drive-in lot. I never even saw a car. And now that dress; will it get by?"

"I tell you there'll be nobody to get by. If you hadn't pried you'd never have noticed the dress."

He did not answer. She wondered briefly if he had noticed her bra; the dress was lined so she wore no slip. A moment later it didn't matter too much; after all he was only one more familiar stranger in the school orchestra, where she as a second violinist played with her back to him.

Why worry? This, the only unpleasant part of the fantastic evening, would soon be over. They had long since left the throughway, and were now on curves of new pavement, bordered at intervals by blue street lights, but so high, so pale, they

8

lighted nothing except streaks of road. Had not the car's lights
swept over a driveway now and then, the place would have
seemed a waste inhabited only by light-bearing poles. The car
rounded another curve; the lights picked out a cone-shaped hill
of loose red earth, beside it a giant digger, the scoop at rest. She
shivered, whispering: "Those things make me think of mad
monsters waiting to tear you to pieces."

"They're handy things," he said, preoccupied with the rear-
view mirror, worried. "I think that same car has been following
us for miles, but it's always too far away for me to make it out.
I'd say from the head-lights it looks like it's some kind of foreign
job."

She looked around. Good old Uncle Jeff and Aunt Margaret
were coming right along. Silly things; why didn't they get on
home to bed? She wished she dared tell Robert old friends were
following because they were worried over their Susie out with a
strange boy. Pretending she knew nothing wasn't very nice. Yet
the truth would make him even angrier; and here he was quarreling again.

"Now, are you all set to go home?"

She nodded. Home. Home where you would start thinking
about that letter delivered in homeroom this—no, Friday was
yesterday now—morning. She gave Robert a quick glance. Had
she shivered? Had he noticed? She pulled the *rebozo* more
closely about her, carefully arranged her arms over it, and sat
silent, staring at nothing.

"And what happened to that happy tune?" Robert wanted to
know after a few minutes.

"Tune? Oh. —I guess I was thinking of my trouble."

"Too bad you didn't sooner. But like you say, they may not
be home, so we might get by."

She looked at him. "We? You don't have to come in. Anyway
this is a trouble at school."

"Trouble at school? For you? That write-up of 'Susan
Schnitzer, Outstanding Junior Girl Student,' in the 'Purple Sunflower' yesterday will make you automatic all-*A*."

"So what? The IBM and I," she said, no gladness in her
voice, "we get along fine together. This is a people."

9

"People?"

There was now no quarreling in his voice; kindness, almost, but more curiosity. She ignored it. If that psychologist now demanding still another session with her at school thought she was sick-sick, nobody but nobody was going to know it. Something had blown out her circuit-breakers—she was so careless; singing songs out of French Canada, and now bringing up her trouble. She saw her hands were bare, and remembered gloves. There'd be no one home to see, so she would put on the beautiful new long white ones Angie had given her tonight, straight from Paris.

She carefully drew on the gloves, but before the second was finished, she forgot and again started singing a sad, hymn-like song. Finished, still singing, she spread her fingers and considered the gloves.

"Now you *are* set up," Robert said. "Paris?"

She broke off the song as she covered her hands in a fold of the *rebozo*. "You—you know just by—half seeing them in this light?"

"Mostly guessing. Last summer in Paris I bought some like those as a gift—for my mother. Don't be scared." He sounded like a kind brother, if you could imagine such, as he went on: "Your people like some I know? So bugged by De Gaulle they won't buy anything made in France?"

She nodded. "If France were the only place. You get tired: hiding things, changing labels, pretending an Italian knit was made in Birmingham, that real Chinese jade is green glass, and —." Where was her IBM? Why had she rattled on so to this cross boy; except, worse, he was suddenly getting friendly and inquisitive. Why? Because he could afford kindness now that he was almost rid of this kooky girl who had never had a real date, and showed it? She didn't know how to act with a boy.

Moments later he sounded actually happy. "We're almost there. Here's the Old Road."

They followed the old asphalt pavement, narrow and root-cracked, for only a few hundred feet before leaving it with a downhill turn onto the wide cement of a subdivision. This road was so new, grease and tires had only streaked the bone-whiteness. Here, there were no street lamps. The car was rounding a long curve when from far away and in front of them, a red glow flickered, brightened, until the long, wooded hill above the road was silhouetted in blackness against the red-washed sky. "They're burning again over on the throughway cut. Green trees. Alive. Ugh!" Susie whispered.

"Just be thankful you'll be clear of the mess like we are on The Hill. And here we are." He was turning into a drive marked by green reflectors in front of two stone pillars, one bearing an entrance sign above a tendril of dead ivy.

The drive crossed one side of a large, bare, slightly sloping lawn, then curved behind the dim bulk of a brick and stone dwelling. A bluish light, glowing, hidden high under a central portico, showed four giant columns rising to the eaves; behind the columns, tall as they, were four rectangles of dark glass. Other blue hidden lights outlined two long wings, each with an overhung upper story supported by squat pillars set into low walls; and as the wings also made heavy use of dark glass, the whole seemed a box of shadows outlined in darkness.

Robert drove at a crawl as he studied, first the whole house, then concentrated on a dim blob of white light from the upper story. Susie, noticing his gaze, whispered: "Don't worry. That doesn't mean they're home. And even if they are, they can't hear us at the entrance on this side. All sound-proofed, sleeping-pilled, they couldn't hear a thermonuclear bomb."

"Nobody will have time to hear that one," he whispered after a noiseless stop.

She had opened a small brocaded purse. "Now, for the unfinished business. I gave you ten on deposit. Right?"

"Right."

"The corsage. Did you have to get such an expensive thing? Still, my mother liked it. That ought to be worth something. Whatever did I do with it? My great-grandmother used to press corsages. Now I guess you put them in the Deepfreeze where they'll keep forever. Seven ninety-five. Prom tickets, four; a regular evening of your services, ten." She looked at her watch.

"Ooh, I've got to hurry; I'm sort of expecting a telephone call. —Two hours and a half at time and a half brings the total to twenty-six ninety-five less the deposit."

"Mileage," he said. "Forty-one miles to the hotel; double that and multiply by ten cents, the state rate."

"And I have only a twenty and a five; and you don't do business on credit. I'll run up to my room." She was out of the car, up a low flight of steps, over the flagstone walk under the overhang, and by the door before he caught up with her. He held the door handle, though she was whispering, begging: "Don't open it. Let me try it first. The burglar alarm could be on. I have to hurry; the pantry telephone may ring in about five minutes. I must be there, and I want to get your money first."

"Skip the money. I'll see you in orchestra Monday."

She was inserting two paper-thin copper discs between door and frame. Each disc was fastened to one end of what appeared to be several feet of thin insulated wire; its central section with a small bulk in the middle, held in place by a clear plastic bag. She watched the bulb. There was no glow. Holding her shawl with an elbow, she pulled out the discs, and returned them to the bag.

"Isn't that dangerous?" Robert whispered as she inserted the door key. "Suppose the alarm had been connected? You could have electrocuted yourself, or set off the alarm, and for all I know brought the sheriff's patrol."

"It's fool proof; quit worrying. There's no need to go in with me." She had opened the door, and the last words were whispered over her shoulder.

"No, you don't walk in alone. Suppose your old man is home and heard the car. What do you think he'd imagine? The truth? On a heavy date like this is supposed to be, the girl just doesn't go leaping into the house—alone. —Oh, Lord, you're losing underwear or something."

She looked down and in the dim light recognized a nylon swinging from the rubber clips of her cast-off girdle. She crammed it back into the sack under her shawl, whispering: "Oh, the hateful thing. My mother bought it. It makes me almost pity Bismarck cursing his girdle—his quote polo belt unquote. But I must get to the pantry telephone."

"Who's Bismarck?"

"My father," and carrying her shoes, she ran down the side hall to a door set three steps above the floor. As her foot touched the bottom step, the door began opening while behind it a light went on to show a cupboard-lined pantry. She hurried across this to a telephone booth in one corner. She closed the opened panel to a crack, then went back to the door she had come through to look for Robert.

He stood halfway down the hall, head tilted as he studied the ceiling. "I heard," he whispered, "a kind of pinging overhead, I think. I'm not certain, it sounded so faint and far away."

She had turned back into the pantry when there came, from over the garage it might have been, an indistinct thump as if something had struck a board or block of wood.

"Hear that?" Robert whispered.

She shrugged. "Probably Lulu, our cook. But, please, come on in here. If this door is open when the telephone rings, the sound goes all over the house."

He came into the pantry, and when the automatic door had shut itself, she explained: "You don't have to whisper here. That electronics man who started to build the house made this pantry into what he called 'a jewel of acoustics.' The serving maid inside can see—it's one-way glass—all that goes on in the dining room, and hear, too. But no one outside can see or hear what goes on in the pantry."

He looked around as if satisfying a long curiosity. "I drive to school over the Old Road just back of this place, so I saw his builders, then all the additions and changes you people made. —But doesn't that noise overhead bug you?"

"Oh? That? I guess I had my mind on the telephone. —Old houses make all kinds of noises."

"Old! This is a practically new house compared to any on The Hill. Why, I don't think it's even four years since they started it. You people haven't been living here two years."

"As if I didn't know," she said.

"You're shivering. Afraid there's a burglar up there?"

She wished he would go. All he wanted was to satisfy his curiosity about the Schnitzer house. How did one get a boy to

13

say good night? —What had he asked? "No, I'm not afraid. It's because I'm cold. This place is always cold and smelly."

"Smelly? Even you smell very little—now. I can't smell anything else."

"That's it," she said. "The nothingness; like a freshly cleaned room in a brand-new hotel before they've brought the flowers. Once, in another house, a long time ago, there were crickets; and a hard wind would bring the nicest creaks and rattlings. There were no thermopanes and I could hear the rain, and always the slap and roar and thunder of—traffic."

She was talking too much again: she had almost said, "the sea"; and Robert listening with all his ears. Or did it matter? He was listening to the ceiling.

She, too, listened; heard, and read the sound; click of a woman's shoe-heel on the tile of Susan Marie Schnitzer's bathroom. Had she forgotten to lock her doors, and where else had those heels been? She gave one downward glance at the *rebozo* bulging over waist and breasts. She didn't dare try to hide the evidence, not now. Her father could be in the breakfast nook. She clutched her arms more tightly across her stomach, listened for more clicks; gave up; feet made no sound in her carpeted bedroom. Robert was looking at her; he would see how scared she was, not by the silly idea of a burglar, but of her parents.

She tried to find words for telling him she must now go meet the enemy; they must not, *must not* come in here to find the telephone ringing. She nodded toward a door of dark glass. He understood, whispering as he went up to peer through the glass. "Don't panic. I guess your folks are home. Do you want me to stay by the telephone or come with you? We could each take half the wiping-out."

She shook her head: "The telephone, please."

The automatic door of dark glass was opening, and they stood together, listening, watching. At first, with the pantry lights behind them, they seemed to be standing on the threshold of some high-walled cavern roofed with darkness and floored with milk. A faint, red-tinged, quivering light mingling with some more-distant, nebulous, blue-white glow, here and there revealed pale indistinct shapes.

Gradually, the nearer side of the cavern became a dining area with the usual furniture. Past this, the living area appeared to be little more than an appendage of a mighty central entrance hall sweeping out from a wide, curving stair with banisters that glinted palely in the light. "Somebody's left a TV on," Robert whispered, nodding in the direction of the quivers of white light. "But that red glow?"

"It's the simulated flame of the simulated wood fire in the simulated fireplace in the corner you can't see," she whispered. She stepped back into the pantry, and stood silent until the door had closed. "They've probably heard us, and—." She stared again at the bulging shawl.

"Couldn't I take some of your load? It's—well, it sticks out."

She looked up into his face; his sudden kindness increased her fright. Careful to hold the shawl with one arm and not let it slide from her hair, she felt under the folds and brought out a paper sack. "I guess this is safe. —If they find it—they couldn't know I wore the flats or that the sweaters came from Granma."

"Granma?" He took the packages. "Granma?"

She never heard for staring at her hands; so white, so white against the black cloth. That was how she would have it be; mourning for the wars and troubles in the world; but not just now, that whiteness, something was wrong. She'd better get going.

Hands tightly clutched on elbows, feet soundless over the lush carpet, she hurried to the foot of the stairs. She had stopped to look and listen when light from the balcony above washed over her. She forced herself to stand even straighter as she looked up to see who watched. She saw no one.

The whiteness of her hands bothered her again; she told herself it was because everything else she wore was dark; even the party dress was granite-gray. It seemed darker now, so clearly outlined by the pale banisters, above the white wall to wall carpeting. She glanced around, though she knew that in this house there was no darkness—of wall or furniture—she could stand against for camouflage.

It seemed a long while she stood, watching, listening, dreading. She heard at last her mother's voice from half way down the main upstairs hall: "Susan, darling. You *are* home. I thought I saw car lights in the drive." The voice was clear, but muted; coming closer, it changed to a whisper as if nearby a not-to-be-disturbed baby slept.

Susie tried to hold back the breath of relief when her mother stopped at the head of the stairs. She called softly, a slight quaver in her voice: "Oh, Mother—dear, you home so early?"

"Your father wanted to get to bed early for golf in the morning," the careful voice continued. "His doctor insists. And all that talk of burglars worried us. Imagine, a holdup in our very own shopping-center bank. I suppose you heard a lot about it at the dance. Have a good time? And was your dress all right? It seemed, as I told you, rather dull, as if you were in mourning."

Susie sent her voice up in a soft trilling. "Yes, Mother—dear, yes it was all wonderful. That is, everything except the robbery. I heard fifty million different tales."

"Same at the club. First, the robbers were caught with a woman driving the getaway car; then they weren't, and no woman at all. —Didn't Robert come in with you?" She came down one stair.

Susie gave a quick glance at her feet. Bare or shod? She remembered taking off the heels. "Thank you, IBM, for putting them on again," she whispered under her breath. "Oh, Mother, of course I'm not alone." She fought down an impulse to step back. Why couldn't she talk to her mother as she talked to Dr. Laughton or even teachers she had had? Was it because all of her could never talk—to either parent? She lifted her head higher so as to look straight into her mother's face. "Robert wouldn't leave me by myself when everyone's so scared of burglars. We heard somebody in my bathroom and were we ever certain it was a burglar. It was awful. Then I realized it was you?"

Her mother ignored the implied question. She came down two more steps; worse, she was studying her daughter. Her glance centered now on the hands. Susie did not look down. She knew why her hands had seemed so white; those new kid gloves from Paris. In another minute her mother would come down for a closer look; know the gloves for what they were, and wonder —without asking aloud—how she could afford them on her clothing allowance; then, aloud, remind her of Bismarck's ukases. She might even learn that new girdle, party favors, and a lot more contraband were what made the *rebozo* bulge. She bared her teeth in a smile she knew was pitiful, and trilled: "Oh, Mother, those beautiful shoes you bought were simply fantastic. I'm afraid they look old now after all that dancing." She wished she could be certain she was keeping the shakes out of her voice; the woman had taken another step downward.

Keep her interested; keep talking. About what? Dancing, that was it. Her mother was a marvelous dancer. She tried to remember the name of one dance, any dance for high school; she might try to demonstrate one imagined step of rock 'n' roll. Better not; her mother knew more about them than she did. Shift course. "Oh, Mother, I just remembered! Robert is all alone out in—."

Her father's voice, loud, angry, came past a door opening from the other side of the balcony: "Is that Susan home and waking me?"

She took one quick step backward, but almost at once was again able to stand stiff and straight to answer: "Yes, Father, I'm home, but I hope I didn't wake you." She watched him stalk away from the slowly-closing door, out of the light behind him that too clearly showed his silhouette without the "polo girdle." She almost never saw him in a bathrobe, and in spite of her fear of what was coming up, she thought as she had thought before, that it was kind of sad to have a milk-tank-truck-bodied father.

"You ought to have hoped sooner," he stormed.

If she had been scared before, she was getting bugged now. He was striding straight for the stairs, fists jammed into the pockets of his bathrobe, its cord so tightly jerked he showed his bulges fore and aft, big above his thin legs dark with hair. She could do nothing but stand on the pale carpet under the shadowless light that would not let her hide so much as her nose. It was even harder not to show relief when he stopped at the head of the stairs. Here, he stood silent, glaring, a statue washed in light, towering above his wife below him on the stairs, but ignoring her.

"I wish," he said after a silent scrutiny that seemed to last an

17

hour, "you would do something about your hair. Looks like it hadn't been combed in a week."

She'd let the scarf slide from her head; she must have jumped or loosened her arms that first time he yelled. She started to lift a hand to smooth her hair; remembered she had to hold the scarf together. Her mother was staring; nobody could ever read her face, but, poor woman, she had loved that miserable hairdo she had insisted her daughter get for the "school party." Why was she, Susan Schnitzer, such a sneaky coward? Why couldn't she tell them she had only tried to get her poor hair back the way she wanted it, the way her hair belonged, not exactly fuzzy, but too curly for the present fashion.

She almost turned her head when she thought she heard the soft opening of the pantry door. Robert could be listening. He and her father had not met. Girls were supposed to introduce their dates; or were they, to angry fathers in bathrobes that showed their bulges? Still, an introduction to smooth Robert might cool him down. The big deal hadn't started. He'd learned something. He wouldn't come charging out of bed to quarrel about her hair when—. She'd debated too long.

"Susan Marie, you must know I am an extremely lenient father, generous to the point of stupidity."

Her fingertips bit into her clasped arms, but only the *rebozo* fringe quivered. She had been caught once in that one when she had given only a: "Yes, Father." Now, she said: "You're very generous, Father, but certainly not stupid." The words came slowly. Her mouth was dry.

"You think I am a good father? Eh?"

"Oh, yes, Father."

His voice was thunder: "Then why do you disobey me in the most important matters?"

Her mother had been struggling to hang onto her smile. She was now able to turn away from the banisters, smile securely fastened. "Please, dear, Robert is—."

"Will you kindly stop your interruptions." He came down one stair. "Susan, you have not answered my question." His wrath was fully collected now; his voice a sonic boom.

She stood, head lifted, breath held to check her trembling.

She had forgotten his question. She looked at her mother, not for help; help would never come from that direction, but there might be a clue to her father's question. And there it was; her mother's hair shining like a freshly unwrapped lemon Popsicle. Her hair? No, this thing was bigger. Somehow he'd learned she'd made a big hole in that heat-proof, cold-proof, acid-proof Schnitzer plastic curtain to be with people she was forbidden to see.

She managed a smile, frozen; everything inside her frozen and disconnected; her IBM had short-circuited, able to do nothing but beg for information. It came.

"A supporter of subversion under my own roof. You know how you have been taught to hate all people and things reddened with Communism. It's this deceit of yours that got me out of bed when I badly need the rest." He stopped for breath and an accusing glance at his wife. "And had it not been for Brandon it could have gone on forever in this house."

His hot words didn't matter any more; old stuff. She felt as weak with relief as an icicle under sudden hot sun. He hadn't discovered her biggest and most precious secret. Still, she must put on a listening face, try to learn what she had done. Instead, her mind slid away to Angie's gift of gloves. Would that cold sweat dripping from her palms ruin them?

"—Don't think I took time to listen to your so-called folk music. I checked the names. That was enough. Most are on the proscribed lists of the patriotic, anticommunist organizations I belong to. That woman is a notorious Commie agitator. And niggers. Imagine, you, my daughter, listening to that filth. And that white man. I wouldn't believe he was the one, the very one who refused to testify, until I checked my list again."

Oh, how wonderful it would be to answer that lava outpour with a cool: "I know he didn't testify. He's no sneaking coward like you; after Brandon got into my study, then you sent Mother snooping." She was having trouble keeping that "I-know-I've-done-wrong look." Her IBM was working again. She licked her lips; drew a deep "your cue" breath as she tried to remember that drama class in junior high. She now had enough wind to give what she hoped was a piteous cry; not easy when all her

19

insides wanted to dance with joy and relief. Shaking back her hair, she was ready when he ran out of words: "Oh, Father, I should have been more careful. I didn't take time to look through all the albums. I'll take them back first thing in the morning."

"You can't take them back. They are burned in the incinerator. And if such a thing happens again your precious hi-fi will follow."

She did a short, sharp scream bit, properly she thought; at least the effort left her able only to bury her face in her hands, and explain in heartbroken sobs: "Oh, Father, I haven't money enough—but I can earn it somehow."

"Money? I have, strange to say, never heard complaints from you on that score." Some terrible thought silenced him. Then he yelled: "Is it actually true that a daughter of mine has gone into debt for—for subversion?"

Better try some more sobs, and that line she remembered from a play: "Oh, Father, how can you so mistrust me?"

"Don't turn on the floodgates act."

She managed to check her sobs—as soon as her computer was in working order. "I'm terribly sorry, but in English we're studying ballads. I went to the public library where we were told to go to get records." She remembered his war with the library; spare it from blame. "The ones we were studying were all out, so I helped myself to what was left; I didn't even look, I was in too big a hurry to get home." Better try a quick tack away from the library. "Brandon, or whoever it was, had no right to go sneaking into my room."

"Brandon did right. The end justifies the means."

Didn't the old fool know that was Marxist? "Yes, Father," she said after two sobs and a hiccup. "I'll explain to the library. I hope I don't get a lecture on juvenile delinquency. The library staff has never liked us too well since last UN Day when Brandon tore up the wrong flags because he—."

"That will do."

She felt the weariness in his roar; frustration, too. Kind of pitiful he was, but this was a good chance for a family lesson in not meddling. "Don't worry, Father. I'll explain—everything; and hope they'll take the money in installments as I earn it. Pure old ballad records are horrifically expensive, but I imagine they will understand—after I explain how you feel."

His mouth was opening. She poured words over it. "Mrs. Johnston, the assistant librarian, didn't do a thing to Rosella Margerita Montinelli—she's a girl from the other side of the expressway—you know, from working class people brought in when their neighborhood was voted into Eden Hills School District. I wouldn't know her, of course. But I've heard she's wild about art. Her art was why she got special permission to take out a very expensive and rare book of reproductions of some cubist. Her father, he's with the town garbage crew, came home drunk. He grabbed the book and he threw it at the girl's mother; she ducked; it went into the spaghetti sauce. But do you know when poor Rosella explained everything, all about the kind of father she had, Mrs. Johnston was most understanding. Now, I—."

"Don't compare me to a drunken dago from the wrong side of the tracks." He had tried to roar his you-shut-up interruption, but his wind had died, sails slack, not even gas for the auxiliary motor, craft drifting.

Then any feeling of triumph she might have had was flattened by that word, *dago,* only now hitting her, hard. How could he? And her mother on the stair. Why hadn't she thought of her mother when she gave that imagined girl an Italian name?

"Not one more word out of you."

She had forgotten to look at her father in trying not to look at her mother. She nodded; he turned and stalked to his door that opened with customary slow dignity. He tried to hasten it with a jerk that said he would like to slam it; but, poor man, he could not.

"Susie."

She looked at her mother, unmoving on the stair. Smile and poise still there; after that word you couldn't help but admire the way she didn't show it.

"You and Robert make yourselves at home—only do be quiet. Tell Robert good night for me. —I almost forgot the thing I wanted to tell you. The water pressure has been so low, your father suggested I check for leaking faucets. And do you know that when I was in your suite, I discovered that neither the elec-

21

tric door into your back hall or your closet would work. Remind me to call an electrician again."

Such a great big tale deserved a great big smile. Easy. She had just been told the rummaging had not gone into dangerous waters—her closet. Her excitement over the upcoming party had caused her to leave the contraband records in her study; she wouldn't let it happen again. "You worry too much about my comfort, Mother. It takes a bit of doing sometimes, but I always get the doors open. Good night. Sweet dreams."

Her mother was already turning away.

Susie watched her legs go up the stairs, then past the widely-spaced banisters. That new dress—black lace over what looked to be pale green satin—with its mini-microskirt and even mini-er neck and back, showed too much. Her ankle-bones looked big between the dainty shoes and thin shanks; her knee joints swollen, they were so big. A door, different from that of her husband, opened, and she disappeared. Somewhere somebody pressed a light switch, and the upper stairs and the curves of the banisters were again only glints in the artificial flames.

She hurried toward the pantry, and had a near-collision with Robert, standing in the opened door. Half talking to herself, half asking, she whispered: "Will I ever be like that?"

"No," he said when the pantry door had closed behind them. "If the *that* means your parents. If you don't take a different road, you'll never live to be their age—not in this house. —It hurts me, but I owe you an apology; I'm sorry I said you were stewed when you got into the car. I've never seen a better act. You were so cool and sweet. You know I couldn't always tell which was Susan Schnitzer and which the actress?"

"I get tangled in my selves sometimes myself." She looked at him as if in his face she might find one untangled self. "Thank you for taking back what you said. But I wonder, now, if—if I did have too much champagne. I felt all singy inside. But not any more. It's all gone. I wonder how it feels—getting high?"

He smiled. "There are all kinds. You'd better just wonder. But my wonder is that you can even stand up after—that—confrontation, I suppose you could call it." He gestured in the general direction of the front stairs, then, seemingly embarrassed by what amounted to eavesdropping, asked: "Say, don't you want my personal tape recording of the phone conversation with your —relatives? —I chucked your grandmother's gifts and the flats in that food-warmer. OK?"

She must be sick-sick; she didn't remember mentioning her grandmother to him. "Thank you. Yes, I'd like to hear, if you can spare the time. But I'd better listen outside. Somebody might come through here."

Shoeless again, she led the way. At the end of the portico, she stopped to search the sky for stars, but found only the gray blackness of rain cloud. "I think I know how it was," she said. "You spoke first to Sheridan?"

"The very British, British voice, not telling a thing with her: 'And to whom am I speaking, please?' I guess I made some kind of sound, for on she went: 'Miss Schnitzer's escort?' You'd think my name was classified. I said: 'Yes.' I didn't like that part, a strange female knowing my name, but not repeating it. Delicate. And you don't know her name or where she is calling from—San Francisco, New York?"

"Sheridan is a kind of housekeeper," Susie explained, walking now toward the back of the house. She had heard the questions in his voice; and more cautious now, was not going to let "Angie and Joe" slip out as she had "Granma."

He questioned her with an "Oh?", but seemed to have given up hope of answers, for he went on with the telling. "Anyway, this Sheridan wanted to speak to Miss Schnitzer, if she were free. I explained you seemed to be tied up at the moment. 'Thank you, Sheridan, I'll take over now.' That was a man's voice, not quite Michigan—hard to place—nice, though? But worried. 'Is everything all right? Hang up if—.' He didn't seem to want to finish, so I told him nobody else was around. He thanked me for the long wait for you and apologized. I was not to blame 'the little one,' he said; it was his fault. He wanted to know if you were all right. 'I imagine she drank champagne as if it were lemonade. She doesn't know too much about it—yet.'

"I liked that; as if champagne were a sure thing in your

23

future. Then he asked, nervous: 'Are you certain no one is listening? Sounds like an extension is open.'

"This woman's voice came on. 'Of course an extension is open. I was worried.'

"I explained you had everything under control. But, blast it, just as I was getting her over her worry, here came your father's roar. I had left the phone booth open a bit, but I couldn't hear enough to know what was happening. They were scared, especially the woman, giving little 'Oh dear's,' and whispering, 'Is he noticing anything?'

"I wished I could tell her; she had the most beautiful voice. Then, too, I was getting scared. I had the feeling your father would come charging in at any minute, grab me, the phone, and that would be it. But I offered to pull the phone booth open all the way, then hold the dining room door wide. By this time your father was on a scat start without a muffler. I stayed there with the door practically pushing me over until he had gone. I went back to the telephone just as the woman was saying to the man: 'Such a father! He's not even noticed the time. And that boy he thought she was with, a complete stranger.' I didn't like that too well. But they were so grateful for everything, I actually felt I had done a noble deed.

"Look, I've got to get home. My father will be having a fit."

She looked at him in wonder. "But you're a senior—you must be around eighteen?"

"Don't get me wrong. He's no comic-strip father. Times I wish he were. Easier. When I get in late there's no row. But even when I sneak in, no noise at all, there he is, always, up on some excuse—the children, a glass of milk, a call to the hospital. He's so full of little lies that when I'm out a lot he has to start using them over and over. It bugs me. Worse, he schedules his big operations for seven a.m. He really needs his sleep."

His voice had something in it along with word sounds. Guilt? She didn't know, and anyway why show she had heard more than words? "I'm sorry I've kept you so long, the telephone and all, but you don't have to stay with me out here."

"I'll go when I see you safe inside again. —Why are we

24

going back here? Isn't that shed where your father keeps his weed and bug killers?"

"Yes, but behind it, Lulu and I have our 'walled garden' as she calls it."

At the shed corner she stepped off the cement into the damp softness of grass, where she searched until her hand felt leaf and flower. Gently feeling, now and then pinching a stem, she soon held up to Robert what, in the dull red light of the far away fires, appeared to be a handful of small round black shapes on stems. "Mexican chrysanthemums. They are little and browny red, but when you smell them you know it's flowers you smell. The gardener at first wouldn't have them, because they weren't in the landscape architect's plan. But Lulu persuaded him, and took care of them while I was gone this summer." She held the flowers up to the pale blur of his face. "They haven't been sprayed. Can't you tell from the smell?"

He sniffed, nodded, then turned back toward the car. "Watch it, now. You could lose a stocking or that burglar probe out here, and somebody might find it. I'm still weak. What if one of your parents had come close enough to get a whiff of wine or see all those secrets under that shawl?"

Her voice was more wistful than frightened as she said: "I thought my mother might—this once. I think I had everything under control—except my hair. You saw my mother. What did you think of her?"

"Beautiful, of course, a brown-eyed blonde. You know, when you people came here, my father's wife saw her somewhere and thought she was a second wife—or even his older daughter."

"It would please her no end to hear that. Mind if I tell her—maybe? She began winning beauty prizes when she was fourteen. But I don't think your mother looked at her too long. What did you think?"

"Tonight I hardly saw her. I thought she sounded—well, absent-minded or worried."

"I mean her appearance. Didn't you think the mileage is beginning to show?"

"That's an impossible question in an impossible conversation. I guess in some women the chassis kind of sags. —What a conversation! I'm no expert on older women."

They had almost reached the car and the blue glow from the portico lights. "I wish," she said, "I could wear a *rebozo* with the art of a Mexican woman; she can fill one with everything from a baby to cotton for spinning, and spin at the same time. I've been wanting to put one of these flowers in your lapel—but if I reach that far, my arms loosen and the *rebozo* slides."

"A flower would be nice," he said, taking one.

"You'll love it," she said. "I like to have them around at night so I can wake up and smell flowers. Did you ever come awake to pure dark—the drapes drawn, and nothing, nothing to hear or smell or see? And nothing will come, and you wonder if you are deaf, blind, and smell-less—or dead?"

"The dead don't wonder," he said. "Why can't you turn on the light and read or study?"

"The light makes it worse. You can see where you are."

"Then think of nice things. You could imagine sailing on the sea."

She stiffened. "Why do you say I love the sea?"

He was impatient. "Why are you always pretending, trying to put me on? You know you love the sea." He slid into the car, but at once turned back to her. "Look," he said, kind again, "when you go to the library you don't have to tell exactly what happened; paying up is the main thing. Your father—look, I'm not criticizing or taking sides—it never pays to take sides, at least out loud—but your father is too loud in his opinions for this neighborhood. He seems to have a Dallas–Chicago–Birmingham syndrome."

"He, unfortunately, pushed his motion of neighborhood-wide weed and bug killers through at the annual township meeting," she reminded him.

"Well, in this neighborhood just like in the rest of the country, the majority has little say with the Establishment. So at the library—."

He stopped as she smiled. "You believed! Friends gave me those records; they were worn, but most were in pretty fair shape. I begged for them. I was going to keep them awhile, then slip them out as a Friends of the Library donation."

He gave a low whistle of admiration. "You are a master hand at—prevarication. Is that word nice enough?"

"I think 'diplomacy at the personal level between the mutually unaligned' a better term."

"You are a cool one," he said, getting into the car.

"The world is a cold place." She looked down the drive to the road. Empty. Uncle Jeff and Aunt Margaret were somewhere on their way home. She wished she could have waved to them.

"Your world could be a lot colder," he was saying. "Those people on the telephone, why they seemed to love and worry over you more than your own parents."

"Don't rub it in." She watched the red light quiver over the wooded hillside above. "Do you suppose the great blue heron will come to the swamp in the morning? Or have the fires and the noise and the earth movers got him?"

"Iggy saw him one day last week." The motor was on; he lifted a hand: " 'Bye now."

She caught the free hand between her own. "I'm sorry you're so late, but if you could only know what a wonderful time it was. I can't explain it. I never dared believe things would work out tonight. But—they did, they did." Standing on tiptoe, she kissed him on the cheek; then, wordless, whirled away.

2

She locked her bedroom door, and stood, face pressed against it, blushing as she thought of the kiss. Why? Why? She turned and tossed back her hair. Why ruin this wonderful evening in trying to find the why of why? She had something nice to remember forever. Not even her own silliness, nor Robert's crossness on the way home, nor the snooping of her parents had spoiled it. Nobody had learned anything. Her mother hadn't found that letter hidden in her closet, demanding she have another conference with that kooky would-be psychologist. No, she wouldn't start worrying over that—now. She would manage.

She smiled into the dark, almost pure dark. The bedroom never hurt so when she couldn't see it. The darkness was not as thick as on most nights in her bedroom of the cottage by a fog-shrouded Nova Scotian bay, but better than in any of her father's houses until this one.

True, every two or three months he had his secretary rework the letter of complaint to the township supervisors, pointing out "—the absolute necessity for a light on the road near my property is particularly urgent now in view of the Detroit riots of the summer." Neither light nor rioter had ever come. And never would, she guessed.

The darkness thinned, grew red-tinged as the bonfire light

seeped through the one window at the end of the room, so heavily curtained and draped that it was, in spite of the light, only a narrow, corner-smudged rectangle. She watched the window disappear as the red quivers trembled into nothingness, leaving only the green night-light. Set to mark the bathroom door, the green eye seemed always watching when she crossed the room at night. She kept the bulb too loosely screwed for contact, but tonight her mother had re-screwed it.

She went over and loosened the bulb, then turned and walked along the opposite wall until the flounced drapery of a bed brushed her knees. She slid one foot far under, pressed the slight hump felt under the carpeting, and at once heard from the other side of the room the faint whisper of an opening door.

She hurried toward the sound, and as the door closed behind her, went down four narrow steps. Bottom step reached, she turned, and with one giant stride touched more carpet, not in front, but to the side of the stair. This time the sound was that of a double closet door sliding open in metal grooves below and above.

The electronics man had had the door built to open with an electric pad in front, as did most of the doors in the house, including the one she had just come through. But she had, for her inner hall and closet doors, bought parts for other electronic opening devices. Much of the assembly was done in the family basement under the guise of building an electronics apparatus for a biology exhibit at school. Compared to beautiful oak or maple floors, wall to wall carpet was horrible stuff, but it could be convenient for a girl in need of security.

Still with no light, she went into the closet. Her mother, when assigning her the quarters originally planned for two maids, had gone into ecstacies over the "huge walk-in closet, the dream of every young girl." Cedar lined and floored, it had space for everything from ski equipment to a library—secret after the old electric opening pad had been disconnected and her own substituted.

Brushing past plastic bags and clothing, she went to a back corner where, kneeling, she loosened her clasped arms, and let all things bundled in and around them slide to the floor. She stood a moment, head bowed, fingers busy with the neck fastening of her dress. It slipped down, and she stepped away to leave the dress as a tent-like covering for the parcels.

She reached for the hanger that held a big, cover-up cotton flannel nightgown and a woolen bathrobe with a slipper in each pocket. She scuffed her feet on the cedar floor, smiling, sniffing, but as always there was no smell. The cedar was deodorized, like the gardener's marigolds. Still, it was good to remember that even here in The House of Usher there was a once-living thing that had felt the wind and the rain, stood perhaps in deep snow and heard from far away the thunder of the sea. She shook her head; no, the cedar had most probably come from Uncle Jeff's country—east Tennessee. She had heard him speak of the cedars in the valleys there.

At the closet door, she turned down the hall toward the back of the house, and had taken three or four steps when in front of her a door began opening with a flood of light behind it. The light showed, on the other side of the opening door, the gleam of bathroom tile and chrome, as well as the hall she walked through; small, low-ceilinged, with the closet doors on one side, steps leading to the bedroom door on the other. At the opposite end of the hall, another door led to her study, planned by the original owner as a second maid's room.

Hurrying into the bathroom, she took off her underclothing, opened a small washer set into the wall, put the clothing into it, pressed buttons, then turned to the shower. She hesitated a second in front of the green, blue, and silvered glass panels. The Schnitzer private water system suffered many ailments; one of the most worrisome to her was an asthmatic cough in the pipes, often accompanied by loud gurgles, even screams. These, because of the system of piping, were the only sounds that could now and then travel from her quarters to those of her parents. More than once her father had complained about the noise of a too-late shower. She shrugged and parted the panels; he was already so mad he was probably not even trying to sleep, but soothing himself with another bottle of beer.

The pipes were quiet. She showered, then dressed in her night things, brushed teeth and hair quickly, though tonight, filled as she was with thoughts of the party, the place bothered her less. The green and white composition tiles, the "miserable fake waterproof green and blue and silver junk" that draped dressing table and window, all had been decided by her mother, her one sister, Charlotte, and the nimble-faced little interior decorator. He had reminded her less of a man than a character in an animated cartoon.

Back in the closet, she shut the sliding door with her secret pad, which also activated a two-minute light. She then rolled out from under a back shelf a large magnet. Almost too heavy for lifting, semi-circular in shape, it seemed to have been made only to suck with its two powerful poles on the metal rims of the double closet doors. Part of a bombsight motor, she had bought it from a Detroit war surplus store for help in the study of magnetic fields, but had never much liked having it around; it too often brought thoughts of the people it might have helped bomb to death.

Finished with the door, she took from a back shelf a thick and heavy book that popped open when she pressed one corner. She turned a few leaves before reaching a cavity cut into the glued-together pages; she took from this a small remote-control box. Simple, it worked on the same principle as those on the family cars that opened the garage doors.

She waited until the light went out, then pulled on the shelf while the other hand pushed a button on the control box. A section of the wall around two feet wide gently and silently swung out. "Thank you, Little Atlas." Her lips shaped the words without sound. Still soundless was her question: "Do you suppose, Little Atlas, that boy, Robert, remembers the dormer windows and wonders where they went? Or does he remember the roof of the back part was lower than that over the front hall and the living and dining areas? Didn't anyone notice my father's architect had the back raised? But that my section, practically finished, plastered and everything, was left with the low ceilings unchanged so there is all that attic space above?"

Telling her worries to "Little Atlas," she stepped over the bottom framework of the blinded dormer window, slipped under the loosened insulation batting into darkness as complete as that of her unlighted closet. She was ready to push Little Atlas to remind him to close the opened wall section on its electromagnetic catches, when she heard a faint ping.

She stopped, smiled; some little animal had struck metal in the jungle of piping between the upstairs of the garage wing and the back of her quarters. It could be a bird or a squirrel, or even a cricket to chirrup. She had always hoped for a cricket—here; the only spot in all the Schnitzer Domain where any living creature save man might be safe from sprays, pellets, traps, and Brandon. She listened, but the sound did not come again.

She pressed the "shut" button on Little Atlas, and, turning to put him in his niche on the upper frame of the blinded window, resumed her soundless conversation: "Little Atlas, do you know why I talk so much to you? No one else around is safe to talk to. Friends aren't. Even an acquaintance like that nosy Robert is dangerous. —And do you know, Little Atlas, I have told no one, not even Granma or Beeto, about that would-be psychologist. Why does he want to probe me again? What did I say or write wrong the other times? Does he think I am sick-sick? I must forget it—now. Where is that flashlight? Its place is next to yours. I must have been crazy with excitement to leave doors unlocked and misplace things."

It didn't matter. She could depend on her radar and her mental map. Three or four feet directly in front was a wall, the back of the help's quarters—two bedrooms with bath between— above the garage. The near one was empty because Lulu, the only help living in, used the front bedroom. All about, in and out, were the insulation-swathed pipes, the hidden arteries of the house, supplying it with all things from sewage drains to electric conduit cables.

Nicer was the good smell of wood from the bare beams and trusses holding up the roof boards, so widely spaced that with a flashlight she could glimpse the cedar shingles. She stood, head cocked, listening to the wind, a very little one tonight, more like the sigh of a weary world. No good gusts to let you imagine it was the sea you heard instead of the trees up the hill, or the one Schnitzer tree big enough to roar. She sniffed. Mixed in with the wood smell was another smell, damp. Could there be a leak?

That would be exciting—and dangerous if it showed below.

She was on the plank she had laid for a walkway over the beams, one hand reaching for a rung of the makeshift ladder she had built to her attic bedroom, when light flashed into her eyes, then disappeared. She stopped, smiled. A storm. Wonderful. No other flash of lightning had shone so brightly through the small louvered windows near the roof. The thunder would be—.

Something, for an instant soft, then hard and unyielding, whipped round her head, pinioning ears, mouth, nose, and eyes. Her flailing arms were trapped tightly against her body; but one hand was still partly free. Her nost hurt; in a second she realized it was jammed against a button. She next knew the thing that had her head was cloth-covered. Arms squeezing her to death; arms on a man's body.

Brandon. She tried to speak his name but could not. Though fourteen months younger than she, he was almost as tall as his father, and heavier. All her insides were ashes running away in the rain. He had learned of her secret attic bedroom. He might have found a clue in it to her big secret. The once-free hand was now pinioned against his body. Her arm hurt; pressed so hard against him that under the layers of damp cloth she felt ridged hardness. Ribs. Brandon was fat.

Her IBM revived enough to remind her that Brandon was not home. Her secret might not be ruined after all. This was somebody who had crawled up her hidden passage above the potting shed—some one who had helped build the house and knew its secret. She struggled against the hands, but stopped after one try. A long leg hooked about her leg, and the squeeze on arms and head tightened. It was a struggle to get her mouth open enough to breathe. That prominent nose of hers was taking plenty of punishment. She thought she heard a garbled whisper but couldn't be certain; her ears were too tightly pressed.

Screaming was out. She couldn't. And if she could who was there to hear? Lulu was fairly close, in feet; but between her was a wall of insulation, an empty room, and Lulu's sound sleep. Her parents on the other side of the house were probably still awake; not quite time for sleeping pills to get to work. But they were walled in by layers of insulation and soundproofing, behind thermopane windows, and with a burglar alarm they were certain would go off after the least tampering with a window or outside door.

Her nose was working again. The wet smell she had first noticed was close now, the man. Closer, was another smell; familiar, one she loathed, that made her think of herself when she was having a heavy menstrual flow—blood. She was shivering. The whispering above her pinioned ears continued. She could make out no words. Was the fault her ears, or was the sound the wordless garble of some crazy man run away from an institution, or a wild, wild hard-core boy from a house of correction? An angry impatience was getting through without words.

The arms around her head was loosening. She might in a second be able to let out with a high wild scream. What good was that? The kind of noise to make a suspicious dog run after you and bite, would make this—. The man sneezed, a violent sneeze that shook the two of them. She felt the wind of it on her hair as she was pushed away. The other hand struck her on the nose as its owner sneezed again. Struggling to keep her balance, she realized the blow on her nose had been only a collision with the hand in its upward flight for a handkerchief in the breast pocket of a jacket.

"Please, excuse me," he said, then got nose and handkerchief together just as she managed a quick, sharp shove. He merely hung on to her shoulder with one hand while he blew his nose with the other. Still holding, he whispered: "Please, Cousin Susan, can't you answer me? You've scared me to death. Twice. This time I thought you'd fainted."

The voice, she thought, was that of a boy or a very young man. She started to cry out that he had so squeezed her ears she could hear nothing, but found she couldn't speak. She sagged. He held her. "I have introduced myself three times. —Pardon me, please." He blew his nose again, then continued, his tone petulant as if it were she who had seized *him* in the dark. "You surely know by now I'm your cousin. I only asked you not to scream."

It was as if she were peeping down from her attic bedroom,

and laughing with no pity for this piece of dishcloth that passed
for a girl; she could only stand and heave, too dead to think or
speak, just enough of her left to remember she had no real
cousins except on her father's side. They lived in Michigan near
Petosky, and no one of them had this shape or voice.

He seemed to feel the introduction settled things. He took
his hand from her shoulder. "I thought you'd never get here," his
aggrieved whisper rushed on. "And when you did come it was
without light or sound. It really shook me. I was already half
dead from stepping into your father's unmarked swimming pool.
Won't you try to understand? I am your Cousin Ter, the one who
missed the party. I had hoped to get into your bathroom to dry
myself right away, but I've been waiting here in this icy hole for
hours. Please, will you show me the way?"

Light washed over her. She whirled to hide her face. She
was still free, and he off guard. One good hard shove and he
would go sprawling off the narrow walkway. Then what? Some
part of him, an elbow or a foot, might punch through the weak
fiberboard of the side hall ceiling. The hole would be investi-
gated. His annoyed whisper hissed behind her: "Please, show me
to the bathroom."

Her numbed brain half made a blurry plan to trap him in
the closet; with neither Little Atlas nor knowledge of the secret
pad, he'd have to stay there until she could think what to do. But
he was too quick for any plan; cautious, too; not as she had
expected, bumping his head on the low back door of her closet.
He slid straight through, so that by the time she had the big
bomsight motor magnet rolled away from the sliding doors, he
was right behind her.

She pointed to the bathroom. He turned toward it with a
quick: "Thank you. Excuse me." As always the door closed
slowly to give the automatic light time to silhouette him in the
doorway. He was tall, taller than her father, or did he only seem
so because he was so slender; slender without being narrow-
shouldered. Young, too, late high school or—. He had stepped
behind the door.

The next thing she knew she was flopped into her study
chair, soothing her nose with one hand. Her steering gear was

out; the wind taking its will of her. She had no memory of coming into the study. She stared at the hand that had rubbed her nose. It smelled. She held it under the study lamp. Blood, a smeared spot on one palm; blood from her poor nose. That button had really bashed it.

She reached for a tissue; rubbed; stared at the unblemished whiteness. Whose blood? She was shivering again. She went out into the hall, but did nothing but stand and watch the bathroom door. The time to do something was now. She could nip through her bedroom, and before that so-called cousin knew what was happening, be down in the pantry ringing up the sheriff's patrol. Deputies would come—with questions: "And where is the prowler, miss?"

Her answer: "In my bathroom."

"Oh? And how did he get there?"

"I—I showed it him." No. That would never do. She'd have to begin with the attic. She shook her head; questions on the attic would be even worse: "How did he get *there?* How did you happen to find him?"

"Please," loud and shrill with a hint of command was coming through the bathroom doorway. A naked arm was beckoning. She didn't move. If that door opened all the way, and he—. She dropped her glance to see a sock-covered foot between door and frame; above the foot a length of trouser leg. The door was opening no wider; he must be holding it to the width of his foot.

She walked slowly up, eyes on the floor. She had meant to keep them there, but her glance went up when he whispered: "I'm sorry to bother you, but could you please find me something warm and dry?"

She looked up into a face, darker than her own, thin, big-eyed, with a nose that was gaunt, slightly hooked, but the way he wore it, you might call it a patrician nose. She wished she could wear her nose that way. If she knew how to practice, could —. He was shivering. Worse, he had a sick look, he was so pale around the mouth, and his eyes watery-red. Still, he smiled, a nice smile.

She managed to tell him to step on the green pad in front of the dressing table for instant, overhead heat. He was, she decided, about the age of that boy she had kissed. She dropped her glance again as shame for the kiss came back. She forgot the kiss. In front of her was a strip of undershirt, wet for several inches above the trousers; and into the wet part, above and all around was blood, several kinds of blood—pinky stuff thinned out by water, spots caked and dried blackish, and a big streak freshly red.

The bloody undershirt was disappearing; the door closed to a crack as he whispered: "Yes, it's blood; only a little. I got it—." He stopped, shivered, studied her as if trying to make up his mind—or make up a tale. She turned away. He called her back with another whispered: "Please, won't you try to find something —anything warm and dry. Your father or your brother must have a spare bathrobe,—if you can't pinch some pajamas—for temporary use, of course."

"Pajamas! Pajamas?" She backed away, staring. He never saw her stare. The door had closed. He must get things straight —now. She must get it into his head—now—that he couldn't, just couldn't, hang around her quarters in pajamas—or in any kind of clothing. She was knocking; there was his face, close above hers. Why, his lips looked blue. It wasn't only cold that ailed him; he was having a chill. His chin was quivering.

Still, he could frown down on her as he asked, impatient: "Yes? Yes?"

"I'm not certain you should—."

He interrupted with an: "Oh, excuse me." The door closed.

Seconds later she heard his vomiting. She stood a moment, eyes fixed on the door, not seeing it, more like watching one of those slow, blown-up slides in chemistry—one drop of this element added, and the compound changes, crystals begin to form. The image of that heartless prowler, pretending to be a cousin, was disappearing; in its place came this sick and troubled boy in need of help.

She looked down to see with disgust she was giving way to that old childhood habit of pulling and squeezing her left thumb in the clenched fist of the other hand. She was being silly. Her computer must have mended itself; it came on for the first time since meeting the boy to remind her he had told the truth—at least part. He was the missing boy she had heard mentioned at the party. She had heard he had a severe cold; some one else had remarked that at least he was not too sick to travel as he had telephoned his regrets from Windsor.

All he wanted from her was to get himself and clothing warm and dry. She might even risk taking his things down to the big laundry dryer—take only a few minutes. He could stay up here in whatever she was able to find in Charlotte's suite. That husband of hers had surely left something the boy could wear for awhile. Nice to know she wasn't completely rattled after all. Her component parts were working. Her radar guided her to the right plastic bag of winter woolens and her fingers came up with the duplicate keys to Charlotte's suite.

She had never used them until now, coming by the keys more by accidental thoughtfulness than cunning design. Bismarck demanded keys and locked doors for the quarters of his children as if the place were a cheap hotel overrun by thieves. "Good training for later days," he said.

All obeyed him, though Charlotte suffered most. She was perpetually misplacing her keys. Usually they were found days or hours later, but never before Mrs. Schnitzer had taken the master key chain from the safe in the master bedroom, and sent Susie biking off to get duplicates made and into Charlotte's hands before "—your father gets home."

Last June when the household was in a great blast-off of wedding preparations, Susie, readying herself to get away from it all by a nice morning of reading and heron-watching at the pond, had been sent through the early June heat to that little key place in the shopping center, a dreary stretch of cement set with box-like buildings. She had not needed—or wanted—the generous pay given by her mother; it would not give her the wild ducks on the pond or a possible sight of the great blue heron. The sensible thing to do with her money was to get extra keys for Charlotte; the next time she had to go for keys, she'd only pretend and bring home keys after a nice long bike ride into the country or a stay by the pond.

She now silently unlocked the back door into her sister's suite, a large L-shaped assembly of dressing, bedroom, sitting, and bath with windows on two sides, and plenty of closets. Charlotte's husband must plan to do a lot of visiting, she thought, as she went through closets and drawers. He had left a fine assortment of clothing with a selection of night things. Too bad he was on the stocky side; you could, if you wanted to be mean, call him a fat porpoise. Nothing would fit her tall, thin visitor too well, but she thought the longest-legged pajamas she could find would at least cover his knees. She also found a long, long-haired bathrobe.

She next raided the medicine cabinet, and came away with aspirin, a thermometer which she took time to sterilize, and a green bottle with four V-Cillin-K 250-milligram tablets left from a prescription for Charlotte's husband. Different from the Schnitzer males, he did not religiously take all his pills. She also remembered bedroom slippers; if he had planter warts or athlete's foot, she didn't want any smeared around her.

Back in her hall, she put everything on a chair within easy reach of the bathroom door. She listened a moment, but instead of vomiting, heard the shower. He was certainly making himself at home; he must have found the bathroom linen closet with plenty of clean towels, cloths, and fresh soap. She was not a very good hostess; she should have got the towels herself; and also advised him to take a sponge bath. Nice, if the pipes should squeal so loudly her parents heard. Would their wonderings on why their daughter was taking a second shower be enough to bring them in to investigate? She shrugged. She remembered no pipe noises from her shower, heard none from the boy's; and anyway it was doubtful if they were interested enough in her non-subversive activities to come investigating.

She was in the clothes closet hanging up her party clothing when she looked around to a "Thank you," and there he was by the closet door. "Short and wide, but not too bad. I am using the socks for bedroom slippers if you don't mind. I don't want to get some loathsome foot disease."

"Sorry you're worried," she told him. "But at least the thermometer on my study table is safely antisepticized. Suppose you go use it now."

His smile was nice in spite of his watery eyes. "At first I

39

wondered if you could talk at all—to me. To Beeto you're different—a broadcast."

"Beeto?" She was shivering again. "You—you know him? —And he told you my secret?"

"You ought to be ashamed. You know Beeto doesn't tell secrets, and certainly not yours. We didn't know your passage over the potting shed was a secret to anybody except around here. I told you we were cousins—not too many times removed. I live close to Chicago; Beeto visits us. His worrying around over that hole I came through is pitiful, always worrying. That's how I heard, his worry."

She couldn't think of anything to say, and was glad when he left to take his temperature. She went to clean whatever mess he had made in the bathroom; there was scarcely any. Everything he had worn except his shoes was rolled into a neat bundle. Planning to dry the suit and launder the other things, she opened the bundle to find blood all over his undershirt, shirt, with some on the vest. He had really hurt himself on something; but what? Nothing was torn. The door was opening and he was whispering: "Do you have to look at that mess?"

"You can't wear these clothes in the shape they're in." She took out her still-damp underclothing from the wall washer, set the washer on *Dry Warm*, then turned to pick up his sopping trousers. He grabbed them and put them in himself. She next got out the loathsome blue plastic bucket for a quick cold-water soak with bleach of his bloodied shirt and underclothes. He saw what she was about, took the bucket, and did the work himself.

Finished, he helped himself to a plastic glass from the dispenser, filled it, then turned to her. "My temperature's almost a hundred and two on that thermometer. Do you suppose those pills you brought will cure pneumonia? I know I'm getting it; that cursed swimming pool. I already had a psychosomatic cold."

"You'll have to imagine the pills are psychotherapeutics. You're going to be all right," she told him. He did look sick, but he was scared more than anything. She wondered, too, if a long hot shower such as he had had could raise the body temperature.

40

Be nice to know such things. And should he take aspirin with the pills?

She followed him into her study. He thought aspirin a good idea, but after a glance overhead, said:

"A good sleep in your cozy attic may do me more good than all kinds of medicine."

She needed several seconds to find her tongue. "You can't, just can't do such a crazy thing—sleep down here in the bedroom. Anyway, you'd be better off in a place where you could have a doctor—if you should need one."

He sighed. "Cousin Susie, I would never have believed you could be so hard-hearted. Why, no humane person would send a dog out into such a cold damp night. The only worry, as I see it, is that Beeto might sometime learn I had spent a night with you."

"Don't put it that way," she hissed. "You're able to stand up and argue. You could surely walk down to the cab-call phone— less than half a mile—and get away."

"To where?" He gave a troubled headshake. "I can't go on—not now. You see—I robbed a bank. And the idiots, they thought I was going to kill them. And—. Please, may I get to bed?"

He made you wonder if he had studied dramatics or was a natural-born actor. What a tale. Chances were he was in a Charlotte predicament—broke—but, different from Charlotte, ashamed to say so. "Be reasonable," she told herself. "He is sick. In the morning when he's better—or well—I'll offer him money." She only then realized how completely he had won. She was already taking bed linen from the bathroom closet.

She slipped around him and through her clothes closet, Little Atlas in her bathrobe pocket. The *how* of her closet doors seemed the only secret left her. She would, if possible, keep that. He followed with the flashlight, and quarreled about her coming with him. He didn't like the idea of "a young girl following a man to his bed."

She tramped on her tongue wanting to tell him that since he considered himself a man, he could at least offer to carry some of her load. Getting the bed linen, water jug with glass, and an old picnic bucket up the widely spaced rungs of the attic ladder she had made wasn't easy. She wavered on the last rung as she reached up and over to settle the water jug on the floor.

"Please," he begged behind her, all that coolness gone from his voice, "come down. Let me go first and carry your load. I've already been up there." He tried to give her more light by lifting the flashlight higher; the beam, after wavering above her, dropped to the floor.

She had one knee over the edge of the floor, when she saw a thing she had never seen up here—a round dark eye with an overgrown pupil; the pupil black nothingness, the rim of iris with the dull shine of oiled metal. The light moved away. She got the second knee up, started to rise, and stopped, frozen. The light had come back to strike what she had decided was a short length of pipe. Now, closer, and under the light, the eye had become the end of a pistol barrel pointing at her neck; a pistol like one of her father's.

The boy, on the last rung, turned off the light, and said, his voice dropped to the faintest of whispers: "Yes, it is a gun. I had hoped you wouldn't see it. It isn't loaded. But don't touch it. I used gloves."

"For what?" she whispered, not moving.

"To rob a bank. I told you."

"I thought—I thought you were joking, telling tales the way Brandon used to brag about sneaking out our father's pistols to scare children he didn't like." Talking helped. She could move again across the floor she had made of leftover pieces of plywood.

"If I have family gossip right, your brother wasn't telling a tale about his use of pistols. The truth came out as he had told it while you were summering with your grandmother, I believe?"

"Sh-sh," she begged, her whisper yet more frightened. "Don't ever forget, around here, to call her, 'The Camp for Exceptional Children;' or 'Camp' will do."

"I know. I just forgot. Sorry. —Say, any danger of that light showing through—there are attic windows, surely—and cracks around the eaves, I guess?"

She shook her head. Surely, his bank robbery story was all a tale. How could he be so cool? The bed-reading light she had switched on was a powerful little thing with its own built-in transformer, yet so hooded there was little seepage past a book's page.

She began to strip the cot, staying as far from the light as possible. She could not see the boy's face, but felt he watched her. Silent, out there in the dark, he had become an ominous presence. Her private TV kept showing her the gun.

"I should be helping you."

She gave a startled jerk away from the voice. She had not known he was so close; sock-footed, he had made no sound. It seemed years ago, instead of minutes, there had been that worry and embarrassment at the thought of letting him be the first to see her "own room;" no plastics, no rayon, no mourning for the world here. Instead, bright blues and reds—her spread and rugs and pictures from China, Russia, Mexico, Canada, sneaked in by way of Canada; and no one but herself would think beautiful the soft gray of the old wooden milk box that served as bedside table.

Everything shook up and neglected in the excitement of the upcoming party—books and papers all around. There could even be some of her silly poems scattered over the wall shelf that served as writing center. None of that mattered now. She drew yet more into herself when, in the cone of light, she saw a long hand smoothing the sheet.

They worked in silence, each kneeling in the shadow, the light above and between them. Shadowy and faceless as he was, she could still make out the movements of his head enough to know when he left off looking at her to study the jungle-like growth of pipes that sprouted out of the shadows above to disappear in the full dark of the passage below the attic.

She didn't feel like talking, but courtesy, as well as safety, demanded she explain to him a bit about the pipes. She pointed to the shadowy outline of a large square duct, sloping out of darkness into darkness. "That's a cold air return. It has a loose joint; when I want cool air I open it. That big one coming down past my writing shelf is hot air; I can open it when I am cold."

He was shaking his head. "So many; so many."

"It's mostly the fall-out shelter. It's under ground and away from the house, so the pipes had to come up here to hook onto the main ducts somewhere."

He said: "Ugh. Your father—."

He stopped, but almost at once said, his tone no longer disgusted, mournful instead. "I wish I had gone to your—that party."

"I wish you had, too," she said. The arranging of the spread forced her into the light. He moved up to help. He was now close and examining her. He would see her scars. She dropped her face, but in a moment curiosity lifted her glance; and so they stared, each at the other; she kneeling on one side the cot; he opposite. He suddenly moved back into deeper shadow.

"Don't stare at me as if—as if—."

"You were a robber," she whispered when it was clear he could not finish. She was at once ashamed; plainly he was not happy with what he had done—if he had done anything. She added: "You were staring at me."

"Sorry, but you see I've heard so much of you—and you seem never to have heard of a Ter." There was in his voice a trace of wonder, not unmixed with pique; he was, she imagined, accustomed to plenty of notice. "My father," he was explaining, peeved, "knew your grandfather well; and more, they were— quite closely related. I've heard of you from my father since I can remember; and now from Beeto it's slides and motion pictures—in color—along with 'My Susie' this, and 'My Susie' that. They still talk of that awful time when you were around six years old, and your grandmother was deported back to Canada because she was supposed to be a subversive or something; and how she had to let your father take you, and in less than six months almost kill you by throwing you through a double window. I had expected, in spite of Beeto's pictures, a face all scars."

She was too agitated to notice she was leaning into the light. "Your gossip is wrong. I jumped through the window; I thought it was open. My father didn't throw me. And as for Granma, she loved the States—in many ways. She wanted to stay and stand trial for what the FBI and immigration people called 'subversive

44

activities.' She'd only tried to help people not much of anybody else would help: like Sacco and Vanzetti a long time ago, and refugees from Franco's Spain, and the interned Japanese in World War II, and the people wrecked by un-American investigations, and—. Anyway, it wasn't her fault some of the organizations she had given money to were later called subversive. And it wasn't what she did—it was what she wouldn't do to please them. The investigators kept hounding her for names. They wanted names of people she hadn't heard of in twenty years, and she'd never known the names of others. She wouldn't try to give them."

"Don't get so upset," he begged. "I know."

"But do you know the worst part? She wanted a trial. Who kept her from having it? My father and my mother, her own daughter. The publicity, they said, would ruin my father's business, just getting started."

"Forget it. Forget it. I'm sorry I brought it up. I was thinking what beautiful eyes you have; big and—gray I guess you'd call them. And you do have a fascinating face. I can't find anything from your German father, but I can see Sicily and Italy, and a lot of Nova Scotia; I mean Scotland or Ulster or England, or where ever your grandmother's ancestors lived."

"All three. They mixed in Canada a long time ago." The bed was finished. She got up.

He was bending his head to sniff something she could not see. He smiled. "I can still smell."

He was cool in spite of his troubles, while she was so shook up, she only now realized she, too, had been smelling chrysanthemums. She had picked and killed the poor little things, then left them to wilt. Where? She didn't need his scolding: "You don't treat your flowers very well."

She took from her milk-box table a small silver vase, bought in Mexico during the summer. When she had poured in water from the night pitcher, he reached the flowers across the bed, but as he did so he winced, angrily, as if the reaching arm were a friend who had betrayed him. He jerked his hand out of the light, but not before she had seen under one fingernail a thin dark line. He tried to make a joke, but there was none in his voice: "Makes you sympathize with Lady Macbeth. I scrubbed and scrubbed and thought my nails were clean."

She backed away; had half a mind to pretend she knew nothing of Lady Macbeth, and so could not know that was blood on his hand. Instead, she heard herself making an inane remark: "In orchestra there is a new girl some call 'Lady Macbeth with her spots all washed away.' "

"Why?"

"I don't know exactly. I think it's because she's from Birmingham, Alabama."

"How silly. They are assuming, I suppose, she has helped bomb and burn Negro homes and churches? There are some good, brave people in the south; and even the inhuman ones are not hypocrites like a lot in the north. But you have to admit there's no hypocrisy about your father. From what I've heard he makes his prejudices plain—in word and deed."

The truth hurt. She wanted to change the subject. "Shouldn't something be done about your wound?"

"No. It's too small and high under my arm to matter."

"But how could you get hurt in your upper arm enough to bleed so, and still not tear your clothing?" She was thinking he could have, in the dark, tangled with some loose strands of the old rusted barbed wire hanging to forgotten fence posts of fields waiting for the subdividers.

"Bullets never make big holes," he said.

Bullets? And what had his own bullets done? No, he would never have shot at people.

"Those fools tried to kill me." His voice trembled. "Do you know they actually shot at my back?—And I wouldn't have hurt them for anything."

She couldn't believe the wild tale. "But did they know you wouldn't hurt them?"

"Oh, they knew all right. That seemed to me the nice thing about bank robbing. Nobody gets hurt—usually—and nobody loses anything."

"Just money," she whispered. "A lot of money is—more than sweat-stained; bloody even. People fight for it."

He nodded. "But bank-robbed money is the cleanest of all.

It's insured, and insurance companies are rich as Midas; and—.
Don't look at me that way. I'll take it back. You act as if I had
killed some poor old lady for her rent money."

"The FBI wouldn't chase you for a dozen old ladies killed
by slow torture; but an attempted, just an attempted bank robbery, that's different."

"Look, you don't have to tell me about the American concern for money over human life. I know. But listen—morally, is
bank robbery any worse than getting rich off this filthy war? My
father's businesses are booming. And your father, his little heat-
resistant plastics plant is getting to be a big thing thanks to the
war."

"Please. I'm not my father."

"I'm sorry. I apologize. I'm only trying to show you that
robbery is really a kind of free enterprise. And free enterprise
can be robbery, shielded, even aided, by the government."

"My father—if he heard you say that he'd take you for a
Communist."

"So what? Has he ever known one Communist?" Wound and
illness were forgotten. "Oh, Susie, can anybody, can any of us
escape our fathers? Can you? You thought just now I sounded
like a Communist; that really grabbed you. Don't be like that,
believing in the one sin only—Communism. Think of all the
murder, theft, falsehood, and torture that go on around us. —I've
heard your brother takes birds out of their nests and pulls them
apart while they're still alive. And what does your father do to
punish him? Nothing."

He towered above her, close, yet his face was lost in the
shadows. Better this way than looking at that thin troubled face
with the wild dark hair falling all over as he emphasized his
words. He had her all wrong. She could not believe he had
robbed a bank; but he thought she was—. "I am not my father,"
she repeated, forgetting to whisper. "Brandon doesn't—do such
things—now. At least I haven't heard of any lately. I wish you
and the others could forget all the bad things I told Granma
when they first got me."

She wished they were biking down some lonesome country
road where she could talk with him of these things that chewed

47

holes in her, and of which she could speak to no one—here. She remembered he was sick. "I'll keep you talking till daylight," she said, and started for the ladder.

"Don't go away angry." He held out the flowers. "And don't forget these."

She gave a sad head shake. "Up here is the only place I can have flowers. My father's allergies. He might see them in my study, and start sneezing—unless I could persuade him they were plastic."

"Plastic flowers. How bloody awful. —I'm sorry."

She loathed the pity in his voice, and hurried to get away; but halfway down the ladder, she remembered she had not told him about tomorrow. She explained she couldn't see him first thing in the morning because she was going to the swamp for theme material.

He was at once interested, and wondered if the swamp growth here were like that near his school in Canada. She managed at last to get him out of the swamp and back to himself. He assured her he could awaken around eight for the next pill, hoped he wasn't putting her out too much, and thanked her for everything. "Oh, yes, and would you please leave your closet doors open, just in case?"

She didn't like that, and explained she had left an old picnic jug for emergencies.

He was angry. "I'm not that helpless."

Little Atlas could only open or close her secret door; in order to prop it open, she had to deactivate. The connection was hidden under the insulation near the foot of the ladder. As she knelt there, seeing with her fingers, she heard the boy's troubled sigh, then the agonized words: "*Seigneur, prends pitié. Seigneur, prends pitié. Seigneur—.*" There came a low groan, not as if from pain aspirin could ease.

She felt herself an eavesdropper, and hurried away. "I am getting old," she whispered, stopped stone-still in the hall. Lately, she had made the responses so seldom, they still automatically came in Latin. How long ago was Latin?

She took two blankets from the bathroom closet, and, trying to forget her distaste, went into the funeral parlor, unused except to walk through since coming home three weeks ago. Shivering, she laid the blankets on the "young girl's dream bed"—quilted taffeta (rayon) headboard to match the quilted, scalloped rayon spread (each an underdone-frozen-boiled-pea-green) above a tiered and ruffled (melted-blueberry-popsicle-juice blue) rayon taffeta underskirt, flounced, "for the contrast one needs," with pink (machine-made) nylon lace.

She crawled between the blankets, and lay rigid. There was time for more than two hours of sleep—if she could get to sleep. She tried to yawn and could not. She tried not to think of the party; all that happy excitement would keep her awake. The worries were just as bad; the confrontation with the psychologist; Ter—she had remembered his name—how would she ever sneak him out of the house? and homework waiting in physics, math, chemistry, Latin, and English. She must write a good theme.

Go to work on the gods. Name and give their relatives; then, the people from the bottom of the sea and the top of the sky will come and bring you sleep. She was puzzling over Asclepius, wondering if he belonged, when a dark woman with long black, water-dripping hair, and sitting high on the spiny branch of a tall cactus, held down to her a little house with vines over the windows. It was a sand house carried away by the tide a long time ago, and now so freshly dug from under the sea, water ran down the pale sand of its roof.

She did not try to take it from the woman's hand, but smiled and snuggled more deeply into the blankets. The prickle of wool on her chin told her she was still awake.

3

The inner time clock that lived without electricity and never needed a windup brought her wide awake. A dim blob of gray marked the overdressed window. This meant it was around seven o'clock of a late September morning, that time of year in lower Michigan when the nights grow long and longer as the sun runs down the sky to winter.

Bed straightened, blankets put away, she hurried to the bathroom carrying her old blue jeans and sneakers for swamping. She showered, unworried by the gurgles, coughs, and screams of the piping. Her father, in the storm he was in when she came home, would have taken so many sleeping pills washed down with beer he'd be deaf to all sounds. That would be something for a poem, she thought, dressing: "My father cannot hear the piping of the pipes."

She was hunting another line, shaking her head to "These are not the pipes of Pan," while, silently as a cat, she went up to check on Ter; that was his name and she must think of him as that instead of The Boy. She forgot both name and poem when she heard his too-loud, too-quick breathing. He was sick, good and sick; nose completely blocked, and, judging from his respiration, fever higher in spite of the pills. She comforted herself with the thought the antibiotic had not yet had time to take effect; but suppose he had a virulent virus? Somebody ought to work out a virus killer.

She dropped to hands and knees, to move quietly over the uneven floor to the secret bookshelf. Working on viruses wouldn't be a bad life. Most of that life would be needed to learn the chemistry, physics, math, biology, physiology you'd need, plus an M.D. Pitch-black as it was, her searching hand found the right book.

She stopped at the top of the ladder to listen again to The Boy. Should she leave him? Did fever have the same effect on him as on Brandon who went out of his head and talked wild and loud? "You're silly with worry. You ought to be worrying about his trousers left in your dryer," she told herself, hurrying back to the bathroom. "He's not twisting about or muttering. And anyway, he's a cool one."

Trousers hidden in the closet, secret pads in place, doors locked, and carrying the book, binoculars, and writing materials, she ran down the back stairs to the kitchen. Here, with automatic temperature still on *Night*, the place was cold when measured by degrees; though no amount of heat could, when empty of Lulu as now, take that other coldness from stainless steel, sick-blue tile, white enamel, and colder blue-white fluorescent light. Even Lulu's two African violets in red earthen pots had in the cold light the look of dead plastic. Shivering, she stayed only long enough to rummage up a slice of bread and a tomato. These she put into her binder; if her stomach growled too much, she'd have something to give it.

She hurried on to the gardening center for her bike. Here, she stopped to look for any telltale signs Ter might have left when coming through her secret passage. He had put the loose square of ceiling that went over the beams, back into place; but in climbing up, first to the rim of the soapstone sink in the corner, then to the heavy herb and pesticide shelf, he had knocked over a can of extra powerful—poison ivy—weed killer.

She righted the can, searched for other signs of use; found none. Not surprising. She had, when home, used the hole for more than a year, and no one had shown any interest in the how of her comings and goings. Even if someone suspected she had a secret passage, it would, covered as it was by loose insulation batting, be almost impossible to find; found, it would take a person a good deal more nimble than her father or Brandon, and certainly much smaller, to reach it and then go twisting sideways through, as the slender Ter had done.

She had found the hole months before moving in, when one day after school her father, proud of the new home in the "tightly restricted" neighborhood, had brought his wife and family to see the progress of the remodeling. What with raising the roof of the back central section, adding another wing, lengthening the garage and giving it a second story, the place looked as if it would never be finished.

The one thing almost completed had been the tacked-on wooden gardening shed with its roof sloping up close to her bedroom window. The shed, she had been told by her father, was to be the storage place for her bike.

The carpenters had finished for the day, so she went inside to have a look. Pesticides and gardening supplies were already moving in, and the place not even finished. There was not yet the beginnings of a proper ceiling, for the planks went above the ceiling beams instead of being nailed to the lower edges. Or were they even nailed? Above them was a lot of nice attic space under that high slope of roof. She had glanced around. Nobody in sight.

She had, by way of the sink and shelves, climbed high enough to find and lift the loose corner square. The carpenters, working from above, had not bothered to try to fasten the square of ceiling from below. She had swung herself up, expecting nothing more than the attic under the shed roof. Carefully soundless, she had put the board in place, and in complete darkness had explored the corner by touch. Much to her joy and surprise, she had found a strip of loose batting where she had expected bricked-over wall. This was at the lower back corner of the shed attic where it abutted on the new second-story wall of the garage. The bricklayers had bricked under the edges of the shed wall only enough to form a beginning for the upper wall of the garage. They had not bothered to brick over a hole nobody would ever see—or so they had thought.

She had lifted the insulation and gone on to find the pipe-cluttered passage behind her quarters. She had leaped down, happy. The new, ugly home would have secrets after all.

So far the secret passage had brought no trouble but Ter. And should she call him trouble? She tried to forget him as she rolled her bicycle out the shed door, then rode over the drive and onto the flagstone walk that led to the swimming pool with "attached elm tree." That was how her father thought of the tree when he ordered the pool built so close to it; the scoop shovel had torn out mats of mangled roots.

She had not planned to stop, yet she did, hoping; but as always there was nothing except the cold blue-blueness of the water above blue concrete, the smell of chlorine—stronger on this still morning—and that other smell, the odor of nothingness, not even the smell of weed or insect killer, now odorless as the newer war gases.

She stared up into the elm. Last night it had dropped more crumpled, gray-brown leaves onto the pool. They, along with whole twigs, fell in an unceasing gentle rain of dying—no sorrow for the dying, only her father's anger. He had spent his money on a fancy pool to be shaded by a mighty elm. He had spent more on spray people who sent dust and pellets and showers of liquid into the tree. Still, the elm died, a slow and ugly death with a continuous messy weeping that enraged her father. The other part of his dream was realized. No living thing save humans ever troubled the pool or the tree or the grass.

She turned away and biked over the stone path to the concrete-and-porcelain barbecue with electric fire and rotator. She then risked a bicycle track across the dew-wet grass to the hole in the screen of shrubbery where a Scotch pine had lately been removed because in death it was ugly brown. The mixture of peat moss and earth—and how Bismarck had roared about the bills and come up with that "When I was a boy on the farm," business—was still richly dark and grass-free.

She was past the spot before realizing that in the dark earth she had seen the print of a man's shoe, worn by neither Brandon nor her father, too narrow. Ter's, of course; she sprang off the bike, scuffed out the track, looked for other signs, but found none.

She pushed her worries over Ter, the unwritten theme, the psychologist, to the back of her mind as she rolled the bicycle through the densely wooded strip that bordered the same old, root-wrinkled road she and Robert had traveled for a short distance last night; except they had been on only the lower end. This part was private, built and maintained by those on the hill above, and only for them. Her father had learned that while planning a second driveway—a back drive for delivery trucks and help. It would be short, with only the back lawn and the strip of road shoulder to cut through to the old road. But somebody had made him understand that not even the owner of a "Custom-Built Executive Home on a Two-Acre Plot" could have an entrance on that road. The plat book called it Ramsey's Hill Road; she had never heard it given any name except "The Old Road." She preferred her private name, "The Sacred Way," because everything about it, including the wide, tree-filled shoulders, was sacred to those on The Hill. The Hill, nameless, was in turn referred to as The Village.

That place with its own country club, gas main, water system, bus for school children and help, had also its own laws and mores—everything for The Village alone. The private bus was visible, but the laws and the mores, Susie had decided, were like the constitution of England, unwritten. She had never seen The Village, but she thought it to be a collection of large, old-fashioned homes set on acres of landscaped lawns inhabited chiefly by old-money people on the shady side of middle age.

True, she had met two young ones from The Village: Robert, who had offered his services for the evening, after she had chanced to mention to Iggy, the other boy from The Village, how much she would like to get away from home for several hours on Football Prom night.

Iggy—she was uncertain of his last name but thought it Soames—was a lovely boy, a few months younger than Brandon. They had first met on a Saturday afternoon a week or so after the Schnitzer settling. Susie had taken refuge from her quarters—her attic not yet in use—to read and look for birds in a back corner

54

of the lawn where a big maple of the Old Road shoulder lent its shade. Iggy had glimpsed her from his bicycle, got off, come over, and started a conversation.

He had stopped for pure evaluation, she had felt at the time, and at first had been icily polite. Her wariness had vanished as he talked of the book, *Pronunciamiento,* she was reading. Not that he told her, but from his talk she knew he had read it in the original Spanish; hers was a French translation. Their likes and dislikes agreed; both enjoyed reading of the Mexican deserts and mountains, but not the guerrilla warfare.

They had since met often, at the back of the Schnitzer lawn, or biking to their separate schools.

The Village, however, was not Iggy. One afternoon not long before escape to "camp" she had decided to explore the Old Road and find out if the lower prong shown in her plat book skirted the farther end of The Hill to come out above the swamp.

The road had been a delight; walled and roofed with trees and shrubs in bud and flower; all wild, she had thought at the time. Later, Iggy had explained that most of the shrubbery by the road had been planted, intended to give a look of nature in the wild, and that the big buds belonged to imported and most expensive rhododendrons. Save for bird song and twitter, the place had been silent with a deserted look about even the few driveways, often neither named nor numbered, and all narrow, uninviting tunnels through still-thicker shrubbery.

She had been sitting on her bike, watching a squirrel on a tree limb, when she heard a smoothly running car approaching at a polite pace. She continued to sit, but instead of passing her, the neat black car stopped gently, as if in that world all things were done with decorum. The voice, too, had been gentle as it asked with the greatest politeness: "Lost? Whose place are you hunting?"

She had already seen the small neat letters on the side of the car, Village Patrol, but had answered with as nice a smile as she could manage: "Am I ever glad to see you. I think I'm lost. I'm hunting Lafferty's Road."

"It's back the way you came," he had said.

Knowing she had not fooled him, not one bit, she had turned and fled from his proffered directions after a quick "No, thank you. I think I know where I took the wrong turn." She had wanted to tell him she had seen no Keep Out signs, but did not.

It was not until her return for school the following fall that she had found, each set on the outer edge of the road shoulder so as to be clearly seen from the Schnitzer backyard, three freshly staked-down, neatly done in black and white, "Private. No Trespassing," signs. She learned from Lulu her father's weed killer had trespassed.

Now and then in the very early morning, as now, she biked the few hundred foot stretch of road between the dead Scotch pine and the gas main cut. Always she felt guilty, though she took nothing from the road shoulders but sight and sound and smell. She touched nothing. The people of The Village wanted not only the trees and the shrubs, but the sight of the red velvety plumes of the sumac, the shaded wild asters—blues, lavenders, purples, and white—the goldenrod, bright yet fragile in the shade, all for themselves.

She reached the gas main cut, a sloping grassy strip across the road shoulder, smooth enough so she could bike down to the road where she belonged. Here, she stopped, first to watch a spider spin, then a long look at the wide sweep of flat valley floor below, though not a great deal lower, at least in elevation, than her father's house. On fair days after the sun had crested the hill one could from this spot see the new development of "Professional Homes. Choose your own from five different patterns—all-white roofs—attached garages—two-storied if preferred," so the signboards said.

Now, the white roofs and patterned ugliness were hidden under the early morning fog and mists. She smiled. She could imagine she stood by the sea on a still foggy morning when the tide is in and quiet. Whether the fog shifted or she only now saw, she did not know, but the far end of her sea was ruined by one of the same broken-backed digging monsters she and Robert had passed on their way home.

She turned away. That meant another basement for another house. Her father would be angry again. Many times she had heard him complain that "—cheap housing, nothing over fifty thousand, is ruining this neighborhood." She had wondered if the people in The Village felt the same way about her father's house and the other "executive homes" on the lower slopes of the hill—new money trying to get close to old money. And did the owners of the professional homes complain of the still less expensive, more closely crowded "first homes" that ringed the shopping center at the lower end of the valley?

Like sets of numbers formed into some kind of geometric pattern. Could you make—? She shut her eyes the better to hear. Yes, it was a car coming slowly, quietly, politely up the Old Road. She had never known Security out so early. She ought, she guessed, to take off and be on the public road below when the car came by. Pride forbade it; anyway, she was on property leased to the gas company.

The spider had finished the strand and was fastening it before she again heard the car; it had been stopped somewhere near her father's house, and now came on slowly as if in extra heavy traffic. She blinked when, instead of Security, here came a dark blue sedan; not new, not old, it was like a million other smoothly running cars; and either of the two men in it could have been any one of several million other men. They were so properly dressed, either might have been chosen, not for the best dressed, but as an example of what the United States business man wears to work.

She wondered uneasily if her look were a stare as one said: "Good morning," in a voice no different from a million other male Midwestern voices.

She hoped she smiled as she good-morninged back; not easy. She tried to lick her lips; they wouldn't lick; as the car moved away she wanted to lift a leg over the bicycle and be gone; the leg wouldn't lift. She couldn't do anything but remember the men who had pestered her grandmother: two homogenized men in a slowly cruising homogenized car out in the early morning, added up to one thing—the FBI. Hunting the bank robber.

Had they found Ter's track near the Schnitzer place? That long silence indicated they had stopped somewhere nearby. The

57

car started up again. Reason came back. Had they found anything the stop would have been longer; one would now be ringing Schnitzer doorbells while the other cruised. What had they known of her grandmother? Nothing, or why would they have ground and ground the questions into her solely because some witness had named her? She wished she had sneaked back more often and listened longer; she had not understood at all, at all—then, when trouble was a smelly fog you couldn't get your hands on.

She had coasted down the gas main cut, and now pedaled through the domain of "Executive Homes." The wide new road, like the concrete drives curving into and out of the two-acre plots was empty. The houses, each sitting against the back of a loop, also seemed empty; easy to imagine this world peopled only by houses.

Today, the houses were those middle-aged ladies glimpsed in the fitting rooms of the expensive boutiques she sometimes visited, places with a clientele of well-to-do teen-agers and old-model, simulated teen-agers like her mother and Charlotte. Walking past the often-opened cubicles, you glimpsed the too-thin and the spread-out ones, sometimes only in bra and girdle, sometimes in ill-fitting teen-age dresses, price tickets dangling; and always those women wore an air of embarrassment. They knew they were out of place in the new dress, or without any at all. It was as if they were apologizing: "I am trying on this dress only for amusement. Do you think *I* would wear an off-the-rack dress?"

The houses were worse. They had not even false eyelashes of quickie shrubbery to soften their staring window eyes. They sat naked on their browning grass, much of it so lately laid the seams still showed, some of it dead, as were several shrubs standing brown and crisped. Even the plantings of small things, though green, stood as if making up their minds to grow or die, for each said: "I was once alive and so don't belong here." The swimming pools of many different shapes, but all of the same hard bright blue that had nothing to do with the sky, had an "in" look. They had never been alive.

The house-people ended at empty lots with "Acreage For Sale" signs. Here she turned downhill, and after bouncing over truck tracks on a temporary road, came out on the new pavement near the end of the "professional home" development, and was soon on Lafferty Road. She thought of this as a "real country road," straight, laid out long ago when the township was platted into sections.

She had first seen this part of the road around two years before; it had been a green-walled and roofed tunnel with fields on either side of heavily wooded shoulders. Subdivisions were far away. Now, the "professional" homes had swallowed the nearer road, and the county had prepared another stretch for widening and paving. The road shoulders, bleeding earth from the widening cuts of the scrapers, were empty of greenery. First, the herbicide crews had gone through to kill all small growing things. Power saws and wood shredders had taken the larger trees. Ashy beds of charcoal told of how bonfires had "cleaned up" anything left.

She bowed her head, pedaled furiously, and tried to look at nothing, though now and then she glimpsed without wanting to the bared cut-away roots of some still standing but dying tree far back on the road shoulder. It was not until she had gone up a short steep rise that she permitted herself a long look ahead.

She pedaled still faster. She could now see, close, the remains of the green tunnel, walled by trees and underbrush and flowers, roofed by the widely reaching limbs of white oak, beech, maple, and other trees she did not know. Silent, save for birds, she liked this stretch of road better than any seen below The Village—all this was wild, planted by God for the public. Trouble was it made her sad—now; so little left. She biked slowly, stopping often to study a wand of goldenrod, pick up an acorn, or hunt the sky through leaf and limb.

She was abreast of the last big white oak before she again looked straight ahead, and then with a sniff and a frown. Bare of any plant, the road with its raw earth shoulders rose gradually for a short distance, then after a shorter, steeper rise appeared to end in nothing but smoky fog. It did. The bridge approach was finished and waiting for the metal frame work of the deck that would carry the country road to the abutment on the other side; below, the six-lane, limited-access superhighway was being built.

The old gravel road had dipped low to cross on a causeway set with drains, a sluggish stream bordered by thickly grown swamp and woods plants. It had been easy to see from a moving bike the ferns and shrubs with many flowers in early spring. She had never learned the names of most; Michigan woods were for her a new world of which the more she saw the more she wanted to know. Now, she could never know the names of those flowers; they were buried under many feet of fill for the roadbed. The newly made detour on Lafferty Road was but a bumpy stretch of sand and gravel with a scattering of mud holes.

A few feet past the big oak, she rolled the bicycle through the road shoulder underbrush and on into the still thicker growth of an ancient fence row, marked less by a scattering of empty posts than the jungle-like brush interlaced with wild grape vines. She left the bicycle behind a large glacial boulder, then walked around the rock to stand and smile on the overgrown pasture that began at her feet and swept out and down to the highway cut that bordered the pond.

She helped herself, with no feeling of guilt, to a bunch of wild grapes. The field, as far as she could tell, belonged to some absentee who wanted nothing of it except a fine price from a subdivider. Last fall barbed wire had been on the posts, and behind it an old plow horse grazed. Now, the land was empty, turned open to the world, no owner's name printed above it in the plat book, no sign of any kind; nothing but a thin line of red stakes near the road embankment.

Carrying her binder and eating wild grapes, she walked for a short distance through dew-wet dried clover and knee-high yellowing grass. She stopped by another boulder, and there, careful to send her glance straight out instead of down, she looked in front of her. Trees ringed much of the landscape; glimpsed between them was the corner of what she thought was a big old barn. She let her gaze drop lower to a sloping green pasture where cows grazed, with the lowest cow smudged by smoke and fog. More smoke mixed with curls of fog covered the lower field, the swampy shores of the pond, and she supposed the throughway cut. She would not look.

She ran then, straight down across the pasture. Wet grass whipped at her bare legs, yet the running was good, not so fine as running down the beach to the sea at sunrise, but better by far than anything here; a long run, no reason except something inside her cried for the running; no one to watch or wonder, just the running down through the grass and clover. She did not stop until mud sucked at her feet; rivulets of mud streaked the grass, but the smell of mint was pleasantly strong.

She looked up to face the fifteen-or-twenty-foot wall of earth and rock that held up the new roadbed and had smothered the swamp on this side of the pond. She took off her sneakers, and skirting a drainpipe higher than she was tall, climbed up in a steep diagonal, slowly, as loose earth and gravel swallowed her ankles and small boulders rolled down.

Top reached, she picked her way across the strip of un-graded sticky clay, wet sand, and rocks of what was to be the three east-bound lanes. Then it was down and up again to the second three-lane strip. Here, two lanes of packed clay carried the imprint of many tires, most made by construction machinery, for few people came to watch the pond, save Iggy now and then.

Halfway across the last lane, she stopped, and like one com-pelled, took a long look in the direction of the bridge abutments. Up to and for a short distance beyond them there was nothing but torn-out earth with here and there a bed of charcoal to mark a tree-trunk bonfire; farther, the smoke of smoldering log piles thickened into a slowly moving curtain done in bands and whorls of gray.

Closer, beginning on her side of the bridge approach, were the machines at rest on this Saturday: cranes pointing to the sky, cranes crooked to the earth, dump trucks, bulldozers with wheels higher than she was tall, and the even uglier and bigger two-en-gined earth movers. Drawn up in a row, they stood like warring monsters ready to charge.

She turned and looked at the other stretch of road. Here,

most of the work was still in the get-the-trees-out-of-the-way stage. The swampy, fertile black soil had supported a heavy growth of beech and maple on the higher spots with giant willows ringing the pools, where late last spring she had found tall blue irises.

She dropped her glance. The devastation of dying trees was too much. Many leaned far over as if they wanted to fall but could not; sap-oozing tree trunks, bark torn away by bulldozer blows, showed their white, glistening wounds. Others lay as the bulldozers had left them, their torn-out roots silhouetted in the reddened, smoky light that seeped in long rays through the wrecked woods.

Head bowed, careful to see nothing but the ground in front of her, she turned away to run across the lane and down to a high red pump pipe with a spout on the upper end and its lower end in the edge of the pond. She kept her glance lowered as if afraid of what she would see.

She smiled. Her downward look had chanced upon three stones rolled into the pond, and on top of each a little turtle sat, undisturbed by her coming.

She lifted her head, looked far out, and drew a deep happy breath of relief. Like a small statue in front of the cattails on the farther shore, one great blue heron stood, and behind it in a dead tree near the edge of the pond was another, motionless as the tree. Her lucky day; she had never until now seen two herons together. Fog and smoke hid patches of the pond; one swampy shore was cut completely away, and replaced by a man-made wall spilling alien rocks and dirt into it; fire control trucks were taking its water; yet the pond was still alive.

Far out a duck quacked; red-winged blackbirds, disturbed by her coming, cut curves in the sky; close, one frog, braver than his brothers, resumed his croaking. Dragonflies and butterflies were in and out among the reeds; and neither heron showed alarm as she went in a cautious tiptoe toward the place she wanted.

Sometimes wading, sometimes leaping from hummock to hummock, she reached her "secret nest," a large and fairly flat glacial boulder, so hidden in buttonbush, willow, and reeds, she had found it only by chance one winter day when she had come to chop a hole in the ice to get temperatures of the ooze and mud.

Still secret in spite of the road work, she had grown to feel the rock was her own forever undisturbed nook in her pond that nobody else wanted or claimed. No farmer lived near it. True, there was the barn on the other side, but down here she could see only one gable window, high, like a small eye; even in winter, evergreens hid everything except the one window and a patch of roof. The pasture was rented, she supposed by the owner of the cows; she had never when biking past glimpsed a house beyond the narrow, overgrown drive.

It was from this rock she had gathered material for last year's biology paper and a science-fair exhibit. Yet all those facts collected with camera, tape recorder, microscope, test tubes, thermometer, and other instruments were not what she needed now for her planned paper in English.

Using the binoculars, unobtrusively pushed through a hole in the leaf screen, she watched the heron in the tree, then dropped the glasses and wrote: "One heron is a crooked branch in the tree." She read the words; said, "Ugh," and drew a line through them. She should have the name of that dead tree; worse, the heron was upright; the branch of a tree was never perpendicular to the ground.

She took the glasses again and gave herself up to enjoying the life around her. In a short while all the sounds, hushed when she came, began anew. A killdeer began a thin crying from the nearby shore; red-winged blackbirds returned to bounce from reed to reed; a muskrat slid back and forth a few feet away; a duck dived to come up only inches from her side of the rock.

The sun crested the trees on the eastern end of the pond to send searching fingers of light into the grass and reeds of the opposite side. Now, in the stronger light, there was an oddness about a little shrub in the grass; the top tapered up to a sidewise point; made you think of a bird's bill pointed skyward. She caught her breath. It was a bird's bill that of the least bittern; closer than the other time when, puzzled, she had looked it up in her bird book. Please, least bittern, take one step out of your camouflage of brown-yellow grass, and let me get a good look at you.

She watched and waited, smelled peppermint, and caught the warm, earthy smell of the pond as the sun warmed its water. A shadow crossed the rock to send a duck's feather drifting down; a dragonfly bounced, almost touching her nose; and somewhere behind her she heard a little fish leap.

Still, she would not look away; she could in the strengthening light now see the bittern more clearly; surely he would take one step, and—. He had, with no movement she could see, melted into the weeds and grass behind him.

"I'm sorry. That was my fault."

She sprang up, too startled to recognize the familiar voice. She watched a sheaf of cattail spikes rise, then slide away to show dark hair above the back of a jacket, camouflaged with spots and streaks of green, brown, and yellow. "Iggy," she whispered.

"I'm sorry," he repeated, frowning as he laid a camera on the stone. "I knew when I moved I would ruin the bittern-watching, but first my feet went to sleep, then one hand; and I was afraid for the equipment." He was awkward with his gone-to-sleep hand, and she helped him bring up a tape recorder and a large tin chest from a buttonbush-covered shelf of the stone. "I was too greedy for equipment," he told her as he stood on one foot flexing his leg. "There wasn't room for all of me on the shelf so I sat with my boots in the water. It's cold."

"Wiggle your toes and fingers," she suggested, determined not to show any of the shame and sense of loss his presence brought. Still, better he than anyone else; Iggy, save possibly for Katy, a senior at school, was her most familiar stranger in this part of the world.

The pain of awakening hands and feet was going, and he could give her his warm, wide-open smile, as if a gentle light switched on somewhere inside him. Iggy was different from what you'd expect. Rather tall for his age, nimble, well built, a splendid skier, loving his horse and an excellent horseman, she had heard; neatly dressed most of the time; perfect vision, beautiful teeth; yet he was the neighborhood genius. She had heard

Katy speak of his intellect with awe. He, like Brandon, attended a special school for special children, but the schools, you'd have to say, belonged to different sets of numbers. His was for exceptionally bright children selected from diverse backgrounds and several school systems.

Besides herself, Iggy was one of the very few who biked to school, and as his school and Eden Hills High were close, they often met. She had since returning from "camp" seen him several times, but today there was something in his face that held her like a vivid but placeless memory. Not that his looks were unusual, but for an instant his face seemed familiar, as if she were re-seeing someone she had once known well, especially the eyes.

She realized she was staring and said: "Don't worry about my bittern watching. I know when I came I ruined a lot of things for you."

He shook his head, congratulated her on not having disturbed the herons. "But I really goofed things when I settled in not long after good daylight," he told her. "I wanted to bike over at dawn, but Mr. Soames, you know, my mother's husband, insisted Renfro drive me. You know what happens when a car stops; wild things know people are on the way. But they must have been glad." He nodded toward the herons.

"They?" she asked.

"The people watching on that side—students and professors of zoology, botany, biology, ecology, from colleges and universities round about—Wayne State or even U. of M. This is or was one of the few swampy ponds left in its natural state. Sometimes they camp overnight so they can be ready to watch before daybreak. The Primitive is glad to have them. She's frantic to see her pond so blighted; oil from the machinery is already making a scum and the public's swarming in."

"I—I guess I am part of the public," she whispered. She pointed toward the field she had run through. "Does that belong to—to this woman?"

He nodded. "But I'm sure she doesn't think of you as part of the destructive public. The Primitive—and I'm not being rude to call her that instead of Mrs. Nevels; better to be a primitive than one of those barbarians who are ruining her property and the rest of the world. Anyway, she went to the science fair. She saw your pond exhibit and thinks it should have won top prize."

His glance had wandered to the book she had brought, a work on Michigan wild flowers—or so the jacket said. Susie separated her hands; she would in another second be twisting her thumb. "Please, Guardian Angel, Jove, Cloud of Probability, feed some conversation into my IBM to take his mind off that book. Keep him from opening it." She had been careful not to move her lips, and, still careful, let her head say: "Thank all of you."

Iggy had looked from the book to the other side of the pond. He turned to her and smiled; she smiled back. The sound of a beautifully lonesome flute floated across the water, playing "Death and Transfiguration." Unusually good, the flutist, she thought, but wondered if she imagined it. She had no ear for judging music; this was beautiful because it came across the water in the still morning air. During a pause she whispered to Iggy: "I could almost think it Katy, our best flutist."

"It is," he said. "Early practice in Katy's home on Saturday mornings brings complaints from the neighbors. The Primitive encourages her to use her barn or house; she loves it."

"You know Katy, too? We're in orchestra together."

"Oh, yes," Iggy said.

She didn't want to pry, yet she wished he would talk of Katy, the only one in school she could think of as something more than a familiar stranger. She was like an unsolved equation with no knowns. Last fall both had been strangers in Eden Hills High; Katy's problems had seemed worse than her own; she at least had come into the system as a sophomore, the first year of senior high; but Katy had entered as a junior, harder still. Then soon you learned she was no stranger to the community, friendly with many, even boys from The Village such as Robert.

Susie had been drawn to her partly by her unprying friendliness, but more because Katy seemed to need her as much as she needed Katy. Neither was exactly an outcast, but they were certainly strays at school, because neither belonged to any of the nameless, invisibly walled cliques that made for togetherness both in and out of school.

There was also that something in Katy's face. It came and went like a cloud above the sea, too quickly gone to learn the shape of it upon the water. Times, she seemed to shrink from certain people the way she, Susie, shrank when she thought someone was staring at her scars or ready to ask a question about "camp." You wondered—a silly wonder—if Katy could be ashamed of her poverty. Judging from her clothing and the long hours she baby-sat or worked in the public library, Katy's people were terribly poor. You felt she skimped on many things to pay for music lessons and keep that splendid silver flute.

Why so poor, her people, Susie had wondered? Her maternal grandfather had been a doctor in Eden Hills. She had also learned in a roundabout way her parents were well educated; both worked. The family had moved a lot, but Katy had never traveled. She was particularly curious about Canada; after learning that Susie had spent much time in "camp" there, she asked, in chance meetings at the bike rack, many questions, some wistful as they were curious. Was it really true there was in Canada no committee to investigate un-Canadian activities? Now why would she—?

Susie roused to Iggy's whisper: "I imagine you all keep 'Death and—' well polished. Robert told me once that each former student killed in Vietnam gets a special assembly with the orchestra playing that piece."

She shook her head. "That was the plan but there were so many deaths. Twelve just last year, that was too many to work into the schedule, so there was only one memorial for the year."

"How horribly efficient! And what about the wounded?"

"Nothing." The flute was beginning again, running in and out like a singing bird through the small west wind that had come to riffle the water. She was staring across the pond, lost in the music and Katy, when she smelled Mexico. She looked around.

Iggy had quietly taken an insulated box out of his tool chest, and from it had set out a spread she had never expected to see in Eden Hills—a pile of still-warm tortillas waiting for what looked like steak *asado*. The smell made her mouth water, and when Iggy handed her a napkin and a tortilla filled exactly right with meat and sauce, she took them with no pretended unhunger. It was good, though she did have to smother a gasp after the first bite; it was even hotter than in Mexico. She remembered her tomato and divided it between Iggy and herself.

He was grateful; and when the flute was silent, said: "Nice you came along, or some of this would have gone to the frogs and fish. What do you suppose it would do to a frog's croak? But I can't hurt Callie's feelings; she tries so hard, and overdoes the pepper. I wanted to bike off with nothing, or make a sandwich, but she would get up at some ungodly hour to cook a spread for me. But her chocolate is perfect." He unscrewed a thermos with two plastic cups under the top, filled both and handed one to her.

Taking the chocolate, thanking him, she again had the feeling she had known him in some other place.

They were sipping chocolate, when he said: "We wished last spring when it was so chilly you had some kind of nice arrangement like Katy has now. It must have been miserable writing on this cold stone."

She gave him one frightened, unprogrammed glance before she could collect herself enough to answer with careful unconcern: "Mostly, I was just taking notes."

"I mean when you wrote those letters to the editor of the paper, the ones against the weed-killing campaign sponsored last spring by your father."

He read her terrified look, and was hurt. "You don't think Robert or I would tell, do you? But I was really tempted when my grandmother, eager to meet a kindred soul, tried to ring you up. Of course she couldn't ever get a number for that name at that address. I don't blame you for faking things; and don't you blame us for knowing. The wind told us. Robert and I found several scraps and one whole sheet of paper that had blown away while you were working on this rock, writing, writing, tearing up, writing."

He stopped to watch a fire-control truck roaring up to the pump pipe, then pump water, all done with so much noise conversation was impossible. She refused to watch the truck steal the pond water, but Iggy studied the operation until the

68

truck had disappeared in the smoke beyond the bridge approach. "I hope," he said, turning back to her, "there's not a fire out of control up that way; the truck hurried so. Do you know what the township people, some right around your place, are doing? Burning their trash on the log fires—cheaper than paying to have it hauled to the dump. The burning paper blows all over. The Primitive is really worried; her property is so close. —But, look, you mustn't worry over the letter-writing business. I certainly would never tell; neither will Robert."

He was looking at the book again. Iggy was her friend, but more dangerous than some familiar stranger; she thought hard, and in a moment was able to come up with: "Robert doesn't have a very good opinion of me, I'm afraid; not after last night."

That did it. He turned from the book, happy, clasping his hands. "You did get to go. You looked so kind of—sad—I thought. I was afraid to ask. Now, I think you only look sleepy. What upset good Robert: late hours or a sip of wine? His bringing up, lately anyway, has been pure WASP, you know."

"Both. He thinks I'm still a child. I'm sorry I didn't tell you right off; after all, you told Robert and made it possible for me to go to this really wonderful birthday party for—a friend. I still feel as if I'd dreamed it all." And then her private TV tuned in on Ter in the attic; that was a nightmare, unbelievable.

She tried to shove *that* dream away with talk of the party. Iggy's listening grew into a sharing. He was happy for her as she told of the fun: the chef who helped sing "Happy Birthday" and then got a song himself, in French; the party favors and the real gifts; the music and most especially the guitarist; and the champagne, not just the taste, but she had never noticed how beautiful it could be; and—. She had already told too much, for herself —and Iggy, too. There was a growing wistfulness in his eyes that caused her to switch the conversation back to Robert's reaction to her wine-smell.

"He must have really suffered," Iggy said, laughing. "I wouldn't want to walk Robert's road: everything duty; this is right; that is wrong, as if right and wrong were in labeled barrels, with love in another to be pumped out and sold for good behavior." He had stopped laughing, and sat looking at nothing. "Robert's been good to me. I shouldn't talk about him like that. I'm sorry."

He refilled their cups. Susie accepted with apologies. "I know I'm being piggish, drinking so much, but this is the best chocolate I've had since Mexico."

Iggy looked quickly around, then bent so close she could see herself in his eyes as he whispered: "It's The Primitive's goats' milk that makes most of the difference, but the chocolate is richer and fresher too."

She did not puzzle over his eyes again. She had recollected the face with eyes so like Iggy's—yet very different. Those other eyes had been set in dark, wrinkled skin, that in spite of all the years of desert sun and cold and blowing dust, had been more a delicate brown tissue paper than coarse and leathery. Those brown eyes had been smiling, friendly, but also wistful, one might almost say hungry, as they studied the rented Vauxhall, not too big and very good on hills. The eyes had gone back to her grandmother's face, as one long brown hand, palm like old ivory, had from the basket of purple cacti fruit taken one and held it as an offering in her opened palm, the eyes smiling, giving, not begging—yet still wistful as were Iggy's.

"What is it?" he asked.

In avoiding Iggy's eyes, she had looked too hard at the water. "Nothing," she answered, carefully casual. "Silly wishings; wishing our concert had not stopped, wishing I could see a silver fish, wishing I were on another visit to Mexico."

Iggy's voice was also carefully casual as he asked: "Since you told me you went to Mexico this summer, I have meant to ask, were you by any chance in San Luis Potosí? It's my favorite place."

He was herself running down to the sea on the first day back —while she walked sedately down the grand stair to join the Sunday-dinner-waiting Schnitzers. She nodded, and hoped that in her face he could see no memories: dust devils across the plains; the thin burros; the poor, poor people sitting along the curbs on fiesta night; the little adobe huts with—there had been pots of flowers hanging from the walls. "A fantastic place where everything was beautiful. And the market, wonderful. I especially remember the cathedral filled with people for the blessing of the fiesta; women on the floor with babies, the splendid *caballeros* loaded with leather and silver, little children all over, and the nave blue with incense smoke."

"And did you see the dark Christ?"

"Yes," she said, nodding, though uncertain in what village church or town cathedral. She remembered dark-faced Christs and many saints by many walls, or only a face here, a lifted hand there.

"And in the market do they still sell those laughing, pink-nosed, white ceramic pigs?" He had forgotten to whisper.

"One whole stall of them, beautiful. We bought some." She could not tell him how her grandmother, on a buying trip, had smiled on a pig she held: "These, a few, might do well in the shop. They seem genuine, no tourist-trade look."

"I always wanted one, but—they're quite large."

So he too had the problem of hiding things. "I'll give you mine. It's one of the smallest." She hated to part with the cheerful pig, but Iggy looked so happy—now, she was glad she had it to give.

He protested: she should not give away something she loved when it was such a long way to San Luis Potosí to buy another. She wished she could tell him she could easily get another from her grandmother's place near Halifax. She was struggling with that guilty feeling over what amounted to a lie, when from across the pond there came a growling drum beat.

A flood of drum beats followed, with a horn and a guitar joining in, all tuning. The herons would be flying; she looked in their direction to find them motionless as if they listened. Iggy had sprung up. "Oh boy, they got together after all; part of them; Robert couldn't make it. Listen, that's Katy with the horn —and they're short on bass."

The sounds had become a tune and Iggy cried: "Come on. Let's dance." He caught her wrists and began to pull her up from the stone.

She tried to hide her shamed embarrassment. She had had dancing lessons, but not for these sounds she felt in her insides more than she heard them. She had sometimes seen the teen-age tourists dancing on the porches of her grandmother's cottages; their gyrations, strange as they were wild, matched the music thumping out from the record players that traveled with them. She had secretly tried a few of the motions—and had felt herself a clumsy fool. "I can't," she now told Iggy. "I don't know—."

"Of course you don't know my style. Just watch and do what I do. You'll get the beat. Look, even the duck family out there has it."

Laughing at the idea of a dignified drake shepherding his family across the pond while flopping his head, flip-flapping his wings, stamping his feet, bending and twisting as Iggy was doing, she relaxed. "You've got the beat, but good," he chanted in time to the music. "Now don't fall off the rock and frighten the fishes."

She didn't know if the chanted words were advice or song, but, laughing, repeated: "Don't fall off the rock and frighten the fishes," while trying to follow Iggy's movements.

She was sorry when the music stopped; the frisky, limber-legged feeling it gave her was so good. Better, that wistful look was gone from Iggy. "You like their music, or you couldn't dance that way," he said.

"It's—at least that piece—it's like being in a good storm," she told him.

"That's it," he cried. "Swinging, rocking up a storm. We'll have to make this a habit."

"That would be nice," she said, and meant it.

More music came across the water, happy enough, but no storm of drum phrases. "Does that say anything to you?" Iggy asked.

"I don't think so."

"Me neither. And anyway I shouldn't take any more time for dancing. I want to give you some advice I think you need." He picked up the book, hefted it, and at the same time did a wonderful job of not seeing her reaching hand, by turning slightly to leave the hand in mid-snatch. He could have been an old routine-frozen teacher, so precise and all-knowing his words: "You must learn to be more careful. The weight's about the

72

same, the size is a fair match, but the headpieces very different. And why make the mistake of picking for a jacket a pretty thing that practically invites you to open the book?"

She didn't try to answer. He continued: "When hiding proscribed books, always choose a dull jacket; and if you want to do a perfect job, go to some of the buy-a-book-for-my-cause sales; they always have awful old things nobody wants that you can buy for a nickel each. Tear off the back, paste it lightly on your book; and there you have it. —Please don't look so scared. Nobody's going to tell. I know what it is to walk that road."

She nodded toward the remains of the good food, just for him, then the expensive equipment. "Someone helps you walk your road." Her whisper dropped, and her sad, smiling glance rested on the rock. "They must love you a very great deal."

"Possibly. But how can I separate their love from their duty, or what they consider dutiful attentions? A certain kind of love can be a weight on your back. I mean the stuff we're talking about, not the exercises in marriage manuals."

She wondered if, remembering, she blushed. "No, I don't think love, real love, is ever a weight. It's light, but warm, like an ermine coat."

"But suppose you had to wear that ermine always? It could be awful on an August noon at San Luis Potosí, for example."

She searched for words to make him understand—without telling too much. "You don't wear love. It isn't always within arm's reach. You just know it's there; it waits forever, so warm, but never a weight. I don't know how to say it; ermine is no good. Love doesn't have to be insured, or worried over, or begged for, or—."

Iggy was studying her face too intently. She'd better get off the subject of love. Truth, a little, wouldn't be too dangerous— not with him. "I wasn't trying to learn about love from that book; I wanted some psychology—if possible."

He opened the book. "*The Adolescent Female;* one trouble is, it's out of date. Mr. Soames has this whole series. I've sneaked a look at them now and then. They all seem to dwell on the *dangers;* but Mr. Soames is too busy even to know, I'm sure; he is nearing the most dangerous time for a man—middle age."

He put down the book to use the glasses for a study of the bridge approach: "Oh, no. I think I'm about to be cheated of twenty minutes' time here," he quarreled.

Susie looked to see, silhouetted in the smoky haze, a man-sized figure with a child on either side standing on the upper edge of the bridge approach.

"He is really putting the mint in the cod-liver oil today," Iggy complained. "If he wouldn't let me bike, he could at least have let me go with Renfro to my music lesson." He briefly studied the figures through the binoculars, then moved to the highest part of the rock where he stood a moment. "I had him wrong," he said, dropping down beside her. "I will get my full time. He is doing the 'Every-father-should-give-his-children-time' duty; big deal, like walking the dog so many minutes each day. I also let him have a look at me; claims they worry when I'm around this pond alone. Can you imagine?"

"Yes." Once again she could not explain how her grandmother, Beeto, and the others had questioned her about quicksand—but never her parents. "Perhaps," she said, "it's his way of showing love."

"Duty," Iggy declared. "It's a lot easier to be a parent than a child; follow the books and the crowd, and not give a damn; if things go wrong blame it on the book. Overprotectiveness in my book is just another name for nosiness, or the quieting of guilt feelings brought on by rejection of the child."

"Possibly," Susie said. His happiness was gone. She tried to think of something to change the conversation from both the book and love, but wasn't quick enough.

Iggy was off again: "My sorrow was, and is, nobody can agree on love. The early love I remember best was cheap and stupid—to some people. Can you imagine bringing a child and his mother a bunch of not-too-fresh daffodils from the five-and-ten when every sock the child has is full of holes? I really am giving you the book; but you're like Robert, you know we can't all live in Candyland with the Candy Man."

He paused for another brief study of the figures on the bridge approach. "He may come this way; he's looking over the pond, but is too polite to use the glasses again. He knows it

74

would be embarrassing to do the eyeball to eyeball deal with binoculars."

Susie had already slid under a willow bough over a lower edge of the stone. "He might not like seeing you with me," she whispered.

"Oh, he'll be glad to see me with a girl. According to his moldy information I am only now getting past the girl-hating stage. I can even have crushes on females, older ones as I recall. You're about fifteen—chronologically I mean. You aren't that old in other ways."

"Tell me," she whispered, frightened, ashamed, "do, do you notice it very much, that—well, part of me is behind?"

"I was only putting you on," he soothed. "You know all that jazz about absolute norms went out with the absolute I.Q."

The thought that she might have abnormalities noticeable to the world so terrified her she went off guard. "But, but suppose you were up against a kooky sort of would-be psychologist working on his master's or his Ph.D.? And you think he follows the old ways?"

Iggy considered. "I know almost no psychology. And I certainly don't know much about the female, but I've heard that girls about your age are supposed to eat, sleep, and dream boys; and so you are supposed to hate your mother—jealous of her mate-catching, her child-bearing abilities because you are afraid you can never catch a man or have a baby. —What's the matter? You look positively ill."

Her smile, forced and small, died as she asked: "How would this—this psychologist evaluate me if I—were to say I pitied my mother? I have wondered if my father was the same now as when she caught him—before he was so much the army man. Would that make a man think I had a horror of marriage—or worse?"

"You worry too much. We can't all go wide-tracking forever. Whatever your answer, what's it to some nosy creep, anyway?"

Iggy's sympathy did what questions could never have done. The story of her bedevilment by the student of psychology seemed to pour out as if from some gone-wild tape recorder with no turn-off switch; one that must go on to the end of the tape done in a squeaky, scared-stiff voice that at times seemed sound only. She couldn't keep track of the words.

Last March she had received notification that she was one of a group chosen by this man to "help with an in-depth survey." She hoped it wouldn't take up too much of her time, and though not exactly flattered she had not minded too much; he had not, in that first note, said anything about psychology. Then, when they had an after-school group conference, she had learned the horrible truth.

She had gathered that the rest of "the group"—none had she ever before seen, and most were boys—were chiefly general course students with a susceptibility to drop-out. She had learned the real deal from the man's chummy little talk. He had thanked them for their willingness to help him study alienation, and also hoped he could help them in "matters psychological." And she had never before suspected there was anything wrong with her.

That first meeting had been only the beginning. They were all together again at the next, an "evaluation session, written," he had said when giving the date. He had told them not to worry; no study, no materials were required. She had known from his talk it would be a big deal, magnetic pencil to fill a million spaces, after you'd knocked holes in your head trying to figure out tricky multiple choice, true-false jazz. They were not to worry, he had told them; the "written evaluation" would not come up for six weeks, time enough before school finals to have each "respondent" in for oral discussion on "an individual basis."

She had really worked in those six weeks; brought down the wrath of her father by missing dinner—she'd telephoned of course—and the wonder of her mother on why her daughter had suddenly started giving all her spare time to "shopping in Detroit." Those trips to Ann Arbor had taken an awful lot of time, no direct route, first by bus into Detroit, then out again. Still, she had felt the U. of M. libraries would be the very best place to learn how a normal American girl should be in matters psychological. She had even skipped some Saturday morning science clubs. Every Saturday afternoon and the Sunday afternoons she could manage she had spent sneaked away in a corner of that big main library. And was she ever scared she'd be asked to show an Id. card.

She had hoped that with all that study, and the books she had bought to read at home, she would come out as normal on the examination. But it had been longer and trickier than she had expected. Then, a week or so later, when she'd thought the whole deal was over, she had been called in for a long discussion, alone with that man. Worse than the written examination, his probing personal questions had been like pincers pulling on her brain.

Now, after all that, she'd learned Friday she'd have to have another discussion with him soon. Now, what had she done wrong the first time; and how could she correct it, not knowing what to correct? She had learned from his talks to the group and the individual discussion that he had chosen her and most of the others for a "study in depth of alienation"; she, because of the—scars on her face; and well, her parents *had* moved a great deal.

Iggy, angered by the story, gave a sharp head shake. "Your scars are too faint to be noticed by any normal person. And as for your family's moves, all the new people moved around on their climb up. That brain peeler isn't even a member of your school staff. Your parents might—." He was suddenly embarrassed.

He had never met her parents, but he had heard of her father and his weed-killing campaign. How much did he know of her family? How much had she let him learn now? Lies, must it always be lies? Could he or anyone suspect her biggest reason for being afraid of the psychologist; that he might, if he had not already done so, learn "camp" was her grandmother?

Iggy had turned from her to look across the pond. He smiled as if he watched a beloved creature. Wild or human?

77

Susie, frightened that Iggy was watching some human who had overheard, looked to see a swath of grass and willow bough, bent above the water, rise to become a camouflaged, wide-brimmed straw hat. Under the hat was a tall boy in work clothes, not faked but real; faded old blue shirt stuffed into worn blue jeans that disappeared in waders beginning at mid-thigh. Her heart thumped up into her throat. He made her think of the real men who fished or gathered sea weed along the Nova Scotian coast.

The boy, she saw with relief, was showing no interest in the talk on the rock, but was studying the dead trunk of a big willow. She continued to watch as he cut out a rectangle of mushroom-studded bark and dropped it into the burlap sack held by rope over his shoulders.

He turned in their direction when Iggy said: "Hey Angus, we danced up a storm. It was groovy."

She was chewing the name, certain she had heard it before, wishing she could see the whole of his face, when he turned and smiled at her. She gave back the best smile she could manage; not easy; it was as if she had spoken her wish aloud: "What I see makes me want to see more. Please turn." And so he had, he turned to smile and show her that fantastic face; too thin, rather long with plenty of nose and jaw and lower lip, weather-beaten as a Quebec skier's in March. His cheeks went in instead of out; the bridge of his nose rose in a slight hump, and his longish hair was the rich red-brown of upper Bay of Fundy mud, and his green-brown eyes were even more beautiful.

He acknowledged Iggy's praise. "Yeah? Why, thank you. Glad you liked it."

A shadow crossed the water. Iggy sighed, "The heron, and we didn't see him take off."

Susie glanced at the bird, then back to this Angus. He had tilted his head to watch the disappearing heron; and when it had gone, he continued to look, taking in all things: a streamer of cloud, the old rail fence on the other side of the pond, and the dead tree where the heron had sat.

He made her think of her great-grandmother looking out to sea, loving all from the pebble to the wave. She thought it was the light rising from the sunlit water that gave his face that radiance; nobody could be that happy just wading around in a muddy pond on a fine September morning. Or could he? She watched from under lowered lids as his gaze dropped to another dead willow. He cut from it one great shelf-like mushroom; and then as she watched his hands, she recognized him as one of the percussionists in orchestra.

She marveled that a boy could change so. The orchestra practice room at school was small and square with seats in tiers, so that a far-down, far-back second violinist could see the drums with little turning of her head. She knew his hands; flat on drum, holding drumsticks, lifted above the timpani, waiting with cymbals. Times, he played the piano, and she again had scattering glimpses of his hands.

She had also in swift stolen glances studied his face, that is the face he wore in orchestra. It was different from the hundreds of other boys' faces in Eden Hills High. They were neutral mixtures running to shades of brown in hair, blues and browns mingled in eyes; noses not prominent as her own, and jaws that were nothing but the lower parts of cheeks.

A still greater difference in his face was the look it wore—at school—a remote, inward-listening gaze as if somewhere inside him, a drum, heard by him alone, were out of tune, and on the tuning of it he must concentrate. Now, the face seemed no kin of that shut-out-the-world-so-I-can-listen-to-my-untuned-self she had studied in orchestra.

He had seemed so far removed from her, that now she was surprised and flustered when he said: "Congratulations on that write-up in the 'Purple Sunflower'; your grades I mean, not getting into that sheet. It really showed up Old Maddox; giving you a B in his AP course when you go on to get practically the best score you can make on the College Advanced Placement." He smiled. "Robert told me you were the only one who dared ask the old boy the wrong kind of question: 'But doesn't our constitution give us the right not to believe in God?' I remember that one."

"Robert?" she asked.

He smiled again, nodded. "Yes. He probably kept so quiet you didn't notice him—but he made A under Maddox, and didn't do well enough on the College Placement exam to get college credit."

Iggy wanted to hear more of Susie's honors and troubles. Angus waded over to sit on the edge of the stone, waders trailing in the water. Susie retreated still further behind her hair and the willow bough as Angus told Iggy what Robert had told him of her troubles—and courage—under Mr. Maddox. She never wasted time on the *Purple and the Gold* as everyone but the students called "The Purple Sunflower"; nothing but a shining little sheet that weekly came out with news of sports, school social functions, and pretty articles that added to the glory of school; the real news of student complaints and sneaky administration locker raids it never mentioned. Still, when Iggy started to congratulate Angus on *his* achievements, she began to wish she had read the paper instead of giving it to her grandmother, always eager for copies. Apparently Friday's paper had carried news of the semifinalists in the Merit Scholarship business and among them were Angus, Katy, Robert, and a Ben whom she was expected to know.

She was thinking how nice the honor was for Katy, who hoped to get a scholarship, when, from out a clump of willows, a boy's voice asked: "What's up? Classified conference?"

Angus and Iggy at once began begging Ben to come over. He had, whoever he was, a beautiful voice, slightly familiar, but she knew no Ben. When she saw another tall boy in work clothes she knew she was wrong. Her ready-waiting smile did not get any bigger while her private TV showed her father as he had been last night. Interesting, his reaction if he could see her now, smiling up at a Negro.

She had never until last year's first orchestra session sat in a room with a Negro. Now would be her first time of speaking to one, save family laundresses and heavy cleaning women. She managed a smiling: "Good morning, Ben. Thank you for that fantastic music," then discovered in some confusion she had picked up her binder to make room for him beside her. And *that* book still in sight.

"Thank Angus, our star." Ben appeared to take no notice of the book or the difference in their races. He sat by her with the same air of unconcern as when, the only Negro in orchestra, he stood by Angus in the percussion group, his only thought the music.

She congratulated him on his scholarship and he congratulated her. He told them Katy was biking over. She sat silent while the others answered Iggy's questions on the mushroom business.

The florist in the shopping center (*Dreamland*, "of colonial inspiration throughout, completely glass-enclosed") was having a run on mushrooms. The garden club clientele needed all sizes for their autumn arrangements that permitted no flowers. Angus and Ben had permission from The Primitive to take what they could find. Ben planned to sell all of his, unless his mother wanted some; but Angus said he had to give most to a decoration committee for, "the adornment of the temple of Christus Suburbanus Restrictus."

She wondered if he were speaking of a church, but did not ask; his voice and his face told her he didn't like that temple, whatever it was. Iggy also heard and changed the conversation. "How did things go last night? Did the hawks tear down your signs like last time?"

Angus wore the orchestra look as his glance flicked Susie. "The usual," he said.

"Susie's O.K.; a little dove in a nest of hawks. And anyway she has too many troubles of her own to worry over you."

Angus smiled, a quick warm smile that made him again the boy looking at the sky, except he was looking at her. "Troubles? Try not to think about them." He turned back to Iggy. "We had all kinds—doves of course on our side, and even girl hawks."

"A girl hawk seems a strange beast," Iggy said. "But it must be nice to be able to picket when you please."

"Won't it though," Angus said. "Without this q.t. business."

Susie wished she could think of something to say that wouldn't give away the fact she had never been in a sit-in, kept a vigil, or walked a picket line. Well, there had been that one time when she was so young and stupid her picketing didn't count. She had been sent to the store and on the way had come upon about a dozen men walking back and forth in front of a cleaning shop. Each had carried a big sign that said the shop was unfair. She believed in a fair world and had walked with them until a surly policeman had ordered her home, "where you belong."

She roused. Iggy was having a fit unbelievable for him, a perfect storm of name-calling: "—The Lazy Dogs, The Stinkers, The Drop-Outs, The Underdogs, The Unspeakables, The Worms."

He stopped as Ben wailed: "All those and a million others are already taken. We don't want to steal a name."

"Couldn't you use something nice, like The Supremes, say, or The Vibrations; or something truly awful? How about Mini-britches? No, you'd have to dress to match that. What about The Merry Wanners? Would they get it?"

"Get it? They'd be coming around to work up a deal, buy or sell," Angus said. "No, if we're going to play for church dances we need a name not too nice to scare off the young, but not too far out for the old. Some parents still have influence."

Ben agreed. "Robert would never go for anything wild; not

for the church groups he's lining up for us. And the real causes you care about never have much money and have to be careful. 'The Worms entertained the last meeting of the local Youth-for-Peace group'? How would that sound in the paper? Not that a paper around here is going to mention a peace group."

Susie nodded, her puzzlement gone.

"We haven't heard from Susie."

That was Angus, looking at her. Might as well tell the truth. "I don't know much about—rock and roll stuff. I could only think of silly names: Weeping Willows, Quacking Ducks, and one I like except it's crazy—The Humans." No need to struggle further. He was interested.

"You know we might just be The Humans. I don't know of any group with that name. How about it, Ben?"

"Nicest I've heard," Ben said, pleased.

Angus was staring at the water, soundlessly moving his lips to frame over and over "The Humans," when Katy pushed through the willows. Everybody began telling her the name Susie had come up with.

She said it was great and then while Susie was trying to get in a compliment on the flute solo and congratulate her on the scholarship contest, Katy exclaimed: "The very book I've been wanting to own. May I look at it, Owner?" She looked at Iggy.

"It's Susie's," he said. "But the jacket has all the flowers, period. The book is something she is studying for a brain-squeezing, coming up one of these days."

Katy let out a troubled "Oh." Ben showed sympathy, and Angus seemed angry as well as sympathetic.

Susie could only sit huddled under her hair and a willow bough while Iggy told her troubles, free with them as if they had been his own. She couldn't be angry, she hadn't told him this particular trouble was a secret from all the world, including her grandmother and Beeto. Had she in her talking fit let either name slip? She wasn't certain how much she had told; the truth; but truth was usually dangerous—for her.

Angus was saying: "Nobody has any right to put her through the third degree. It's not required at school—and she certainly is no loonier than the rest of us."

The thought that she could hug him for that kind remark, caused her to turn hastily away. Her glance fell upon Katy's shoulder-length hair, free, wild, and beautiful, even wilder today than usual. You couldn't call it anything but red, for red it was. And wild compared to the smooth, self-conscious, bleached and /or tinted hairdos of Eden Hills High; on warm dampish days the ends twisted and curled all over. More than once after an assembly program that featured a flute solo by Katy, Susie had heard the whispers of other girls: "That flutist, why doesn't she have a hair stylist tone down and straighten that mop. What a mess."

They didn't know, or care, that Katy, with a heavy school schedule, music practice, and baby sitting or working in the library, had no time for proper care with big rollers and ironing at home—and no money for hairdressers. You felt she didn't worry about it too much; when she mentioned her "subversive hair" at all, it was with a resigned shrug. Now, streaming down the back of her faded gray sweat shirt as she leaned forward listening, the hair seemed brighter, more alive than the sunlight that touched it. Susie's trouble slid to the back of her mind as she wished she could paint the beautiful stuff.

Her worries settled in again when Katy turned to her. "A lot of make-up might help. He couldn't see the real you."

She was trying to think up words to explain when Angus said: "That wouldn't work. What's under the make-up always comes through. I've watched so many faces as they waited for my father. Made-up faces. No matter how much they're made up and smile and talk and wiggle, the scare shows through."

"Why're they scared?" Ben wanted to know. "Your father never hurt anybody. He has a wonderful reputation as a minister."

"Right, that is the last part. Those waiting women, and the men, too, know they'll at least try to do what the old boy tells them to. I can't help seeing them. He puts them in the music room. And do they ever interfere with my practice. But he feels that in 'the intimacy of the home' he can get 'responses of greater depth' and a 'more intimate dialogue' than in the church offices.

84

"And so they sit, waiting; some afraid he can't put their marriage back together, and some afraid he can. He always makes them wait; the only way he can get a tape of their reactions alone together. They never notice the tape recorder. It's in a bookcase behind a missing pane of glass."

"Forget it. Quit chewing holes in your insides," the Negro said.

"Boy, you're being un-American. Nobody's supposed to forget *The Christian Family*. Sixty thousand copies in print. At home it's the one big deal. It has more than enough sex to make it sell, and just enough religion to make it respectable. What knocks me over is that he's turning these people's problems into money. How will they feel when they recognize themselves in the book?"

Iggy, after again locating Mr. Soames, sat down and turned to Angus. "The book is certain to be a success. Your famous father will be a status symbol; wait and see; the ones with saved marriages will run around telling of how they went to him. The ones he couldn't help will feel that if a great man like that couldn't, nobody could have saved their marriages. Same principle as having a relative die under the hands of Robert's father. If that status-symbol surgeon couldn't save him, nobody could."

Angus turned on him. "Don't say that."

Iggy was unruffled. "You know what Robert says when anybody asks him what kind of surgeon his father is: 'He confines himself strictly to good addresses.'"

"He's only joking," Angus said. "What's up? Cows out?" He sprang up to look, as had Ben.

Iggy grabbed his glasses. "Somebody's running away with The Primitive's truck. She'd never let anyone drive it so fast over that rough detour. —No, it's stopping—almost skidding off the road. The Primitive was driving! She's speaking to Mr. Soames. And is she ever mad!"

Angus slammed on his hat with an angry thwack. "I'll bet some of those miserable new kids are chasing her sheep again. That bloodthirsty weedkiller's boy—."

Katy didn't shush him by saying: "That 'bloodthirsty' weedkiller's daughter is hearing you"; but you knew why she interrupted with a quick: "Oh, it must have been the bulldozer crew who knocked a tree across her fence and let the cattle out. I know she planned when the fog lifted to go to the barn and take another look from the loft."

The Negro, already off the rock and running, called back that he was going to finish track practice by running up the road to have a look for strayed cows. Angus, carrying Iggy's tin chest, told him to yell if he had to round up cattle; everybody could help.

Susie found herself alone on the rock, frozen. She had heard the pickup start with a roar; it was now getting closer. In another minute or so that woman, already angry, would be here; and she, Susan Schnitzer, who tried to be so proper about other people's property, would have to walk up, and under the eyes of all, ask permission to visit the pond—when she was already by it and had trespassed for more than a year.

She got off the rock, but froze again, head bowed among the cattails. There were many things in the river of her mind, some garbage of which she would like to rid herself but could not, always floating, never touching, disconnected from the before and the after, come by chance, but eternally there, an eddying backwater that would never move on to the sea.

And now an ugly thing came floating in to make her wish she could hide deep in the pond's black mud and never come up. The floating garbage bore no date, but it would have been on a Sunday morning, a breakfast scene, for Sunday was the one day when the Schnitzers had to have togetherness with breakfast.

She knew it was breakfast because she could see the piece of apple *küchen* stopped in mid-air on its way to her father's pink lips. He loved it, this dish of his childhood his wife had learned to make. It always mellowed him into praise of both food and cook. She could see her mother, beautiful in a morning robe and a fresh face put on for church, smiling prettily as she said: "Seems to me I got a wee bit too much cinnamon"; her eyes cold as the freshly-bought, frozen *apfelküchen*, unwrapped, re-wrapped, labeled "old yeast dough," and slipped into the bottom of the basement freezer.

You couldn't blame her for trying to keep her husband in a good humor. And there he was, holding a huge piece—manners were strictly for eating with away from home—happy, smacking his lips, and not just over the *küchen.* "I tell you the community won't stand for such lawlessness. Our side has a lawyer just as good as that old hillbilly's. How anyway did they ever let hillbillies into this neighborhood? Precious little better than Negroes. Mark my words, she'll get a year in the county jail."

Her mother had nodded; plainly, most of her mind was on a greasy gob of *küchen* about to land on the breakfast cloth. Brandon was happy, declaring: "She ought to get ten years."

Susie had let the sounds roll into her ears and out, absent-minded in her uneasy search for a proper excuse to get away from the table. Words, laughter had flowed around her while she sat staring at the philodendron that stood in the dividers—the decorator had said no one could know it was plastic, but Lulu on her first day of work had asked how often the artificial philodendron needed washing and if it could stand hot detergent water. The plastic plants disappeared under a rolling wave of her father's words.

"The lawless old woman has land somewhere out in the township on a gravel road." Brandon had been able to give the exact location; at the time she had not stopped to wonder how he knew; her father's talk had continued: "—went out with a gun to stand in the road where her property began—insisted she had control over the road shoulder next to her fence rows. Imagine. She looked so wild with that gun, the men stopped the spray outfit and waited until she left. They had just started to roll again with nozzles open, when here came a bullet right under one of the men's feet; it nicked a tire."

Susie had at this point thought of the woman with distaste. She hated guns; they made her think of war, and her grandfather's death. Her father mimicked the woman: " 'Hit's June,' and the young birds in the tangles of wild grapevines on her fence rows had not come off 'their nesties' "; a bluebird had eggs in a hole in a " 'fence postie.' " And then her relief for the woman she had never seen. "That pinko lawyer Soames has got her case continued, but she'll get jail, just you wait and see. Weeds and messy birds," her father had roared. "Imagine doing all that for weeds. She belongs in an institution."

And that was the green tunnel she loved to bike through; and the field she had run over was—. "Look out." A hand grabbed her shoulder, just as her foot went down, down. The hand belonged to Angus. She had thought him gone with the others. "You shouldn't wander around this pond alone. There are quicksandy places that can suck down a tall strong man."

She freed herself both from the chughole and the hand, remembered she had not thanked him and turned to him. His kindly looks instead of the anger she had expected again switched on that uninhibited tape recorder. "I wish I could go right down to the bottom of the swamp and never come up. My father—and my brother—I just realized—."

"Buck up," he interrupted. "If only this once in your life you want to go to the bottom of the pond, you'll be lucky. Come on. She's looking this way. Mad as she is, she'll still remember we're not our fathers."

Head bowed to keep the cattails and buttonbush out of her eyes, she was plunging on through mud and water when the pickup stopped.

The voice came, strong without being overly loud, the words twisted by an accent, strange to Susie: "Oh, Angus, honey, didn't you get your mama's message? She's been telephonen all over hunten you. She put Mr. Soames on th' lookout, too."

Angus sounded sorry, no pretty white lies for him: "I've been too busy. It's a shame you've been bothered by something so unimportant."

"Your mama thinks it's important," the woman answered, some sharpness in her voice now. "Lotsa people thinks them reporters comen out to write about your papa's book an' take pitchers of his family is mighty important."

Her tone changed as she cried, worried: "Oh, law, Angus, I'm just now getten a good look at your head. Did you get that haircut your mama called me to remind you about? These days I can't tell a fresh haircut. But honey, you'd ought to be gone. Your mama said it's the last chance to have you all together; your sister's goen back to college, an' when th' man come last time at Christmas for the book jacket pitcher you couldn't be found, your mama said."

The knife edge had gradually dulled on The Primitive's voice until by the time she finished you could almost call it a butter spreader. Angus apologized, and wanted to know if she'd had to drop her work to get out the truck and bring him a message when she was busy stringing okra and making green tomato catchup.

It was then her voice and words matched her driving; though the most that got through to Susie, shivering in the reeds, was anger. Yesterday, she told Angus, the last thing before they quit work, a bulldozer crew had pushed a big maple across the fence of her "back middle twenty." She had seen it from a barn window, and telephoned the road builders. A man had promised to have it fixed right away. The fog had been too thick for her to see when she'd first looked it over from the barn window this morning. She had looked again, later; with the sun higher, she had seen it plain as day, the top of a big maple smashed across her fence. The cattle might already be out, and some of "them wild new boys" chasing the poor things all over.

Angus told her that Ben had run up to take a look; if he'd found cattle tracks on the road cut he'd be yelling by now.

The woman said that was "mighty nice" of Ben. Her next words fell like stones on Susie's ears. "Whar is that little Schnitzer? I'll declare she's driven me crazy. Harder to see than a quail."

Susie gave one longing glance behind her: "Swallow me swamp and let me never come up." She wondered if she had spoken aloud. Angus turned her about, swung her over a mud hole, and stood behind her as if to say: "If you can't walk, I can carry you."

Surprised that she could move, she found herself clawing up the road embankment. On a level with her eyes was a pair of heavy work shoes, intended for a man, and big enough. A reaching hand caught her upper arm; its mate took the other arm, and she was picked up out of the red, rolling earth. She was for a moment little again, finding refuge in other arms that, strong and kind as these, had comforted her after big or little hurts to mind or body.

The anger she had heard in the voice was not in the hands as they stayed on her shoulders after she stood on her own muddy feet. She looked up into an old woman's face, big, gaunt, with a nose that was a nose, and large eyes, black-seeming under the heavy brows that almost met in a black line across a weather-beaten forehead. The darkness in her face contrasted sharply with the strings and wisps of white hair slid from under a bonnet.

Susie stood, less afraid, but silent while the eyes went over her. They missed nothing: the mud on her feet from the woman's pond; the grape stains from *her* grapes; the swamp grass and cattail seed—. She wondered what was on her face; the woman's glance was centered there, searching.

The woman was hunting, waiting for explanations and apologies. She heard at last her squeaky voice as it tried to explain: she had not known the land or the pond—she meant after the fence and the horse were gone—had belonged to anyone, except possibly the state or some absentee owner who didn't care about it; she found no owner's name in the plat book. She must now find words for telling of how last spring she had gone into the woods above the pond. She couldn't go on; it seemed she'd been hearing that shamed, choked voice forever, and all the others gathered about the woman's truck; they were too polite to listen, but—.

The anger was yet in the woman's voice. "Oh, child, I knowed you didn't know. You couldn't. The land had already gone to law when th' last plat book come out. They didn't put my name on it, they was so certain. An' I've never seen you hurt a thing. —All I wanted to tell you was, you make me nervous, allus by yourself. You must be careful, real careful goen around th' swamp an' th' pond; parts is terrible dangerous. Now, I wouldn't have you quit comen fer anything in th' world. That rock where you go is safe enough to git to; but I do wisht that when you aim to do much walken around in th' swamp you'd come by th' house an' do it on yon side; it's safer. I've been asken th' youngens to do that ever since Angus when he was little might nigh got sucked under. —Angus, oh law."

She waited until he had finished loading Katy's bike into the back of the pickup, before she continued, and then with a kind of dreary dutifulness: "Angus, honey, don't you think you ought to get home? It's too late fer that haircut, but mebbe they's still time to get ready fer the pitchers. They's lots a boys do sich things; recollect that boy from your hill, the one allus on his papa's circulars?"

"You mean," Angus said, smiling, "the son of Solid Substance and Free Enterprise?"

The woman said: "Oh, child, that's a nice family." She turned back to Susie. "Honey, you're goen to pull your thumb off. Don't be so nervous on account a me. It's so nice in th' woods now, jist enough leaves down to make a little rustlen when they're dry. If you can spare th' time, I'd be much obliged to have you come along with us."

"Thank you. I'll be happy to come some other day; I'm behind in my homework now." She tried to put on a nice bright smile in spite of that choke inside her. She felt as if she had found a friend—two friends—Angus and this woman; and she might go to prison.

The woman was smiling. "Now, when you git th' time, come by th' house an we'll go take us a walk in th' sugar bush when it colors up real good. Th' sun a shinen on them red and yaller maples allus puts me in mind a that old song, 'Where th' streets are made of gold.' An feel welcome to th' pond. But do be keerful. Pick anything you want, flowers, er grapes er nuts in th' fence rows." She had started toward the truck. Susie walked with her, stopping while she stopped to remind Iggy Mr. Soames had said he would be ready to leave in five minutes or so.

Susie had forgotten Iggy. He had taken off his coveralls, and was now a proper boy in proper dress, a familiar stranger, to whom she had spit out her secret. She tried to smile and act grateful when, after every one else was in the truck, he said: "Don't worry so, Susie, you'll be all right with that idiot psychologist. I am sure I can find some books that might help; not that I think you'll need any. 'Bye now." He turned to wave at those in the truck, and call a thank you to The Primitive for a fine morning in her pond.

Susie waved and everyone in the truck waved back. The truck was soon lost behind leaning trees and log piles. Still, she stood, staring after it, Angus driving. The first invitation she had had in this neighborhood to take part in something outside of school and her father's church; and she could not accept—because of that miserable boy in the attic.

She turned away, and saw, running up from the other direction, a little boy with a smaller girl not far behind; back of her a man came, more slowly. All were smiling at Iggy, eager for him.

She had scuttled across the last lanes, slid down the embankment, and was hidden by the earth wall before she thought Iggy might have wanted to introduce her to his family. Politeness had demanded she at least speak to the young children. Had she even thanked him for offered help or told him good-bye?

She saw by one muddy foot a bunch of peppermint threatened by sliding mud. She broke several sprays; Ter might enjoy the smell. As she walked up the pasture hill she searched out the finest bergamot and other mints she did not know; higher, she gathered goldenrods and took two each of the many varieties of wild asters from the big dark purple ones down through shades of blue and lavender to tiny white ones near the top of the hill.

She stopped by the rock to arrange the flowers in her bike carrier, carefully so they would not crush. Finished, she sat and rubbed the palms of her hands round and round on the weather-worn granite boulder. Sitting there, with the feel of the stone on the backs of her legs and her hands, she could on cloudy days half close her eyes and imagine the pond below was a far inland bay of the sea. On sunny days such as this, the position of the sun was too strong a reminder this place was not *that place*. Yet it was good to feel rock, real rock.

She had not known until she felt the wetness of tears that

she wanted to cry. She sprang up, reached for the bike; it wavered through the thickening curtain of her tears. She dropped face down on the sun-warmed stone. Crying was for children; it left traces and stains on your face so that people asked you why. Still, she luxuriated in her tears. They came without exact reason, though often, as now, after a time of warm happiness like last night.

Lying in the sun, a hand caressing the rock, she wondered which was worth the weeping: the lost secret, the lost freedom of the pond, her own stupidity, The Primitive on her way to jail, or Angus? Why Angus, when for these many months she had thought that pond hers alone, a bit of worthlessness unloved by anybody? And all the while it was watched over as if it were the flower garden of a queen.

She had thought it hers without taxes as her grandmother said of the shells she gathered in the summer dawns when she was the first to make footprints in the sand. Depending on the time of the tide, there were often half-alive jellyfish glistening in the gray light; while high in the sky gulls screamed and wheeled, angry at finding only starfish and sand dollars; and in their outrage dropping the pretty things to fall in the sand near her feet.

She had never told her grandmother it was not only shells to sell in the shop she went out to find or the dying jellyfish to be rushed back to the sea, but the sunrise. She knew from where it came; for if you stood and watched the soaring, circling gulls you could see the sunrise first, not on the sea, not on the earth, but on one gull risen for an instant higher than the others, gilded, golden, as if instead of a herring from the sea it had caught the sunrise. So many mornings she had stood in the gray dawn, the water of the bay lapping over her feet, looking up, waiting for the gull to drop its piece of sunrise, as the starfish had been dropped to fall like widely opened flowers.

Morning after morning she had watched and waited, even in fog when out on the Duff Rock the warning bell tolled like a bell for the dead, and beyond a few feet the gulls were but gray shapes, moving, then nothing. Yet, even on such days she had known that high overhead where she could not see, some gull held a piece of the sunrise and might at any moment drop it near her feet.

Then, one morning she had known—and no one had told her, save possibly the sun and the gulls; the brightness would never fall near her, nor would she ever go running or even swimming far out into the bay to pick it up. The sunrise would never fall because it could not. That knowing marked in her mind the end of babyhood.

And now the lost pond was the end of something else. What? She searched for words; couldn't find any; realized she was sobbing aloud; so what? Could any passerby hear? Home, she'd slip through her secret passage; nobody would see the tear marks. Ter would—? She sprang up.

5

She found all parts of Ter worse—except his tongue. He quarreled because she had been gone so long, and shook his head to the flowers with a whiny: "You know I can't smell a thing, not even the vervain and other mints you brought."

His seeming self-pity so annoyed her, she thought of telling him she had seen what she thought was the FBI, but decided against it. He might sneer and want to know how she knew the FBI. She wouldn't be able to tell him, not exactly; it was something of the same learning that guided her around the deep holes and bottomless quicksands of the pond.

He woundn't eat, refusing even orange juice. He didn't want her trying to sneak anything out of the kitchen for him, too dangerous. The cook might get suspicious.

"Lulu and I get along fine together," she told him.

"Is it that Polish woman who cooks German sauerkraut and pigs' knuckles and potato pan—?"

She jammed the thermometer into his mouth. "The Schnitzer family must have been your main research project, but please leave Lulu out of it. How would you like pretending to be someone you rather hated, just to get and keep a miserable job? Lulu is good; and she is very intelligent in spite of an unfortunate marriage. The man left her with a child to support when

95

she was very young. She did all right in a factory for several years, but when automation came in they phased out women. So, she took a cooking course in Detroit, and became a cook. My father wanted a German cook and would pay well, so she rented German language records from the library, got help from a German neighbor, studied German cookery. Open, please."

She could have thwacked him. He grabbed the thermometer —103.2°—before she had time to shake it down. He was scared. "Do—do you think I might have pneumonia, like my mother?"

"No, of course not." She hoped her voice held more conviction than her mind. She sat a moment, lax-handed, staring at nothing. Only one more pill; no hope of finding more antibiotics in the house—provided she could get the chance for a good search. "I'll get more antibiotics for you," she told him at last. "But first let me examine you, at least a little; I'll have to describe your symptoms."

He was so terrified he sat bolt upright and bumped his head on her bed shelf. "You can't go telling a pharmacist you have a sick visitor."

"I'll get a prescription from my doctor for myself—if I can. Now, get into the light."

"What would Beeto say to all this?" he quarreled, still lying rigid, back toward her.

"We'll know when you tell him." She switched the light from low to high, picked up the flashlight and waited. She soon heard an angry snuffle; the blanket heaved, and there he was below the light with all of him under the blanket except his face.

He did look pitiful and frightening, too; eyes glazed, mouth too pale, almost bluish under the tan, and the pulse in his neck jumping like the ball in an IBM typewriter. Still, his wrist pulse, though much too fast, was as strong and steady as Angus on the drums. He refused to obey when she asked him to unbutton his pajamas so that she might use her ear as a stethoscope and learn if his lungs were clear. "I don't like this any better than you do," she told him with considerable anger. "You came here; I don't want to have to drag you back down the way you came, and pretend I know nothing when they find you half dead—or worse."

Finally he took the blanket off his chest, and unbuttoned the top two pajama buttons with a: "There, I hope you're satisfied."

"Thank you, I am," she told him after she had laid an ear at the proper places on his chest, and heard nothing but clean, clear whooshings of air.

He was so angry, she hesitated an instant before unbuttoning the third button of his pajamas. He grabbed and held the opening. "Listen," she said, "I have a hard deal ahead of me, pretending. I have to know if that wounded arm is infected. You'd better pull it out and let me have a look; that is if you plan on help from me."

He gave one angry sigh, then bared and lifted the arm, fist clenched. Getting the flashlight into proper position was not easy; she could see nothing but hair until he cried through gritted teeth: "Look on the underside, high on my upper arm. Only a scrape; not worth all this."

He was right; not a real flesh wound, little more than a small scrape, deep enough to have bled, but healing with neither red streaks nor swelling.

When he was buttoned up again, she said: "Open, please." He obeyed without thinking. She brought from behind her a toothbrush, the handle dipped in alcohol. She got it in as a tongue depressor before he knew what was happening. He gagged nicely, but rolled away, teeth clamped before she had finished looking. Still, she had seen enough to know he had a throat infection; tonsils and surrounding area were much like the inside of a burst overripe tomato, only redder.

She next jerked the pillow from under his head, seized him by the hair to hold him still, and got two drops of nose-clearing medicine into each nostril in spite of his attempts at head twisting and jerking her hand away. "Keep your head well back so the medicine can go where it should. I don't want to take the time to do the job all over again—now," she told him.

He gave her one speculative glance, and limited himself to a frown. He looked so doleful, she tried to cheer him with the news that he had no symptoms of pneumonia, or infection in his wound; only a feverish cold with an infected throat.

"Get this up-coming deal over before you jam a circuit breaker," she told herself as she hurried down to her bathroom. There she pulled the folded-into-the-wall ironing board from the wall, set the iron on Dry, Linen, and while it was heating took a shower in water hot as she could bear, standing until the water began to run warm, a signal the electric heater was losing the battle. She dressed quickly in flats, skirt, and blouse, taking pains to give her clothing a slightly disheveled, I-am-too-sick-to-care look. She next took the blue pencil she used in math and physics diagrams, rubbed a thumb and finger hard around the point, then gently with her blued fingers rubbed the skin under each eye just enough to give her that crumby menstruating look. The shower had not taken all the wild grape stain from her lips; she liked the effect—an indication of poor circulation.

It took only an uncomfortable moment or so to create with a swab dipped in Mercurochrome an infected throat—reddened tonsils and vicious-looking streaks. She then ran cold water over wrists and hands, taking care not to dry them too well and lose the clammy feel. Last of all, she held the hot iron within a few inches of her face, giving especial attention to cheeks, forehead, and ears.

She stopped by the bathroom mirror for a quick study of the total effect. She wondered if she had overdone it. Her face, ordinarily the color of pale Chinese tea, now had rosy cheeks; her eyes, from the iron's heat and overlaid with gagging tears caused by the paint job in her throat, had a glazed and glittering look, somewhat akin to the porcelainized finish on a new car. She shrugged.

Careful to leave her inner doors set on their secret opening pads, she hurried down the side hall, then into the main hall, above the grand stairway and on to her mother's door. The job ahead was a bit like a first high dive into a strange pool, only worse; you wanted to get it over. Still, she stopped a moment in front of the closed door of her parent's upstairs living room to check her IBM. Was it properly programmed, and in her mother's presence would it go on automation and stay there? She drew a long shivering breath; she couldn't answer that one.

Flashlight in one hand, thermometer in the other, she

knocked, gently, until there came a muffled, uninviting, "Yes."

"Please, Mother, may I come in?" She had no trouble in getting the properly sick quavers into her voice.

"Come on."

The "accoustically perfect" gadget in the door was now on, working so well she could read her mother's voice; tired, frustrated, exasperated, ready for another tranquilizer—perfect; she wouldn't examine her daughter too closely. She overdid her incoming stagger, she guessed, for her mother, kneeling on spread newspapers, squeaked and sprang up, so hastily two small dried mushrooms and a tuft of lichen fell from the lap of her "gardening apron."

"I'm sorry. I didn't mean to scare you," she said, trying to swallow between words so as to get that sore throat into her voice. "I must have caught cold or something last night; too much dancing I guess; but Robert is such a wonderful dancer." Mention of the dance took some of the irritation from her mother's eyes, focused now on her daughter's hair. "I thought I felt peculiar, so I took my temperature. It is slightly above one hundred three. I looked at my throat. It is dreadfully red."

All that work wasted; her mother had not glanced at the proffered thermometer or flashlight; she had eyes only for her daughter's neglected hair. No, not entirely. The news her daughter had an infected throat that could be strep, bringing a possibility of rheumatic heart disease was slowly getting through. "O-h-h, n-o-o," she wailed at last. That was an expression she had picked up from Charlotte, who used it when she was prettily exasperated, but now from her mother it was a wail of frustration with life in general, but most particularly with her daughter. "Just when I thought I would have a few minutes for practicing on an arrangement, after fighting all morning for time, and—. Oh, darling, that hair."

Susie waved the thermometer—carefully. "I'm sorry, Mother, but I'm sure a round of antibiotics will clear it up."

Her mother took the thermometer, but after a good deal of head-twisting—she should get bifocals—turned toward a door. "I am going to get your father's. Thermometers can be wrong; his old one was more than a degree off. All that worry."

Thoughts of that second thermometer, instead of pretended illness, sent her to her knees on the spread newspaper. "Now don't let this rattle you. Think of your poor mother, so eager to win a prize in the garden club's Autumn Arrangement Show." She had worked weeks on a Spring Arrangement, and had not so much as received one of the very liberally scattered honorable mentions. Since that failure she had spent a mint on practice flowers, books, suitable containers, and lessons.

The other thermometer was descending. Susie tipped back her head, mouth widely open, but her mother did not glance in the direction of the beautiful paint job. Susie lifted her right hand. Her mother stared at it a moment before understanding she was expected to take the pulse. She began a search of the wrist, her fingers too quick in their wanderings. Let her keep her little lies; she could find no one's pulse except Brandon's, and then only when he had a high fever. She did, however, notice the clammy coldness of Susie's hands. "Just the way poor Brandon gets; he'll catch it now from you. Darling, your knee is almost on a mushroom, and do you know they're charging fifty cents each at the florist's."

"I'm sorry—."

"Please, remember the thermometer."

Susie had to put her mind on deciding on the proper moment to slip her wrist from her mother's pulse-hunting fingers. If she waited too long—. The fingers, no longer hunting, were lax, scarcely touching her. She pulled gently away from the unnoticing hand, and crawled off, head bowed, searching for spilled mushrooms. She was now turned, back to her mother, and in brushing hair from her eyes—a perfectly natural gesture, for she had to see to hunt mushrooms, didn't she—she struck the thermometer lightly against her teeth with a forefinger.

She crawled on, and retrieved an acorn from under her father's wing chair; while doing so she got in another tap; head hanging low, she pushed out the thermometer with her tongue, crossed her eyes and read. Scarcely a hundred. She'd have to do better than that. She took a cautious look around. Her mother was staring at the beginnings of her arrangement. Susie rolled a mushroom, expertly, so that it went under the TV. Using only one hand, she crawled slowly toward it; the other hand took the thermometer, turned it upside down, and under cover of her shoulders, gave it two quick, sharp sling-downs.

Physics was a good thing to know. True, she could not at the moment think up a governing law. Some form of trigonometric identity applied to Susan Schnitzer's law of force? Anything that shook down must shake up, given up for down and down for up. Oh, Cloud of Probability! She had overdone it; close to 104. She debated rolling an acorn, and trying to sling the reading down a bit; she decided against it; thermometer time was long since up; and, anyway, better too high than too low.

She crawled back toward her mother, and for the first time looked at the spread-out newspapers. She was reading before she realized it: "Housewife Grilled Three Hours by FBI." A pretty young mother with a baby in her arms stared at her. What had the poor woman done? Somebody think she had a faint streak of pink? She saw the words *bank holdup;* and read, grabbing only phrases: "—family held by police until FBI reach scene. — thought to have been driver of bank robbers' getaway car."

Lower on the page a two-column spread screamed: "Crime Invades Swank Eden Hills." Smaller type told: "Daring robbers aided by false tip and confusion over burglar alarm—dark glasses, crew cut, blonde hair, plump cheeks, black and tan reversible raincoat—thought to have been blue-eyed—at least one accomplice—familiar with neighborhood and bank. —very large sums of money—one of the few banks open until eight on Friday. Emily Dexter in state of shock. Mrs. Ashton fears possible miscarriage—."

"Susan, we're forgetting the thermometer."

She remembered to hand it to her mother. That miserable accomplice gone with the money, to leave poor Ter with the gun. She had never believed him; and had put his tale in the same category as the gossip overheard at school about theft rings and "grass" parties. True, the average daily paper, according to Uncle Jeff, never printed any news that might interfere with advertising and the Free Enterprise system, but no Detroit paper went in for whopping tales of nonexistent robberies.

She came to; gathered her mother must have read the thermometer, for vexation had changed to worry. She was backing away so as not to get the dread disease. "You're pale now as a ghost. You should be in bed." She looked wistfully toward her flower arrangement materials, while with a kind of: "I loath that man, but I must do what I should do," she said: "I'll have to call your Dr. Laughton; and he'll never come out here." She gave a great big sigh. "I'll have to drop everything and take you in, for it's impossible to get a prescription out of him by telephone. Why oh why have you insisted on keeping him after we moved away from his—?"

Susie shut her ears. She was weary of that old quarrel over Dr. Laughton, the finest man and the best pediatrician on earth. How would it be lying to him, tricking him into a prescription—? She wouldn't think about that. Chances were she couldn't anyway; she might fool her mother, but not him. Her mother was already gone to the other end of the room, the sacred place reserved for her father's work and his telephone—unlisted. He had a den across the hall, but seemed to prefer his upstairs living room. She crawled quickly toward her mother as soon as she noticed the woman was hunting the number; she carried it in her head. Her mother had found it.

Susie hoped the line would be busy; she could use the time to check her IBM, half wrecked as it was by the thought of lying to Dr. Laughton, plus being fed all that unprogrammed information from the newspaper. She fixed her glance on her mother's face. Made you think of a frozen chicken pie, a new kind with a painted crust; every once in awhile it forgot and seemed ready to frown.

One thing ailed the face was its owner's attitude toward Dr. Laughton. Years ago after Dr. Heffer, Susie's surgeon, had called him in to care for her general health, she had shown such improvement her mother was soon begging Dr. Laughton to take on Brandon. Susie had never been able to learn exactly what did happen the one time her mother had taken Brandon to him. Angry roars from her father ("No child of mine needs a headshrinker. What an old fool.") had led her to think that possibly Dr. Laughton had felt Brandon needed help for his multiple fears, his tantrums, and his inability to get along with either teachers or children at school.

She thought now of how afraid she had been her father would decree no more Dr. Laughton for her. He never had. Her mother might not like him, but she did respect him, Susie thought; it was hard to say what went on behind that beautiful face. At least she was polite, thanking Miss Armstrong the nurse; nice to have a well-brought-up mother; she was thanking Dr. Laughton now for interrupting his work to talk to her. The next minute she was in trouble as she tried to answer questions for which she had not bothered to learn the answers before bothering him. She turned sharply away, her voice dry ice as she handed the receiver to Susie: "He wants to talk to you."

Susie choked, managed at last to drag out a thank you and an apology for the interruption. Between cooking up lies for someone she loved and wondering if they'd work, sickness in her voice was requiring no effort. Dr. Laughton made things worse; he was his usual self, believing her. "And why didn't you come biking in? You're not quite up to one hundred and four."

She managed a choked laugh while she marveled at his memory. That little incident had happened a long time ago when she was in elementary school. She had one morning felt too sick to go to school. Her mother had felt her forehead, then gone away to do the errands and keep a hairdresser appointment. Susie, feeling worse, had, after a time, taken her temperature; too high; she had biked in to let Dr. Laughton have a look at her; no great feat as by then the Schnitzer family had reached a rung on the ladder around a mile west of upper Woodward, not far from his office.

He had, after failing to reach either parent, sent her clanging away to a hospital where she spent a very pleasant ten days in spite of a severe strep infection—and he had come to see her every day, often twice.

She mastered her chokes enough to answer his questions on temperature, nausea, pain, appetite, and had she looked at her throat? Yes, she had looked with a mirror and a flashlight; it was red with a few streaks. "No, sir, it doesn't hurt, exactly; just— kind of scratchy sore. Oh, no, sir, my chest doesn't hurt, not even with a deep breath. No, I'm not coughing. It isn't really much."

The doctor didn't seem to know it, but he had a lot of violin in his voice, beautiful, usually; but now it growled down to low G as he cut her off with a: "Suppose I decide how much it is." He next wanted to know if she had done anything unusual lately. It was getting harder and harder to spit out lies in answer to that warm, sweet voice; still, she managed to tell him of the dance last night; crowded and too warm inside; outside she had felt chilly, but had not done anything about it.

"Natasha at the ball," he said.

"She had sense enough not to catch cold," she said.

"Long after you are well of this bug, you'll have the memory of the fun you had last night. Right?"

"Right," she said, and knew if he kept on talking that way, she'd start bawling like a just-had-a-shot baby.

There was a short silence. He was debating. "You still there, Susie?" She held her breath as he continued: "I have had two emergencies this morning, with a hospital consultation yet to come, and the office full; otherwise I would insist on seeing you. Instead, I'm going to do something I don't like to do and have never done with you—order a prescription for telephoned symptoms."

Plainly, he was not happy with what he was doing; he quarreled a moment about how she should have a throat smear and possibly a blood test; then it was over—almost; he was asking her to hang on while her file was checked. She dropped her head to the telephone stand; she was too ashamed to hold it up. He made you feel he had nothing on his mind but taking care of you and nothing else to do, with the waiting room full of crying babies and older children in for fall check-ups. He would probably miss his lunch.

He was back; and she was glad she didn't have much more talking to do. He went through the same painstaking directions and warnings he always gave when she had to take antibiotics. Furthermore she was to call him at once if she should get worse; in any case have her mother call him at home around seven; he then told her where he would be during the afternoon and gave numbers. She gave the name of their closest pharmacy; and from her mother got the promise he demanded—if the medicine could not be delivered at once, someone would pick it up.

"Now, you get to bed and stay," he told her. "By the way, how is your brother?"

"One-ninety or something, growing in every direction; he's gone camping today." She had the feeling he wanted to learn more of Brandon, but politeness rather than lack of curiosity forbade his further questioning. Strange, his interest, and amazing his memory after seeing him only that one time. She wished, if he had time, she could talk of Brandon, anything so she could hear his voice, but her chokes were worse again. She could get out only: "Thank you so much, Doctor Laughton. Good-bye."

His good-bye seemed even warmer when she turned from the telephone to find her cold-faced mother watching her. Suspicious because her daughter had forgotten to play her role of half-dead girl. She slid out of the chair so abruptly, her mother sprang toward her. "I'll be all right in a moment," she said, and heard her voice, quaky as her insides. Was there such a word as *quaky*? Granted there was, why should she feel that way now? Puffed up she should be as a victorious general with "only fairly heavy casualties."

It was pitiful to hear her mother try to put sweet chitchat into her voice as she asked: "Whatever was it the doctor wanted to know about Brandon?"

Brandon, Brandon, always Brandon. Here she was with all manner of alarming symptoms, but supposed to remember a conversation. Her mother had been eavesdropping, the lowest—. She was ashamed of herself for being so shook-up she had not sooner thought to come up with the symptom that always alarmed her mother. She did; giving such a great big urp, the woman put a hand on her shoulder as she cast an apprehensive glance at the white wall-to-wall.

The question in her mother's glance came back. So much interest for such a little thing; but nothing, absolutely nothing, a mosquito bite or a sniffle, was little if Brandon were concerned. She gave an even better urp. "I think I should help you back to bed," her mother said.

She was showing symptoms of one of her sequential fits of

tender motherhood; all of it out of some cruddy magazine—a semiannual it must be—written by an underdone dope who had never seen a child except as something to test and measure.

The telephone rang. "Your father! I do hope we didn't keep him off the line." Her mother rushed to the other end of the room to leave her daughter gasping, reeling, dying—yet crawling onto the door-opening pad.

She was in pajamas, but putting off the chore of getting into "that bed," when she heard the ladylike knock that meant Lulu. She managed a choked, "Come in," and wished she could flop down and have another good cry. She had thought Lulu long since gone on her twice-a-month weekend off; but as the "extra leave" began only after Lulu had served Bismarck's breakfast, straightened the kitchen and the rest of the house a bit, the Saturday off was largely theoretical.

Lulu got only part way through the door before Susie forgot she was sick and ran to help her with the tray overflowing with ice, orange juice, tea, extra hot water, arrowroot biscuit, and various cold comforters. Lulu insisted on readying the bed, helping Susie into it, and paid no attention to her protests that she was plenty able to wait on herself. She was in bed before she learned just how much she had done to ruin what was left of Lulu's Saturday. Dressed for going out, Lulu was on her way, not to her home, but to the pharmacy to pick up Susie's medicine. She now wanted to know if there were anything else she could get for her like lemon sours or throat drops.

Susie wanted nothing except to get that medicine into Ter, but since it wouldn't cost Lulu anything, and might even make her feel she was doing good, she asked for lemon sours and nose drops.

Lulu gone after a lot of advice on taking fluids and rest, Susie downed an impulse to lock the door and dash up to check on Ter. She would then hide in the closet for her second good cry of the day; trouble with all that was her mother might come at any moment.

It seemed ages while she listened, but it was only half an hour by her watch before her mother came, beautifully dressed for going out, filled with apologies for leaving, and bringing a key and a plan. She would call to see how Susie was. She had unlocked the back door to Charlotte's suite—closer; she didn't think Susie was up to running down to the pantry telephone even if she could hear it. Susie could rest on Charlotte's chaise longue while waiting for the telephone call; however, she must be careful not to muss things. Charlotte and her husband had promised to meet them at the game in Ann Arbor and come home for the weekend.

Her mother was going to meet "your father and his guests" for lunch; they were then going to the game, and what with dinner and crowded traffic they would not be home before "midnight at the earliest." Now, would Susie please be in Charlotte's room between halves; if her mother couldn't make it to the telephone then, she would call after the game—around five, she imagined.

Susie wondered if she were too sick to bring up her old peeve—no telephone of her own when Charlotte had had one from the age of twelve. Today, her mother could not give the usual rejoinder: "Wait until you're dating, dear." Last night was now proof enough that she was dating.

Words were shaped for bringing up the matter when her mother cried: "Mercy, your father will be furious. I'm late!" She was gone.

A short time later, Lulu, perspiration on her nose, came knocking, then tiptoeing in with the medicine, huge black and yellow capsules which she insisted on giving Susie while she lay in bed. They had quite an argument; Susie closer and closer to tears; Lulu gentle as if she were dying, yet determined to keep her in bed, "—with all that fever." Suppose she did vomit, she could use the little vomit pan made for that.

Lulu dashed off for it. Susie made a soundless run for the bathroom where she sprinkled water in each eye for vomit tears. She heard the opening of the bedroom door, and began a great urping to show she was trying to swallow the capsule. Lulu heard, rushed in, and after one glance began helping her back to bed.

She had overdone it again. Lulu did not want to leave her. Susie, getting chokier and chokier, suggested Lulu ease her worries with a telephone call as her mother was doing. She knew Lulu had planned a big weekend for her daughter and her daughter's girl friend; a trip to Belle Isle, possibly to the zoo, and some shopping late this afternoon.

The argument went on intermittently between Lulu's trips for sickroom supplies; among these a vaporizer with plastic tent which she insisted on setting up. Susie let her. It could be inconvenient at times, but still a Lulu-mother would be nice. Leaving out her daily kindnesses and concern for your health and happiness, she looked the mother part; she certainly wasn't fat or soft, but her gentle curves and roundness made a pleasant change from the fashionable thinness of her biological mother. Instead of being coldly beautiful, her face was warm and pretty, blonde with a real nose, and eyes that were blue but never cold.

Susie's feelings of guilt multiplied when she realized she had caused Lulu to miss a ride with her mother. True, her mother would pay Lulu's cab fare as she always did when she couldn't get a ride to the bus station, but she knew that Lulu, no matter how tired, walked to the bus station and saved the cab fares she collected. Now she was somewhat cheered when Lulu, worry and apology showing in her eyes, explained she would have to be leaving, if she meant to "catch that ride with that nice Mr. Haber; they had him out to take another look at the well pump." She went slowly away, looking over her shoulder at Susie in bed, and plainly certain she ought to stay.

Susie, kneeling by her window, peeped until she saw her get into the pump man's car. Lulu got along well with all men, from the firemen who had rolled out the cars from the garage when her father belatedly discovered he had knocked a hole in his gas tank, to that multitude of men who were always coming to diagnose and treat the forever ailing House of Usher.

6

Safe, with Lulu out of sight, Susie gathered up all the sickroom supplies brought for her she could carry, and with the medicine hurried up to Ter.

He was so thoroughly nasty, she decided he was better. First, he wanted to know why she was going around "undressed in a bathrobe"; then without waiting for her explanation, asked if she had managed the medicine. She gave him the bottle so that he might read the directions: before she could stop him he had swallowed three pills.

She told him with some heat he was only supposed to take two, two hours from now. Had he forgotten the man-size doses of V-Cillin?

"I am probably close to half again as heavy as you; according to the directions you were to begin with two," he told her, turning his back.

The sharp hurts of the lies to a man she trusted and loved— and who trusted her; running Lulu to death; plus all that homework, undone because of this spoiled brat who had not even thanked her for the medicine; all so crushed her that, wordless, she turned toward the ladder.

Her feet were feeling for the top rung when here came his

quarrelsome whisper: "Please, won't you get dressed? I keep thinking of Beeto. What would he say?"

"I wish you'd quit talking about William Anthony Herrick as if he were some kind of ogre; and also quit using a nickname only his real friends and family use."

"He hasn't any family. He's an orphan."

"He is not. His mother is still alive, and he has Granma and me. And even though his father was killed in World War II, he and his father's people around Halifax visit back and forth a lot."

"You are not his family. His mother went back to Italy and married again; but wouldn't let his father's people have him because they're not Catholic."

"Neither is Granma."

"She brought him up in the Catholic faith, the way she would have brought up you because your mother and your grandfather were Catholic. Don't forget that."

"I don't forget my grandfather; my mother changed her religion for father," she told him, going down one step where she stopped to remind him: "Beeto's mother has never forgotten him. She helped him through college."

She thought he sniffed at that, but did not linger to make certain. Talking of Beeto's scattered people and her lost religion was not pleasant. She had no memory of life without Beeto. He had been in her grandmother's home for around ten years when her own mother left her—all of three weeks old—to grow up with her grandmother while she rushed back to her husband, a quickie captain with the Occupation Forces in West Germany. She had lived six years with her grandmother and Beeto; he had always seemed like a brother, then, and now, closer than Brandon—in spite of silly talk that he might some day be her husband. She went to her closet.

There, using real Chinese tea bought in Canada, water heated on her forbidden hot plate, and a beautiful Russian pot, that U. S. Customs had thought from Sweden, she soothed herself with two cups of good tea before starting homework.

She was just getting into a math problem—find the variable

in a series of equations, then graph the resultant function—when there came quick taps on the ceiling. She continued to think on $x = y^2(y-2)^2$. She had not started the graph, but it was in her head. The taps came again. He could be in pain, nauseated, or choking.

She was scarcely off the ladder before out of the dark came his sad, troubled voice telling he had been so dizzy on his last trip to the bathroom he had almost fallen off the ladder. The antibiotics, fever, and lack of food were causing it, she told him; then wanted to know why he had not used the old picnic ice bucket she had provided.

His answer was angry and embarrassed: "Please, such a subject for conversation. Remember, I'm not locked behind your closet the way you left me for hours this morning."

She switched on the light. He flopped into the shadow on the other side of the cot. "Were you trying to knock a hole in the plaster to get me up here just to quarrel?" she wanted to know.

"Nurses are supposed never to be cross, but I don't blame you. I am causing you a lot of trouble."

His voice had changed to sweet politeness. This worried her; taking the meanness out of patients was not one of the properties of the many-propertied antibiotics. His wounded arm was on top of the bed covering; she looked at it with the flashlight until he jerked it under him; still no sign of swelling or blood on the pajama sleeve. His coordination continued splendid; he had flopped all over while trying to be an unpatient. She reminded her IBM to remind her at the proper time to find out if there were such a word as *unpatient*.

He was whispering from out the shadow: "A priest, I need a priest." And as if to show death upon him he moved into the light.

He made her think of some old-time hero; Julian, she thought, after a long term of semistarvation in a moldy prison while awaiting execution. His sad dark eyes were so big and beautiful below that pale forehead with the fine dark hair dripping down over it, she found herself wishing Lulu were home; from her she could learn the whereabouts of a priest. She took his hand. It was neither icy cold with the chill of incoming death nor burning hot with fever. She was being an awful fool. "You're getting better, and feeling worse," she told him.

He gave a great sigh. "Don't be silly! I think I am taking pneumonia—just like my mother."

"You're young and strong," she said. "The young and the strong don't generally die from anything but accidents. Study your statistics."

"That is exactly what my father did for me, quoted statistics." He so forgot himself in his agitation, he lifted on an elbow, the better to see her face. "I was scared when I heard that doctor on the phone calling the hospital for an ambulance with emergency care for my mother; 'urgent—critical,' I heard him say. I could go to day school then, a very good one, and live at home. I wanted it that way—then. My father wasn't home that morning; gone all the night before. Some sort of 'business trip.' He didn't know she was sick when he came whistling into my room about ten to see why I hadn't gone to school.

"I've wondered if my mother knew, while she was still able to know, where he was that night. He had known she had something like a cold, except it wouldn't go away. He was real, real cool, took his time about starting for the hospital while he quoted statistics to me. 'Women,' he said, 'don't die like men. Look at all the widows. Getting her into the hospital is nothing more than a wise precaution.'

"And he rattled on with a lecture for me on how I should have gone to school; I'd scare my sisters and have them crying when they got home. Had I sent flowers, and what kind should he send? She liked them all, he said. And when they'd carried her out before breakfast—they'd just taken time to put one of those portable oxygen tents over her—she was already past liking or loving or hating.

" 'Lilies,' I yelled. 'Lilies are the only flowers she'll need. Save the others for your girl friends.'

"I never did know whether he slapped me or hit me with his fist; so old to be so quick. I was plenty black and blue around one eye for awhile. We were glaring at each other there in my room when Rosa tapped on my door. 'Somebody to see you,

Master Ter,' she said. She wasn't crying any more; her face was just a face.

"And I knew, and I said: 'Father Amari.' She didn't answer because I knew, but just with my head—then. I had rung him up to go to my mother at the hospital.

"I walked round my father and out the door. I was ashamed, walking out to the priest as if I were the head of the house with no father. We had learned to manage without him.

"And all she had was a severe virus pneumonia, something about her heart, and a few other complications. She had worn herself and her heart out waiting around and worrying over him while he was—well, while he was."

"You're feverish or you wouldn't talk so." She added, hoping, why she didn't know: "Perhaps he loved her, after all."

"You know you're an awfully little girl in spite of those terrific grades you make. Love? But she was his wife. He brought her over when she was not quite seventeen, not as old as I am now. Why, they had been married around sixteen years. She was old for love, past thirty. A man needs a wife, especially one like my mother; she knew how to do everything from raising children to being President of the Altar Guild Society or how to dress for cocktail parties—which she loathed. And was my father ever shook up when he didn't have her around any more."

He was getting chokier and chokier as well as hoarse. She wanted off the sad subject. Her godfather who also lived near Chicago had also lost his wife; but sadder than thinking on death, for every living thing had sometime to die, was the wonder if this beautiful boy, filled with mother-love and religion, had actually robbed a bank. "Your mother," she said at last, "the way you speak of her, reminds me of Angie—you know Angelica, Joe's wife."

Angie was the wrong direction. "Why, you can't compare them! Angie's parents were peasants—rich grape-growing Californians. And she spent four years at Berkeley where she learned things that didn't improve her wifely qualities. My mother was educated in a convent; her father was no peasant, but a professor of archaeology. Joe's Angie would have done better to—."

"I wish I could tell you half the things Joe and Angie have

done for me," she interrupted. "Joe is my grandfather's nephew; Angie's no kin, but she means just as much; if I couldn't visit her and the boys, I would die of loneliness—here." She flounced to the ladder.

His plaintive: "Please, Susie, wait. I apologize. I didn't mean to rattle you," stopped her. "Talking to you makes me feel better. Even if I'm not dying—yet—I still have to get my—someone to get me out of here. It's awful. I thought that by tonight I'd be able to sneak out and walk to a cab stand or even that bus station—but I'm too dizzy. So, you will have to do some telephoning."

"Will I? It depends on where your accomplice is. My father has a telephone bill syndrome. One little long distance call on the bill and there are, plus the usual static on the waste of money, questions on the who and why. 'Father, dear, it was the bank robber's accomplice.'"

"I tell you I had no accomplice."

"I suppose I could go to a pay phone and use the credit card Beeto pays for—if I do it."

He reared straight up in bed, and never noticed he had dropped his role of the dying. "Beeto? Are you crazy? He would recognize the number."

"Do you think he's so petty he'd check the numbers? His secretary gives him the check to sign, period."

"O.K. I won't argue. If only you had a license you could drive me to a bus station, and there'd be no need to telephone. But I *have* to be back by Sunday night at nine; if I'm not, they call my father. He probably thinks, if he's thought of me at all, that I'm spending the weekend sailing with Joe and Angie. I accepted their invitation; then after I caught this cold, I telephoned your grandmother, and after I had made my excuses for her birthday party—I must get her a nice present—I asked permission to use her Windsor cottage for the weekend; and please to tell Joe I could not go sailing."

He had taken pen and paper from the milkbox-bedside table. "I'll give you three numbers to call in the order I write them. You'll have to get one man—Lanny is his name." He looked at her. "If you won't call from here, you can bike to a pay-station."

"You forget I'm supposed to be sick in bed. What if the neighbors saw or I ran into Dr. Laughton?"

He was sharp in an argument. Dr. Laughton would either be busy with the sick or sailing or golfing or gardening. And as for the neighbors, everyone on a fine September Saturday afternoon would be at their country clubs, or riding clubs, or yacht clubs, or like her parents gone to the football game in Ann Arbor. Furthermore, he had gathered, the neighbors were not much on togetherness with the Schnitzers. Who was there to notice her?

She shook her head. "Give the medicine time. You seem livelier; and I would say your temperature has gone down. I could walk with you after dark; you might just be able to—."

He was sighing again. "That's what's so discouraging. My temperature is down, not quite one hundred and two. But I *feel* worse."

"Gordie Howe could play a whole hockey game with a temperature no higher than that," she told him.

"Please, won't you get going? I'm sorry, but I have to reach —that man."

She looked at her watch; plenty of time to get back before her mother called. It was a dangerous, stupid thing to do, sail out into the teeth of gale-warnings; yet what he said about her not being noticed was true—she thought. Getting out of the house again would be nice; a bike ride of three miles to the shopping center, then back, would get her brains in better shape for homework.

She hurried away to dress and get started. Less than half way to the pay phone, she had to admit Ter had been right about the habits of Eden Hills. Nobody around to notice; even the vast expanse of shopping center parking lot was dotted only here and there with a car.

She went first into the block-size drugstore, not the pharmacy from which her prescription had come, and bought a small tin of aspirin. Next, carelessly, as if it were an afterthought, she bought a Detroit newspaper, folding it quickly, to show she was not the least bit interested in the two column spread, "Police Chief Backs Officers." Careful to betray no hurry, she studied the paperbook rack a moment—mostly popular junk—then went out to her bike.

She had almost reached an exit when she stopped with a jerk; frowning, she stared back over her shoulder as if searching for something; after a second she quickly turned around, wearing an exasperated look for the benefit of the nice middle-aged woman in a beautiful Rover coming up to the same exit. The woman gave a little head shake of sympathy for this girl—like a million other girls in black skirt, black poorboy, and extra sweater—who, it was clear, had just remembered an errand.

It would not have done to have remembered in the drugstore where the telephones were not enclosed, or gone to any other exit with their plastic wrap-around booths that gave no privacy, but only here where the closest phone was completely enclosed in an old-fashioned little wooden house, particularly fine today; not even a parked car nearby.

She laid a pile of change on the counter, and saw with shame for her cowardly self that dimes were sticking to her sweaty fingers. She tried to tell herself this was exactly like a long-distance call to Beeto, without her credit card—the second number had the same exchange as his apartment address. The weakness in her legs kept reminding her she was doing a miserable job of lying to herself; in spite of what Ter said, this Lanny was undoubtedly an accomplice. And she wanted no bank robber to have a voice pattern of Susan Schnitzer. So how to speak.

She debated. Fake a French accent? No. Better to speak United Statese. What kind? Hard-core Detroit? And supposing there were such a thing, how did it sound? Her TV sent Joe, good in such things, mimicking a man from Chicago with whom he had had a conference; he'd gargled his words in the back of his throat before sending them through his nose. She'd have to be careful or she'd lose the sour ball in each cheek.

She fed two nickels in, gave the operator the first number, learned what change was needed, made a separate pile of it, but got nothing save the lonesome sound of a ringing telephone. The second unanswered number sounded even more lonesome. Her hands were getting stickier and stickier; the third number would be it. Keep your sour balls in position.

She counted rings, reached three, and heard one word. "Yes?" The operator demanding money came between her and the man's voice. She fed her quarters in, and wondered how one asked for a Lanny. The operator was gone, the line clear; the man's voice came again, impatient in spite of good grades from an excellent charm school, soft yet strong, steel soaked in oil. "Yes? What is it? Who is calling, please?"

She was bugged. She kept thinking of Iggy's eyes. This voice was doing the same thing to her—a memory with no frame. She'd better be thinking not only of what she was to say, but the way to say it. "I'm talking. I have a message for Lanny," she gargled through the sour balls.

"I am Lanny. What is it?"

Floating past on that river of forever moving, disconnected bits of life was another voice, exactly like this man's. Whose? She had forgotten his question, until he again asked: "What is it? Can you hear me?"

"I am I," she managed at last. "I was told to ask Lanny to send word to a certain boy's father that—anyway—this boy won't be able to get back to his school when he's supposed to. He is the same boy—with a bad cold so he couldn't come to a party Friday night."

"Ter?"

"Yes. He picked up a virus and a bug."

"Pneumonia?" The voice was edged with worry.

She felt, more than she reasoned, this man was Ter's father. She tried to soothe him. "No. Only a little sore throat." She wanted to detail the improvement in his symptoms, but while she was chewing over words and accent, the man so pounded her with questions she gave up.

He suddenly dropped the questions, and said in a cold hard voice that made her glad there was a long stretch of I. 94 between them: "If you don't tell me what I need to know, I will call the telephone company, the FBI, a private detective agency,

117

and have this call traced. What are you calling from? A cathouse? You had better—."

She never heard the rest for chewing that one over, unaware she was doing it aloud and in her own voice; but the word was strange as The Primitive's "okra stringen." "Doghouse, possibly. No, this is too high for even a big dog, and certainly for a—."

"Never mind. Never mind. Please tell me what I must know. I can now understand you better."

No wonder. She had swallowed the lemon sours. The operator broke in with the thirty seconds more business. The man, impatient, worried, begged: "Can't the call be reversed?" She hastily fed in the needed change, and when she was certain the operator was off the line, said: "I wouldn't go messing around with any kind of investigative outfit if I were you. He wouldn't let me call any one except Lanny."

He wanted to know where Ter was.

She hesitated. He had dropped his threatening line, and now seemed more than ever the frightened father. "A Detroit suburb," she told him. She closed her eyes, the better to see the map of southeastern Michigan. "It's several miles north of I. 94 on the northwestern side of Detroit, and a few minutes east of U.S. 23."

"But won't you please give me a number I can call, at least close to him?" he asked with pitiful beseeching.

She debated. "You can't call even me—not any old time."

"What time? I should be there around seven."

She let out an involuntary, "Oh"; then collected her wits enough to ask: "And where is there?"

"How could I know—now? Some motel, hotel—close."

"I would make a reservation for—him—too; tonight." He said nothing, yet she felt the state of things was getting through. "You can call between seven and eight. I wouldn't use a credit card—cash. And if I should not answer, the call will be from Mr. Williams, my physics teacher. Please remember."

She wondered if she had kept the same voice throughout, and if telephone operators ever listened in, and—. He was again begging her for a number.

Poor helpless man; he must love his son as she loved his

voice; but the wife was a sad business. She gave him Charlotte's number. He next asked: "And who are you in case I have to be the physics teacher?"

"Why, I am I, Priscilla, the young lady of the cat—."

"Please," he said, and let out a heavy breath; frustrated, as if he might enjoy choking her or himself or somebody. "Thank you," he added. The receiver clicked, though there was more time on the quarters.

As she picked up the leftover change, she saw with shame it still stuck to her sweat-wet fingers.

Home in a hurry, she took time in the kitchen to check the robbery story in the paper. It was much the same as that she had read on her mother's floor; no further arrests, not even a suspect as yet.

Ter's impatient question of had she got through to Lanny came while she was climbing the ladder. He was plainly pleased by her answer; but when she started to tell of Lanny's loving worry, he showed no interest.

As it was almost time for her mother's call, she collected study materials and, after propping open doors so as to be able to hear Ter, settled herself in Charlotte's quarters.

She got little done. Ter's complaints of boredom and of the slow passage of time increased along with his wishings and his wantings. He was sick of orange juice, even freshly squeezed. She tried pineapple, apple, grapefruit, and tomato; most he drank to the accompaniment of a complaint that the juice was tinned or not properly chilled. She struggled not to let his ill manners take her mind completely off homework. Not easy; and sometime during the afternoon she remembered his trousers, dried and brushed; underwear washed and dried, but nothing ironed. She finished his laundry; and after the last math problem went to work on the theme—two hours later than she had hoped.

A "creative description" it was supposed to be, making liberal "use of similes and metaphors"—and the only theme so far returned had brought from "Mr. Twitty," teacher of this accelerated English course, only a C; her first in all her years of school. Now, how to bring the pond alive and up her grade?

She could see, hear, smell, and feel the pond and its life; yet the search for words to tell all this seemed always to lead into some dead-end street. Framed at last in her head, the words slid away before she could get them on paper. Part of it was the dashing around; each time she went to the kitchen on an errand for Ter's appetite, it was hurry, hurry for fear her mother would call and she couldn't hear the ring. More worry when she rushed to the attic; there, even with all doors propped, she felt within hearing only when she was on the ladder.

She tried to read what she had written, gave up, and only stared at the marked out words as she whispered: "Be honest; quit telling yourself lies. You can't be listening for your mother —not now. The first half of that game must have ended long ago; there'll be no call now until it's over. —You're letting that green-eyed monster, jealous envy, short your circuits."

True. Here was this undutiful brat in the attic, thinking only of himself, while that old father of his was now burning rubber on I. 94 or in the air. She lay sick with the same symptoms, only worse when her mother left, all alone, and the woman couldn't even bother to ring her up.

Sick? How sick was she? She had neglected to write down the symptoms she had given Dr. Laughton. How well could she dare be by seven? Well as Ter, of course. She tried to make a list of all things from pain to nausea, presence or lack. Aching from the page of lies, she put the sheet by Charlotte's telephone.

She tried to forget her lies and her mother through work on the theme. Should she say: "At twilight the killdeer is the crying of a lonesome wandering child," or make a simile of it? The telephone was ringing.

Lulu, apologetic and worried. It was such a pretty day they had spent the whole afternoon on Belle Isle; after looking at the flowers, they had visited the aquarium, then gone into the woods where there was no telephone. And how was Susie? She had tried to reach her twice, between one and two; and when she couldn't, she'd been scared Susie was too sick to get out of bed.

Susie, trying hard to keep the chokes out of her voice, guessed she had dozed off, and not heard the telephone. She asked if there were any little Mexican chrysanthemums in the flower display, and had Lulu had time for the maritime museum? As for herself she was much, much better, practically well; and she recited the list of improvements she had prepared for Dr. Laughton.

Lulu was again apologetic; since Susie was so much better with her temperature down, she wouldn't bother her with another telephone call tonight; but could she call tomorrow morning? Somebody ought to be there to fix Susie something to eat, and that somebody ought to have been herself. Talking of eating, she wished Susie were with them. The girls had wanted to top off the nice day with a "supper in that high-up cafeteria in Cobo Hall where we can sit by a window and watch the boat lights on the river." Pretty those running lights were, Lulu thought, as well as looking out to Windsor. Oh, yes, if Susie felt up to it, she ought to remember to watch the sun set; she could see it from Charlotte's windows. Now, was she certain she was all right, and didn't need anything?

"Just the sight of a boat's running lights reflecting on the water. They are about the prettiest things on earth," Susie told her, then urged her to get on to dinner; she and the girls must be hungry after such a long day with all that walking.

She went back to the theme, but in trying to read what she had written found the words blurred. If—if what? If she had a mother like Lulu? If her mother had called before Lulu? She had better be fishing for words to describe a clump of cattails. Instead, she fished up *cathouse*, tried to throw it back, probably the kind of word her grandmother did not want her to hear. What ailed a person's mind when it forgot names it ought to remember, but clung to strange words like sandburrs to tweed? And what ailed that boy? He was pinging the pipes. He might know what *cathouse* meant, but she had better not ask.

He wanted limeade, "not too sweet," and not "that frozen concentrated stuff." This meant a search in the larder for bottled lime juice, mixing, getting out ice, hurrying, hurrying, trying to listen; her mother would telephone any minute now.

Ter tasted the limeade with a critical holding in his mouth; Beeto tasting the wine. "Tinned," he said, staring at the liquid as if wondering were it worth drinking. He then drained the glass.

"You're welcome," she said, and left him. Downstairs she remembered the newspaper; that ought to keep him quiet for awhile. Less than ten minutes later while she was trying to read what she had just written—and finding "The sedge is withered from the lake and no birds sing," a poor fit with her own junky words—she heard her tuning pipe. The patient was using it to call the nurse.

Sitting up with the light on, paper across his knees, he made her think of the dog the tin soldier saw—eyes big as mill wheels. "I didn't think it would be spread all over the paper," he said.

"Any thirty-thousand-dollar robbery is going to be all over a lot of papers," she told him.

"Thirty thousand dollars, why, why it—. That paper is wrong; it couldn't be that much; such thin little stacks they felt. —Say, tell me if you know, is shock ever fatal?"

She knew he was thinking of that banking clerk girl he had scared to death. "Not often," she told him. "Trouble is, shock can deteriorate into mental illness, or make her sterile for life, or give her nightmares for years." Dr. Laughton with his: "A good and active mind should be able to absorb the shocks of life," would not agree, but this boy ought to suffer a bit, just a bit.

He was. "And could fright make a woman—ah—lose an unborn child?"

She nodded. He was quiet for about ten microseconds, then he was pitching into her: "Susie, you shouldn't know so much about causes of sterility and all that."

She shrugged. "Sorry." Angry, she dumped words over him. How would he like to be a penniless young girl on her first job, nothing but a servant to a computer and a money-stacking machine, low pay, "and get shot at four times?"

"I didn't shoot at her one time. I didn't shoot at any human being. That's more than I can say for them."

His words were so heated she tried to switch the conversation. "I hope you're thinking of some way to get that money back. Just be thankful you boys aren't dead."

"Boys? Won't you ever believe me when I tell you I did it by myself—with some props. They're over there drying with the raincoat by the hot pipe." He dropped back onto the cot, and lay prone, face in the shadow.

Susie, determined on another try at describing the pond, asked: "What did you want when you called me?"

"Oh? Food and drink I guess it was—but not any more when I think of that business. I wonder why I did it. I had a cold, and felt miserable because I couldn't go to your grandmother's party. I wasn't going without a gift, and I was broke."

"Horses, I suppose?"

"No. I was lucky on the few bets I made, but there were so many other things. Part of it I had loaned an unlucky chap. Why I didn't try to get it back or borrow, I don't know. I don't even know why I caught a free ride to Windsor with some other students. I wasn't planning anything." He rose on one elbow. "You know, I think it was that gun."

"Gun?"

"Yes, the pistol you saw. I'm certain your father left it with your grandmother while she was still in the States. He must have brought a dozen home from West Germany at one time or another. I've heard he tried to give one to Dad. He wouldn't have it; that was when they were still on speaking terms, before the fight over lawyers for your grandmother. Anyway, I had a few U.S. dollars and some change, but no Canadian, and I wanted to call about buses to Detroit—you know, your grandmother has her phone disconnected for the months she's gone. It was when I was rummaging in her cottage for coins, I ran into the gun."

Susie hoped he had finished. She ought to get back to work; she'd let that lonesome listening for the telephone interfere with her writing. This listening wasn't much better. Who wanted to hear about a bank robbery, and most especially a tale made up from what he'd read in the newspaper she'd brought? She'd waited too long; he was talking again; and up here could she hear the telephone while he was talking? She'd better sneak down and take a listen. The shadow was so heavy, he couldn't see what she did.

She hurried soundlessly down and up again in time to learn

123

he was now on his way to Detroit with that gun "in the pocket of my made-over raincoat. The rush hour was coming on; nobody looked at me; I had nothing for customs, and my passport was enough for Immigration. I had only one plan; that was to get close enough to you, I could ring you up on a local call, so if the wrong person answered I could be some boy from your school."

"But why did you want to talk to me?"

"I've told you that all my life I've been hearing of 'Little Susie.' I thought that even if I couldn't see you then, we might make plans for a get-together sometime. That was why I took the Dreamland Shopping Center Bus."

He gave a sad head shake. "It was while I was hunting a telephone booth that I came onto that bank, the drive-in or walk-in outfit. Such a sweet setup for a foolproof robbery! And the time of day was perfect: not too late for rush hour traffic, but still early enough for people to stop and shop on the way home. So everything was crowded. Lights were coming on, enough I could see there weren't any at the back of the bank."

"I suppose," Susie said, starting down the ladder, "that makes the robbery my fault."

"Don't be silly. It wasn't anybody's fault but mine and everything laid out just right, like that hamburger place close by. I don't think I'd had much of anything all day but tea—I wonder did I rinse your grandmother's teapot—but I wasn't hungry. Still, I went into the place; why I don't exactly know. I had almost no money, but I got in line with a tray like everybody else. And what a joint. Like everybody else I was expected to pay when this guy wrote out my order slip for a hamburger and a malted.

"I felt dirty, so I left my binder and order slip on the tray—it seemed to be the custom—and went to their little hole of a washroom off a back hall by the kitchen. Nobody was around. I washed; still nobody. I nipped out a back door at the end of the hall; in that place they don't have to worry about customers slipping off unpaid. You must know how it is back there; half street, half delivery alley, not too many lights.

"I stepped over the Kiddy Keeper wall, and bent down as if I were picking up something. When I came up I had on my blond wig, wax gum in my cheeks, dark glasses ready to go, and as I walked on I buttoned my raincoat—all the way. Just like practice for the on-stage change in my skit. The glasses are blue, so I looked blue-eyed.

"The next thing I remember is the bank, the walk-in side. I seemed all alone there by the window—except for this big-eyed girl. Something strange about her; she was meek as a servant girl dressed up to do banking. I wondered why she stood so still in front of me with her mouth open, until I finally knew I was pointing the gun at her head. Then, I had to say: 'This is a holdup. The money, please.'"

Susie, under cover of the shadows, gave a head shake of doubt. Had he really said that, and remembered to take all the precautions he was describing now: cheap cotton gloves, cheap watch so nobody would see his own, and a change of voice?

"You'd have thought those little stacks of money belonged to the girl, the way she hesitated about handing them over. I reached so she could see the inside of my sleeve and the police would start looking for a man in a black and tan raincoat.

"She finally ducked below the counter. I could shoot then with no danger of hitting her. I shot three times as I backed away, that blasted money cradled in my other arm.

"I heard pops, not awfully loud. I had turned around to run before I knew those pops meant somebody was shooting at my back. The cowards! I fired two more times, straight up. The money kept getting in my way, but as I ran by the side of the building toward that shadowy back with the shrubbery, I jerked off the wig and raincoat, shoved the money and gun into its pockets along with the glasses, and spit out the gum."

He suddenly sat upright, and turned to her. "Now, can you tell me why, why didn't I drop the money—then. I'll see no peace till I can get it back to Miss Emily Dexter. I think," he went on as if she had asked a question, "I robbed the bank for kicks, or to see if I could do such a thing. I don't know. I'm wondering if I need a psychiatrist?"

Susie figured any kind of answer to that one would be dangerous. Instead, she asked: "But why didn't anybody chase you when you ran?"

"Everybody was gawking at the sky—when they weren't

125

running and screaming. I forgot to tell you the most horrible part
—that awful racket. It started, I think, about the time I got
through the bank door. I can't describe it—like fire sirens mixed
in with ear-splitting, out-of-tune gongs. I wondered why I didn't
throw the money down. It would never be of any use to any
human being. And I thought what a miserable deal for the
U.S.A. to get bombed when all my family and myself were in it. I
was for a minute a fool like everybody else; I knew that racket
was the air raid warning.

"Nobody had any mind for me in that riot. All those
screams: 'Detroit's been bombed.' Where's the closest air raid
shelter?' Women screaming for their kiddies and kiddies screaming 'Mama.'

"I had to get back to my tray. I figured that even with the
bomb falling it would look suspicious for me, an American, not
to grab my paid-for hamburger. And I wanted my binder, for by
the time I got out of the shrubbery and onto the walk, it was
getting through to me that noise was the bank's burglar alarm. I
figured I'd better get away from the place—and quick, before
they learned what the racket meant. While I pushed my way
through the crowd, it was no problem to act like everybody else
—scared to death.

"The hamburger place was almost empty. The customers
had rushed outside. I spotted the tray with my binder, and made
for it. When I picked it up I noticed for the first time a sting of
pain in my underarm. I figured I'd been shot. Blood might be
running down my back. I flipped my raincoat over the shoulder
on that side, and started for the door, just as a crowd surged in
like an ocean wave.

"Such a gabble. Detroit hadn't been bombed; not even a big
accident; nothing but a bank holdup with nobody shot; but the
robbers would soon be caught. A bank teller had spotted the
license of the getaway car. The FBI and police cars would take
off when the address came through.

"I wondered how it felt to faint. I knew I'd have to confess
when they pinned the deal on an innocent man. Then, I heard
the accomplice was a woman." He sat up and looked in Susie's

direction. "Such idiots; they ransacked the homes of innocent people, and grilled that man for hours, just because somebody had seen the woman stop her car in front of the bank to give him a lift. The police wouldn't believe he was the woman's brother-in-law, with his wife sick, and his car—. I suppose you read the paper?"

Susie nodded.

"But you couldn't read how the wounded robber felt when it got through to him the catchup he'd noticed on the underside of his wrist was blood oozing from under his coat sleeve. For all I knew my blood could be dripping from my coat tails; in another minute it could make a big puddle on my tray. And there I stood, hemmed in by that crowd still pouring in.

"I got scared of myself. I so wanted out of there and into the dark, I was afraid I would start knocking down guys to get to the door. Then I saw some were clearing the trays, and making for that back hall with their food—all on paper. I did the same. I'd been too shook up to remember there was a back way out.

"And what a relief to find a dark corner with a trash can and dump the hamburger and malted. I began to feel better after I found a cab. The cabbie couldn't see my back, and between watching the road and talking of the holdup—he'd been held up five times—he hadn't any mind for me. He said the robber was some hard-core kid from Detroit. What an insult. 'A decent robber,' he said, 'wouldn't have shot after the money was handed over.'

"I was sorry I couldn't tell him why I shot so many times. When I put in five bullets I wasn't certain any would fire. I thought they might be old, but from the way they went off I don't think they were. I don't know anything about guns; furthermore I'm not eager to learn. I knew if I didn't empty the gun by shooting it, I might never get the bullets out. I'd already discovered I hated carrying a loaded gun.

"I told the cabbie I only had a little over three dollars, and that I wasn't exactly sure where I wanted to go. I was supposed to meet my parents who were looking over model homes in the new professional subdivision in the valley below The Village. He knew at once the place I meant. He said, 'The Village' the way a priest would speak of paradise. I had just enough American money to pay my fare with a decent tip.

"It was full dark by then, misting rain, and all I wanted was a quiet place where I could sit and shake—your attic I'd heard the old ones worry over. You know the rest: how I went up the hill so as to keep off roads where car lights could spot me, then let your blue lights lead me smack into that swimming pool."

"You're a good storyteller," Susie said.

"Story? It's all true."

"I know. Of course it's true." She was sorry she'd hurt his feelings, but it seemed to her there were holes in his tale. "Makes you realize that most of us don't notice much of anything. Why, for example, didn't they start looking for somebody in or carrying a raincoat like yours? You said you took special pains to let the girl see it."

"Susie, you didn't listen. I explained at the beginning how at your grandmother's I had made a reversible raincoat. I cut pieces from the inside of an old one I found at her place, and glued them to the lower inside of the sleeves and the tails of my raincoat, so I would have a reversible like everybody else."

"I understand—now," she said. Another lie; she'd missed that part when she'd sneaked down to listen. And when had she listened? She sprang down the ladder, as she did so, remembering another forgotten thing—the sunset. She'd probably missed it.

She had missed the actual going down of the sun; the sweep of western sky she could see from Charlotte's windows held only some after-light, smudged by log pile smoke and cut by jet trails. She turned abruptly away; seeing more than remembering, her wanting like a hunger for a particular sunset, the sky pale as a peeled lemon above the black silhouette of a spruce-covered hill crowned with the black, jagged spires of the tree tops.

She heard her tuning pipe; Ter again to tell her that talking with her had made him feel so much better, he again felt like eating. And was there any decent wine on the place? Be the best thing in the world for him.

She told him she could supply food, but no wine; no need to

tell him of the small cellar of cooking wine Lulu and her mother kept behind the potatoes in the cold cellar; a secret from Bismarck, she thought.

"How uncivilized to live without wine," he commented in disgust, but grew happier over his food order of: "a nice thick little tenderloin steak with mushrooms, good French bread, unsalted butter, and a salad of fresh fruit."

She hurried downstairs to see what she could find. She could give him unsalted butter at least; Lulu bought it for herself, Susie, and cake-baking; but she'd have to get more from the basement Deepfreeze. And her mother liable to telephone at any minute. She propped open the pantry doors and the basement door on her way to hunt butter and anything else she could find.

She had the butter but nothing else when she glanced at her watch and remembered Dr. Laughton. She rushed back upstairs, and was so harassed that when she reached him he said: "Susie, you sound mad and tired. Getting better?"

"Yes, sir; lots better. Able to wrestle with old Aeneas and try to write a miserable theme." She picked up the prepared sheet, and, careful not to sound as if she were reading, reported her multiple improvements. And could she go to school Monday?

"We'll see." Most certainly she could not bike or bus, but if her temperature should be normal by tomorrow morning and stayed that way, he would consider the matter; she would have to go by car; and no gym. She should quit worrying about homework; relax: "Write something you enjoy writing, or read a good book—for pleasure. Your parents are gone?"

Those violin-timbered tones had unmistakably framed a question. "Yes, sir."

"Everything under control?"

"Of course. Don't scare me, doctor."

"Oh, just precautions; precautions like carrying an umbrella on a cloudy day. One precaution I should like to take is to suggest to your township sheriff that he direct the night patrolman of your neighborhood to go round your drive and check the house. You are quite sick and alone there, except for your brother."

Her head drooped. She had never thought how much those

lies might worry him. She wanted to sound unafraid and light-hearted, but knew she didn't. "If you wish, doctor. Brandon is at camp, but I'm not a bit afraid, and I hate to give the patrolman extra trouble."

He didn't exactly say, "Oh," but there was an "Oh" of relief in his voice as he asked: "Brandon gone camping for the week-end, eh?"

Listening, she thought telephones were deceptive things. Voices without faces to read, they caused you to misread them. He sounded as if, well, as if with Brandon gone he wasn't worried about her safety—any more. Criticizing that sweet, kind man, she was; to ease her guilt, she said: "I love you, Doctor." Wrong; now he couldn't know she always had.

"You say the same thing to Dr. Hefler. Practice your flirta-tions on someone younger. Still, I don't mind serving as a pre-practice warm up; ski exercises in summer without snow. That it?" He did not wait for her answer, but asked her to call him tomorrow morning around seven-thirty; any time, if she should get worse. "We'll see about school." He wished her pleasant dreams and a restful night.

She thanked him, wished him the same, and after they had exchanged good-byes, she continued to sit smiling at the tele-phone. He was, she thought, close to the age of her grand-mother; still, it was nice to imagine he was her father, thinking about her comfort and safety, with little jokes and sweet words.

She had better be thinking of putting the swamp and its pond into similes and metaphors. Could she say the cattails in September were unlighted brown candles? She wrote, read, put fierce lines through the words. They had made her think of a "gift shoppe" sales pitch. A cattail was a cattail, and what else? A wand? No. A club? Of course not. Oh, metaphor, meta-phor, come to me. She'd hunt one for cattails while she collected Ter's food. Get that much done. She couldn't try to cook any-thing until after her mother telephoned. She was half way down the basement stairs when she heard the rings. Her mother at long last. She ran.

Old Lanny Bear too shook up to recognize her voice; or could it be because she had, thinking she would speak to her mother, put neither sour balls into her mouth nor tried to change her speech? He began: "This is Mr. Williams, math teacher at Eden Hills High. I would like if possible—."

She hated to cut off that concerned voice, but the poor man didn't even know for whom to ask. "I don't remember giving you that high school, but things are coming along fine here."

"And things are better?" The happiness and relief plain as words in his voice still left room for caution. "Are you by any chance using an extension?"

So polite he was, so meek, so changed, she had no heart to make him suffer. She assured him the telephone had no extension and that she was alone in the house except for the "patient." "Everything is even better than expected; temperature almost normal, quarreling at his quarters, getting hungry."

"Sounds like him, all right."

She had the feeling he knew her name and who she was. He couldn't have learned from getting Charlotte's number checked; it was listed under her married name of Lutz, and he couldn't know Lutz was Schnitzer. Yet, whatever he knew of her was only one microgram compared to his knowledge of that spoiled baby in the attic; more than a million times as much as her father—or her mother—knew of Susan Marie Schnitzer.

He understood her patient so well, he was sympathetic. "I know you have a handful, he's so high strung and sensitive. He should be in a hospital."

That voice was like a long-gone friend come back; but now it hurt, questioning her nursing and medical abilities. "Well, blame his untrusting, unempathetic father; how stingy he was to put his child in a foreign country with no checking account. He came here after—he got wet wandering around in the rain when he already had a cold."

She was at once ashamed of what she had said. This old smooth-voiced he-bear must be the boy's father. He sounded ready to cry as he wished Ter were able to get out of bed and come speak to him. She had an impulse to go after the lazy thing. He had been coming down to the bathroom, but had not even suggested he try to talk to his worried father.

Lanny was asking if she had pencil and paper; he would

greatly appreciate her writing down his number, just in case.

She assured him there was little chance of an "in case," but took the number, the exchange figures the same as those of the Schnitzers. Smart man. She told him to call next day, Sunday, between eleven and twelve—but he must be careful. She thought that by then the "patient" would be able to come speak with him. His relief at such news did not check his advice, and it was only after a great deal on what her patient should and should not eat or do that he gave her a grateful good-bye.

She had told Ter of the conversation, and was back in the kitchen, when the telephone rang. She charged upstairs to answer to her mother's tinkle.

The woman was touchingly grateful to learn her daughter was getting better; she had been able to call Dr. Laughton, hadn't she? Traffic had been terrible; the restaurant crowded, with service slow; and goodness knew when she and "your father" could get home. "Oh dear," she was keeping "your father" and their guests waiting. She was gone after a quick "Good night," and a reminder not to forget her medicine.

Susie continued to stand, receiver to ear; she pushed buttons; the dial tone came on; that was better than nothing. She roused at last to wonder on what she had been doing before her mother called. Listening, hours and hours of listening. Ter called. She remembered his hunger, and called back: "Food's coming soon." She would look into the store of food kept for emergencies and unexpected company. A small tenderloin steak—if she could find one—probably wouldn't hurt him.

Somebody ought to have it nice in this cruddy world.

7

"The great blue heron so still among the reeds is a promise that life will remain in the man-wounded pond." It was no good; yet better than nothing for a first sentence. "Get up and get to work before Ter starts wanting things; first, though, you had better go listen on the ladder, just in case."

Pulling a bathrobe on, she rushed through her back bedroom door, and was on the bottom step in front of the closet when Ter said: "Oh, Susie, how embarrassing."

His voice came from her study door. She would not look, but scuttled into the bathroom before remembering she could not dress until she could get clothes from the closet. She showered, tidied herself, and hoped he would get back to the attic. There was no sign of him when she tiptoed to the closet, but when she came out, dressed, there he was waiting; "Remember, you're sharing your suite today. I am practically well, with a normal temperature."

She urged him to stay in bed, at least until her parents went to church and his "friend" telephoned.

He was polite, dignified in spite of the bathrobe above his knees and the black stubble on cheeks and chin—but handsome with that beautiful dark hair straggling across his dying-poet's forehead. "I am sick of the attic," he told her, one hand on the wall, for it was plain he was weak as a jellyfish washed up on the beach. "There's too much time to think up there."

She thought of telling him he had a lot of thinking to do, but listened instead to the list of his wants: first, he needed a good hot shower; he had a razor and clean handkerchiefs in his binder —crazy as it was he had brought nothing else; he needed something to wear; he was of course starving to death and needed something substantial on the order of bacon and eggs.

She was shaking her head before he finished. She couldn't get bacon and eggs, not now; and explained a bit about the homemade coffee cake her mother came up with on Lulu's Sundays off. A shower was unsafe; the water pipes could cough and squeal until her mother might, just might hear—and well, come up to see why her dying daughter was taking a second shower so early on a Sunday morning. She realized his glance was on her thumb; she was pulling it.

She turned away to get his brushed and pressed trousers from the closet along with the underwear she had washed. She held out the trousers. "I—I hope they're all right. I've never tried pressing trousers before; I just followed what was left of the creases."

His reaction was a sharp: "I didn't mean for you to mess with those filthy clothes." He stalked toward the bathroom.

He faltered in his stride, but kept going when she said: "Remember if somebody knocks on my door, I'll have to leap right in there with you. I can't be in my room and taking a shower at the same time."

She, after a good listen, left her outer door ajar on neutral while she dashed to Charlotte's quarters where she helped herself to a white sweater she thought could serve as a shirt. She put it on a chair in front of the bathroom door, then straightened her bed. Now, there was nothing to do but sit by the door, listen by the crack for footsteps, and stare at the miserable beginnings of a theme. She heard nothing save the almost inaudible shower; the pipes, as if they knew her trouble, neither squealed nor coughed. When the shower stopped, still studying the theme, she went to sit by the bed.

She was trying to write that opening sentence when Ter

said: "Thank you for everything. Nice to be wearing some of my own clothes for a change."

She sprang up, embarrassed; he was no longer her patient, but a tall, handsome stranger, a man in trousers and her brother-in-law's white turtle-neck sweater that served very well as a shirt. He was, she thought, apologizing for his uncivil acceptance of her laundry work. She stammered out a "Thank you,"; wondered why she had not instead said: "You're welcome," and felt even worse when he reached for that cruddy theme. She did manage to tell him he must stay out of her bedroom at least until her parents were gone to church.

She fled to Charlotte's suite; there, wondered why she had come; remembered after glancing at her watch, she was to warm her heart with Dr. Laughton—and no memorandum ready. She would make it short, for she must not eat a chunk in the little time he would have left for golfing or sailing after making his home and hospital calls.

He sounded as always as if his time were hers alone. She knew it was not, so quickly told him of her continuing normal temperature and loss of other symptoms. Still, he asked a good many questions, especially about her stomach, food, and appetite. She couldn't remember what she had eaten the day before, and had to roll out more lies. They hurt, even though they were the right kind, for he remembered her question of yesterday about school, and thought she could try it—if things continued to go well. Call him if she grew worse; and in any case call him again tonight around seven, and tomorrow make an appointment with Miss Armstrong to see him no later than next Saturday morning.

He was gone. She wondered with some worry how she should be by Saturday. Suppose he wanted blood tests? Would the lack of antibiotics show, and the corpuscle count tell tales? She'd better be thinking on the theme and some way of keeping Ter under control. Such a big deal he'd made when she came out in that cover-up nightgown and bathrobe; yet, he insisted on reading an unfinished theme that showed her mind completely naked; not even underpants and a bra on the miserable thing.

She left to ask for the return of it, but was not half way

across her bedroom before he was coming in to remind her he was starved.

She tried to point out the dangers, the suspicions; girl with never any appetite for breakfast, filling up like a Montreal longshoreman at Seaway opening time. He only smiled and pointed out that, officially, she had eaten practically nothing the day before, and should be hungry to play the role of a sick girl getting better.

Winning was the word for his smile, she thought going downstairs. Things in the kitchen were as expected: her mother, in a freshly-put-on face; oven-heating for the *küchen;* mother eager to be rid of daughter so as to keep the secret of her "homemade" cookery.

She expressed wonder at her sick daughter coming down so early. Susie, leaning against a work table for support, explained: "I was so hungry it woke me up. I haven't had a bite since Lulu brought tea and biscuits yesterday."

"You poor child," her mother cried as if she were just home from a lecture on the need for giving the children as well as the husband a dose of TLC now and then. "Let me help. I can spare a minute from the *küchen*." She went from there into a perfect whirl of Mother-Love-Shown-Through-Service: teapot and covered dish put to warm, butter and marmalade arranged on tray; and didn't Susie think it a good idea to take the tea and toast to her room? Wouldn't it be more comfortable to have tea in bed? She was still sick enough to follow "your father's rule"; no food outside the Proper Places except in illness—that is for his family. No different from many of his other rules, it was not for him.

Susie agreed with a great big smile; her mother had to have her safely out of sight in order to finish the *küchen*. Past this, conversation consisted chiefly of questions put in and answers pulled out at a cautious crawl. Made you think of an information desk in some gone-to-sleep airport where you asked into a receiver, and the answer came back to leave you wondering if you had spoken to a human being or a sound track geared to an IBM machine.

Her health, one question from her mother; the football game, one question from Susie; she also posed a question on the evening after the game. Each brought an: "Oh, very nice." There was a shade of variety in her mother's reference to Charlotte: she and John had not even bothered to telephone excuses for not showing up; their father had been "dreadfully disappointed, and put out, too, after he'd spent so much money for the best seats, then seen it wasted. Poor Charlotte, I know she wanted to come, but John is getting to be an awful grind."

Susie only nodded. It wouldn't do to tell his mother-in-law that if John wanted to get into any kind of medical school, he'd have to grind out some fine grades in that "take-just-about-any-high-school-graduate-provided-he-can-come-up-with-our-fees" college that had accepted Charlotte with her flock of D's. Now what did her mother want? Purse in hand, she had come so close, Susie could see the false-eyelash line of demarcation. She was glancing swiftly around as if expecting a holdup.

"Yesterday, when I was in Ann Arbor," she began in a quick whisper, "I spent every spare minute telephoning; so many music stores and record shops in that town, but not one had it in stock."

She was taking a billfold from her purse. Why? She never carried much of anything but credit cards, and cash enough for supermarket staples and the laundress's pay. She was whispering again: "I want no more scenes. Buy a duplicate; return it, and say nothing."

Susie groaned without looking at the bill. "Simple? To buy a whole album of representative folk songs of—?"

"Sh-sh," her mother begged, holding out green stuff.

Susie glanced at the bill, a twenty, then gave a look of polite indignation before turning away to empty the warming teapot. "Mother, you'll elevate my temperature. You couldn't find it in Ann Arbor? That means I'll have to spend hours and hours hunting in Detroit. I can't even telephone; you know how father blows a gasket at long-distance bills. It will certainly be easier and a lot less expensive just to tell the truth, and hope the library staff will—." She took pity on her mother's frantic sh-sh-ings, and was silent while through the toaster glass she watched the browning bread.

"Thank you, dear IBM; it's nice to know you are not too religious to work on Sunday," she soundlessly whispered. The thoughtful little thing had reminded her to tell her mother of Dr. Laughton's no-biking command.

She did so. Two twenty-dollar bills came round above the toaster. She'd better take them, or Ter would be complaining of overdone toast. A pity; she should have at least ten more for cab fare. Be as ladylike as possible, but don't overdo the gratitude.

Tray in hand, she was by the pantry door, when she suddenly turned about and looked at her mother, who was so plainly waiting for her daughter to be gone. "Shouldn't I get this money from father? Won't it make a dreadful hole in your allowance—after my party shoes you bought and—." What would happen if she should go completely crazy and tell her mother the truth? She had not planned a forty-dollar lie. Her mother's sh-sh-ings, her frozen smile, and the explanation didn't make her feel any better.

"Your tea will be ruined, dear. My allowance is big enough, I manage to keep some cash for emergencies such as this. As for your shoes, I charged them. Forget it."

Forgetting, at least for the moment, was easier than expected. Ter's insistence on eating in her study instead of the attic both annoyed and frightened her. There was little danger, but her mother might come up with more hot water or something.

She turned the fan on and went back to her bedroom. There, she found her theme. Ter had corrected the few mechanical errors and here and there made suggestions or asked questions. Most she ignored, but: "Should you describe the frogs?" stopped her. She should. She wrote: "Three gray green knots of wood sat on three separate stones." Knots didn't sit.

She was marking out the words when Ter came tapping. He apologized for disturbing her, but had thought the tray should be left by her sickbed, just in case. She warned him that if he should hear her father, he must nip into the closet, pull the prop that held the folding doors apart, and keep going until he was out the other side with that door shut behind him. He showed no alarm, but did agree not to come out and introduce himself. "Chances are," he told her, "if the old boy does come to see you, he'll stay about twenty seconds."

She checked the room for neatness, put the messed-up

theme out of sight, and after arranging her books in a straight stack, picked up her Latin text, the *Aeneid.*

The class went so slowly, old Aeneas was still getting ready to tell his story, *Liber Primus,* 423–63. *Instant ardente Tyrii,*—. She'd already translated most of Monday's lesson; she'd write it out after doing the homework sheets of questions in Latin to be answered in English. *"Quibuscum se miscuit?"* "With men," of course. She went over the lists; all easy; she would type the answers when Ter got out of her study.

She had finished Monday's translation, and was reading ahead, when there came a heavy knocking on her outer bedroom door. She knew that knock, sprang up to open the door, remembered she was sick, flopped down again, and called: "Come in," forgetting to put sickness into her voice.

It didn't matter. Her father, standing on the outer edge of the opening pad to avoid her germs, had already activated the door. "Susie, are there any niggers in Eden Hills High?"

She jerked the bed sheet over most of her face. Early as it was, he had reached the bellowing stage. Her mother, a few steps behind him, was wearing her, "Peace-at-any-price-without-negotiations" look. Susie turned to try to face him. The noise and the unexpected question had knocked out a circuit breaker in her IBM. Her private TV could do nothing but show the black boy sitting beside her, close under the willow bough. Bismarck couldn't know that. Brandon couldn't have snooped; he had been in camp.

"Answer me."

The IBM was now getting a bit of juice; enough to come up with: "Father, I am trying to think."

"Think? You mean you wouldn't even notice one in school or out. You must have heard a black family is moving into that cheap subdivision around the shopping center. One family, just one, will cut the value of my property in half. And you don't know!"

He stopped, unable, she judged, to find either breath or suitable words. She tried not to flinch as another cascade of sound poured over her. "And so you can't be bothered to notice? But thank God for people like Mrs. Weatherford, a most trust-

139

worthy woman. She has seen seven, mind you just when driving her daughter back and forth to school." He held up seven fingers. "Seven. This time next year it will be seven hundred. She's also getting the location of the house."

The IBM, chewing over who this "trustworthy woman," was, was still able to spit it out: "But, Father, there are close to three thousand students in our school. I have no Negroes in my classes or home room." True, orchestra was not a class. "I see only a small percentage of the school."

"You could at least take the trouble to watch for them in the halls and the lunch room. And don't you get with everybody in—in assemblies? Excuses, always excuses. And you aren't getting out of target practice any more. You're sick or you haven't the time. Well, you're going to take the time. We'll begin with pistol practice on a big black dummy at close range."

"Thank you, Mother Mary, he is going away."

He had looked at his watch, and part of his wrath was now turned on her mother. "You must have served breakfast late. It's three minutes past time to get out the car."

His heels clomped down the back stairs. Her mother could spare only a moment to remind Susie it would be their usual Lulu-off, fair Sunday; church, dinner out, possibly at the club since her father was golfing afterward; no, of course they wouldn't be home to change; use the club for that. The last was spoken over her shoulder.

Susie sprang out of bed, and holding the door to a crack, listened to the heels tap down the stairs. She scarcely noticed that Ter had come to stand beside her. The long, angry blast of a car came up to them; the heels tapped faster until distance swallowed the sound. Susie turned away, and as the door shut behind her, stood staring at nothing, whispering: "I am supposed to learn to shoot hu—."

"Susie. Susie."

Ter sounded far away to be so close; close enough so one hand was shaking her shoulder. "Forget it," he begged. "Learn to faint. Get a statement from that nice Dr. Laughton to say you're not up to it."

"I wonder," she said, still talking to herself, "will it be a big

140

black man, the kind Brandon so enjoys shooting at, or will it be a little-child dummy or a baby?"

"I tell you it won't be anything but a big round target. Come on, snap out of it; bawl me out for eavesdropping—your father set the mobiles dancing in your study—so I held the door open a crack. He couldn't possibly have seen me. Is he always like that? What ails him anyhow? Is he bugged by his partners? Are they actually going to try to sell the business over his head to that oil company? Weatherford still works for it, you know, on the sly."

She roused to the name of Weatherford. She had heard it some other place, some other time; and not this one who counted Negroes. "Weatherford? Weatherford?" She had spoken aloud without knowing. Ter was answering:

"You've let your father knock you out. I just told you he is the oil company man your father's partners brought up from Alabama to look over the plastics plant with an eye to buying. His wife is the Negro-counter. Come to think of it, the girl you mentioned on my first night here, 'Lady-Macbeth-with-her-spots-all-washed-away,' would be his daughter. —You wonder if your old man's got wind of what's up? Say, what about a real nice—brunch it would be now?"

"Give them time to get settled in church. You never know."

"Isn't the phone ringing?"

It was. She had heard it as a noise with no meaning. She ran. Lulu; happy, not long home from mass with her parents and daughter. She was still happier when she heard Susie was "practically well; eating everything in sight and going to school tomorrow." Some warmth and life returned as she listened to Lulu.

Could Susie guess; no, she couldn't; what Lulu had done yesterday evening? Her daughter and some of her friends had wanted a rock-'n'-roll session. Lulu, believe it or not, had also danced—mostly out of sight. Susie ought to have seen her dancing to wild music.

Enough of Lulu's happy confidence in the goodness of life got through to Susie, she was no longer afraid of target practice. She knew she'd get out of it someway: she'd pretend to be violently nauseated; no, fainting would be less—. The telephone again.

Lanny Bear, that would be. Where was Ter? She'd find him, but first she'd answer. And was the man ever happy to learn he could talk to precious. Kind of choked her up inside, but she managed to tell him to ring her up again around five to finish plans for meeting "his friend."

Ter was in her study working on his Greek. He wasn't so eager as the man on the phone. She couldn't blame him. Sooner or later he would have to tell somebody—and that meant his father, the man on the other end of the line—of what he had done. Sick as he was, he couldn't get that money—if he actually had it—back without help. Was he just pretending coolness as he smiled and whispered. "Remember now, that real feed coming up."

She had forgotten food for Ter and left to search the freezer, refrigerators, larder, and fruit closet until she had collected the makings of a decent meal.

She would have fruit compote made chiefly of frozen strawberries—bacon, a French omelette (a nice dish for the cook; if not as expected, it could always be labeled scrambled eggs). The frozen English muffins would toast into fair edibility and that Scotch marmalade was good. She was well into the breakfast-getting when Ter came to smile and say: "That's a real feed you're fixing."

"I don't know how real it will be. In this house I don't even know when I'm real," she told him.

"Who does? Once, I thought dialing a number to learn if you'd lost your last cent on a horse would be real." He shrugged. "It wasn't. —And the bank business—nothing but a big role in some kind of important, very important play; only I don't think I had half as much stage-fright as usual. That came after."

Susie, turning bacon, spared him a glance. "I think you are a hunter of sensation. Try being a sea-moss gatherer or a small-time fisherman—know you won't eat too well if you come back without moss or fish. Or you could be a factory worker on a long strike; go walk the bricks with the automobile-plant workers. And if you want real reality, join the U.S. infantry and get into Vietnam."

"No, thank you, no begging for death while being burned

alive with napalm dropped by mistake by your buddies in the sky. You don't understand. A girl couldn't. It's not sensation I am hunting, but myself. How will I be, fencing with raw blades and no mask?"

Susie pretended the mixing of the omelette demanded all her attention. She didn't want him to get from *her* face any glimpse of her hopes and wonders: Could she get into a good medical school? Could she make it as a long-time resident in a good hospital? If she did, could she ever be a doctor who would mean as much to some little cruddy kid as Dr. Laughton and Dr. Hefler had meant to her?

She'd better start talking in Ter's style—"around the world perhaps; and I shall picket when and what I please—a President or a fascist mob; and—." She'd caught his look of horror.

"Susie, you shouldn't even think of doing such things. If Beeto knew he'd go crazy. He thinks of you as a sweet obedient girl; his 'Little United Nations with the piquant face.'"

She started to say: "O, Gawd," but her IBM, which must have taken a nap to let her tongue run on so, awakened and put in a prissy: "You will some day find self-realization in your work."

"Work? That depends. I wouldn't want to work just for money, so that when I die Mr. Fer—Ter—would be nicely labeled as 'Executive Vice-President of Soak-the-Public Corpora- tion.' —Look here, I came down to help you, and haven't done a thing. What can I do?"

So he did have some future on his mind over and above bank robbing; else, he wouldn't have changed the subject. She suggested he fix his tray while she toasted muffins and shook up the omelette.

"Tray? We'll eat together. I have a card table set up and laid in Charlotte's living room—fairish view."

She pointed out the dangers—smell of food all over the house, parents unexpectedly coming home, a mishap with some- thing sticky on Charlotte's white wall-to-wall. She shut up with a shrug. He would get what he wanted.

He did, and showed so much pleasure in the meal, she forgave his stubborn ways. Her cookery was a shocking success

—for her; though the food was only part of it. Ter had, while she was in the kitchen and basement, selected from the pantry good china, the best silver, and a nice teacloth. He had even remembered flowers, the ones she had brought him yesterday, and pretty they were in her Mexican silver vase.

Ter seated her, said grace, and praised all he ate, especially the omelette—but no word of kindness for that poor theme. "Well, I'm glad you like it," she told him. "Everything came out all right mostly by accident, I guess. I don't exactly pride myself on my cooking. Who wants to be a cook?"

"But every woman wants to learn to cook something; special dishes for her husband, sauces and salad dressings, dream up luscious desserts and nice hors d'oeuvres."

She wrinkled her nose. "She'd do better to learn how to catch a husband able to afford a fine cook and a cook's helper; if she can't she'd better stay single."

"Beeto," he said, helping himself to more omelette, "will keep you in so many servants you can't get along with one cook; you'll have a real chef and a second cook for the help."

She gave a little unplanned shiver. "Oh, by then, Beeto will be walking that keep-fit road, grazing in those dry cholesterol pastures. He'll need so little cooking, the chef can devote himself entirely to lovely food for the help." She felt the conversation needed a change and commented on how well the flowers had kept. The wrong direction, she knew at once; his lightheartedness went like the sun under a cloud; his cloud, the remembering.

"The flowers, the food, everything makes me think of how things were at home on Sundays before—. Always she had flowers all over; many out of our—really hers,—she supervised it and did a lot of the work—conservatory. I wish you could have seen it then. But Beeto thinks it's still beautiful. He talks a lot of how you love flowers. And do you know—I wonder is it a secret I shouldn't give away—he has in our place the beginnings of one for you."

"One what?"

"If he hasn't told you, I shouldn't. A conservatory; don't make too much of it; mostly all he has now are the potted

144

trees—small yet—but coming along; especially one lemon, big."
He lifted a hand to show height.

His hand was high above the floor as the top of his chair post; in looking at it, she would show him her face; he would see how much she hated trees in pots—except in parts of Mexico and other deserts where it was the only way one could have a tree. But a potted lemon tree when you had a lawn with all kinds of trees; worse than a bird in a cage. He had read her face. "But don't you think it's wonderful to make things grow—where— well, they'd die if you didn't take care of them."

She nodded. "I suppose that's what students in agriculture study—or would it be horticulture for the—potted lemon tree?"

He was peeved as well as hurt. "You almost sound as if you didn't like trees and flowers. You should have seen our biggest lemon tree—then." He fell silent, as if wondering how much he should tell. He suddenly leaned closer and spoke in a low, rushing voice. "I'm not even certain I want to go to college—over here—for I don't think I could get what I want. If I could manage the language I would go to Israel."

"Israel?"

"Of course. What's wrong with Israel? I was never taught to hate. I knew a girl; her few distant relatives left were in Israel. She and her brother took music lessons from the same teaching team as my sisters and myself—nothing out of the ordinary, but good enough for the non-genius types we were. Our mothers also met quite often at recitals and children's musicales—both were fair musicians. My mother would always invite this woman and her children to come around for the little informal the-children's-recital-is-over-thank-goodness party.

"Always these were in the conservatory—the woman and her children loved the place. I was getting old for that sort of thing, but I liked to watch the woman and listen to her talk. There was a kind of hunger in her face—the same that got into my mother's, sometimes, I thought. All the woman's close kin had died in concentration camps. 'They are killed,' this woman would say, 'but we are here fattening.'

"And the girl, she was old as I, would sit with me under the biggest lemon tree. We would listen to our mothers and

145

Father Amari, who came often. He was from Sicily and helped my mother's loneliness. They would talk of Israel; this priest was no Schnitzer; he had hidden and smuggled Jews all through that war when he was no more than a young boy. They talked also of Sicily, how the poor dry land could be made to grow crops like that in Israel.

"And this girl would whisper to me, 'I won't stop at talking. I will go there to marry an Israeli and live on the land.' And I would say, 'I won't always sit under a pampered lemon tree. I will be a Sicilian and work on the land and help Danilo Dolci's workers and the poor people.' Father Amari talked a lot of him." He hesitated, glanced swiftly at her face as if wondering should he trust her with his secret, his biggest one, she suspected.

"After I've learned at least a little of what I need to know," he went on more slowly, "I hope to work as an agricultural adviser in some such place as Menfi—or even, live as a peasant—to try to teach the poor farmers in that hard, dry land—have you ever seen it?—how to have a better life—through better treatment of the soil." He was studying her face again; questions in his eyes as in his voice.

"I think you have a good plan—if you're certain you want to be a Sicilian. —I hope to become a Canadian citizen—as soon as I'm old enough to emigrate on my own," she told him, happy to exchange one of her secrets for the big one he had given her.

He was his critical self again. "You can't do that. You'll be living in Chicago with Beeto. He doesn't want a Canadian wife. I've heard you used to talk that way, but I'd supposed you'd got over it, like that crazy scheme of trying to get into McGill Medical School and be some kind of doctor."

Beeto, always Beeto. She began to clear the table. The fact that she had quit talking of the future didn't mean she didn't have any except—nursemaid for a potted lemon tree. And what would she do with Beeto's gift of a potted lemon tree? Fly with it to some warm and happy land by the sea in lower Mexico? She'd never spray it and prune it and keep it in a pot that cramped its feet and—.

Ter, very much the gentleman, was up and taking from her

the tray of dirty dishes while saying something about wanting to help. The lemon tree, loathsome as it was in a pot, had been a nice change from chewing over her troubles—pistol practice, the psychologist, and—the closest—Ter's getaway. "You have to be getting ready for—your friend," she told him. "Check and double-check to make certain you don't leave anything. Also, somebody has to stay up here within hearing of the phone, and watch the drive. Church is over—they might dash home for something. You never know."

Down in the kitchen, she was glad to be alone. The work left her mind free to hunt for holes in her plan for Ter's getaway in daylight—without anyone seeing him. She could find no slip-ups. Finished, she began work on a song for the lemon tree.

How did it go, that hymn they sang in the little Protestant church near her grandmother's place in Nova Scotia? She'd heard it enough so she ought to know. The singers filled the song with a sad hopelessness as if, in spite of the words, they didn't actually expect to gather "at that river flowing by the throne of God." She began to sing: "Shall I tend that pot-ted le-mon tree, that beau-ti-ful le-mon that grows in the House of Gold?"

The syllables didn't match, but by pulling in here and drawing out there the words did very well. She knew she had no voice for singing, and was careful never to sing where anybody might hear. She was having a fine old time, adding stanzas, trying out phrases, singing out her sorrows and her worries as she unloaded the dishwasher, when, in turning with dishes for the pantry, she saw Ter. He was listening as he held the door ajar, and there was in his face more condemnation than music appreciation. "I didn't know I had an audience," she told him. "I thought you were getting ready."

"I'm ready except for a few details. I've propped enough doors so I can hear the telephone; I'm running back and forth to watch the drive, silly as that is. They'd be at dinner by now." Sensing her embarrassment at his eavesdropping while she sang, he said nothing of her distaste for Beeto's planned gift, but went instead into a subject she hated—her father's gun collection.

"More noted for quantity than quality and variety," was his

opinion. "He has at least two pistols identical to your grand-mother's, or the one he loaned her. And does he carry a gun? There's an empty pistol space."

"I imagine Brandon took one to camp for target practice."

"Since when do Boy Scouts of his age go in for pistol practice?"

"He's not at a Boy Scout camp," she told him. "This is some kind of super, super 'Save the U.S.A. for Freedom' group. It was organized in our last neighborhood. Secret, so I don't know much about it. Our father has the leaders here for dinner fairly often—a retired policeman and an ex-army captain. Anybody who ad-mired Hitler might go for them. Big on preparedness; show the "dirty communists we mean business," and all that jazz. Eager for the bomb, for they know they'll be generals in heaven when they die."

"You oughtn't to be flippant about heaven. But I can't blame you—too much. I'd go nuts if I had to live with all the locks and plastic and that ready-waiting cremation vault under me. My father was in World War II; he saw the bodies in those suppos-edly safe cellars in Hamburg. In your crematory there won't even be a body, maybe a little dust, and on top, still pretty pink and green and blue, the plastic flower arrangements that grace your house."

"Please," Susie begged. "I try to forget the fall-out shelter, and never look at the plastic flowers and plants if I can help it. My father is allergic to real flowers—or thinks he is. Further-more, nobody is supposed to go around that place—except my father. When the bomb falls anybody at home is to break the glass case with a key under it. He's the only one who carries a key."

Ter was unruffled. "I didn't do any breaking. I was hunting a flameless incinerator was why I went down that long, gloomy concrete passage. I came to a strange door; made me think of the opening to a tomb. I turned the knob; a ghoulish blue light came on as I opened the door. And there I was looking at the afterlife. Does he think when he's vaporized he'll still be eating and drink-ing beer? There must be several thousand dollars worth of stuff all ready with moldy rot as an offering to the dead."

"I know. I've been dragged on tours of inspection—and instruction. It—."

"Forget it. Forget it," Ter begged. He was taking the dishes she'd forgotten she carried. "I'm sorry I brought it up. Let's think about something nice, like the little surprise I have for you upstairs. I'm in a hurry to see if you like it. So let me help with the work down here."

When they had finished the kitchen work, he caught her hand and led her into the study, seated her, then gave her the neatly typed theme. She read. He had done a perfect job. He had not made one error she could find; he even had the botanical names of the plants in footnotes at the end. Still, it was not her swampy pond. She glanced up to find him watching her face, reading her question of did she want to turn it in. "Don't you like it?" he asked, disappointed.

"It's groovy," she cried.

He smiled. "I wasn't certain you'd like it. I know you do all your own work. But after the misery I've given you, I wanted to do at least a little more than typing that Latin homework sheet."

She didn't have to pretend gratitude for that boresome job she could have done in her sleep. He was in such a sweet humor, she wished they could stay together awhile instead of herself going to Charlotte's suite to do physics problems and listen for Lanny Bear's ring, while Ter went to the attic.

Less than half an hour later, when coming into her study for more graph paper, she wondered how she could bear for two minutes such a self-righteous, narrow-minded, snooping prig. Hearing her, he had come out of the closet with *Father Amaro*, *The Gadfly*, and her beloved *En Attendant Godot*. He wore that I-know-what-is-best-for-you look, mixed with pain and wrath.

She pretended the look wasn't there. "How nice, but however did you manage to find three of my favorites? I've wondered how I lived without Godot so long. Can you imagine I never saw the play until three or four years ago—and Englished then. I bought that copy in Montreal, and when I know I need a pill for self-pity I think of Lucky. And when I get annoyed with the clergy of all faiths for whooping up the war, I think of Father Amaro, and know they are no worse than they have ever been." She had better stop; his nose was white.

"Susie, how can you say such things?"

"With my tongue, vocal chords, breath, and other parts of my anatomy."

"And you, a girl, reading works on the Index. You should be thinking of your disgracefully delayed Confirmation instead of filling your mind with such stuff. I am sure your grandmother wouldn't approve. Even though she was never a Catholic, she had you baptized in the Faith out of respect for your dead grandfather and his people—of which I am one."

So, dignified sorrow was his line. Her Guardian Angel warned her not to tell him her religion was on a foundation of firmly cemented bits and pieces gathered as she went along: Mother Mary, yes; Confirmation, possibly no; hymns when she needed them; many of the saints—she ought to learn more of their lives and teachings. "'Lord, make me an instrument of Thy peace. Where there is hate, may I bring love.'"

She must not, would not quarrel while St. Francis spoke in her head. "Forgive the books and me," she said to Ter. "I like way-out things I don't get in school, especially in French; Granma wants me to learn the language. But I don't get much chance to speak it in Nova Scotia. Instead of worrying over that, we ought to be thinking about—." She drew a deep troubled breath while trying to hit upon the right way to say it.

"My getaway," Ter finished for her. He held out a sheet of paper almost filled with his fine black script. "Read it, if you don't mind, and try to think of anything I may have left undone. I've finished—that is, as much as I can do now—everything, except burning this list."

Made you almost afraid of him; he was so cool, so mindful of every detail from remembering to leave the medicine bottle for her—after taking out the medicine for himself—to removing all markings from his upper clothing "that has to be burned. —Wrap handkerchief on tool and put in binder." She knew what the *tool* was, but she looked up in puzzlement at the next and last item: "Let trouble dry as long as possible."

"Trouble? Drying?" she asked.

He nodded. "It's—nicer to call it that—the money. I forgot to look at it until this morning; there it was, wet. I put it to dry by the cold air return. I had to put the raincoat over the hot—."

She had moved away with an, "Oh." She guessed she had believed him and known with her head he had used a pistol to get money from a bank—but the money, if it existed at all—had seemed someplace else. It couldn't be here, stolen money, in her own secret quarters. "I use a net bag when I dry small things," she said at last. She looked at him. "You—you will see that the money gets back? And Granma might sometime notice that gun was gone. She hated it, but there it was in her things when they shipped her off to Canada. She couldn't give it away because, when my father insisted she take it, years ago, it was registered in his name—and still is, I suppose."

"Try to remember not to go asking her if she got her gun back." He smiled happily, as if gun and money had been returned.

She wondered how he would manage the returnings, then had a fit of the shys. He was so handsome and so tall standing there; for one of the few times in her life she was troubled by uneasy thoughts on how *she* looked. Messy from kitchen work?

"Susie, burning is the problem. Don't you have anything but that tin incinerator in back? My stuff will smoke."

She thought of him. He thought about his business. Were they all like that? "You'll either have to take the things to your home, or use the log piles like half the county is doing. Easy to drive by. I'll explain to your friend." He frowned, plainly not too happy with her suggestion, but unable to think of a better one. She'd better get her mind on the Business Ahead instead of on him. "What about buttons and zippers that won't burn?" she asked.

He thought they could never be identified, even if found by some mischance. "I found some nitric acid in the basement. Yours, I imagine, for science experiments." He had soaked the metal in a plastic cup of acid. "Nobody saw my real watch. People," he explained, "that is people who know, sometimes notice little things like a good watch."

151

At his suggestion, she searched the attic, study, and bathroom, but found nothing except her brother-in-law's socks and pajamas which along with his bathrobe, she hid in the attic for later washing.

She next went to her bathroom, emptied the pale plastic jug of distilled water, kept for the iron, then after telling Ter to listen for the telephone and call her in the garden shed if it rang, she went through her secret passage and down to the shed. Here, after a good deal of dragging and lifting, she managed with the help of a funnel to fill the jug with gasoline from the five gallon can kept for the lawn mower.

She put the gasoline-filled, plastic jug under the sink with more bottles and cans of this and that. She stepped back, head cocked, looking. The pale jug called attention to itself. She looked about for some properly dull covering, and saw, carelessly flung into a corner, what turned out to be an old black and tan raincoat, muddied and torn. She draped the dark side with careful carelessness over the plastic jug, then hurried back to her closet. Soon it would be time for Lanny Bear; her mother might telephone from the club, and she had to dress for—make it The Business Ahead instead of Ter.

She wanted to look nice for that nice-voiced man, and so dressed with unusual care in a new black woolen jumper over one of her best silk, long-sleeved blouses. A pity that in her role of sick girl she would have to cover those lovely silk sleeves with a sweater, but she had a beautiful black cashmere Angie had picked up for her in Ireland. She was in Charlotte's dressing room, studying herself in the battery of mirrors there, when Ter called from the living room.

She smiled at him as she came through the door, but he was looking in another direction—her legs. "Susie," he said with that I-know-best-intonation, "would you mind putting on a skirt, well, a little longer. My fa—friend—hates the short skirts, especially for Sunday wear."

"This jumper is so unmini I could wear it to school. And anyway can't he imagine it's Monday? I should have kept a pair of Mary Janes." She flounced off into her closet where she dressed as for orchestra on stage; that meant an old-fashioned pleated black skirt, practically touching her knees. What a world; childship still a struggle, to master when here comes young ladyship.

No, she was still a child, a stupid, careless little child, she discovered on returning to Charlotte's quarters. Ter was waiting there with that I-know-what-is-best-for-you look securely fastened. "Susie," he began, "I'd go crazy with worry to know one of my sisters was living the way you are. I'm sure Beeto and your grandmother have no idea of the danger, or they would have had something done a long time ago." Her secret passage must be nailed shut; sooner or later a prowler would find it; all manner of people were in and out of the gardening shed with deliveries and work; and the place without so much as a lock. She should dismantle her attic quarters. Had she never thought of the fire hazard: all that bare wood, with no asbestos fire-wall between or above her attic and the garage with gasoline-filled cars; everything close to the furnace almost directly below? Why, she lived in a perfect firetrap.

She listened in silence and hoped her worry that he might try to get some of the relatives to do something, didn't show. She managed at last to bring the conversation around to his business. "We won't know the exact time until your friend telephones," she told him, "but whatever it is, I'll be in the driveway. You watch from Charlotte's windows until you see him in the car. Then nip out with your bundle—if it's not ready, you'd better get packing. Be certain you take everything. When you reach the shed loft, peep down—I made some cracks—and above all don't jump down until I come."

She wondered uneasily if her directions had penetrated. Susan Marie Schnitzer was yet on his mind; he caught her hand. "Oh, Susie, I owe you so much, so very much, I can't ever—."

Wordless, she pulled away. She wanted no eyeball-to-eyeball good-bye; not from this now-sour, now-sweet boy. He flustered her.

He left at last to finish his Greek homework, but it took a while for her to put her mind on what she had planned to do while waiting for the telephone. Wednesday's physics problems? "A watch has a second hand 2.0 cm. long. Compute the speed of the second hand." Simple, too simple to take her mind off Ter and The Business ahead.

Her glance happened upon her big ring binder, open at a blank page. She smiled. Dr. Laughton had told her to read or write something she enjoyed.

She turned on her stomach, heels in the air, and wrote: "The woman is many things. She is an aluminum Christmas tree filled with bubble lights and brittle tinkling ornaments. At her feet and all around her are parcels wrapped as for a queen, but the packages hold only the three-dollar gifts allowed for the office party, though the wrappings cost five dollars each, and are tax-deductible. The ribbons are of gold and silver painted paper. The many colored wrappings are of aluminum from cast-off pots.

"The woman's hair is an arrangement of lemon popsicles. Her eyes are shavings of blueberry popsicles. Her cheeks are painted plastic lilies in the graveyard six months after the funeral. Her voice is the tinkling of glass from the five-and-ten. Her body is teflon-coated.

"She is not always a Popsicle Queen. Mornings very early her face is a frozen pizza, a very old one, so long left unsold the rounds of salami have turned from pink to gray, the cheese is yellow-gray, and the frozen dough is the gray of blue toilet paper, unflushed in the toilet bowl. Other times the face is a frozen pizza dropped from a shopping bag and stepped on in the store by many feet."

She lifted her head. That miserable noise—. The telephone. Not the Popsicle Queen calling her daughter, but Lanny Bear. Nice to have everything ready for him and set to go. How would it be to have that dear old sweet-voiced innocent for a father? He had never read a book on how to treat a child.

8

She made slow figure-eights on the cement behind the garage. Killing time she was; no, time was killing her; bike as slowly as possible, use one hand on the curves; none on the straights; and remember to keep the left sweater sleeve pushed up. No one must see you glance at your watch.

Six minutes more. Would he or could he come at exactly seven? Time to go once more around, slowly, slowly; a sick girl getting a bit of exercise; be languid as you go down the exit drive and into the road. Passersby might see from moving cars. Don't think so hard on the Business Ahead or you'll be too bugged to manage; look at the old brick farmhouse on the other side of the road, and think of it.

She swung slowly out of the Schnitzer exit and across the road to the Schnitzer mailbox, subject of heated letters and telephone calls from her father. "Why," he was forever demanding, "couldn't the mailman cross the road, or why couldn't he deliver at the door as in the old days?"

The mailbox had stayed in its first location, next to that of the family who had bought the farmhouse. The old brick home, now painted white, was so hidden among shrubbery and trees, many evergreens, she had never seen the whole of it, though she had often wished she might, because it was, according to Iggy, one of the few "genuine old farmhouses" left for miles and miles around. The new owners had had sense enough to leave the trees and the lawn as they were, so that in the spring the jonquils and daffodils wandered all over, and later the odor from the ragged row of lilacs by the road had crossed into the Schnitzer lawn— that first spring before the weed-killing campaign had killed the "neglected bushes."

She pedaled slowly toward the Schnitzer entrance as she wondered where the farmer was now. Had he ever been back to try and find his cow spring that used to be on what became the Schnitzer front lawn? Did his wife wonder on the daffodil bloom or miss the smell of lilacs in the early morning? Be nice if you could go biking up to that farmhouse and say when someone came to the door: "How do you do. Pardon me, but I'm Susie Schnitzer, your neighbor." Children had used to do that in Highland Park—or was it in some other place? Somewhere in the twilights the neighbors had talked across their fences, and exchanged flowers along with smoke from cookout fires. And even in that last place in the northwest corner, the neighbors had spoken now and then.

She had forgotten and gone too fast for a sick girl; she was already turning into the Schnitzer drive. She stopped with a jerk; he was a shade early; and driving too fast, brakes squealing as he slowed to turn into the drive. The fool. People hunting addresses did not come like delivery trucks that knew exactly where they were going.

The car honked. She had forgotten she was in the drive. She got out of the way in a hurry. A second later her mother was exclaiming: "Susie!" as her father grunted from the driver's seat. The car whizzed on; the garage doors were squeaking out the news it had stopped and they were opening before she could take in what had happened.

She must be bugged by the Businesss Ahead not to have recognized her father's grade-D driving. Would Ter hear and jump through the hatchway too soon? Quit worrying; your parents might notice. Chances were Ter was passing the time going through her attic bookshelf, clicking his tongue over something not worth hiding. And here she was passing the garage, and no memory of having come up the drive. The electric mouth was shut. Her father would by now be in the kitchen, a bottle of beer in one hand, the other on the fridge door while he looked for some tasty, low-cholesterol, low-calorie goody. And where was her mother? She could be watching through the one-way glass, amazed by the quick recovery of her so-sick daughter who was going much too fast.

Rolling down the exit, she saw the smudgy time of day had come; almost too early to get ticketed for no lights, yet too late on a cloudy evening to see clearly. That man must know his dawns and twilights for all the year as her grandfather had known the tides for his—.

The car came as she had thought it would, softly, in slow hesitation. The urge to hurry, to finish the business was like a hard wind pushing on her back. Still, she forced herself to bike slowly on, a convalescent girl mildly curious about a mud-spattered car which, judging from its slowness, had a driver who was lost. She could not yet make out the man's face, but his voice was even more familiar than on the telephone, as, after the car stopped, he said: "Pardon me, young lady, but for the last half hour I've been trying to find a Blue Heron Road in a new subdivision. Could you please—."

Close now, she had interrupted with a whispering cry: "Why it's you. Uncle Lans. I've seen you so little since that time you saved me; and now you're here." She had found his hand, and stood, clinging, choking like a fool.

He squeezed her hand in both his own, looked into her face, smiled, all in the instant. He glanced into the rear-view mirror, then again at her as he whispered: "Susie, I am sorry; sorry we had to meet this way after all these years. And I can't understand why the boy didn't tell you who he was; Ferrucio, my oldest child and only son. We've called him Ter since his little sister began to learn to talk and called him that. Susie, my godchild, I've neglected you since—. But—that child?" He sounded tired as he gave a slight nod toward the house where his thoughts were—with Ter. Then he was smiling at her; that same old dark sparkle in his eyes. "We can't drop anchor under full sail, as your grandfather used to say."

There was a hurt inside her; so many years, always Ter, and Ter still. It was like a play; they the only living things in the killed land, save a little wind sprung up to bring a yellow leaf from a cottonwood across the road; except, poor actress that she was, she could only cling to the car window frame and whisper: "It is you. Your voice, I was certain I had known it, but I—."

He was the better actor, remembering his lines; perfect he was, the question in his voice as well as the words asking the whereabouts of Blue Heron Road.

Her cue; she came on stage and, remembering to frown, said: "Blue Heron? The newest street isn't on any map yet, but I saw the name on a board; only I think it is Blue Goose Road."

He smiled. "At least the bird is still blue. I could have misunderstood my friend. How do I find the Blue Goose?"

She remembered to shake back her hair; he might not care for girls who hid their faces. "The best way to get there is over the super highway. It's not finished, but two lanes are well enough graded that machinery and cars go over them. Trouble is, I don't think I can direct you without the plat book. I keep it in the garden shed. Could you take time to drive up?"

"My dear young lady, of course. You're the one who is being inconvenienced. Don't forget your bike in the road."

She had forgotten the bike, but not her lines: "I'll be happy to, sir. Only be careful to pull into the right spot. I'd better go in front to show you. My parents just got home. They're in the house, but my father doesn't like cars blocking the garage doors."

It was for a micro-instant as if a bitter cold and hard wind had come to smooth the smile wrinkles out of his cheeks, the tiredness and the worry inside him showing like rocks behind thin fog. He smiled, nodding her forward, and everything was clear, no rocks at all, only happy, sunlit water.

She swung in front of him, and without looking back, biked up the drive, slowly; give Ter time; no, that was not the reason. She had no breath, no breath at all. She drew abreast of the double doors of the garden shed, and, as she sprang off the bike, gave one quick glance around. Nobody.

Fighting down that urge to hurry, she opened the half of the shed door on the kitchen side until it was at right angles to the wall, and thus bit onto the wooden wedge she had left exactly so. As an extra precaution, she pushed with her foot a ready-waiting brick against the inner side of the half door. Finished, she opened, wedged, and propped the other half of the door. The two halves, each at a right angle to the shed wall, now formed a short, walled passage to the doorway.

The car had stopped as she had planned it should. One rear door was between the two halves of the shed door, so close the car's body shut off any view of the doorway. She sprang to open the back door of the car, but it was already swinging out. She had wasted time in forgetting she could depend on those long strong arms.

She whirled into the shed to see above her the whitish blur of Ter's face. He held down his bundle. She reached, caught it, then dived for the jug of gasoline.

"Please."

His whisper was too loud. She grabbed the binder he handed down, and saw some brightness in his other hand before she turned to shove the binder into the car. She was reaching for the gasoline when she heard the soft thud of his shoes on the sink rim. He still held that bright something in his hand as he rushed to her corner instead of into the car.

She put the bundle meant for burning into the old raincoat, set the jug of gasoline on top, jerked the sleeves of the coat together, tied them in a loose knot, then did the same with collar and tail. She turned to heave the whole into the car, but was blocked by Ter. He whispered: "Do you mind if I take the flowers? Five families and so many species. Why can't different people live together the way wild things do?"

She managed to shake her head. Part of her mind was on getting the bundle into the car as soon as possible; the rest was on Ter's whisper—not the words, but his voice. There was a sorrow, a worried fright she had not until now heard from him. Was he more afraid of telling his father of the robbery than of the doing of it? You couldn't blame him; Lans would stand by him, but—. "You could have told me," she whispered, "you were my godfather's son."

He gave no sign he had heard as he took the bundle and put

it into the car. Turned back to her, he whispered: "Susie, oh, Susie," the sad worry not gone from his voice.

She felt something brush her nose, the corner of her mouth. Wondering, she lifted her head so that the last kiss landed on her hair. "I don't know how to tell you—."

His whisper stopped when Lans spoke, calm as always. "Never mind, miss, if you can't find the plat book. I'll try on my own again, easier now that I know to look for a Blue Goose on a board."

Ter, instead of getting into the car, was holding her hand. The kisses had so startled her, his whisper was only words without sense: "Oh, Susie, it slid away."

He dropped her hand and dived into the car. She saw the soles of his rubbers go through the door, the rest of him was already on the floor, under a blanket carelessly dripping over the seat and down. She draped the blanket over his feet and shut the door. She stood a moment, rubbing the corner of her mouth. Came alive, rushed into the shed, switched on the light and gave a searching glance from the ceiling down. Nothing out of place.

She heard the soft purr of the car, jerked the plat book from under her sweater, and rushed to Lans. "I'm sorry I kept you so," she told him. "But here it is." She held out the book folded back to the sheet of paper on which she had sketched the route he was to take. "If you don't mind a bit of rough driving, turn left at our exit, then follow this."

He was already nodding, head bent above the book. A cold wind blew through her heart; time, the hair was salt and pepper where it used to be glossy black. He had lifted his head and was smiling at her as, holding her sketch, he handed back the book. She took it, caught his hand, but remembering she stood where somebody might see, dropped the hand as he said: "Thank you, Miss. Thank you a very great deal. Be careful of that plat book; it has a loose sheet."

He gave one quick, cautious glance around, then was off stage as he bent closer, whispering: "Thank you for the other, too. A weekend of medical care and nursing amounts to much more than that. —Please, remember I ask you not to bike alone on lonesome roads. —And somehow we must get together, all of us. You've never met my daughters—your kin." The car was moving before he finished.

She rubbed her nose, the corner of her mouth as she watched the car disappear with unconcerned slowness around the conservatory-mud-room wing. Was Ter really in it? He could help rob a bank no doubt, but he could not aim a friendly kiss. On the cheek such kisses should go, always on the cheek; Jeff and Joe and Beeto, as well as various sea-captain friends of her grandmother, had always put them there. And why so sad? And what had he said? " 'It slid away.' " What to where? Time? Time had not slid for her, not those close-to-ten-years since Lans had saved her—.

She wouldn't think of that, only Lans. "Thank you, IBM," she whispered. She was checking the loose sheet he had mentioned. She looked down at the limp-backed book, folded so that her township showed; and for the first time she saw the small oblong of green with figures and a face. "Oh, IBM, you belong in the junk heap. You can't even tell me when I'm looking at money." And the IBM, laughing at her, was whispering: "Didn't you hear him mention the high cost of medical services? Put the money out of sight. Next, shut those propped-open shed doors, and do something about your bike; your father will be furious to see it out of place."

Bike properly parked, shed doors closed, she turned her face to the wall, and made a green fan of the money—ten twenty-dollar bills. She closed the fan, and made of it a hard little roll which she stuffed under a handkerchief in her sweater pocket. She put the plat book away, went to her bike, and there stopped, one hand on the handle bars.

She never knew how long she stood. She felt she had lost whatever it was that could keep the wind from picking her up and blowing her away. She still had that good, kind, sweet godfather. That godfather's son had come to her for help. She had given it, and was she ever glad—except: through that son she had learned how much nicer his goddaughter had it than his wife with a potted lemon tree to love. But Ter could be wrong.

She could no longer think for that ugly little noise, a constantly moving, changing tap-tapping; seemed she'd been hearing it for hours. The sound had come through as the car drove away: all around the swimming pool, clicking on the tiles, tapping over the stones to the barbecue, and now on the cement in front of the kitchen.

"Susan," and all the charm-school tinkles were gone from her mother's voice; "must you painstakingly direct every stranger who uses our drive as if it were public property? Remember, only last week your father spoke to you about that rough-looking working man of some kind you directed." The heels had not stopped their tapping, and by now were directly in front of the garden shed.

"Yes, Mother, but that poor carpenter's helper was lost, his second day on the job, and—."

"Don't argue, dear. You know it infuriates your father. —Are you certain you're up to being out of bed? You don't look at all well."

"I was just thinking about a story I read for English. All of it went through the head of a man while he was being hanged; I suppose while his neck was breaking. Makes you wonder on time. It never goes the same. Some new measurement, better than the solar system or even the theory of relativity, is needed; for if time and space are one I should be at least on Mars." Her mother's gawp shut off that gone-wild tape recorder.

Susie looked at the sky through the dying elm tree, and tried to remember what the woman had said about her. Bed? "I have been in bed too long," she said as her mother went up to the shed doors. "I need fresh air and exercise more than rest. Otherwise I can't sleep."

"You know how you feel. —Say, I have begun my fall collection for the disadvantaged, underprivileged clothing drive at church. Have you anything to give?"

Susie watched an elm twig fall. It wouldn't do to ask what kind of clothing underprivileged was, but—. "Please, IBM, get to work on my mother's reaction if I should tell her she misplaces her modifiers. It might help this weakness in my knees; I can't lift a leg over my bike, not yet." She listened for tremors of weakness in her voice, but could hear none as she said aloud: "I'll look over my things, Mother."

"I'm hunting Brandon's old double black and tan raincoat to give to the driver. Have you seen it?"

"No, Mother." So that coat she had sent for burning belonged to Brandon. She waited, breath held, for more questions. None came. There was only the faint sound of the shed door's opening, then heels tapping past it. She glanced around; the doors were shut. She sprang onto the bike without thinking of leg weakness, raced to the barbecue, on through the hole in the hedge, and did not look back until she had reached the thick growth of the road shoulder. She saw no one. Had anybody seen her there would by now be at least a reminder of the rule against biking on the grass.

She raced on; scarcely knowing she was invading the forbidden Sacred Way. She didn't know why she hurried so; to see Lans—and Ter—again, or to get away from the Popsicle Queen?

She had not felt the hand, but when she saw her right one drop to the handle bars, she knew it had lifted to wipe mud out of her mouth. It had been a bleak Detroit April day but warm enough for mud; and she, on the afternoon shift of first grade, not quite six years old.

It was the time of year when skis and skates are put away, and in the cold rains and sharp winds the outdoors was not much good for play. Yet still she felt the uncertain spring less as a season than a Strange Time. Why, she didn't exactly know. It had something to do with the men—salesmen, her grandmother said. Queer salesmen; always two in a car; only one came into the house while the other cruised the block or parked the car and waited.

The strangest thing was that the man who came into the house never brought samples or anything to sell—just questions. Sometimes he was there of mornings; other times when she got home from school. And why didn't her grandmother send him packing? There was a tightness in her face and voice when he had gone. And what was the word they had used over and over?

She was wiping her face again—getting that mud and caramel spit out of her mouth and eyes; running hard, not quite certain all those kids were chasing her; big boys from her school, girls, and the parochial school crowd she thought; there were so many running feet and cries: "Commie, Commie, Christ haters. She don't believe in God."

All seemed part of the Strange Time, especially the squeals and cries of the little girls. Not that she thought much. The main thing was the running, not looking back; wondering, wishing, mostly wishing: wishing she could run faster; wishing she hadn't made Beeto stop meeting her because she was almost through first grade; wishing the pains in her chest and her side would stop so she could have more breath; wishing she had, in spite of the urgings of her one true friend, Clarice, obeyed and waited in the school for Angie with the car.

Angie and her grandmother bringing her to school in the car was part of the Strange Time. But not so strange as last night, a time of much loud noise. She had been awakened by yells and cries that seemed to come from the front of the house. She was running downstairs to investigate when there came a banging crashing jangle from the living room. A broken window? Beeto caught her at the foot of the stairs. Only the wind, he said; so wild it had blown out a window. The shouts? He apologized; he had left his record player on too loud. Which would she have, a song or a story?

The story had gone in and out her head between the puzzled wonderings. She'd heard no wind, but heard other voices through Beeto's words; not those of Joe and Angie—newly married then, with no children; or Jeff and Margaret; all had come in the late afternoon. Next morning, the Strange Time had been there still; Angie and Joe for breakfast; talk nobody wanted her to hear; and worst of all that tight stillness about her grandmother. Going to school in a car when the weather was fine for walking had been strange, along with her grandmother's note to her teacher, asking that she be allowed to wait inside until they came back for her.

"Commie kid. She's got a Red Granma." She had put a street crossing between her and the cries; they were farther away, yet she knew now they were for her. What was a red Granma? Something struck her on the shoulder. She staggered and saw mud fly past.

164

One hope ran in and out. Clarice, her one true friend, her schoolmate, a big girl more than seven years old, who stopped with her every day at the candy store, then went home with her to have an after-school snack, might turn the gang in the wrong direction—and save her. During school Clarice had been part of the strangeness; she'd acted as if she'd never known a Susan Schnitzer. School out, all that had changed. Clarice had come tiptoeing back to Susie, waiting alone in the classroom. She wanted Susie to stop at the candy store as usual; Susie had her allowance, didn't she? Oh, her grandmother wasn't coming, or she would have been here by now.

So many of Clarice's friends were along, Susie used all her pocket money, even what she was saving for another Pooh book, to buy bubble gum and caramels enough to go around. The girls, Susie's gum and candy in their hands and mouths, had, on coming out of the store, drawn apart to whisper and giggle, breaking at last into laughter, bending double with the laughter, and always, always looking at Susie. She had tried not to notice.

There had at times been hurtful words and questions from other children: "You eat books for breakfast?" "You ina first grade, honest?" "A kinda queer kid." This wordless laughter was somehow worse. She had suddenly wanted her grandmother, now, even if it meant walking without Clarice. "I'm going home," she had said, and stepped into the crowd, now crossing behind the safety-patrol boy.

Clarice grabbed her coat. "You must wait," she had said.

Susie jerked free, got across the street just in time, but the next sidewalk was so packed, running was almost impossible. One more street to cross, then around the corner and home. She again ran across the street. A safety patrol yelled at her for breaking the no-running rule. Somebody yelled from the other side of the street: "Wotta yuh expect of a dirty Communist?"

She carried that last word with her like a bundle as she sprang onto the curb. That was the word she had tried to find in *Commie; Communist* was the word the salesman had used in questions to her grandmother. The word must have slowed her, or else her running gave her away to those around her; the taunts were closer, now: "There she goes. Susie's a Commie kid. Her granma's gotta go to jail. Christ-hater. She don't believe in God."

A hand grabbed at her satchel; another gave her hood such a hard yank, the tie strings cut her throat. Where was Clarice? Why didn't she come? She could quiet those squealing, whooping little girls, making more noise than the boys at her heels. She wished for Clarice as she wished for home and her grandmother.

She rounded the corner. And there it was, gate open; but the block was long, that yard gate farther away than the last white-cap on the sea. The feet were closer; she felt fingers brush her flying hair.

She made the mistake of looking back at danger. She saw the uplifted hand, the face above it, mouth open. The face had held her; she was seeing it now, not remembering; always she would see it, see, see; used to be that face would awaken her out of sound sleep to make her walk the floor. The face belonged to Clarice, her only friend in school; the girl her grandmother had treated like her own; and for whom she had saved pennies, nickles, dimes, and even quarters for candy, ice cream, popsicles and little cakes to go into that always-hungry mouth.

She couldn't pull her eyes from the mouth; Clarice's mouth. It had opened as the head shot forward; warm, sticky wetness was flung into her eyes, between her lips; from farther away had come mud. She could see nothing, not even the foot that tripped her; the face, the spewing mouth had her trapped. She was more aware of it than the grabbing hands or even the pain of pulled hair and the grind of dirty cement against her face. Fists pummeled her head and shoulders while boys' feet in heavy shoes kicked her ankles, shins, and thighs. And all around the tongues shrieked out their lies about her grandmother.

Somebody yelled: "Let's feed the Commie mud." Laughter was mixed now with the jeers as they pulled her shoulders and hair while others pried loose the fingers clamped over the curb. A gripping finger came between her lips; she bit it and got her head up, turtle fashion; in spite of the caramel and the bubble gum in her eyes, she had one glimpse of a man of God walking toward her. Hope came, then died, as, on seeing the

166

trouble in front of him, he turned sharp about to jaywalk.

Now, she could see nothing except a blur of grinning faces. The mob had her on her back; hands all over holding her down while fingers pinched her nose until she opened her mouth for breath. A handful of thin mud was clamped across her teeth, rubbed in and down while more hands held her cheeks and jaws. She struggled, retched, tried to spit out the mud, but could not; another handful was being rubbed in.

Nobody saw him; she felt the difference in the hands under her shoulders and her knees before she noticed the only sound was that of running feet. She would always remember the voice: "Susie, my Susie, you're going to be all right." He cradled her on one arm as if she had been a baby, then, walking toward the gate, he turned her stomach-downward and tried to help her get rid of the mud.

She was still face down, vomiting, when a car stopped, and his voice came again, more sorrowful than complaining as he talked to her grandmother. "Susan Elspeth, why didn't you let me know? I started soon as I saw you had been named—from thirty years ago—by that fool witness. If you don't have a good lawyer, I know some."

"Oh, Lans. Lans, am I ever glad to see you. You have your hands full with business; and at home three young children, and Julia not too well." Her grandmother's words were slower, more wandering than her hands feeling Susie, patting her, smoothing her hair.

The hands left her, the feet went past her, and now Lans's voice was sharp, almost harsh. "Don't go over there, Susan."

"I can see it from here," her grandmother said, her words tight now, like pebbles falling. "Susie's blood all over the pavement. They could have killed her. Blood-hungry they are. Why didn't they do it to me?"

Angie begged her to come back to the car. She sounded shook up; they'd been to school and couldn't find Susie. Susie was ashamed.

Lans had almost reached the gate. "It was a bunch of crazy kids. Come on. We must get her to Children's Hospital. Just for a check. She's going to be all right."

And so she was: her body. Half a dozen doctors with everything from X-ray machines on examined her at the hospital. Only nausea, some shock, abrasions, and bruises; bed rest and sedatives, bandages and ice packs here and there were all she needed.

Lans had felt Susie's escape called for a celebration. They had had a party with Angie and Joe, Margaret and Jeff, Beeto and her grandmother, with herself spending most of it sleeping and waking in her godfather's arms. Her grandmother was able to laugh again—for awhile.

The laughter stopped when the army captain and the Fairy Queen came. The beautiful woman who wanted to be called "Mummie" she thought of as a fairy-like creature from some dimly-imagined, far-away world. This lady and the big man Susie had been directed to call "Daddy," the blonde-haired girl, and the fat baby boy, were strangers, not many weeks back from Germany. Business, house-hunting, and settling had left little time for visiting Susie and her grandmother.

Yet they came that night like thieves, taking a cab to within three or four blocks, then slipping up the alley to tap on the back door, not even risking the sound of the bell. They had come to make plans for claiming their so-beloved daughter.

Somebody gave her hair a sharp pull. Who? She was away from the mob, safe in Lans's arms. Lans? Where was he and where was she? Wobbling on her bike in the middle of a clump of small, low-growing aspen; a branch of one had caught her hair. She was facing almost due west where the sun went down in late September, for she was looking into a red sunset sky.

Her radar, with no help from her, had guided her along the lower fork of The Sacred Way to the low spot in the road above the swamp and the throughway cut. She had come here to see Lans again after sending him the long way around so he would pass several bonfires and have a choice for the burning of Ter's bullet-holed clothing.

The light in front of her was wavering; she smelled smoke. She was seeing, not a sunset, but the red glow of embers from piles of oil-soaked trees. She worked her way out of the aspen, left the bike by a large beech, and after walking a few steps came to the edge of a steep gravelly bank. Fifteen or twenty feet below was the edge of the throughway cut at the point where it curved to bypass the lake below The Village. She could see The Primitive's pond, a red mirror of reflected light with the raw earth of the road cut passing by but soon lost in red-tinged smoke set here and there by flame.

The car wouldn't be in that direction—yet. She looked the other way. Here, the swath for the road was a tunnel of light flanked at intervals by glowing embers and roofed by the red-reflecting sky. On the ground more red glowed from what appeared to be broken sheets of glass—small puddles of water, remnants of the swamp left on either side the causeway.

She had lifted her glance to a tall woods maple, alive with all its leaves, though the trunk was smoking from a log pile smoldering nearby, when the whole of the tree reddened. She turned and saw between her and the pond a new bonfire, so close she could see the shape and motion of its smoke-fringed flames.

She watched for a moment the oil truck that had started the new fire come on in her direction; then looked at the pond. Its still water, red in the bonfire's light, seemed to rise and fall and waver with the flames, as did the sky. Somewhere a killdeer flew up with a bewildered cry and overhead a duck quacked. Something tore at her, sharp as the killdeer's crying. Suppose that cruddy theme did bring an A? So what? It wasn't the pond, not her pond. She and Ter had only described a piece of water, not brought the pond alive. How could you ever write of the sea when all you could make of a wounded pond was a spot of muddy H$_2$O? All the botanical and zoological names on earth would not bring it alive as the sea was alive in *Moby Dick*. What was it?

She heard a chorus of quackings; wild ducks coming home, flying low with a tired flapping of wings, black shapes against the red sky until they disappeared into the pool of red that was the pond. Others circled above the bonfires; or were they ducks or only pieces of debris, some falling, some whirled away in the draft?

She had not noticed the closeness of the oil truck until flame roared up from a pile of logs and brush on the other side of the road cut, off the embankment in a swampy spot. The sickening smell of burning green leaves and oil floated over her.

The flames, higher, closer, redder, changed the place into a world she had never seen. The barkless patches of trunk left by bulldozer blades on the yet-standing trees became bloody red wounds that with the darkness behind them seemed alive, moving in the leaping light of the flames. A piece of drainpipe crosswise of the road became a black cavernous mouth ringed with red; others, lengthwise, were red-backed reptilian monsters. The line of earth-destroying machines she had looked at yesterday now appeared as one long red and black beast, wriggling, readying itself to obliterate the earth; for in the wavering bonfire light, red reflections on metal were constantly changing into black shadowy mouths that spread to become black bodies, so that the whole seemed alive and moving.

She looked away to search out a sad, mixed-up chorus, half a quacking, half a terrified crying. She saw soon, low above the trees on the other side of the last bonfire, the wavering, bobbing stream of little shapes. They were ducks, lost and blinded by the fire as they tried to find their summer's nesting grounds, now under the road-fill and fire. They dropped lower to circle aimlessly; a few were able to rise high enough to get away, but most flapped lower and closer above the fire. Soon, they were no longer ducks flying, but only the litter of the world falling into the fire, or, with feathers aflame, whirled away in the updraft.

She shivered and looked away to see a car stopped a short distance up the road, the driver waiting, it appeared, to see if he could get past the oil truck now on her side of the cut. Lans. She could not have described his car; dark, she thought, a quiet motor, but no new look. She had watched the car as he drove away, and briefly wondered if it were his or rented; the license had beeen so mud-splattered she had not even been able to learn the color.

This was the same car, for there was Lans driving with Ter beside him. She could not make out features, yet she was certain. She stood, eyes on the car, wishing she could drive with them to the pond. If the oil truck man were not—. A loud "whoosh" sounded close; but she was too lost in longing to think what it meant.

Not until hot smoke rolled over her did she notice the log pile on her side of the cut had been oiled and fired. An instant later red light was all over her. The truck driver shouldn't see her. She slid down the bank, what noise she made drowned by the truck and the fire. The slide ended with her feet in mud and water at the bottom of a narrow ravine, walled on one side by the hillside, the road embankment on the other. She climbed this in a long diagonal that took her closer to Lans, but not above the top where the truck driver might see her.

She was close enough to hear the truck driver suggest the car wait until the fire died down.

"I realize," Lans said, "we are trespassing—my son hoped to hunt botanical specimens along this cut—but why burn now when the ducks are coming in?"

"These trees have gotta be outa the way so the drains can go in before freeze-up."

Lans continued politely critical. "But this time of day, burning their nesting grounds, is worse than cruelty to the ducks; it's killing a lot."

"I know," the other said, "but orders is orders." He went on to explain the danger of fire spreading from the smoldering logs; people were burning their trash on the embers; wind-scattered, it could set everything on fire. There was also danger from the oil. "Sometimes she just seeps down getting hotter and hotter, until, wham, she explodes and no fire truck around." He then told of how he had seen, "somewhere along the way you've come" a quick, bright flash of fire. He'd been too far away to tell whether it was trash or oil.

Susie nodded; the sudden flame on the other side of the bend would have been Ter's gasoline-soaked clothing. She admired the coolness of Lans as he told of how he had stopped the car until it seemed safe to pass the flaming pile, then added: "The fire didn't seem to have spread, though."

"Good," the truck driver said. "I'd say it's safe to pass this one now."

She stayed long enough to hear Lans's, "Thank you," followed by the going away sound of the car. She slid down the bank; if she hurried she could find a thick nest of undergrowth on the hillside where—. A duck, either blinded by fire or crazed with pain or both, was running back and forth in front of her; she saw the spurt of smoke from one wing. She grabbed for it. A wing brushed her hand as the bird rose, shakily, faltered, rose higher, high enough to flop into a tongue of flame. Running down the ravine, she had reached the place where the big, fiercely burning log pile was just above her. Too low to see all the fire, she never knew if the bird fell into it or was whirled away on the updraft.

She saw another duck, back down in the mud, feet treading air as smoke curled from its breast feathers. She grabbed it, soused its breast in a puddle, but could only watch the proud neck droop, and the unclosing, unmoving eyes. A quacking, crying duck, head and feet alone showing through the flames, fell a few feet away. All around her ducks, some smoking, others with feathers ablaze, dropped in an agony of beating wings and hoarse cries.

As she grabbed at them, hoping to save at least one, her IBM kept trying to interfere. She paid it no heed until she felt a hot stickiness across one foot; oil, thinned by heat, was racing down the embankment; one sneaker was half covered. Flame was following the oil. She sprang from the oil puddle.

She was clinging to a little aspen, oil-covered swamp water below her filled with flame, when she heard the roar of another truck.

More oil? Seconds later the truck stopped to squirt foam, then water, into the gulley, and more water on the hillside below and around her. Let all the ducks in creation be burned alive, but not one fallen leaf on the sacred soil of The Hill must be charred. Late as it was, straggling ducks were still hunting home; she heard their scattered cries, and tried not to think of Vietnamese babies being burned alive.

By the time she reached the bicycle, smoke and flame had thinned enough, she could make out a car parked near the pond. Standing on the road bed, as if he looked over the construction, was a man, no more than a smudged silhouette in the smoky distance; yet she was certain she looked at Lans. A few steps away where the swamp growth gave place to open water, she saw another figure stoop as if to pick up something. That would be Ter gathering mint, but wet feet wouldn't be good for his infected throat. He suddenly straightened and appeared to look overhead.

She, too, looked and saw against the red-tinged sky the leisurely flapping wings and crooked black lines of a great blue heron. He was so awkward he made you feel he was an alien in the sky; yet the sure serenity of his flight, high around the hill away from the fires, told her he would get safely home. She watched, head turning with his flight, until he was lost behind the hill. She blew a kiss in his direction, and another toward the figures by the pond, but they were gone and she saw only the receding rear lights of a car. The heron, safe, was a good omen for Lans and Ter. The ducks already burned to death or dying couldn't be helped; but there was one nice thing about being dead.

You didn't know.

She was half way home before she realized full dark had come, and she was wet, oily, cold, with mud all over her from sliding down and climbing up those banks. Well, if some of her people saw her before she got cleaned up, she would just have to say she'd kind of fainted and fallen into the mud. She'd get under the shower first thing. No. How could she have forgotten Dr. Laughton? It was past time for calling him.

She reached the doctor at the hospital, listened to more congratulations on her quick recovery, and received a firm permission to go to school next day.

No one saw her until about two hours later when Brandon banged on her door; by then she had showered and was dressed in night clothing and bathrobe. Brandon wanted to know if she had a Saturday's paper. Nobody had thought to save it for him; and he could learn almost nothing of the robbery either from today's papers or his parents.

What made it "so positively disgusting" was that he and his father had been in the shopping center buying camp supplies when the robbery took place. "And here I had to leave and never know what happened until I heard it on my transistor. Dad thought it might be an air-raid warning, and beat it home to be close to the shelter. But nothing happened."

Susie didn't want to hear about the robbery, but did, she thought, manage a fair look of listening. She wished she could work up a little sisterly feeling for Brandon, instead of remembering his snooping that had led to those beloved voices being burned. He was always so much the frightening stranger. His sheer size was part of it; now close to six feet and two hundred pounds at fourteen and a half years old.

The real strangeness, though, was in his face; big, fat, and pale with something in it always behind, not growing up to match that big body. She forgot and stepped back when he suddenly dropped his voice to a whisper. "Susie, have you seen my last spring's raincoat? I've got to find it on the q.t. so Mummie can get me another one exactly like it. She has to do it before the old man comes round for inspection. You'd think we was beggars the way he quarrels about how much my clothes cost."

She managed a head-shake, not believing his coat, new and expensive last spring, could be the rag she had sent to be burned. She grew certain the rag was his coat as he went into details of how he had torn and ripped it here and there, dirtied it when he fell into a mud puddle, then hidden it in the "gardening center" so his dad wouldn't see it before his mother had a chance to buy another. He had to have it so she could buy "—the same brand, and size, and everything."

His growing feeling of persecution could end in a tantrum; at such times she was half afraid of him. "I hope you had a nice time at camp," she said, trying to get his thoughts off the raincoat.

His look worsened. "How stupid can you get? My preparedness group is not out for a good time." This was the beginning of a long angry tirade against the "traitors" who would neither build fall-out shelters nor undergo "even one day of the rigorous training I have endured this last weekend."

Susie wished she had not brought up camp. She ought to

174

have known better. The outdoors and Brandon never got along together. First, he was afraid of all things from a thick wood to a tiny crawling insect. He was the kind that if there were one mud puddle within a mile, he would fall into it. Bees, hornets, yellow jackets, mosquitoes, not to mention poison ivy, nettles, brush, briars, and the sun, all stung and bit and scraped and scorched his soft, juicy skin.

His disconnected quotes on patriotism, chiefly from Bismarck and his camp directors, led to Susie's crime of having "subversive records." She was saved from what promised to be a lengthy diatribe by the ringing of the pantry telephone. "I was expecting a call, so I left the pantry doors on neutral. Get out your violin for me."

She went for her violin, forbidden to Brandon by Bismarck. He felt a boy, unless he had real talent—and he was certain Brandon had none—had "no business messing around with a violin." He felt drum or bugle more suitable. The sad thing was that Brandon, though he had never had a lesson, could get more music out of her violin than she ever would.

She ran. Brandon, disappointment in his voice, was calling from the side stairs that a boy wanted her on the telephone.

Iggy. He spoke in quick whispers, first explaining he had a "security problem," and might have to hang up in a hurry. He had raided Mr. Soames's private library, and found two works on psychology he thought she might like to see. Could she meet him tomorrow as she biked to school? She was ready to give a happy "Yes," when she remembered her faked illness and Dr. Laughton's "No biking." She loathed spreading the lie, but had to explain to Iggy. He was sympathetic, and suggested he leave one book hidden in the dead evergreen, if she wasn't too sick to walk that far. She was thanking him when he suddenly began in his normal voice to tell her she must take care of herself and not neglect her illness.

Security must be passing by.

9

She liked this time of day before Old Harp came. Homeroom, fake togetherness, and Mr. Twitty's English class were behind her. Now, head bent low by her violin, she plucked softly string by string, but listened instead to the muted vibrations crossing and recrossing around her: the clear notes of a French horn, the low growl of the Negro's bass drum, the perfect and beautiful tones of the new girl's violin—the one, she thought, whose mother counted Negroes—or Lady Macbeth-with-her-spots-all-washed-away. She sat only one chair removed from the concert master. Then from the last chair in the second section came the troubled wail of Benny Schlotmann's A-string, forever out of tune.

The lowest of the low was Benny, a special target of Old Harp, who threatened him daily with eviction if he struck one more sour note. Yet, sweaty-handed and goggle-eyed with fear, he stayed. She thought she knew the reason: parents like her own; "—and all that money for music lessons, wasted?"

Her glance happened upon a corner of her binder under the chair. The money she owed Robert was in it. How would she get it to him? He was somewhere behind her in the brasswinds, she thought. She pretended to listen with particular attention, and hoped those hot waves of embarrassment didn't show. Why, oh why, had she kissed him?

Percussion was still; and Benny's A-string was Old Harp's A-string, the correct number of vibrations per second. She wondered if Angus wore his tuning face. She carefully looked up and around. Some of the remoteness was gone from his glance as he watched the door, then with an almost imperceptible head-shake looked at someone behind her but closer to the front of the stage. She twisted around enough to get a cautious glance in that direction in time to see Robert reaching a violin across two bent heads into Benny's outstretched hands. Did Robert charge Benny for the tuning of his violin?

A dangerous job, that. Old Harp would have no one in orchestra who could not tune his instrument. She wished she could see Katy, but on the little squashed-up practice stage a far-back second violinist could not see even the back of the first flutist. A few sounds were fluttering up, quickly dying; nothing out of tune. Why did she like it better the other way, the mingling, the out of tune, the too loud, the too soft?

If she could write a symphony, the name would be "Notes Out of Tune" or "Flames on Living Flesh at Twilight." Somewhere on earth there should be a place for notes out of tune— and people out of tune. The people who did not say the proper words at the proper time; and the sounds that did not make the proper number of waves per second—crooked they were in their circling, like the burning ducks; no, not that; gulls in a high wind were—.

"Fifth Chair, in the second violins."

The girl in the fourth chair nudged her. She jerked up her head to face Old Harp's cold blue glance that often, as now, reminded her of Bismarck. "How long have you been in this orchestra?"

"Since tryouts last fall, sir."

"Answer in sentences, please. And have you not in that time learned even this one signal?"

"Yes, sir. It means silence, instrument ready, eyes on the conductor."

"Then, pray tell me why you don't obey it?" His words, not loud, were spewed out with the suppressed fury of ice water, rushing through the one small hole left in the frozen faucet.

She choked, struggled for words, felt the sweat on her hands as she started to lift the violin, remembered he had not named the music. And all the time he waited, freezing her with his eyes; and the orchestra waited in a silence that screamed all ears were listening. "I, sir, was—."

She jumped, then grabbed the violin as it slid part way off her lap. Something had fallen with a clattering crash that sent thunder-like roars and rumblings over the room. She did not dare take her glance from Old Harp while she held her breath. The whole of him appeared to quiver as his glance encompassed the entire orchestra. Whoever had caused that noise was pretty certain to be sent to Mr. Yakalong, First Assistant Principal in Charge of Discipline.

"Sir, I somehow let my foot touch the music stand when the thing was unfolded to its full height. It fell into the timpani, then against the bass drum when I grabbed for it. I'll try to mend it." Standing straighter than usual, Angus gazed from the top tier with no bending of his head, so that Old Harp must lift his glance to confront him. There was no insolence in his voice or face. He did not even show sign of remembering he was considered one of the best musicians in the orchestra.

The orchestra waited so long, the collectively held breaths must at last go out in a long sigh, not of relief, but for air. Angus had stopped looking at Old Harp; his face was the familiar one of listening to that inside drum. Susie remembered her conversation—if it could be called that—was not yet finished, and again fixed her glance on Old Harp but could not tune out her private TV that kept showing Angus. He now seemed no kin at all to the Angus at the pond. Even his hair looked subdued; part of the change, she guessed, came from the decorously dark gray jacket with dull trousers, proper shirt, and tie, about the same as other boys wore to school.

"You know the rules. Don't touch the music stands while orchestra is in session. Try now to get along with it." Old Harp spewed the words, but stronger than the anger was his weariness.

Susie had thought of him as one of the younger, more alive teachers: "A real musician," she had heard, "with a great future."

Now, his body finish was going; the blond hair, long as the mores of the school would allow, she had thought rather nice until now when it was greasy enough to show its thinness; and his forehead, instead of seeming poetically high and thin, was today only old-man bony.

Oh, Jove, tell me what he has been saying. She had been staring straight into his face without hearing one word. She relaxed. Nothing except the same old warnings; be careful of the old music stands, the old music, the folding chairs that squeaked; and hope the request for a "more generous funding of the music department" would be heeded by the school board. Plain it was he did not on this morning love the school board.

During the first week of school he had given each of them a set of mimeographed sheets outlining orchestra programs and schedule for the school year. Now, his humor worsened as he told them to disregard his schedule. American Day would be observed and also Veteran's Day. The program of international music had been canceled as had UN Day; the vacancies would probably be filled by a memorial service and a "Salute Our Fighting Men" assembly.

"There has also been an addition," he continued, and dry ice would not have smoked within sound of his voice. "It has been decided—" There was on the "it" such a vicious hammering, Susie wished she could tune him out, but dared not. He was soon explaining that all assemblies were henceforth to begin with "The Star Spangled Banner." And before each rendition the orchestra was to rise with the audience, salute, and give the Pledge of Allegiance.

And since, he continued, the orchestra had never saluted as a group, encumbered as the members were with instruments, it would be necessary to give considerable time to practice. Furthermore, they must practice from both their on-stage positions as on Parents' Night and their orchestra-pit positions as on American Day. The on-stage position would offer no great difficulty, except of course for the encumbrance of instruments and the problem of rising without touching music stands; few would have to turn completely around in order to face the National Emblem. The orchestra pit position would offer more problems.

There was in the orchestra practice room as in all class-rooms, central halls, auditoriums, lunch rooms, and also offices, she supposed, a National Emblem presented by the American Legion. Here, the small flag stood, as in other rooms, on the floor near the door, but since the seats rose in tiers, Susie, like the others, must lower her gaze in order to look at it. She did not. Instead, fixing her glance straight out and hence well above it, lips firmly together, she rose amidst the muted clattering of chairs and carefully put down or held instruments.

They first practiced the on-stage position so that she scarcely had to turn as did the first violinists. Old Harp, turned completely sidewise, gaze rigid on the limply hanging cloth, led off with The Pledge. Susie crossed her fingers and moved her lips now and then—without sound. Already a citizen of Canada by her own proclamation, there were not too many more years of waiting to be the real thing—if Canada would have her. Now, she felt sick. The world had her by the nose and a mud-filled hand across her mouth. Why couldn't they salute the Michigan flag? She liked Michigan—Detroit and some other parts—but had she ever seen a Michigan flag?

She risked a dropped glance. It fell upon a red, half-wilted rose, tied with what looked to be the lace of a man's work shoe on that head of shining hair; too pale for ripened wheat, not so pale as Charlotte's fresh from a "rinse" at her hair stylist's. A petal was sliding from the rose; it stopped on the shoulder of the black sweater worn by the girl she hated on general principles, though she had never spoken to her, this daughter of her father's employee, Lady Macbeth of Birmingham with-her-spots-all-washed-away. Who had given her the name? and from whom had she first heard it? Did she help her mother in the counting of Negroes?

Old Harp was quarreling: "More life. Now, again." He led off with an overstressed, *I*. The arm on her breast felt as if pulled by a great weight; she hooked a finger under the neck of her blouse, let the arm hang.

Standing, it was easier to see Angus. He stood as always, save now he seemed straighter, taller than she had ever seen him. The orchestra look was gone; in spite of his clothing, he was the Angus by the pond, his inside drum in tune. Her crossed fingers slid apart to let her arm drop. Her IBM must have suffered a power failure, only now telling her after this long look that Angus was in danger. He stood as always when waiting for the next drum phrase—arms crossed on his chest.

Old Harp would yell in a second, then send him at once to Mr. Yakalong. Worse, some Salute-Counting-True-Blue-Patriot like her father would report him both at home and at school. Cause a great stink so he would have to be expelled; he could not then get into college. Straight into the armed forces he would have to go. What there for a non-saluter? The black hole four by four by four?

Old Harp shooting words like carbon dioxide bullets, was leading off again. Angus looked at her; she flushed, took her glance away to let it fall on Old Harp. He had an arm up, baton clenched in his other hand, gaze riveted on The Emblem. Susie breathed more easily. The uncanny, encompassing ability of the man's glance was gone. Normally able, with scarcely a look or a listen, to catch a note one thirty-second off, a woodwind vibrating one micro-instant too long, spot gum behind unmoving jaws, one loose hair on a sloppy violin bow, he now heard nothing save The Emblem and The Pledge, saw nothing.

Smart man. If there were in his orchestra any Jehovah's Witnesses, non-saluters on purely moral and nationalistic grounds like herself, anti-undergodders, absolutists as was Angus, peaceniks, and general nonconformists, Old Harp wasn't going to know about it. Angus was safe—from him.

She turned her head for another cautious glance at Angus. Their eyes met; something crossed his face, weak sunlight through thin cloud; his version of a smile. And what was she doing? Why, beaming on him with all her eyes. Rattled, she turned from him to the rose. It had dropped another petal that lay on the upturned ends of that shoulder-length hair like a baby in a cradle.

The petal was turning because the hair was turning. Everybody was turning. A music stand clattered to the floor, a chair scraped, but Old Harp had mind only for The Emblem and The Pledge as he reminded the group they were now to imagine they were in the orchestra-pit position. Susie wondered on the psychology book Iggy had left by the hole in the hedge as he biked to school. She had had a time sneaking out to pick up the book, sneaking it in with Lulu come early to the kitchen because of Susie's illness. So far, she'd had no chance to read it; perhaps during Latin. The violinists on either side of her were sitting down. Poor Old Harp; his face made you think of a wild apple in March after it has lain frozen all winter under the snow.

Things continued to go badly. Old Harp's face went colder and colder, older and older, tireder and tireder. Was there such a word as *tireder?* If not, there ought to be. When you spoke it slowly, letting out your breath on the end, it had a weary sound. Possibly for Old Harp desolate was better; he was desolate over the dissolute music. He was now giving them the snarling reminder that, though TSSB was an anthem, it was not a funeral dirge; he wanted more joy. Joy she must take in the rockets and the bombs because they were killing foreigners. She was doing all right thanks to that deal at home; her father forced her to play while he and the rest stood at attention and sang.

Where was Ter by now? Canada? How had he made out in the telling of his father? Did he say: "Look, Dad, I robbed a bank? Here's the money. Get it back." And that strange goodbye? "It slid away." What slid to where? Time?

Time wasn't sliding now. Somebody in brasses had blown a sour note. Old Harp was correcting with motionless arms and a silent stare. They started over again, no longer an orchestra; only a collection of disgusted students who banged and tootled, sawed and blew on and on in spite of one sneeze, three coughs, and at last somebody's foot pat-patting. More silence, then falling into it the icy reminder: "This is an orchestra—supposedly —not a bluegrass band."

The sound of the class-closing gong was an opening window after months of sealed thermo-pane. Old Harp, in common with other conscientious teachers, never held you one second after the blast-off bell. Music was in A-Building of the school complex; most academic classes were in C-Building, second floor; but Susie's next, chemistry, was away off in E-Building. And who wanted a flock of tardy slips?

So, forget Angus, Ter, the psychologist; everything except getting to that chemistry test on time. "Jack be nimble, Jack be quick": fold the music stand soundlessly; close the music carefully, remembering loose pages; grab binder from under chair; carry everything down to the front of the room; there, leave chair and music stand in their proper places; go next to Music Storage, shove music into proper slots; take violin case from your numbered space, put in violin and bow, return to proper space; if out of proper storage during school hours the insurance is off. Take binder and scat—without running.

E-Building could be reached by the exactly-alike, seemingly endless halls, crowded worse than rue Sainte Catherine late on Good Friday. A second route lay through the tunnel, shorter, but badly ventilated, and with even worse crowding. She preferred to cut across the inner court; nothing but a wide expanse of cement, no flowers, no fountains, but never crowded in any weather. Best of all you had the sky, not much, hemmed in by walls like a prison sky, but enough to let you remember there was outside of school a world with a sky.

Even in the court, running was forbidden; points off if you got caught; enough points and to Discipline you must go; you would then not get the Principal's Recommendation Without Reservation; the college you wanted would then not have you— and so, McGill, I will not run. Few tried to run; for in spite of the General Course and Trade School divisions, every child—no, every parent in Eden Hills—was certain his brilliant offspring was material for "some outstanding college," if not Harvard or Radcliffe.

Her IBM and radar as always took care to keep her in a long-strided, flat-heeled walk that even when the knees bent way down to keep those heels on the ground, could not be called running. She made it to chemistry on time: take end seat in back row, unzip binder, get out pen, take out the two well-sharpened pencils carried for emergencies, re-zip binder and slide under chair; everything finished well before the unit-test sheets were given out.

Fifty questions for fifty minutes; a mixture of multiple choice, true-false, and head-work problems. Easy. "One kilogram equals 2.2046 lb." —True. "H_2CO_2 is the formula for carbonic acid." —False. She sped on, lifting her head now and then to stare at nothing and think. "What is the weight of one liter of oxygen? You may use the back of this sheet as a scratch pad." "No, thank you. My computer doesn't need a scratch pad."

She finished in time to check her answers. Paper in, there was still time to hear without wanting to the frustrated sighs, angry mutterings, and, three chairs away, the girl who cried with a quiet sniffling. The blast-off bell clanged, and she, like most of the class, was shot into lunch, the time she hated most.

By this time you felt thoroughly dirty; chalk dust gritty under your fingernails, feel of those bodies that had thumped and jammed you all morning; yet, there was never time or space for a good wash in the packed girls' washrooms—that is, if you planned to eat. She had wondered if in the school, built for fifteen hundred students, now with close to three thousand, even one washroom had been added.

The sixty minutes given to lunches for the whole school had originally been designed for two thirty-minute periods. The hour was now divided into three periods with some classes split, so that the school day ended at the same time for all. Extra class-rooms had been added where classrooms were never intended to be, but the washrooms were sardine cans filled with oversized herring, all alive and wriggling—and dirty.

True, as in any good free-enterprise system, the poor fish had several choices. First, he could go dirty straight from class to lunch, and so have time to go down the full hot-lunch line and do a lot of eating—provided the cafeteria lines were moving well and offered something edible. Eating dirty was out for her, so that her first choice was that of a washroom; she passed several on her rush from E-Building back to lunch in A. She usually washed in Building D, the special place for general course students. Since this group lunched on the last shift, and Susie in the middle one, the washrooms were, at this particular time, less crowded, usually. She was in luck today; not room for another nose in front of the mirrors, but she found a cold-water faucet—there was no hot—and a bit of basin all to herself.

Washed, she must finish getting through D-Building, cross

the wide intersections of B and C, up and down two flights of stairs in C to her locker, get through B-Building and on to the cafeteria near the end of A.

Another choice was the snack from home; in that case spend, as she usually did, half the lunch period in getting to and from your locker, for any sandwich or fruit was inedible after being squashed around in a binder all morning. Also food needed some kind of wetness you couldn't bring from home, so down the short lunch line you must go, more time.

Still another choice was a small tin of something on the order of antipasto or crab meat, but she had eaten such stuff daily most of last year, and now sickened at their very sight. The best solution would be to eat enough toast on the way to school to carry her all day, but even when she forced down three pieces she still growled in her last class until the boy who usually sat next her would study her with an unsmiling analytical gaze as if he thought she had swallowed a live dog.

The greatest hazard in her rush to the locker was the first flight of up stairs. Like other stairs, one way, and packed between periods, yet fairly speedy, unless a flock of not-yet-completely-oriented sophomores tried to come down the up stairs or vice versa.

Today, though the going was slow, she was half way up the first flight of C Stairs Number 4 when the back in front of her stopped so suddenly she jabbed its buttocks with her binder; while behind some tall somebody's binder punched her shoulder-blades. She braced herself, and managed to leave a bit of breathing space between her and the jacket in front. Muted groans mingled with cries of, "Quit pushing. I can't move"; suggestions that all turn around and go down; along with wonderings on what was wrong, as nobody was trying to come down, filled the stair for a moment or so before weary silence fell.

Soon, however, waves of stories began to run up and down: a teacher was having a cart of books moved; Mr. Maddox, Chairman of the History Department, a true-blue American first and history teacher second, had carried the National Emblem into the hall, and was forcing all passersby to salute, give the

Pledge of Allegiance and the Scout Oath; while in and out were the behind-the-hand whisperings, meant to be heard, and done as usual by a certain-kind-of-boy.

She stood, feeling dirtier and dirtier, shrinking from the bodies that pressed on all sides, their sounds, their smells. She'd take a well-run fish market any day for the collection of deodorants, toothpastes, cheap perfumes, mouths foody from the first lunch period, after-shave lotions, with here and there whiffs of body sweat and feet. Second by second the stair, walled as it was on both sides with doors above and below, seemed to grow hotter and more airless. Equally bad were the whisperings; she tried, but could not completely shut them out. Once a whole sentence blew over her shoulder: "School security said Big Red lost his virginity in the freight elevator, but the state troopers are hunting it under the football stadium. Ha. Ha."

She stared at the checked wool of the jacket six inches from her nose and gave no indication she had heard. "Think of something nice—your grandmother's spruce woods," she told herself. "Or perhaps you'd better think about that autobiography coming up in English, or decide on what character in American Literature you can do a paper. No, you've decided, or have you, on Captain Ahab?"

"Look, Brain, get out of neutral and into gear. Can't you see the line's moving, Susan Schnitzer?" She turned to see an acne-faced boy with the wrong kind of shirt, a strange stranger who would always be a strange stranger. Your picture in the school paper was at best a questionable honor—at least here at school. "Quit worrying and learn to love the thermonuclear bomb, Kiddo."

The acne-faced boy again, now beside her on the stair. She gave him a big bright smile. He gave back the smile, then followed a line of long-legged boys taking two stairs at a time. She gave his back an interested glance and rather wished he had stayed beside her. She might have found a peacenik. How did you go about finding people who believed as you believed? She thought Katy hated the war, but Katy like herself was careful in her talk. Why? How could she have forgotten Angus? He of course was a peacenik or—.

She had almost bumped the body ahead; this time that of a girl. Movement had slowed, and again the stair was filled with groans and sighs; but for a different reason. Had the first traffic jam lasted a minute or so longer, the whole stairful would have been late to class; and when there was a great fall-out of tardies for one period, the cheap little computer could not accept all the information at once. Last year in a blizzard, the little thing had been so overworked with absences and tardies, it had been sick for days—and nobody was absent or tardy. Thus, when slips ran above a certain percentage, they didn't count, though the teachers made them out just the same; a teacher couldn't short-circuit or pop a circuit-breaker. Or could he? As things now were, most of the half above the middle stair would get there on time—provided *there* was not too far away; the lower half would—.

She had reached the packed hall. She was slowly worming her way through when a thicker swarm clustered in front of a freight elevator stopped her again. She saw only the last stretcher bearer, a foot or so of purple clinic blanket, the back of a school nurse's cap before the elevator closed its mouth on everything, and the feet around her quickened as did her own. You wondered each time you saw a loaded stretcher, but never heard; like driving past a wrecked car on the highway shoulder after the blood is black on the pavement. Death or wounds that mutilated? You never knew. She had seen no blood in the hall—insulin shock, low-sugar shock, epilepsy, cardiac failure, simple fainting, or a bleeder? You never knew.

"Thank you, Dear Direction-Finder, and Dear Automatic Pilot." They had taken her up the second flight of stairs, turned her left, sent her six paces down the hall, given her a right turn to face the proper locker. Automation had spun the correct combination, opened the tin door, put texts and notebooks of the morning away, taken out materials for the afternoon, and a cloth case of a thing that smelled of cheese; must be her lunch, but why the dress-up outer dress? She always used a paper sack. Computer had arranged everything in or on binder; Direction-Finder had brought her downstairs and put her into the short lunch line, short for a change with nobody horsing around.

She had been thinking; of what? Angus, then medical

research; or rather wishing she knew enough about the endless field to think on it.

She bought her Strontium Ninety in no time at all, but stopped to search out a vacant seat. The cafeteria was its usual honor-system bedlam, a blast-off with all the controls gone wrong, and nobody, except the few who wanted to eat in peace, caring. The teachers were all in their safe pillboxes of classrooms or lounges. The quickies who never bothered to wash and lunched chiefly on candy bars were already living it up on the narrow strip of recreation space left for the jukebox and dancing by the arithmetical progression of lunch tables.

She had never bothered to watch the dancing here, or bought a record of the thumpy music and howling songs. Still, that dancing on the rock with Iggy had been fun; and if a boy asked you it would be nice to know at least a step or so, or should one say a body or so—if a boy asked you. And most were girls dancing alone; practicing for that boy.

She abruptly turned from the dancing and pretended to be looking over the tables. The back of a boy watching the dancers had seemed a shade familiar. He turned slightly, and she saw that TV-ad profile—Robert. In another second he would find her looking at him. And wouldn't he just know she was gazing "upon him with longing eyes."

Rattled, and taken up with pretending she looked for a "Special Person," she at first saw only a beckoning arm. Her overworked IBM was slow in coming up with the information that the arm belonged to Katy, and was beckoning Susan Marie Schnitzer to come sit with her.

She started in that direction after one quick glance to make certain the boys so close to Katy were not at her table; for, though in the halls of Eden Hills High one often saw kissing and other forms of necking, custom demanded that boys and girls eat at separate tables. Another custom decreed that foreign students should have a separate table; this one made some sense; she suspected the foreign students themselves had demanded their own table as a recess from United-States togetherness.

As she drew nearer the table, she remembered another custom, one of those so unspoken you were never certain; but seniors ordinarily ate only with seniors. True, Katy sat at the end with vacant seats on either side, but the other girls must be seniors as was Katy; at least she couldn't remember one of those faces in any class.

Katy's welcoming smile was making her feel better when a familiar voice said: "Welcome. We'd like to hear your side of the argument."

She looked up to find Angus smiling at her. He and the Negro, Ben, sat on the opposite side of the next table, so close to Katy's they might as well have been sitting at the same table. She wanted to thank him for his accident that had saved her neck; but that would imply he had done it on purpose; he wasn't the kind to make a noise like that in orchestra, but there must be some way she could show gratitude without—.

"Ah, Susie at last;" and here came Robert nimbling up to her chair.

She glanced up to find his eyes, not on her face, but her legs, encased at Lulu's insistence—"Remember, chick, you're still sick enough to take antibiotics;" in knee-length black woolen socks. Now, he was of all things pulling out her chair. The whole room would see—and hoot.

Her confusion was so great, she tipped the tray as she started to put it down; the overly long straw in the flimsy little milk carton followed the slant of the tray, and the milk followed the straw. There she was with a puddle on her tray before she had even started to eat. Robert cried, "Oops," and picked up her binder, purse, and lunch container before they were wetted. "You sit down," he said, again behind her chair. "I'll take back this dirty tray, and bring you another with more milk."

She had the feeling the others were bursting to whoop with laughter, but she couldn't stand there forever.

Satisfied she was safely seated, he took the tray and went off in the direction of the short lunch line, she supposed. The main thing was he had gone. She was not aware her face was un-zipped with puzzled confusion showing until Katy said: "Don't worry; Robert seemed normal in orchestra. Makes you wonder, though, if that tale of the chemistry student who took the pure grain alcohol from the lab—he put the rubbing stuff in its place

—and keeps a bar traveling through the boys' washrooms isn't true. I don't think there is a school rule against selling liquor in the washrooms."

"Nobody says they're selling liquor; pure alcohol from the lab is a chemical even when diluted. —Susie, you better start eating; not much time left." Angus turned back to Katy. "And anyway Robert thinks too much of his reputation to risk liquor on his breath at school."

"I suppose he'll have to stick to vodka," Susie said. "But his reputation has such a high polish, you wonder how anything could—could tarnish it." She had let her tongue run away, and never noticed until it was almost finished with its nasty remark. She began a hasty opening of the flowered lunch container.

"You wonder," the Negro said. "Is he putting us on for fun? The Establishment's not that low, telling a guy to do articles against miniskirts and pretend the idea was his own." He looked around. "He's researching the dancers again."

"And Susie will never get her milk," Angus said. He turned to the Negro. "What they want Robert to do with his series of articles on quote Good Taste in Dress unquote is the same kind of brainwash they used three or four years ago when they were having pickles because some boys were wearing low-slung, tight jeans. My sister was a junior, an associate editor of the *Purple Sunflower,* same as Robert now.

"Then, the administration practically ordered the student editors to come up with a series of pieces with the same overall title they have now given Robert for miniskirts. Quote, You may choose your own titles for the individual pieces but emphasis must be on those awful jeans, unquote. Seems a very big fish, member of the school board and a lot of other things, came to sound off in Assembly. He saw kids in pants slung on their hip bones, and went into hysterics. 'Important visitors from out of the state,' he was said to have said, 'will think this outstanding community produces nothing but hoods.' So the school paper went into the business of manufacturing public opinion that would get the guys out of the wrong pants and into the right ones."

190

"Why couldn't the Establishment have made a rule against the pants they didn't like?" Katy wondered. "Or against miniskirts, if they're worried about them—now. The style's so old."

"I guess they got tired of hoping it would change," the Negro said. "And if they made a rule it would let the world know the perfect students in this perfect school were dressing like what they call 'the grease.' It would have been in the papers. Also, the powers want the students to think they have freedom under God and student government."

Susie nodded. "So Robert has been chosen to guide us in dress? And—he was—unusually polite to me because I'm not wearing a miniskirt." She was feeling better in some ways, worse in others, mostly because of the lunch—enough for a football team. Taking out the first sandwich, she remembered. Lulu, worried by Susie's illness, had risen early, and had a lunch before Susie went into the kitchen. There had been nothing to do but take it. Ben, she saw, was doing what she liked to do, looking at Angus's hair.

"Let's all hope," he said, "the paper doesn't unplug its trumpet on hair lengths."

Angus smiled. "It's already at the bend me, break me, shame me, till I lose my hair, stage."

Susie gazing at that fantastic Bay-of-Fundy-mud hair, gave an unprogrammed, wailing, "Oh."

"You'll have to come to a 'Mourning Hop-In For Lost Hair,'" the Negro suggested. "It's a high-school group in Detroit, wild about Angus. He can sing his sad songs with the guitar, or take the drums. No difference. The girls flip and forget to dance for looking at him."

"Aw, go plug your trumpet," Angus begged.

"But can't you cut it real short, or even have it shaved, carefully, and make a wig?" Susie asked. "You can't ever buy a wig that will be as—." She anchored her tongue until she could think to substitute, "to match it" for the "beautiful" about to come out. One trouble was she had glimpsed Robert working his way in her direction.

Angus was shaking his head while the Negro nodded.

"Work on him. The Primitive suggested the same thing, and so did Pryor. We could find a wigmaker who'd do it some night while we had a Wig-In."

Susie whispered: "Oh, please, Angus." She couldn't say any more; he was looking at her, smiling.

Then she had to smile—at Robert. He was putting a clean tray with fresh milk in front of her. Politeness demanded some show of gratitude; impossible to use words; Robert was pouring them out on a subject she loathed, her health. Iggy had told him she had had a throat infection and could not bike to school for a week. He'd tried to ring her up this morning to offer a ride, but she was already gone. "This afternoon I'll be waiting for you in the first rank of Parking Lot Number Three. Remember now. You know my car. If it's raining I'll pick you up at the Confused Goose entrance. —You must be well by Saturday."

He apologized for leaving, then stayed long enough to explain he must get back to miniskirt research; the dance floor was; "—an exceptionally good place for that sort of thing."

He had talked long enough to let Susie think up words for thanking Angus. "I know it's kind of kooky to thank anybody for having an accident, but yours with that old music stand saved my neck in orchestra. So, I thank you."

"He wouldn't have said much more to you. He's mad at the whole world. You can't blame him for that. He has the title of Director of the Orchestra, works hard, neglects his own music. Then, somebody else—and I'll bet they don't know a harp from a harpsichord—selects the music, over his head."

"It wouldn't have been so mean," Katy said, "if they'd forced him to change his programs before he mimeographed them for us. Like somebody wanted to prove to us our orchestra leader has no power."

"Who has the power? Who is the boss?" the Negro wondered. "But I guess it's classified."

"The power is shared."

She had thought Robert gone, but here he was bringing up Lady Macbeth, no subject for hot color or miniskirt research. Susie hoped her face didn't show the emotion she hated. Envy. It had come down on her the other afternoon as she had stood unlocking her bike in the September rain.

Here had come this long black roadster, a man driving, a nice-looking man considering the company he worked for, but old, past forty. He had smiled at her while the woman with him got out of the car. Dried up and bleached out, a kind of desert blonde you might call her, a desert, that is, that you know will never have another rainy season. This hard dry woman had hurried to the portico with an umbrella and a raincoat, waving at her Lady Macbeth to stay under shelter as if she were magnesium liable to explode in a bit of water. Such a rushing to help her daughter into the coat, carry her binder as they went back to the car; and all done in a perfect fall-out of "honeys" and "dahlings" and askings about school, and was she too "tahd" to go with them to look at a car for herself?

And the man had held the car door open, not honeying so much, but smiling on his Lady Macbeth as if she were the only girl in the world. Still, he had, behind the backs of the other two, sent a second smile across to Susie. She had, batting the rain out of her eyes, watched the car slide away, and wondered how it would be to have one parent, just one, meet you that way—once.

She came to. Here was Lady Macbeth in person at the corner of the table, smiling like an old buddy at Katy in her "underprivileged" clothes. If Susan Schnitzer were like this girl, her parents would be different—or would they? Everything perfect: the way she walked, so straight as if she knew she had breasts and was glad she had them; and her head so high, not stiff-high the way Charlotte carried hers after a week's tune-up and overhaul at a Beauty Retreat, but naturally as if that head could never think of holding itself any other way. She was slender in the waist, but no angles or bony legs for her; and that hair, long, smooth, unsalted-butter color, with never a fuzz or a string; you wondered if she washed and ironed it every night.

Susie pretended to be hunting some tidbit in the lunch bag. Gawking she had been, like—like Robert. Was he ever getting a shock. He was trying to introduce a girl to kids who knew her

193

better than he. Katy was wishing they could have lunched together; or had she had time to eat anything?

"Ah ate two whole cans a baby food. You can cahy them in yo bindah an they don't spoil."

That *mousse de bananes* accent, though not easily understood, did make you realize the language without *R* and *G* was rather pretty. The girl had everything—and more; along with love and TLC, musical ability and long dark, curling lashes— real—she also had brains. Why had Susan Schnitzer not thought of canned baby foods for school as well as skiing?

She was being introduced by Robert. The girl's smile was a fluorescent light with a slow switch. The button was pressed; a microinstant of nothing; then flickering dimness for a second as if the light didn't know whether or not it was connected; on at last, big and bright and full—just for you. "Ah'll be so glad to know you. Ma fathah wuks in th same company as yo fathah; an yo mothah has most kindly invited us to dinnah—next Sunday ah think."

Susie never knew exactly what she did say to that news; most of her mind was on trying not to show her distaste for dining with—. Robert was going to introduce the Negro to her. What would this girl who probably helped her mama count Negroes do? Faint, as had those girls in a southern college a long time ago when a Negro walked into their classroom? The Negro was up, looking at the girl as Robert spoke her name: "Mary Lou Weatherford."

She was smiling; the light was glowing, a big desk lamp with two oversize bulbs; every electron bombarding the mercury vapor at such super speed, each molecule of phospher glowed. Made you realize the other smiles had been, at most, only the second switch of a three-way bulb. "Ah'll certainly get to know you, Ben. We have math, orchestra, and *a cappella* choir together."

The Negro had plugged in his full Christmas tree set—bubble lights included. You'd think he'd be embarrassed and suffering as much as the girl; if so, he was doing the same good job of covering up as she.

Robert didn't bother with introducing Angus. It was clear there was no need as she smiled at Angus. "All these times Ah've seen you, it wasn't till Sunday when we visited yo papa's church, I knew who you weah. My mothah so enjoyed his sermon, 'Prayer not pickets.'"

"And did you dig it?" Angus asked.

Her voice was sweet as ever. "Trouble was Ah'd studied th' wrong lesson. Th' one wheah Christ drove th' money changers from th' temple." She was unzipping her binder, and so couldn't know of the smile Angus dropped on her down-bent head.

"Sit with us tomorrow," Robert said, trying to catch Lady Macbeth's glance. "I believe you'll take my side in our argument: Is it better to be the poor little sophomore Angus met crying in the washroom because he is being flushed out of College Preparatory and must go into General Course and so can never go to college and be a professional man like his father who is determined on college for his son; or is it better to be a Messner—you know, our orchestra leader? He was a child prodigy, the violin. And look at him now. In other words, which is better, to live half your life on a rocket, certain it will get into orbit some day, but that some day never comes; or always know you'll never reach the launching pad like the kid in the washroom?"

Lady Macbeth's only answer to Robert was a smile, and a quick one at that. The "Lunch Period is Ended for You" gong was crashing down. As always in the lunch room, it was a kind of earthquake shaking up the inmates. Those finished and fooling around dashed for the doors; unfinished ones ate even faster, some with drink in one hand, sloppy joe in the other. Most, however, could spare only one hand for eating; second hands must be picking up books, binders, zipping, unzipping, loading purses, shoving wallets into pockets, loading trays with dirty dishes and paper. Still chewing, sipping, swallowing, late ones rushed into the squeeze around the dirty-dish belt where they sipped and chewed even faster as they unloaded. Rearranging binders, books, purses, wallets, while still chewing, swallowing, they waded into the Big Squeeze around the exits.

Everything gone into high gear, only partly to get to class on time; third lunch-period eaters, already oozing through the doors, were massed by hundreds in the hall; the lunchroom, as well as all doors, belonged to them. If you got trapped in the incoming tide, you could get a good buffeting along with a tardy slip. At such times Susie was glad she was scrawny; made ducking easier. She was picking up her tray when somebody lifted it out of her hands. Angus. "You haven't much," he said. "I can take it with Katy's paper sack and mine."

She smiled her gratitude, helped him clear her tray, stack it under the other two, and caught another smile from him.

Memory of his smile made her next class, beginning calculus mixed with other math, nicer than usual. The memory went into temporary hiding when on the way to physics she glimpsed ahead the black sweater and shining hair that meant Lady Macbeth. Come to think of it, one of the most hurtful things about the girl was the way she dressed. It was as if she had been hooked up to Susan Schnitzer's thought waves when one morning in late August, at a fiesta mass high up on the Mexican desert, she had watched those poor, barefooted women, all in black, save sometimes for a glimpse of baby carried in the black *rebozo;* and there below the incense-shrouded heads of the dark Christ and the saints, she had made the basic plan for her school wardrobe: as much black as she could get by with at home. —"But black isn't your color, dear. It's not as if you were a blonde."

Now, did this girl wear black as a mourning for the state of the world, as Susan Schnitzer wore it, or because she was a blonde and beautiful in black?

She forgot her wonderings in physics where, because she alone of the class had solved them, she put on the board and explained three examples. Latin was next, and the trip from here to there was a daily dive into frustration.

As the need for classrooms mushroomed, Latin had been stuck off in F-Building, which housed the Trade School Division. The quickest way to get there from physics was to go to the War Dead Rotunda; from there exit into the court, cross this to E-Building, go through E, down six steps into F, then on to Virgil at the very end behind the gasoline engines and across from metal-working.

She was rushing across the court in her heels-down run when somebody behind her said: "A moment, please, Miss

Schnitzer." She stopped with a jerk; the rummer she had been expecting; that moldy fool of a would-be psychologist was waiting for her with his brain-probe. "What did you think I was, the FBI?" And Robert was walking beside her.

"No. I feel my crimes are important enough for the CIA," she told him, at the same time remembering the money, not thought of since orchestra. She, with no lessening of her stride, unzipped her binder, groped until she felt the envelope of bills, and after one quick glance around gave it him.

"Thank you. There was no hurry," he said as he shoved the envelope into an inner pocket of his jacket. They were split apart by a crowd pouring out both doors of E. She was going down the steps into F with almost two minutes to spare before he found her again. "You know, you might have trouble in finding my car; so why don't we meet in Music Storage where we both go after school? Then, I can take you. O.K.?"

She had forgotten his suggestion at noon, chiefly because she had still planned to call a cab. She managed to drag out: "That would be nice—if it isn't too much trouble for you."

"Not a bit. Say, you love boats and water?"

She nodded.

"I thought so." He glanced around, and seeing no one in the jigsaw section they walked through, went on in a low, careful voice. "I'm giving a little boating blast of a thing, Saturday. —Oh, we won't be alone," he added, misreading her unhappy stare. "Katy and Angus are coming; Ben might." He gave a quick look around. "Don't tell a soul, not even the wind."

She looked across the huge warehouse-like room, and saw, between the metal lathes and the motors, six short rows of folding chairs facing a small portable blackboard—Virgil, without one wall or a desk for the teacher. She was almost there with less than a minute to spare before she could turn to Robert with her squeaky asking: "You mean a real boat—on water?"

He was annoyed. "What else? And don't think mine is any ordinary cabin cruiser."

"Oh? An outboard? Or is it a skiff? I'd rather have a dory, but I'm no good at rowing."

"Susie, Susie, you're putting me on. You don't really think

that. If you do you're in for a big surprise. This boat has everything, even a galley. You'll flip when you see it." They were nearing Virgil and a handful of students; he came very close and spoke even lower: "Now, don't forget; Science Club hasn't started yet so you'll have all day Saturday. I'll pick you up at ten."

The bell was sounding; he was hurrying to his seat in the second row, with nothing but a pleased smile for her weak "I don't know."

Automation came on, to carry her through; still, she had to struggle to keep her mind on Virgil. The homework Ter had typed caused her to think of him. What would he say to such a kooky deal—strange boy, strange boat, no chaperone; she was tangling herself; she'd prefer a real sailor to a chaperone. Did Robert know that even shallow Lake St. Clair could be treacherous, and especially at this time of year when sudden gales and squalls were common?

Her grandmother would think her a disobedient little fool even to consider a ride on dirty St. Clair in a boat she'd never seen with a boy she scarcely knew. She tried to get rid of her grandmother, but all that drilling in respect for water and seamanship came back. She had no memory of when it began: no swimming alone; no getting into strange boats; no going out with friendly tourist families unless a local seaman was aboard; and as if they did it on purpose to give weight to her grandmother's words, each summer a handful of tourists drowned themselves along the coast.

She fought her way back to Aeneas. The old boy had troubles, but at least he was a man instead of a girl in Eden Hills High where if you turned down, for no reason except you didn't want to go, a date with a boy, word got around and you might never be asked again—by any boy.

"Susan Schnitzer, quit telling yourself lies. You've made yourself believe two whoppers. First, you knew you'd go when Robert told you who was coming. Angus. You're going because he'll be there. He's probably Katy's boy friend. Chances are he knows nothing of boats, but—."

She wondered if she'd spoken aloud; a cautious glance around showed all eyes on Virgil now being murdered by a stumbler who made you wonder how he'd got through first-year Latin. She tried to follow, but her thoughts slid away: would Robert really drive her home? If so, why hadn't he waited until they were alone in the car before asking her to come on that so-secret boat ride?

Answers to her wonderings came when Robert, after meeting her at Music Storage and taking her violin, had walked with her to his car. Two boys waited by it, regular riders, she gathered; one a strange stranger, the other a familiar stranger—or at least she thought she'd seen him somewhere. Their names as Robert introduced them slid in and out her ears and made no contact with her brain. Seated in the car up front with Robert, the boys in back, IBM came on to remind her the tall, tanned one with the nice smile was a big wheel of some kind; she'd heard him speak in Assembly. His name? His name? What was—?

Robert was asking a "Pryor" if he had really decided to give up debating.

"I decided last year when they handed out the topic for the interscholastics," he answered with something in his voice the words didn't say.

She thought she knew him then: Pryor, a real big wheel, son of bigger wheels on The Hill, Solid Substance and Free Enterprise, big in the automobile business, big in politics, big in Detroit's social life. Or were they *the* Pryors? Be fun to ask. Why bother? He, like the other boy, was only a nice bit of homogenized, pasteurized boy.

Their exit drive, Number Three E, was so choked with cars that by the time Robert was able to ooze into the main drive, her watch said five of four. Biking was much more efficient, nor did it cause fumes to pollute the world. That was all she could think of to drop into the silence, and her guardian angel kept her from saying that. She chewed over the feeling in Pryor's voice not put into words. "Robert, wouldn't it be better for the students if you did a series of articles on their rights to choose debating topics

199

—and other things—instead of trying to persuade them to dress in Establishment Style?" That too clear, too precise voice was her own.

Pryor yelled: "Yea, yea." The other boy clapped.

They then began to ask silent Robert about his "crusade"; and didn't bother to hide their laughter, mixed at times with sharp—"needling," her father would have called it. She thought Robert was put out. She must keep her tongue on a rigid diet, words counted and weighed.

She stared at the car stopped next to theirs. She, Susan Schnitzer, could learn from the girl there how to keep a boy interested. Well, Robert was plenty interested in fending off the questions and comments she had started, but he was not as happy as the boy in that other driver's seat, with the girl almost in his lap, one arm around his neck, hand stroking his shoulder. Her other hand held a cigarette shared by the two of them, puff by puff. And with all that, she could still say things to make him laugh; she must be whispering as she kissed his ear; his shoulders were shaking.

"Make him see the light, Susie—if it's not too late, and he's not already part of The Establishment, the part that keeps its fist on the school paper."

"If you don't like the way the school paper's run, you ought to have stayed with it last year instead of resigning in a huff," Robert cut in, his voice less smooth than usual.

"I resigned in protest at their policy," Pryor said. "To that outfit—I mean the administration—desegregation or peace, or family planning, or anything that might cause what they call 'political controversy' is out. Also out is any truth or complaint that might give the school a bad name—the fights all over, the small size of the library compared to the space for football and parking, the liquor and drugs that find their way into lockers— and—aw heck. Don't mind me. I tried last year to get an article published on the miseries of lunch: only twenty minutes to do everything from washing to eating—after trying to find something edible in that mess."

Susie smiled and forgot to watch the cars around her for looking at Pryor.

Thursday Latin finished, she made for the door. The third full week of school almost gone; that was something; the week of her "illness" when she could not bike, almost gone; that was something, too. Yet, this meant four days come twilight since Ter had gone; no word from him; and no mention, that she could find, in either the Detroit or suburban papers, of the return of the money.

Where was Ter—Chicago or Canada? sick or well? He could let her know. Ter was only part of "this gritty time" when the wind blew sand between your teeth; worse this year than ever; more things to bug you: the psychologist from whom she had heard nothing more; the visit Friday after school to Dr. Laughton; this dread of him was a new and miserable feeling, but then she had never before lied to him. Would he learn from blood tests or simply by looking at her that she had never been sick?

That upcoming dinner with the Weatherfords could be much worse than she had first imagined. Only lately she had learned Lady Macbeth had attended the football prom with Pryor. Would that sweet, innocent thing wonder aloud before the elder Schnitzers where their daughter had been on the night of the first football prom? She'd better get an answer ready; and should she tell Robert? Their tales—in case he had to tell one—better coincide. Thoughts of Robert reminded her of another future misery—the boat ride.

She gave an impatient head shake. She wouldn't think of *that*—without remembering Angus would be there. This was one of her grittier days when all good things and people seemed left behind and only bad lay ahead. Home in her attic, she'd feel better listening to Pete Seeger and—. A body bigger than her own bumped her from behind as a binder jabbed one shoulder.

In spite of leaving Latin in a rush, she was being smothered in the school-is-out tide of E-Building she had hoped to avoid. "Think of something nice," she told herself. "Imagine these bumping bodies are spruce trees and you are walking through your grandmother's woods." Her body wouldn't join hands with her head: her feet kept remembering, and hunting the softness of moss in the twilight under the old, wide-limbed spruces. Ferns brushed your knees as you picked your way between the gray trunks with their gray, dead lower limbs decorated with garlands and knots of pale green crinkled moss; but over your head were the green, living branches, so thick you couldn't see the sky. Now and then you stooped to pick up a cone that seemed to want picking up, or measure your height against a fern. Now, you leaped the brook, deep in the black earth and silent in summer.

Her legs, surrounded by legs all trying to move, refused to leap. Instead, careful not to send her feet treading on heels, they worked their way to the court entrance.

There, she was almost alone. She made of the gray-cement-floored-and-walled court her grandmother's lawn she crossed on the rounds-of-wood path to the kitchen porch. She could see the late-blooming roses, the old stump aflame with red and yellow nasturtiums climbed all over it; the phlox in spite of their beauty, their begging of you to linger as you hurried past because you wanted to walk between the dahlias that, heavy with flowers, bent over the path; red and yellow, white and lavender, their falling petals made spots of brightness on your shoes as you walked between them. You could not hurry past although they made you sad because when the dahlia petals began to fall it was almost time for you to go back to your father's house.

The Here-Today-and-Gone-Tomorrow rose by the kitchen porch never made you sad; its great shiny red pips were almost as nice as the wide pink-purple flowers that bloomed all—. "Susie, you're not forgetting it's Thursday; no orchestra, so you don't go to Music Storage."

Robert's Middle Western United States voice and words destroyed the flowers. "But I have to go to my locker," she said, her feet no longer on a cross section of red spruce, but gray cement. She listened as he told her, with apologies, that he not only had to go to his locker, but also had to see a "faculty member" connected with the school paper.

He was gone to leave her wondering. Why did he say "faculty member" instead of teacher; or why didn't he say "big fist" for that "guiding hand" on his miniskirt articles? She couldn't make him out. She was certain he was anything but wild about Susan Schnitzer. Yet, he went out of his way to be seen in her company, even walking with her to and from orchestra and Latin—when he could catch up with her. Why?

Time to ask a question about Miss Schnitzer. Why, since there were so many things she didn't like about this puzzle of a boy, did she promise to go with him where she didn't want to go —on that boat? Be honest, Miss Schnitzer. You keep remembering Angus will be there. Also, don't you think it's kind of nice to be dating a Big Wheel from The Village? Your few schoolmates —if you can call them that—are impressed; your parents more so; even Brandon is less rude to you.

Automation had taken her through a back exit and onto a cinder path that led to Parking Lot C. She left the crowded walkway to cut across the Board of Education's version of grass —chiefly weeds killed by herbicides, then moved close to the ground. Now wondering if The Establishment would actually force Angus to cut his hair, she absent-mindedly picked up a piece of litter, a pale gray sheet of coarse typing paper. She had walked only a few steps further, when two more sheets of the same paper came on the light wind to settle nearby. She crumpled one without looking at it, reached for the other, but stopped, staring. She had noticed only the blank backs of the other two.

She was now looking at some kind of picture, with a few words in large print under it. She picked it up, looked an instant, then crumpled it. She had seen a charcoal black silhouette with thick protruding lips, hairy naked arms around a white neck, the white head thrown back in struggle. The paper was gray enough so the head of the white woman had shown clearly; but not too dark to smudge the big black words: "Do you want this? Keep them separate as God intended and Christ preached. Keep Eden Hills High free of Reds and Blacks."

What a cruddy, cruddy world, the human-being part. Nice to be a Canada goose and fly away from it; no, a herring in the sea where you'd see none of it. Something brushed her lightly on one shoulder; another sheet was sailing in. They were all over. Most appeared to be in the parking lot; before school was out some dirty soul had gone up and down, scattering; more and more blowing near her on the lawn.

She put down her binder and lunch kit, then went to work, picking up the sheets; clean, but they seemed to dirty her hands. So thick, she never lifted her head as she hurried from one to the next. Her hands were overflowing when a large plastic trash-can bag, held open by two hands, came under her down-bent face. Startled, she looked up to see the sack was held by a boy in orchestra, a first violinist whose name she didn't know.

Silently, she emptied her hands, then moved on to others. She stopped suddenly to study the printing on a sheet. Brandon, at his father's urging, had made and spread Universal-Weed-and-Insect-Killing literature on the same size sheets, hand printed as were these. She crumpled the sheet. Mean of her to blame Brandon. The E in his type was nicked at the bottom; nor did the H have a thin place in the middle as had his.

Her next load went into a trash can bag held open by an old man, so bald his head glinted in the sun. "Thank you. Thank you," he said. He seemed familiar; some teacher she supposed she'd seen around. Minutes later, she straightened to look over the lawn; there were no more sheets within hands' reach. Now, she saw only people, a dozen or more of pupils and teachers, some with bags, some with handfuls of paper, others with only a sheet or so, but all like herself looking for more.

She thought of the Negro in orchestra. He drove to school. His car in some parking lot might be covered with the dirty sheets; since she didn't know his car or which lot it was on, she'd have to check them all. She began with the closest, but instead of hate sheets, found students hunting like herself. Among them were Pryor and Burlingame, each with a stuffed sack, and the news that the parking lots were clean; everything was clean.

She was waiting by the car with the boys, who had long since returned, before Robert came. She looked at him and wished she could say she preferred walking home to riding with a boy grinning like a fool when she wanted to cry over this miserable business. His "dialogue" with the big fist must have gone very well.

She didn't ask; neither did the boys who sat as glumly silent as she. Robert at last wanted to know whose funeral they had attended. "That of common decency," Pryor answered, and told of the hate-sheet shower.

Robert nodded, still happy. "Mr. Stahl and I heard what had happened, so we went out to check the front side of A-Building. We could talk there as well as in his office; not that he had much to say. He liked my piece."

"Shall we cheer or clap hands for your successful campaign against miniskirts?" The boy who almost never spoke had spoken.

She remembered his name was Burlingame; he also lived in The Village. He didn't seem to be such a big wheel at school, but his parents were bigger than wheels. His father was more like an earth-mover motor for one of the Big Automotive Three. Strange that the Hill People with all their position and wealth, and the money wasn't new, should have sons like Pryor and Burlingame. Did they have to keep their mouths shut at home as did she? No, at least not Burlingame. "Dad said that Negroes-moving-in tale was all a lie, started by a real-estate company to make the white fools in such a hurry to get out and sell before the price goes way down, the company can buy almost new homes at low prices. Negroes of course don't show up; so the company sells the same homes at a high price."

Pryor said: "Ugh. Bank robbing would be more honest."

"Robert, instead of miniskirts, why don't you do some articles for the school paper on the really indecent things? This hate-sheet shower and the lies about—."

Robert had interrupted with a groan, and disregarding the cheers of his riders, said: "Susie, Susie, we've been over this road before. Free choice of debating topics you wanted the other day. You must realize the policy of the school paper is never to get tangled in politics."

"Politics?" she asked. "That hate sheet?"

Robert only nodded, but Pryor answered: "To The Establishment anything from civil liberties to peace that could cause what they call controversy is out. Worse, the decent side gets smeared as 'Communist-inspired,' or at least 'leftist leaning.'

"In Eden Hills High that computer curtain hides a million dirty spots; but mention of one in the school paper would show the school was not perfect. There's lots of money here; criticize the school and you go knocking holes in the Free Enterprise System. So, keep all ugly stories where ugliness belongs—among the poor, the Negroes, the goons, and the grease in inner Detroit, or some white suburb of little boxes."

"I'd give a year's allowance to hear you say all that on the platform in Assembly," Burlingame said.

Pryor nodded. "Wouldn't it be nice, though. I might just do it the next time I introduce a speaker. —But don't hold off the allowance for that. Try to get a few months in advance; I'll see what I can do, and we'll have another underground paper." He turned to her. "I'll bet Susie would help on the editorial side."

"And money, too. That is, a bit," she added. An underground paper, something, she supposed, that spoke the truth, would be a good way to get rid of the Lans money. It was still hidden in the attic because she'd not yet had a chance to put any of it into her secret savings account with a Detroit bank. She'd have to do it bit by bit not to arouse suspicion; in the meantime suppose snooping Brandon found it? Explaining her attic quarters would be nothing to thinking up a whopper on how she'd come by the money.

Robert had switched on. She ought to listen. One nice thing about riding with the boys was you learned a lot. She had not until this week known of student vandalism—kept secret by The Establishment, that also kept its raids on student lockers secret. Now, she gathered from Robert's talk there had last spring been an underground paper; a "filthy sheet" to hear him tell it. "Imagine Susie even reading four-letter words, not to mention writing them."

She thought of *La Jumente Verte*, bought because she had enjoyed a children's book by the same author, but said nothing. Burlingame mourned: "The Powers got wind of it, confiscated and burned every copy before one pupil could see it."

"We did have some wild seniors, bright though. Trouble was they wanted to shock more than enlighten—I guess. But you'll never make me believe The Powers burned our sheet for the four-letter words our crazy editor put in; there was too much truth. What if parents of failing kids had learned Mrs. Pickett was fired because she couldn't in honesty give a football star a passing grade. Or—."

Robert interrupted Pryor with: "Gossip, that was."

"Gossip my eye." Pryor was red-faced. "Three of us interviewed the woman at different times. She wasn't sick. That tale about an extended sick leave put out by the school—when we asked—well, you can't call it anything but a dirty lie."

"Sh-sh. No need to tell Susie's mother." Robert said.

Susie, looking at Pryor, absorbed in what he was saying, had not noticed they had reached the Schnitzer drive, decorated by her pretty mother with a pretty basket gathering chrysanthemums from the driveway border. She smiled and waved; and continued to watch, Susie suspected, as Robert let her out at the side entrance. Quite a sight, she guessed; Robert with all the flags of his manners unfurled, leaping out to help her as if she were an old, old lady with six pieces of heavy baggage. And today she did not even have a violin.

She had finished tea with Lulu in the kitchen, and had started to her quarters, when here came the Popsicle Queen to let her know how closely Susan Schnitzer had been watched. Her mother put on that old, old record—her daughter's appearance. The wording unchanged since last spring, volume no greater, but more urgency in the song.

The beginning was the same: "Susie, darling, this is one of your beautiful days, so please don't think I'm criticizing, but—." That *but* was a great big tow-truck bringing in a block-long line of disabled cars: her hair; didn't she think it was time to start having regular appointments with a good hair stylist, not all year, "—if you don't want to, but at least until you have it in good shape after a summer's neglect at camp. And, darling, your skirt; isn't it awfully long for the present school styles?" Not that she cared for those "awful mini-minis, but you could wear something a little livelier, not necessarily a hot color, but one of those nice plaids."

And what was she wearing to Robert's picnic; slacks, her mother imagined, would be the expected thing; but did Susie have any decent ones? When Lulu took her for a check-up tomorrow after school, if she had any time left at all she must hunt a nice pair of slacks.

Susie, knowing she would wear a pair of beloved, torn-off-at-the-knees, salt-water-faded, blue jeans, assured her she had "decent walking shorts." She then put on her own record: A clothing allowance such as her own would stretch only so far; furthermore what with five academic subjects, gym, driver ed. and orchestra on alternate days, she had no time.

"You should have plenty of time. You're not taking one thing outside of school, and I do feel you should at least be taking more dancing lessons, not to mention music, and more horseback riding, or tennis, or both. And all the wonderful youth activities in this neighborhood; our church alone has a lot to offer; there's even a 4H group if you don't want the Girl Scouts."

She realized she was getting off the subject and returned to Susie's appearance. "One has to take time to dress properly. Charlotte not only found the time, but long before she was old enough to go to school had loved going to her hair stylist and the beauty shop. I know school—. School; —I had completely forgotten. And I meant to tell you first thing. A few minutes before you came, the nicest, politest boy telephoned you. —Oh, dear, I didn't get his full name—Terence was his first.

"I thought you would know because he was absent today; he said the Virgil class was small, and apologized for bothering you; but he said that if anybody knew whether or not he'd translated a certain passage correctly you would. I was so flattered. Do you know he either read or recited—in Latin mind you —the passage to me, as if he thought I understood Latin. First I think I've heard since high school. Might be all right for you to call him back after while. One doesn't often meet such a polite youngster."

Susie could only say: "Yes, mother," while she tried to hide her puzzlement. She remembered no Terence in Latin roll-call, nor had she noticed any missing. —Whatever ailed her. That polite Terence, charming her mother, flattering her with spouted Latin, had been Ter. He had remembered her. He was all right. She turned from her mother to hide her face; all that joy might be showing.

No need. Her mother was looking toward the pantry door as she said: "Yes, Lulu."

"The telephone for Susie. It sounds like that same English girl that called you a few times last year," she added to Susie.

Angie, that would be; her Scots housekeeper Sheridan had put the call through. She started to dash, remembered she should not be dashing for mere girls—not any more. She forced herself to walk slowly and thank Lulu on the way, even taking time to remark she wished it were Terence.

Lulu gone into the kitchen, pantry door closing, she leaped into the booth. In another instant she was listening to Angie, worried, asking all in a breath: "Is everything all right, Susie? Did the call from that crazy Ter—I understand your mother answered—arouse any suspicions?"

She remembered to ask: "Ter?"

"Of course you wouldn't know who Ter was. How stupid of me; he's your godfather's oldest child and only son—his real name is Ferruccio." Didn't Susie remember that school boy in Canada who had been too sick to come to her grandmother's party? One reason he had so wanted to come was to meet Susie; he'd heard so much about her—but nobody had expected him to try to ring her up as soon as he and Lans reached a place close enough so the call would not be long distance. It was still dangerous.

Susie assured her Ter's call had caused no trouble, then, hating herself, wanted to know if he had changed schools or why wasn't he in school? She then listened to an account of Ter's cold that had brought on a throat infection so severe he'd telephoned Lans who had come for him last Saturday, then kept him one night in a motel because he was too sick for the drive home. Only by today had Lans felt Ter was able to return to school, but he was still so worried he had driven the boy to Windsor rather than have him take a plane from Chicago.

Oh, somehow, some way they must get Susie and Ter together; such a handsome boy, the tall, thin type, but not effeminate; making a wonderful scholastic record, and so unspoiled, so thoughtful. One reason he'd left in such a rush was he wanted time for Lans to drive out to Riverside, so Ter could check to see if he'd left her grandmother's place neat and straight; he also had wanted to leave her house key with a neighbor, gone when he left.

"Wonderful," Susie cried. "I mean," she quickly amended, "he must be a wonderful boy." Angie's news meant Ter had taken back her grandmother's—no, her father's—gun. And certainly he had returned the money; the papers may not even have bothered to use the story; or she could have overlooked it.

Angie was now hoping Susie could go sailing with her and Joe Saturday. Susie explained she'd promised some kids at school she'd go picnicking with them—if the weather was good; if not she ought to stay home this once and get organized; homework, clothes, orchestra practice, everything needed attention. All those lies to Angie hurt; and worse, in a way, they gave her a greasy, no-good feeling. At least she could tell the truth when she told her how sorry she was she couldn't go sailing—this weekend.

The edges of her sorrows for the lost sail and missing Ter's telephone call were dulled by the thought that Ter had remembered her; and more important, all was well with him, at least money- and health-wise. You couldn't help but wonder though, what poor old Lans had done and said when he learned his son was a bank robber.

It was late, with homework finished, before she remembered

the "gritty time" that had so grabbed her at school. Then, she'd planned to listen to a lot of sad songs and maybe have a good cry. Imagine! She wasn't a baby any more, to carry reminders of her grandmother's world in Nova Scotia, so she could touch them when she felt the need. Now, she kept such things as shells and dried Here-Today-and-Gone-Tomorrow rose pips in her secret-secret attic drawer where the Lans money was.

Miserable deals were coming up, but she'd pull through them all. At least the going was not as rough as say in the last year of junior high. Her parents had seemed determined she should take every out-of-school lesson, join every group the neighborhood offered. When she wasn't in after-school dancing or something else supposed to improve her, she was messing around with Girl Scouts or with a church young-people's outfit. There'd been no time left for Susan Schnitzer to use alone as she pleased.

She was smiling as she rubbed a pale, sea-smoothed sand dollar between her palms. The nicest one, not too big, but big and sturdy enough to keep in her purse. The little sea urchin shell she had fortified with plaster had a nice prickly feel; she would also keep that in her purse along with one small spruce cone. She stopped suddenly; she didn't remember opening the drawer, or getting ready for bed, or anything but thinking she wasn't a baby any more.

She shrugged, then continued to fondle with hands and eyes the treasures in the drawer: many varieties of sea shells, from the long thin razors to fat little "pennywinkles"; varieties of seaweed and moss, small pieces of drift wood, several sand dollars and sea urchins, pebbles, along with reminders of the fields and woods—cones, dried flowers, land and tree moss, a sprig of hackmatack, dahlia petals, and rose pips. When she closed the drawer she had, along with shells and cones, a still-red Here-To-day-and-Gone-Tomorrow rose pip, bits of driftwood and rock-weed.

She didn't really need them any more, but when foul weather settled in at home or school, something nice to touch could remind you there were other worlds with weather always good for sailing.

Next day at school, she touched nothing from the sea or woods; good sailing with the looked-forward-to landfalls all there: Angus in orchestra and again at lunch; Katy, too; a one hundred on that chemistry quiz; and at last Lulu with the station wagon, and happy to be out of the House of Usher, though the trip for her included grocery shopping.

It was not until she was in Dr. Laughton's waiting room that she, pretending to hunt something in her purse, fingered the sand dollar. The doctor was so wise; he would know she'd never been sick; and what would she—. His office door was opening; he was smiling at her.

She tried to return his smile and down her shivers. She was glad he examined her at once; gave her an excuse to say nothing while he looked and listened. The throat examination was worst of all; he would see; he would see; nothing, nothing.

It was over with only congratulations from him on what a fine patient she was; the infection had not left so much as a fresh scar. Satisfied with her body, he left it for her mind, with more congratulations on that Outstanding Junior Girl business—she wondered how he learned such. He hoped she was still interested in medicine and medical research.

Relief made her talkative, and he was the only mortal to whom she could speak of her one big dream. "I'd like to be a doctor, and work with children; try—well, not just to cure their bodies, but hope to help them into happiness—if possible." He was listening, closely. She felt foolish. "I don't know. I might try only research. There are so few women doctors."

"Some day when she gets back, I'll introduce you to one of the best doctors I know—Dr. Marta Thorberg. She's also a wonderful person, now in a civilian Vietnamese hospital; she works chiefly with burned children. Let me see, I went to her send-off party back in June. She'll be gone at least two years, but meeting her will be worth the wait."

"I certainly hope I can get to know her," Susie said, and meant it. "Not just because she's a great doctor; but, well, people who help other people they don't even know are kind of—rare."

"She's a rare one all right," he said, getting up. "You couldn't know how rare she is unless you knew her life: married while she was still in medical school; her husband a resident in surgery —that hospital didn't pay too well—then. A child came along; she dropped out of school to work at a well-paying but hard job. Her husband trained until he could practice; there was a divorce, and for some reason nobody could understand the courts gave the child—Robert must have been five or six years old at the time—to the father. Come to think of it, you might know her son, Robert Hedrick, a senior, I believe, in your high school."

Fortunately for her he was rising, his signal, or so she had always thought, her time was up. "Everybody knows Robert Hedrick," she told him. "He's on the school paper, The Student Governing Body, and oh a lot of things. I do thank you for telling me of his mother. She'll be an inspiration for me."

"She is to all of us," he said. "Now, don't stay away too long. I should see you as usual early in December."

Outdoors, she crossed streets to walk around two blocks with no wonder on why or where she walked. Robert couldn't be as priggish as she had thought; not with that kind of mother; and how could she get him to tell about his mother? She wanted nothing prying or personal, but something about her work and her life in Vietnam, the kind of stories Iggy loved to tell about his father. The world was quite a nice place after all; everything all right with Ter; and come to think of it she should be grateful to Robert; if he were not dating her the Popsicle Queen and Bismarck would go into one long nag about how she "should become part of the community, and use the opportunities your parents afford you for self-improvement." This meant joining a lot of cruddy organizations you couldn't care less about.

She remembered she was supposed to meet Lulu at the "real butcher's" where Lulu was to buy, and charge, "the finest prime beef roast, standing rib, I can find, or the best steaks—they'd be close to three dollars the pound—for these people coming Sunday. They must be something."

She found Lulu buying prime standing rib, but shaking her head over the price. They then shopped here and there for picnic supplies, but thoughts of neither Saturday's picnic nor Sunday's dinner could ruin the happy afternoon.

Next morning as she drove away with Robert, much of her

distaste for and dread of the boating trip returned. Still, it was nice to be able to visit with Katy, Angus, and Iggy in back; the Negro yet to be picked up. She had not expected Iggy, too young and happy for this mess. Perhaps the good times would hold, and the weather not do what she feared. Much too warm for early October, a thunder storm with squalls was likely in the afternoon about the time they got well into Erie—or wherever they were going. Why worry on the weather? She was a good swimmer; there were on any boat life-jackets, preservers, and a ship-to-shore telephone for distress calls. Yet no matter how pleasant the ride, it wouldn't help that greasy feeling she got each time she thought of her grandmother—she'd never be able to tell her of this any more than of Ter; and keeping quiet was a kind of lie.

The car had stopped to pick up Ben. Dressed in faded blue jeans with a roll of what looked to be foul-weather gear on one arm, picnic hamper on the other, he looked very much the sailor, as did Angus. While he and Robert stowed his load in the trunk, she looked at what she could see of his home; for, surrounded by trees and shrubs, set well back from the street, parts showed only here and there. Still, enough to let her know it was even nicer than she had expected since the afternoon she had learned from Robert and his riders that Ben lived in the home built by his grandfather Holmes, who had in turn lived for many years in a home built by his father. The Holmeses, coming from New England, had been among the early farmer-settlers; always buying more of the then-cheap land, they had through their generations held it until the current wave of subdividers bought the adjoining farms, ruined their world, and offered unheard of prices for the Holmes land.

They had clung to the big old brick house; with its white woodwork, wide eaves, many gables and verandahs, on a lawn three or four times as large as those on either side. Old maples and hemlocks with plenty of shrubbery and flowers, and though there was nothing new or fancy, not even a swimming pool, the house was still the grand old lady among the new "custom-built professional" homes that surrounded it.

The new houses, in spite of living in close togetherness on

undersized lots, had a lonesome air that seemed to touch the silent street. Why? It was no different from other middle class subdivisions in the United States where children watched TV or went to group activities instead of playing outdoors. Then she saw the FOR SALE signs on the front lawns on either side the Negro's lawn. There was another in front of the house across the street. The three houses looked to be empty.

The Negro was sitting down beside her. She smiled at him as she touched the sand dollar in a raincoat pocket. This could bring trouble if somebody like that Negro-counting woman saw and told her father.

The car was stopped again, now in the right-turn lane, close to the curb, as Robert waited for traffic to thin at the intersection. Susie watched four children come running up the walk, and suddenly halt by the car as if it had been a stop-sign. The nearest was a small girl with blonde hair in silvery rollers. She had not known the child was so close until her spit struck the partly rolled down window by the Negro. Her shrill cry of "Nigger-lovers, Nigger-lovers" taken up by the other three seemed loud enough to bring people running to their doors.

Susie lurched as Robert rushed the turn; she scarcely noticed; she could only think of the Negro, watch him as he reached for the box of cleaning tissue. She turned her glance to the road ahead. Was she a ghoul to watch torture? She would tell herself it was only the car window he had to wipe; spit had not struck his face as spit had struck her own a long time ago.

It was Iggy, pretending he had seen nothing, who was the first to speak. "Did everyone see how The Primitive set off her gift—two bottles of wine for my father?"

Robert groaned, and wondered if he shouldn't stop and try to hide the wine in the trunk. He was seeing tomorrow's headlines: "Carload of Teen-Agers Foiled in Alcoholic Orgy."

Didn't Robert remember, Iggy wanted to know? They had carried wine on buses many times since Robert had started baby-sitting for him when he was six and Robert eleven. Each fall when The Primitive bottled her last year's wine so that she might have kegs for the new, she used a different set of labels

215

designed and furnished by Iggy's father. She sent in return a labeled bottle or so to let him see the look of his labels on the wine.

The words went in and out of Susie's head. She had during the past week learned that Iggy lived with his mother and her second husband; his real father, an artist, lived in Detroit. Iggy, she guessed, was going to see him. Did it matter? Would that spit gnaw holes in the Negro the rest of his life? Had there been hate-sheet showers in his neighborhood—and nobody to clean them up?

She grew aware of pain, both in her hands and on her lap. She would not look. She knew. It wasn't enough to make a fist to twist and clench a thumb, but both hard fists were pushing and boring into the flesh above her knees. The Negro was turning toward her. "I like your home," she said, and wished she could smile. "It makes me think of ones I see in Canada, where they don't tear down everything in a hurry."

He only nodded as he reached around for The Primitive's package Iggy was handing to him.

"And she calls it grass sack, the covering," Iggy said.

The covering was burlap, so old, parts were almost the color of a weather-worn canvas sail, gray-mottled. Tied with ribbons of plaited, greeny-brown cattail grass, the package, she decided, was autumn; fastened to the ties or worked into the burlap were small clusters of wild rose pips, little acorns, a hickory nut with the shell curled back, and half-opened beech and hazelnut burrs.

She did not clench her hands again. A package tied with old sail, bits of rope and cordage fished from the sea, would be a pretty thing; you could decorate it with moss and rockweed, and here and there put pennywinkle shells, sea urchins, and sand—. Had she with those clenching fists broken the sand dollar in her pocket?

The sand dollar was unbroken; her purse had slid to the floor. The movement of picking it up roused her enough to realize she was in a place she loved—Detroit, "my kind aunt." The city could never be as alive, as exciting as Montreal; nor quaint like Quebec, an old great-aunt you loved to visit. Certainly Detroit was not as good for people-watching as even dear little Halifax, and could not compare with Edinburgh or London or Paris or Milan or Palermo or Mexico City, or many places she had visited with her grandmother on the yearly shopping and educational trip. Yet, whatever Detroit might lack, she was real and alive after the freezing chills of the ersatz world of Eden Hills.

She tried not to think on that one time—the mouth spitting her gift of a caramel back at her, the taste of dirty mud—and instead to remember Detroit's kindness when she was part of her grandmother's home. Later, in those first awful years with Bismarck and The Popsicle Queen when often she wandered alone for hours on the excuse of "reading at that big main library," Detroit was still kind—and always interesting.

She pitied, not just the Negro, but the others in the car. They'd had to spend most or all of the years behind them in if not Eden Hills some other deadly dull suburb, where even the voices had a grating sameness. They had never eaten at that wonderful little cafeteria on Eastern Market, or spent hours in the Museum of Art, the Historical Museum, other museums and walks and woods on Belle Isle, the public libraries; and when you were really lonesome, wanting smiles and peoples' faces, there was the great store on Woodward where you could shop for anything from school supplies to a mink coat—that with Angie.

Such a mini, mini-soul she had; so busy hunting nice memories to comfort her poor self, she had forgotten the Negro. He had no sand dollar, and did he have even one nice memory of life away from home? She was also being rude, going off on her own private cloud while the others talked; Iggy now: "You'll remember, won't you, Robert, if anyone should ask? I'm in the Detroit Historical Museum hunting material for a paper, or possibly the main library or the Museum of Art, so it will not be my fault if the Soameses can't reach me by telephone at my step-grandmother's. I'll get over there around five or so, but I expect she'll be going out—ah, the bakery—I wish—oh, heck."

Susie glanced back and saw the Mexican bakery, where she still went with Angie to buy, among other goodies, one of her favorites, the large, flat cookies, never sticky or too sweet. She

217

had not until now noticed exactly where they were, partly because everything was torn up and blasted around for another
expressway. Still, Robert knew exactly what turns to take so as to
come into a quiet street of old homes and big trees where
dark-skinned barefooted children played. They seemed happy,
and color-blind, too, the dears. Robert drove slowly, but not one,
after getting out of the way, so much as stared at the Negro.
They'd never make it up the golden stairs and into a subdivision
of "professional homes."

The car stopped. Iggy sprang out, crying: "There he is." He
ran, but was scarcely across the walk, before a tall man who had
run down a flight of porch steps was clasping his shoulders.

Susie came alive. How would it be to have a man like that
for a father? Unpasteurized, unlabeled, unhomogenized, no IBM
card could ever measure him. He reminded her a little of those
Mexican men riding their beautiful horses amid a jingle of silver
and creak of leather. No, he was no kin of them, none at all; they
dressed in fancy outfits and rode with the hope of being seen. He
didn't care; yet he was more handsome than Betto barefooted in
a sailboat. Sockless, he wore huaraches, a perfect match for the
faded, paint-streaked blue jeans, and the coarse linen shirt,
flapping as he ran, clean and freshly ironed.

You saw as he came closer something of Iggy's bouncing
happiness, but you felt that in him—now—it only came and
went. He wasn't as old as her father, and even younger than Mr.
Soames; yet, in his life he'd logged a lot of mileage, and not all of
it in smooth, safe ships' lanes; the threads of lightness in his
longish hair were not sun bleach, but gray.

She was so taken up with him, she didn't notice they were
being introduced until he said: "I know you, giver of the smiling
pig. I thank you." His accent, though slight, was pleasant as his
voice, and his smile a real smile just for her. Made you feel that
anything or anybody who mattered to Iggy was important to
him.

He was pleased with The Primitive's package; no faking, as
he said. "I'm afraid we'll never open this, Iggy; more art here
than in a lot of stuff so labeled."

He invited them into his house; he had finished work for the day, he said, and would enjoy their company. He'd cook lunch for them or take them to Little Mexico.

"We have stuff for a picnic, but it would be nice to eat in your—."

Robert, with no apology, interrupted Angus to invite Iggy and his father to come picnicking with them; but not a word of where the picnic would be.

Susie tried to hide her disappointment as she joined in the round of good-byes, warm and friendly, with the man and Iggy lingering on his porch to wave and watch them go.

Robert drove around the corner as Katy said: "He thinks Iggy is still a little boy."

"In a way he is," Robert agreed. He drew a long relieved sigh. "Well, everything was all right—this time."

"And how many times have you found things wrong? Wasn't it years and years ago, when you hadn't let him know Iggy could make a sneak visit, that you found him half drunk with a strange woman?" Angus asked with some sharpness.

"He was so stoned he didn't know me; and wouldn't have known Iggy. And as for the woman, it wasn't her strangeness I objected to," Robert said, sliding into a parking place.

"But don't you think he will be—sober—most of the time from now on?" Katy wondered. "He's selling his work, and getting accepted. Mom was saying the other day that art students were coming into the library trying to find reproductions of his work and learn about him. So why can't Iggy live with him? They'd both be a lot happier. Or at least let them have vacations together. The way they did before my family left for California and Iggy was little."

"You're way behind on your gossip, girl," Robert said as he cut the motor. "His old man ruined that nice setup when he sneaked him off to Mexico. And a grand time they had. He began painting as he had never painted; and Iggy got healthy again on goat's milk, tortillas, and love. But in a little over a year the Soameses' detectives found them. He came back to the States, but was only allowed visiting privileges with Iggy in his mother's house. —Officially that is. I was baby-sitting for Iggy. While his father painted the pond and everything about it, Iggy and I explored it. The Soameses saw the makings of a great biologist in Iggy. —Look, we're supposed to be having a little snack. Ben brought enough sandwiches to hold us until we get to the real picnic on the boat."

Robert and Ben went for the sandwich basket in the trunk while the others listened to Katy. "Ugh, I am behind on my gossip. I remember when we moved everyone was talking about the affairs of the beautiful, talented, intelligent, well-bred, but not so wealthy, Miss Elizabeth Granville who at nineteen or twenty, while studying Spanish, or was it art, at the University of Mexico, had married a poor art student with the wrong kind of name. She and he with their cute little boy came visiting her parents."

"You're still behind in your gossip, that was before she became Mrs. Soames," Angus said. "Let me quote a well known divine: 'It was the influence of a fortune hunting, Communistically inclined Mexican of the lower classes, plus existentialism and the loose moral climate of Mexico, coupled with the giddiness of youth of that pure and innocent girl.' Unquote."

"Please remind your divine that Miss Elizabeth Granville had no fortune, and that her so-called spell of giddiness lasted a long time. Iggy was past three, or even older, before she met Mr. Soames. If she hadn't loved Iggy's father, she could have had an abortion. And all of Eden Hills will forgive a discreet abortion, but not an indiscreet marriage."

"Nice speech, Katy," Robert said, as he put the Negro's basket of sandwiches onto the front seat.

Susie figured Iggy's mother could have used the coil or some other means of birth control if she had not wanted a baby, but didn't want to ask. Anyway, Robert was urging them to eat, at least a sandwich; then Angus said something about a "good old man" he wanted to see.

"Some other time," Robert suggested.

Angus was insistent: "Do good. Let him pick up a few nickels to beef up his social security. He's honest, never takes more than twenty-five per cent of the cost. Some want double. I know one boy paid down his cash, double, and never saw man or money again, no liquor. He couldn't report it, of course; end up booked on all kinds of charges. When you're about old enough to be forced to kill men, women, and children, I figure you're old enough to have a little beer."

Robert was reaching for his wallet. "O.K., but keep it to beer, and for the boat. Count me in, but no drinking while driving—too many cops."

Susie, taken up with the Negro's torture and Iggy's split-apart life, had more or less forgotten the misery of the boat ride. Her TV came on with no help from her. She saw her grandmother, heard her after a tourist's drowning last summer: "Alcohol for farmers in boats; never, never." Her grandmother had agreed with the manager of her shop: a sailor on the North Atlantic usually needed something in the way of beer or liquor; but seamen knew what they were doing; most Sunday sailors of rented pleasure-craft did not.

Susie turned to the Negro for hope. He looked even more worried than Katy, but one hand was going for that wallet. "I'm not asking for a case," he said, as he handed Angus two one-dollar bills.

"You'll get change," Angus promised. "And thank you for the sandwiches. I'll take some with me to eat while I wait for the old man to go up the street."

"Tell him to step on it," Robert urged. "My telephone call won't last but a minute."

"Oh, yeah?" Angus said with a strange kind of smile.

Susie, though not hungry, had taken one of the Negro's nicely made and wrapped sandwiches. To her surprise, she had enjoyed the first bite. The second choked her. She, too, had a telephone call to make—Beeto. How could she have forgotten; because she had to tell more lies?

She, too, carried a sandwich, after explaining she had a telephone call to make. Nobody seemed to think it anything out of the ordinary. Katy was suggesting to Robert he leave the car keys so that Ben might give her a sight-seeing tour of the neighborhood. Robert, after warning Ben not to take too long a tour, yielded up the car keys. He then suggested Susie come along with him; there were two booths in the drugstore half a block away.

Susie thanked him, but kept silent on her hope at least one was entirely enclosed.

Both were.

Her conversation with Beeto was not so greasy as she had feared. What with all that warmth and kindness from someone she'd known and loved all her life, there was no room for greasiness, though it might come later. First, he chided her for not telling the big news at the party. He hadn't known she was Outstanding Junior Girl until he got home and read her school paper. Her necklace must have another pearl for that. He wished she were in Chicago to go with him this afternoon; he'd left the office early, and was all set for a long sail on Lake Michigan. And what was she doing?

There was no meeting of the Science Club until late October, she was explaining, when she heard the buzz of some I-want-to-get-in body down at the building entrance. "Excuse me; it's my sailing buddy, I think."

He was back in an instant, but, "Thank you, Cloud of Probability; the thread of our conversation has been broken just as he started to ask questions." She hoped he had a splendid sail; look at the moon for her if he came back by moonlight. Nothing much was happening at school or home; Brandon seemed to like his new school; her father was happy because duck-shooting time was close.

Long as Beeto had kept her, she was out of the booth before Robert had finished. She could see his head through the glass, and briefly wondered as she went back to where the car had been who it was on the line able to make him so happy.

Ben was just driving up, and Angus was already there with a big cake-box on which much fancy print and pictures told it held a German chocolate cake baked by Zappi Brothers, Inc. The four of them waited several minutes for Robert, more than time enough for Susie to watch leaves from the big sycamores go whirling away in the wind. Given the unbroken sweep of a lake, the wind would be much stronger; too strong for an unskilled sailor in any-old-craft and a big cake-box of cans of beer.

Robert came running. Then, though careful not to go over the speed limit, it was rush, rush for the marina. She had supposed that people on The Hill all belonged to yacht clubs, but he had used the word *marina.*

She was wondering uneasily on how much beer was aboard and how the marina treated Negroes, when Angus suggested to Ben that if the others didn't mind this would be a good time for some practice. The two of them, he explained, were helping with a "kind of cheer-up party" for a bunch of teachers out on strike.

Mention of songs for strikers brought to her mind Driving Pete, lumberjack, roustabout, I.W.W. sympathizer from a long time ago, and at last a common seaman. She turned to Angus. "Would they like those old Joe Hill and T-Bone Slim songs? Or I suppose teachers would feel more at home with 'The Internationale' or 'The Marseillaise?' "

Angus was both pleased and surprised. "You know you're the first person outside the groups I've met who knows there ever was a Joe Hill or an old labor song. The way the teachers feel right now they'd love them all. —Ben, what about tuning up on 'The Popular Wobbly?' "

"And get picked up for obscenity? I've heard a version of Casey Jones. That was enough," Robert said, surly.

Angus was surlier. "Who do you think we are, including Susie? There's a million versions of most old popular songs. Some guys like one version; some another. —Now, everybody join in; don't be scared of making noise."

Singing, Angus was happy again; and so was Susie, singing with the others, but careful to keep her voice low. She wasn't by the sea or listening to Driving Pete; but down on the expressway, walls on either side, overpasses above, she felt free and far from the House of Usher.

They were going well on "Casey Jones," had him working away in heaven, when happiness left her. Robert had put on the turn-signal and was trying to get into the exit lane. That meant the marina was close; those she had visited on the American side of the river were, she thought, like yacht clubs, all white. How would the gate-keeper treat Ben; refuse to let him in?

223

11

The marina appeared to be pure white. Still, nobody seemed to notice Ben's color. Overcrowded, the place was a mess, with people hunting dock carts, rounding up children, scrubbing boats, rummaging in gear boxes, loading, and unloading, with a good many staring at the sky, mostly clear except low in the southwest where rounded hills of dark cloud showed themselves. Susie, too, looked at the sky now and then as she with the others worked her way along a cluttered dock where the few empty slips showed floating beer cans and fish, also floating; they were dead.

They had reached the end of the dock and deeper water before Robert stopped, and said: "There she is, the real thing, all good oak and mahogany; built somewhere on the Canadian coast. She's not very pretty, but she came up the Seaway under her own power; and wait till she's painted and fixed up."

Susie could scarcely wait to board in the proper style up the cute, collapsible gangplank Robert insisted everybody use. It was something to learn the craft was not one of those cabin cruisers, some with less than two feet of draft, unsafe in even a good breeze. This boat had been an honest little old trawler type, built by real men who knew how to build a seaworthy craft. She was between thirty-five and forty feet long with a draft of possibly six feet—when loaded. The kind of honest boat you could love; except she wasn't honest any more.

Now, she rode high on the water as if she thought herself a catamaran. Somebody along the way had added so much to the original superstructure there was little of the main deck left. You could almost think her a houseboat. And was there ever plenty for the wind to hit? Old as she was, somebody had fitted her out with a diesel. Still, Robert couldn't do any racing; her top speed was probably no more than eight knots; something of a comfort that.

Boarded at last with cargo loaded, everybody poured into the wheelhouse after Robert—except Susie. She catwalked to the bit of rear deck left. Here, she was certain she could smell the sea in the old, yet still sound, salt water bleached planking. She went next to the galley; there were newly installed plywood cupboards, a refrigerator, fancy sink with running water, but also a pleasant surprise—the little charcoal or coke stove was a real ship's stove with a railing and everything; it could be part of the original boat.

She moved on, hunting some inconspicuous hatch that would take her down to the bilge; everything could be rotted below the water line.

She stopped again in what she supposed Robert called the main salon. Sad, sad; part of the now enclosed space had no doubt once been open to the sea, filled with tubs of line and bait with bare-handed men pulling in the catch and at the same time sending out the rebaited line; wind so cold ice glazed the line in the little time it was out of the water. Now, with rubber tile over what she suspected was plywood, a great square of thermo-pane instead of ordinary portholes, and all the built-in stuff, you'd never know you were on what had once been a working boat. If only you could write a poem; where were the men who—. You'd better be hunting that hatch.

She'd overlooked a hatch almost under her feet. Lifting it, a light popped on below, but seeing brought frustration. She could only see, possibly three feet below, the bottom of the ship's hold that completely covered the hull, rotten perhaps. The planking of the hold looked solid—and old. Whoever had stuck on the extra superstructure had used torn-out deck planking in the hold. Be nice to feel the good old wood.

She pulled off her sneakers and slid down, and stood head and shoulders above the hatch while her feet luxuriated in the feel of the planking, and her head struggled with a poem for the boat. You couldn't separate the boat and her first owner. Some Nova Scotian fisherman a long time ago on some little bay had, like her grandfather when he was young, worked and saved and dreamed until he could have her built to make his living or his starving by. And when the starving time had come for the go-it-alone fisherman, he, or more probably his son, had tried to pretty up the old girl for the tourist trade. They had not done enough, or could be too much. Many tourists would rather go "lobster hunting" and get soaked in an open dory—for two hours; gave them conversation material for years.

The motor went on. She dropped to her knees in the hold the better to listen; not that she was motor-wise, but it did sound overly loud, stiff and uneasy as if it were thinking of stopping. She also for the first time since boarding noticed the movement of the boat; quite a bit, when you remembered her moorings were fairly tight. She wished the motor would stop and refuse to start again. Instead, it took on an air of certitude, grew calmer as if, after the bit of excited worry, it knew it would not stop.

She went on exploring, crawling now. She was past the circle of light below the hatch, when she thought she saw, in the darker space ahead, a bundle of some kind. She reached to touch wooly softness. She pulled it into the light and found she held a red Hudson Bay; imagine, a good blanket left to rot in a ship's hold. She was shoving it through the hatch when it unrolled to let something black and slinky slide away. She grabbed and came up with a black slip.

She stood up, the better to examine the slip; it belonged to a tall somebody with large breasts. Robert's mother must have taken it off to put on a swim suit, and while mother was in St. Clair one of Robert's little siblings, always investigating, exploring, experimenting, like other children, had chucked it and the blanket into the hold. She sniffed, held the slip closer; perfume, sickly sweet, and what else? Not nice like the Givenchy given her. "You are too young for certain kinds," he had said.

Imagine a woman with all the money and social prestige The Village demanded, using cheap perfume and wearing a piece of ersatz junk for a slip. Flounces and laces in plenty, breasts all black lace, but not a stitch of real lace or silk; everything machine-made. Still, it meant dollars, always important. She was sitting on the edge of the hatch, refolding the slip to leave on the cabin floor with the blanket, when she heard her name.

The Negro, almost directly below her in the hold, was asking: "Susie, have you seen a bucket?" She saw as he crawled closer, he carried a flashlight. "It doesn't have to be a bucket; a good-sized pot or pan would do." He sounded as if a bucket or pot were important as a lifeboat on a sinking ship.

"For bailing?" she asked, worried.

"No. I'd say she's sound. Pumps work; no bilge water to speak of." He hesitated. "What I'd like is some water in that little engine hold. Not that water would do much good on oil—but. Oh, it's safe enough, I'm sure. Thought of fire just bugs me."

"You mean—what you're saying is there are no fire extinguishers on board?"

His "Yes" was a kind of groan.

"Will none of the flare buckets hold water?"

"There's no flare bucket."

She heard a faint squeak. "Listen," she whispered, leaning above him. "She can't be too bad; I heard a mouse. Mice like dry, cozy places."

"I'm sorry," he said, "but that was a loudmouthed advertiser on my transistor. I had it very low."

She sprang down to crouch beside him. "What does it say?"

"Why, like any radio, it says all kinds of things."

"The weather?"

He studied her a moment, then said all in a breath: "Gale force winds down Toledo way; small craft warnings all over Huron, Erie, and St. Clair, with possible thunder storms."

227

She felt relieved. "Well, we'll just have a picnic here. If you don't want to tell Robert, I will."

"Try, but I think he'd say: 'If you don't want a boat ride that's O.K. with me. Ben's been whining about the weather. I suggested he take in a matinee.' —I'm scaring you. I'm sorry. We're all good swimmers, except I don't know about Katy; and for her I found a life-jacket—kind of damp, though."

"You mean there's only one life-jacket on board and it— damp?"

"No. No. I know there are more. I've been too busy trying to find a bucket to hunt for anything else. Robert will tell you how seaworthy this boat is."

"Did you," she whispered, "try telling him it's the sea that decides what boats are worthy to live? I hope you reminded him she's riding too high, and she won't need much wind and wave to push her over—without expert handling."

"I said considerable in that line. But how do you tell a good guy like Robert you've known most of your life that he's all wet? Don't worry. Angus is a fine swimmer and I'm not bad."

"Robert will manage, I'm sure," she said, mostly to cheer him—and herself, too. "It's just me. I can't help but worry and wonder if his charts are properly corrected, and everything works."

"I haven't seen a chart since I came aboard."

"There is not," she squeaked, "a pilot on all the lakes who would go out at a time like this without charts—even if he knew the lakes by heart."

"Our friend is not a pilot. But quit worrying, and—."

The boat moved sidewise for a few seconds, then stopped with a slight jar. Somebody or -bodies had cast off the stern moorings. She had slewed around and struck a piling. The next minute, Robert on the rear deck yelled some kind of order as Angus dashed forward past a porthole.

She had known in a vague way the Negro was a good athlete—track, possibly basketball—such sports were not in her line; but she would never have believed any boy on earth could come straight up out of that hatchway, already running, and at

228

the same time whispering in a kind of agony: "He's casting off and the wheel untended."

He was gone. Seconds later Angus got busy with a cant hook; the boat straightened, then moved gently out. The old girl continued on her careful course through the marina channel crowded with home-coming craft. Susie relaxed. Robert and the boat were doing better than expected. She remembered the Negro's worry about fire, and went into the galley where she found two picnic jugs of something wet and the five bottles of beer left in the cake-box. These, she carried out and placed within easy reach of the engine-hole.

Now, for the life-jacket search. She found behind the sofa cushions a life-jacket tied with many knots into the long cord of a life-preserver. Somebody's little Cub Scout had really gone in for knot practice. As she stood untying knots, she felt as well as saw that shallow Lake St. Clair was already kicking up white-caps. Yet Robert was doing all right.

They were entering the heavier traffic of the ships' lanes when she saw a salty. Bad weather and an inexperienced captain together could not keep down the lifting of her heart that always came when seeing a salty on these inland waters. A little Dutch freighter, perhaps on her way from Glasgow with a cargo of whiskey to be exchanged in Chicago for wheat.

The salty had disappeared, and only two knots were left in the life-preserver cord when Angus and Katy came. Katy, wearing a life-jacket, was enjoying what amounted to a sight-seeing trip for her; but Angus looked dour as he glanced at the cloud hills Susie had watched in the marina, now changed to mountains. Sight of the life-jacket and preserver seemed to make him happier, and he insisted on untying the last knots. Finished, he had the life-jacket over her head and onto her shoulders before she could stop him. "I meant it for Katy, but she has one, so it was for you," she cried, annoyed.

He adjusted a buckle. "Don't worry about me. I can swim almost as well as Ben."

"Swim? Why?" Katy asked, laughing because an unexpected pitch of the boat had sent her sprawling onto the sofa.

Angus glanced again at the cloud mountains. "Because the weather is so warm," he said.

Susie wished she could cheer Angus, but could only think that wind and water were worsening by the minute, and she couldn't say that. Katy was wanting her to come with them to the little forward cabin; sight-seeing was better there. Angus was insisting to Katy she'd be more comfortable here with Susie when the clatter of falling pots sent him hurrying to fasten galley cupboards.

Katy followed, after Susie said she'd be along in a few minutes. She didn't say so, but she'd just as soon be alone when in the next few minutes they passed Grosse Pointe Yacht Club. Katy might see the red pennant flying there and want to know what it meant. She wasn't going to ruin Katy's good time by telling her it was the small-craft-warning signal. And what would Angus say to Katy's question? She was being silly. The red pennant might not even be flying.

It was. Seconds later a mere red pennant didn't seem to matter. Robert must have left the wheel untended—in this weather. The boat had slewed around to take a fairish wave amidships. Now, they'd gone into such a roll, one half the sliding door had slid open.

It stayed there until the boat rolled in the other direction; closed itself as the other half opened. Her sneakers, forgotten on the floor, had traveled to a wall where they had stopped, heels close together. She watched them go in the other direction, heels backward, but this time they changed course about midway, and after a moment's deliberation, started aft. No, they had changed their minds and were going to starboard. The door was sliding again, driving her crazy.

She sprang to lock it, and almost collided with the Negro. He spoke in quick whispers: "I don't mean to give you orders, but please get up there with Robert—you can at least be on watch. He let me take him out of St. Clair—I scared him with mud talk—and into the main channel, but now he's thrown me out, mad as a hornet. You can't blame him too much. I mutinied."

Susie clung to the door. "Can't you stay, please? You've done a good job. He'd throw me out in a hurry. Imagine a girl crashing a wheelhouse and trying to give the captain orders."

He gave her a pitiful look. "Imagine me. I kept the wheel long after he asked for it. Grabbed it when he went off course. I don't think he's touched a boat in two or three years—. Oh, my gosh. Get up there, please. If you can't steer, use your tongue."

He was staring out the big window. She looked once, then dashed for the wheelhouse. Robert's curve was taking them straight into the path of a rushing speedboat already giving her I'm-overtaking-and-passing-on-your-starboard blasts.

Susie slid between Robert and the wheel, grabbed it with one hand, swung hard, while the other jerked the whistle cord to give the boat behind a You-can't-pass-now warning. With both hands for the wheel, and Robert with some understanding of what was happening, she was soon able to give the speedboat a passing signal. It whooshed by.

She kept the wheel. The boat managed well enough, and the old girl could take the wind and water. That is if the steering gear didn't break, or the engine act up, or they got her into a collision, or went off into mud, or took broadside one big wave too many, or she caught fire. There was, insofar as Susie could see, nothing else to go wrong: no compass, not to mention direction-finder, no ship-to-shore telephone; no radio, no depth-sounder, no nothing. Oh, yes, there were window wipers—two sets, too small. She had also forgotten fuel—plenty.

"You could go around the world in this—with proper equipment," she told Robert when she had the boat about where she wanted her to be—fairly close in to the American shore, but not too close.

"You don't need extra equipment on a little trip like this. We'll hardly be out of sight of land," he told her. In addition to his annoyance, or anger, at her taking over the wheel, there was in his voice a more unusual sound. Uncertainty? She spared him a glance. He was looking kind of greenish; good; if seasickness could put him below, Ben could take over.

"I was thinking of necessities, not extras," she told him, then tramped on her tongue geared to tell him plenty of boats had

231

gone down within sight of land—and with them a good many people. There were a lot of other things he ought to know, but she couldn't spare time or mind for anything except the river, the boat, and the weather. That wasn't all spray hitting the glass, but wind-driven rain. Seconds later it was roaring in bucketfuls all around the cabin. The wipers had been unable to keep the glass half-way clear of spray; now with the rain they were no more than little dark lines moving through sheets of water. She could see only gray nothingness ahead.

And she had thought she was scared. Now she *knew* she was, as Robert took the wheel with a "Please get out of the way, and quit acting like I was some idiotic goon out to drown us all."

She could only watch as he let the boat slide away from the waves and get out of her lane; or so she thought. She couldn't see. Could that gray wall be the Canadian shore? Was he, in spite of the rough water and the traffic, trying to cross the river? Here, of all places, where the river would soon divide into different channels, and craft entering or leaving were—. He'd let the sweet old boat go into a wild shingaling of rolls, yaws, bounces, and pitchings.

She grabbed the wheel. A gray ghost, so high you had to crane your head to see half way up her, was almost on top of them; she hadn't even seen the boat, but looked when she heard the first angry warning hoot. One wrong move would mean the end.

They were getting away from the long laker. In a few minutes she was again able to head their boat down-river. She wished she could see the Michigan shore—any shore, anything. She felt the wheel turning against her hands. Robert. She moved aside as he said, teeth gritted, she thought: "I wish you'd go below and stay there."

She did not answer. She was trying to figure out the blobs of light all around. Running lights would reflect from the water. She was nuts. They were running lights; too smothered by rain and murk to show more than a weak glow. Were their own running lights on? They ought to be. She found what she thought was the right switch, but could only wonder if the lights worked.

She continued to stand near the wheel, trying to see but mostly listening, feeling. Flying sheets of rain whipped through the half-closed portholes. She was getting wet; rain even in her eyes; she batted it away, hoping, but still she could see nothing. She ought to close the portholes. No; the wetness, even without cold, made you feel you were sailing in a fair wind somewhere beyond the bay.

She heard the wind and the rain, the groans and creaks of the boat, smack and gurgle of the water; and then from upriver the hoarse bleats of an ore carrier. The sound made you think of some huge, unnameable beast in pain, patient in the pain. An ore-carrier, in forever the same lanes with forever the same load, had to learn patience. And so would Susan Schnitzer. All sounds were drowned in a long roll of thunder, close. The funeral guns of summer, Driving Pete called October thunder. No, this was the roaring of a giant as he tilted his big bucket to drown the river in a lake from the sky. Rain and the river came harder on her hair, but still she stood to watch the lightning make shimmering curtains of the rain and the spray.

Thank you, Lightning. The first with thunder on its heels must have been so bright she'd squinched her eyes. These quivers showed they were getting well into Trenton Channel. Robert ought to move out a bit in order to put Grosse Isle between him and the American side; otherwise he'd get into water too shallow for this boat.

She made out the lighted buoy that marked the beginning of shallow water around the upper tip of Grosse Isle. Their boat was almost straight across the river from it; too late to get where they belonged without risking mud. So what? Robert would be embarrassed and angry when he had to be pulled out of the mud. But mud wouldn't hurt the boat.

What had her first owner called her, she wondered? He had probably had a name for her, but always in his mind, after the long stint of working and saving, she had been above a name; a beloved "My boat," the only boat. Chances were he had not cared much for names—an anti-name man. *Antiname,* a fine name for this good boat. Pity she had in her old age such an unskilled owner as Robert Hedrick III.

Still, he was doing better as a wheelsman; he was in the channel more or less where he belonged. The first of the Grosse Isle drawbridges was coming up. He should be swinging to port to get into proper position. He wasn't. She stood and watched, fingernails biting into folded arms. Did he think he could go under the bridge? Did he see it? They would crash, get a bashed boat. But let him learn the—. "Don't you see the drawbridge?"

He saw. She helped at the wheel. No thanks when they were safely through; instead: "You should have told me sooner. I could have managed alone."

She clamped her teeth on her tongue that wanted to ask if he had never heard of a chart. Nagging wouldn't deepen the channel, but enough warnings might make him understand he ought to stay between the markers. The *Antiname* with a deeper draft couldn't go so far to starboard as that little outboard trying to make it to shore before it was completely swamped. "Robert, please—you ought to keep between the red nun and the black can."

If he heard her, he gave no sign.

Instants later, she felt the pull. Gentle, but strong enough to let you know the *Antiname* was in mud. She grabbed the wheel. Frightened, Robert let her have the controls all to herself. Reverse? Or could she? Was this an old, old diesel you had to stop before you could reverse? Beeto would know. He wasn't here. The Negro would—if she killed the motor this would be it.

The dear old thing was wriggling like a fish in too-shallow water as a big, kind-hearted wave, helped by the wind, whomped, pushed, lifted, and in sheer joyful play slewed the *Antiname* off the thin ridge of mud. No part of the boat was damaged. Sheer luck. She only then remembered, what now seemed hours ago, her hard heart had told her to let them stick in the mud where they would at least be safe from angry Erie. A respectable sailor would not let a boat get stuck if he could avoid it.

And was Robert damaged? Staring back at the spot where they had almost stuck, he showed no interest in re-taking the wheel. His green tint had deepened.

She wondered if she ought to try turning. The water was wide but shallow and the channel narrow. Her wonders and her worries slid away as she felt the tapping of Erie's hands on the hull through her bare feet. Erie, set in motion by the gale down Toledo way, was rolling into the river. Here, she could reach you only with her hands, gentle as yet, not fists, only reminders of what Erie had for you out there. Were the hands warning or calling? Take them however you wished. You knew that fists would follow the hands, and soon would come the butting shoulders of the waves, stronger, always getting stronger.

The tapping hands were calling, not warning. The rain came now only in scattered spatterings so that she could see the widening water ahead. Shallow, but deep enough for this—if she went in exactly the right places—except she didn't know the right places. Still, she went on down Trenton Channel; smiling, she stood like a queen when the second Grosse Isle Bridge turned to use all that great machinery, just for her. She gave a short clearance thank-you toot along with a little bow.

Fun. Not as sweet as the old fun in the *Betsy Joe* on a June morning with Beeto at the wheel and her granma walking the decks to see the world on the Detroit River—long laker ore and coal carriers, cutters and yachts, dinky, dirty salties from Greece and Panama, shipshape ones from England, Canada, Norway, Holland, Denmark, Sweden. You saw them all because with Beeto at the wheel in the main ships' channels on the way to Nova Scotia you passed them all, for Beeto and the *Betsy Joe* were made for overtaking. The gulls would be crying their promises of a wonderful summer ahead, and already the misery of life in her father's house was a garbage scow to be left behind.

This dear thing was not of an overtaking nature, but she could get you out onto heaving Erie where you were part of the world instead of one more ticketed coffin waiting for burial in a killed and frozen land. Provided, of course, they could make it through this channel, a strip of water on which this she, Susie, had never been, known to her only through chart studies.

She remembered Robert and glanced his way. He was staring at the whitecaps ahead, a worried wonder showing through the green look. She smiled. Compared to the *Antiname* and Erie waiting for her, Robert was only a familiar stranger. Her friends were the water, the wind, and the boat. The waves were coming harder; the motor singing with the joy of having work to do; and to this song and the wind's song, the creaks and groans of the *Antiname* made a nice accompaniment.

"You don't," she said, after another quick look at Robert's face, "act as if you felt very well. I'll bet you didn't take time to eat much breakfast or lunch either. I know Lulu put extras in that big insulated basket; everything nice and hot. Might be some cheeseburgers; wouldn't you just love one now with lots of onions and pickles and catchup and mayonnaise, and a chocolate malted loaded with whipped soy-bean oil? I forgot you'd rather have beer. I've heard beer goes well with garlicy, greasy corned beef; or maybe you'd like it with chocolate peppermint marshmallow cake."

He made some kind of sound. "Ugh," it might have been. She left off work on Robert to give her mind and heart to Erie. The hands were thumping fists now; Erie really rolling up the river—except the river was almost ended. Whitecaps were curling and breaking and crashing over the bow; a really good one thwacked the wheelhouse to send spray over the tiny top deck. And did the *Antiname* love it.

"I—I'll—go below—for just a few minutes."

He sounded as if he were speaking with food in his mouth. She glanced around to see him, one hand on his mouth while he balanced himself with the other as he cautiously made his way to the door. He mumbled something about sending Ben, then disappeared.

The Negro's tapping came only moments later. He must have been standing one leap from the motor, two from the wheelhouse. "I've done a miserable job of navigation," she told him straight off. "I should have gone into the ships' lanes on the other side of Grosse Isle, but I goofed."

He shook his head. "You don't know. In that downbound

236

speedy channel you could have been stove in by some big boat that couldn't make you out in all that rain—with the running lights poor as they are."

She saw he was wet; so he'd been out on deck in the blowing rain and sloshing water to check the running lights. She wondered what he'd learned, but did not ask. Instead, she insisted he take the wheel. He did after telling her she'd been doing fine.

He didn't have anything further to say—not now. Each understood the problems: they had to get out of this too-shallow water before they dared try turning back. That meant going on into Erie, where, when deeper water was reached, they must in spite of rollers and waves turn to go home by way of the upbound ships' lane on the other side of Grosse Ile—Amhertsburg Channel.

"I can't promise anything," he said. "But with Erie rolling into the river, it'll be deep enough for this boat to get through—if I handle her right."

She liked his sound, recognizing they were in trouble, yet feeling they could come through it. She liked the look of him, too. Bare feet planted easily on the deck, hands firm and sure on the wheel, he was at home, enjoying himself.

She left him to get something she had not until now remembered. Anyway, without charts, it would have been useless to Robert in the channels, but it might help the Negro as the river widened into Erie. This was the small compass, now in a raincoat pocket. On bike, boat, train, car, or plane she usually carried a compass, because it was nice to know where you were, or at least headed.

Getting her coat from the locker, she paused to listen; Angus was singing in the main salon. Half smothered by the sounds of wind and water, she could not make out the song. She almost had her ear to the door when it slid open, and there was Angus. He invited her to do the "Life-Jacket Frug"; he was certain she would have no trouble with her footing, as had Katy.

She made an excuse—she'd told Ben she'd be right back, and wished aloud she could stay. She wished more loudly in her heart that she knew how to do any kind of frug. She could keep her footing on the pitching boat, and it would have been even more fun dancing with Angus than with Iggy on the rock.

Ben's joy at sight of the compass cheered her. Though they had no charts and the variation and deviation were unknown, the compass would still be a big help, he told her. He knew that to keep in the deepest water, he had to steer south by a few degrees east—and until now he'd been wondering.

No longer afraid, she gave herself up to an enjoyment of the world. The waves were getting higher, whitecaps curling, breaking into waterfalls, their spray streaming like smoke in the wind. She watched a wave, the biggest yet, roll over the bow, then listened to the crashing, breaking, trickling as it whomped over the wheelhouse. She shivered with the joy of a long hunger, never completely satisfied, but less gnawing now—it was being fed. As they neared Erie, more and more waves smacked the top deck, but the *Antiname* creaked happily on, and the Negro seemed as confident as the boat. Susie, in spite of her joy in the ride, wished he would talk more. She wondered where he had learned to handle a boat. She thought his father was on the administration staff of a Detroit school, but that didn't change the color of his skin; so how, with the American side of the river and lakes reserved for whites, did he and his friends manage to use boats?

They dove on into ever wilder water. Moments when the bow went down under the crash of a roller, it was like skiing old Thunderboard when everything was ice under a thin film of snow; and the first aid sleds busy as the chair lifts while stories floated up the slopes; a broken leg that one, a wrenched back, a cracked head down there. You saw a broken ski go sliding by, and still you skied. One second, certain you would make it down on your own two feet; the next, ashamed of lying to yourself; though you had so far stayed on your legs, you knew you had never been certain.

She was studying the sand and mud in a big roller, when she thought she saw southward a salty. She couldn't believe it. She looked in the other direction to see markers across a field of blowing whitecaps. They couldn't belong to anything but

238

Livingstone, the downbound channel of the Detroit River. "We've made it! You've done a great job," she called to Ben.

"Just luck," he said.

Not long after Angus came bringing coffee for Ben and tea for her. "You may not be able to drink it with old Erie kicking up her heels. Mostly, I guess I wanted to give you two some kind of reward for getting the boat to a place where I'm not lost. I don't ever remember a trip through that water—no channel."

"It was my fault we got into it," Susie told him. "Ben got us out."

"It wasn't her fault," Ben said.

"It's a wonder, dark as it got—and all that traffic—you kept afloat," Angus said, smiling at her.

She wished he could stay in the wheelhouse as he said he would like to do, but he thought he'd better go look in on Robert again.

The Negro crossed both lanes in a long diagonal, careful not to put the boat broadside to Erie's rollers. He was biding his time for turning when here came Robert. He wasn't walking with much confidence, but there was too much in the hand he laid on the wheel, and the other that tapped the Negro's shoulder. Ben did not look around.

Robert tapped him again as he said, playful, as if it were his turn for the shovel in the sandpile. "What about letting me in on the fun?"

The Negro looked at Erie. "You still look sick," he said, but not talking to Erie. "She's rolling in, but good," he added.

"Look," Robert said, both hands now on the wheel; "the man who brought her up said she took a thirty-knot wind on Lake Ontario with no trouble."

The Negro left the wheelhouse.

Susie was scared again. The boat was wallowing like one of The Primitive's pigs in its mud hole. Robert didn't seem to mind the movement of the boat or notice the compass as she picked it up. She studied him, greenish, weak; perhaps he was even dizzy from his bout of seasickness. Such stupid courage would make her flip—if he were alone.

239

Erie was not so pretty as when they left the river; fewer smoking whitecaps to brighten the hills of water rolling in. That must have been a whole gale down Toledo way. You could almost think you were on the ocean; the waves were not exactly bucking mountains and heaving valleys, but when you went down, down into one, the water wall coming at you seemed—.

And here came the granddaddy of them all, nice and big, looked to be fifteen or twenty feet high; not that big of course, but it would be fun to see this little old boat climb right out. The course of the wave had suddenly shifted; waves didn't do that. The fool was trying to turn and run.

She didn't know when she grabbed the wheel. Her TV tuned in to her grandmother hearing the news and not believing. She would never call Beeto again, never see Ter, or Angus again, and she ought—. The water mountain was hitting them broadside; the whole of the boat caught in the suck of it; water spurting through the portholes, cascading in from starboard. And that was only the surface wave; the bottom was the wide, wide mouth running into a long, long gullet, all sucking; they had to be filled.

She was swinging onto the wheel; her feet were on the deck, but the door was almost below her. Where was Robert? Beeto, Beeto, what would you do?

The wheel was minding; the boat trying to mind the wheel. She noticed then the long, strong, brown hands on the wheel, helping, not fighting. Ben, Ben Holmes.

Wallowing they now were in the other direction. She'd better let him manage alone. They were upright for an instant, and away out there was the old gray bow; she was seeing it through the lace of muddy foam on the glass; how fancy. Lace and bow disappeared as Erie rolled them expertly in the other direction, but not so far.

That was the last good roll. Ben managed to head the *Antiname* in the direction of the channel markers about north by west. Back to home port they must go—with Erie walloping them in the stern all the way. Ben was looking around; he wanted her to take the wheel. He gave her a quick, lighthearted smile. "Don't be scared—not any more," he whispered. "This boat's charmed. She won't stick in the mud, and she won't capsize."

Ben left, and she remembered Robert. He was upright, but in a corner as if to avoid the water, almost ankle deep as it tried to get out the drains and into the scuppers. He came soon to stand by her, but did not ask for the wheel. He was no longer greenish; fright had knocked seasickness out of him.

"Did I make that happen?" he asked after a while.

"You didn't make the wave, of course, but you did try to run from it, and we got caught broadside."

He nodded. "I know that in my head, but I forgot why. It's been years since I've done much boating. We keep a boat at our summer place in the Upper Peninsula; but I don't remember any waves like that on our little lake. I had hoped," he went on with a hesitancy strange for him, "to get in some practice; run the anchor down and all that."

"Not in these seas—at least anchoring. You're young enough to wait for fair weather."

"I have to—I want to learn all I can as soon as I can."

He was wistful, but made no move to touch the wheel. There had been an urgency in his voice she had never until now heard from this gleaner of money, this confident walker of roads. Erie was still rolling along; but Ben, she guessed, was right; the *Antiname* must have a charmed life to be still afloat. Biding her time, she turned southward so as to take the waves head-on. Then, after a few words—to which he listened—on what and what not to do, she gave him the wheel.

He took the waves in proper style with no more tries at running away. Confrontation broadside in a strange boat with his first good wave had taught him a good deal, Susie decided; or perhaps on that ride downriver he'd been too seasick to see well. Whatever the reason, he had improved as a steersman, and grew even better during the hour or so he struggled with Erie.

Night was a long while away, but the early autumn twilight of a sunless afternoon had closed in until more light seemed rising from the gray water than falling from the gray sky; a lonesome time out here with silent Robert and the gray, heaving rollers. She was glad when Robert suggested they start home.

"You're the captain," she told him. "Go to port whenever you want to." They crested a wave, and, though paled by distance and too much daylight, she made out the Detroit River Light with the still fainter channel markers below it. The first half of Robert's "practice" had been south; she had turned the boat so that the last half had been north over much the same course. They were, thus, only a few miles south by east of the river's mouth.

"Is this the right course?" he was asking.

"I hadn't noticed you had a course. Most any spot in Erie is a sort of crossroad—until you come to shallow water. This strong old thing could take you to Toledo, Cleveland, or down the stairs to Montreal."

"Susie, tune out that station. Tell me—where do we go—now. You know—I think—I think we're lost."

The quavers in his voice were not caused by any vibration of the motor or vessel. "Well, then, steer for your marina," she told him, half ashamed of herself. She should bring out the compass, but he did need a good lesson on the stupidity of trying to steer without one navigation aid. Did he even know in which direction he should go? She asked.

He didn't know whether the Detroit River channel was east or west of Erie, north or south. He grew more and more frightened as she let him plow north for half an hour or more; though with no idea he was going in the right direction. Too confused to remember the rollers were heaving in from the southwest, he kept insisting he should turn southeast.

Hollows of darkness were beginning to form at the bottoms of the waves, before he saw the Detroit River Light, but had to ask her what it was.

She told him, not minding too much; he was learning.

They were chugging up Amherstburg Channel, cozy with traffic light and Bois Blanc Island to cut the wind, when Angus tapped. He wanted to know if they could tie up at some "civilized Canadian dock where Ben won't get insulted while we picnic."

"We'll eat on the boat," Robert told him. "And nobody in my

marina would notice Ben while he's walking around. They use Negro help."

"Ugh. Nice, if somebody orders Ben to fetch a dock cart." He suggested they stop at the Bales Marine Supply near Amherstburg. He turned to her. "I'll bet you know the place; has a wonderful restaurant and carry-out; if they're not crowded they'll let us dock long enough to eat, even if we don't buy anything but the chowder I'd like to get for all of us."

Susie nodded, and hoped her face didn't show. The Baleses were old friends of her grandmother who had taken her there many times, as had Joe and Angie. Now, through the Baleses, everybody might learn she'd been stupid enough to go out in weather like this with an ignorant, unskilled captain in a boat without one safety device. Too late to change anybody's mind. Robert was agreeing to stop there if it were a "respectable spot."

Angus snorted at that one, and was gone.

Less than half an hour later, Susie stood on the deck of the tied-up *Antiname* and looked over Canada. Mr. or Mrs. Bales might see her, but the familiar sights were worth the risk. She had helped the others set out the picnic supper, waiting now for the chowder. Robert, she supposed, was gone for it; he had insisted that he instead of Angus buy it; he'd contributed little food to the picnic.

Food? She touched the sand dollar in a pocket and wondered how she could eat. She felt so lonesome and homesick, the only way to part-way ease it was by telling herself that in a minute her grandmother would come with Mrs. Bales to show her around the new *Betsy Joe*. The old *Betsy Joe*, much older than Susie, had been conscripted by the United States during World War II and never seen again. Her grandmother, still a United States citizen, had spent years in collecting payment for the old boat; more time was needed to get the new *Betsy Joe* built. Susie remembered the christening; she must have been four or five years old, big enough to feel the honor and glory of christening her grandmother's boat—her grandfather would have loved it, they had all said.

All that was a long time ago, as were long trips on the *Betsy Joe;* these had been mostly in those first years of her attendance at "The Camp for Exceptional Children." During the last several seasons, money-dripping hands were always reaching out for the *Betsy Joe,* offering unheard-of prices for short or long chartered cruises. Crew, furnishings, and victualing were all under the capable hands of Captain McChesney, a retired naval officer. He was now on his way to St. John's with passengers who wanted an autumn cruise around Newfoundland. And Beeto was long since grown and gone—except for visits.

"Why, it's Susie!" Her fear of being seen forgotten, she sprang down into the upstretched arms of Mr. Bales. She hadn't seen him since late in the summer when he had been "down Nova Scotia way" to take delivery on a boat. She loved to be with him, for as a boy he had known her grandfather, and still talked of him.

Now, he stood smiling down at her, holding both her hands, as he asked after her grandmother, Beeto, and the others. He led her toward the store, commenting on the weather as they went along. The question in his voice as to why she was out at such a time was strong as if he had put it into words. He told her about the cabin cruiser with a family of six aboard reported in distress off Point Pelee.

Neither liked to talk of ships' disasters; and, teasing, he wondered if she had served as pilot for her trip; considering who she had for a grandfather, she must be a natural-born pilot. No man, on lake or sea, could ever match his sure navigation at top speed, come fog, come dark. Talking all the while, he led her into the room off the restaurant where he put her by the old stove she remembered from childhood, never too hot and never completely cold. She must dry a bit, he said, or Mrs. Bales would be worried. Susie could take time, couldn't she, to run up to the cottage for high tea with Mrs. Bales and himself? He had just started when he saw the boat come in. This was their last chance for a visit before spring, as it was almost time to leave for their winter place in the Bermudas.

Susie was mostly silent, smiling, listening, melting that lump of frozen ashes inside her with the familiar face and voice, sights and smells. Her smile grew forced when, as he warmed towels for her, he commented on her wetness, but was too polite to ask prying questions. She was glad she had, at the insistence of Katy and Angus, changed the soaked jeans for the dry knee-length shorts she had brought to wear home on the chance her mother might be around.

He grew easier in his mind when she explained that, though the boat she had come on was in fine shape and "safely fitted," the "experienced seaman" in charge had decided because of the weather to stay in the lee of Grosse Isle as much as possible. So, they had come only part way down Livingstone Channel, and turned back as "soon as he found a suitable crossing."

The old man nodded, listening. She was glad when he sent her with the warmed towels to the washroom to dry. She returned to find her raincoat, the extra sweater Lulu had insisted she bring, and her sneakers. Mr. Bales explained that one of her friends, or possibly the "captain's boy" had been waiting in the door to get chowder; he had sent the boy back for Susie's clothing. Mr. Bales had also told the boy of his wife's eagerness to see Susie, an old friend; he had made apologies for her, and everything was now in order for a nice visit.

It all ended with her having high tea in the Bales's cottage while the others ate on the *Antiname*. Rude, but the visit was worth it. She had been filled with all manner of good things; the best, that warm, happy talk of the old days and old friends. Now, running down to the pier under the maples, she discovered she was crying. Why?

She didn't know. Yes, she did know; it was that great big lie she had told to keep the Bales's from knowing so that her grandmother who trusted her to act with some sense could never learn what she had done. She catwalked around to the rear deck where she planned to stay until, tears gone, she could go make her apologies to Katy and the others.

She stood and stared at Canada, forgetful of her tears and the others on the boat, until she grew aware of music. Careful to stay outside the square of light, she peeped through the glass to see the rest still at table, listening to the music with the concentration of knowledgeable musicians. The boat didn't have a compass, but it did have a record player. Nice.

She turned away and went to the foredeck, the better to feel the wind and see the sky, clearing as the wind shifted from northwest to north. Unless the wind stayed fairly strong, there would be heavier frost tonight. She must remember to cover those cruddy little chrysanthemums, or tomorrow they would not smell so, or dance—. That was it, the music, "Dance of the Flowers"; kind of a mixture; now a sad part.

"Susie," Robert was whispering, "I want to tell you I appreciate your help. Will you go out with me again?"

"I don't know. Ben and Angus seem experienced, real sailors, especially Ben. And practice isn't all; you can study books, manuals, take courses, and still there are things you can't learn from any of these." She looked away to search for tomorrow's weather in the sunset sky as her great-grandmother always did. One pale reddish streak coming through the cloud could mean tomorrow might be fair—for dinner with the Negro-counting family. Forget them. Listen to the going-to-bed ducks talking to each other in the reeds.

"What things?" Robert was asking.

"Too many to try to tell you.—The most important one for a boat captain is: 'When the sky falls all our heads will be blue.'" She lifted her head to a gull's crying; the bird was high and circling. As it tilted to the turn, the yellow sunset light caught one wing to change it into gold; only for an instant, then nothing but a dark circling shape. She wished Katy could have seen that —the gull with the golden wing.

"Susie? You understand—you're not to tell anyone—not even Iggy—about our boat ride?"

His whisper was so low she could scarcely make it out. More secrets, more lies by silence, and why? She wished he would go away. This keen little wind had been trying to clean her up, washing out the greasy feeling from the lies she had just told, and the lies ahead when she went back to that mud-flat life with the Schnitzers. Did he ever feel the same way? Did he get lonesome for his mother the way she did for her grandmother?

That was probably the reason for his secrecy; afraid that away off in Vietnam she might hear—and remember how little he knew of boats.

She wondered if she'd nodded. He was whispering again.

"This Beeto? When you thought we were going under you called to him. Does he stay with the markers?"

"When he needs them. He charts a course and follows it, come wind, come rain, come fog."

"Must be quite a boy! A pilot or captain?"

"No. His sailboat's for fun. He is a businessman on his own. He would also like a garden, all covered with glass, and under the glass a potted lemon tree—and someone to tend the tree."

"Oh?—while I was on my way for chowder—I couldn't help but hear that old man talk. Your grandfather must also be some man?"

"Was. And by now the was is getting close to forty years old."

"And people still talk of him? I take it he was a pilot on the sea."

"And captain of his ship—and owner." In a minute he would ask: "And what did he ship of nights at such speeds without running lights?"

And she would answer: "Various brands, but his specialty was Cutty Sark." She shook her head to knock away the tears her tormentor could not see. The only place for real truth was with her sand castles at the bottom of the sea.

247

It didn't make sense; you'd think the Queen of England was coming to dine, instead of an employee for Sunday "potluck" that had thrown everything and body into high gear. The Popsicle Queen's directives, questions, and suggestions blew down in a perfect gale over the intercom: Susie was to select the "prettiest parsley"; slice the lemon thin; and to remind Lulu she was to use the recipe in the "pinkish cookbook" for the Yorkshire pudding.

Lulu, without too much strain, could manage any kind of company dinner alone, but for this one Susie had been sent to help as soon as the family got home from church. She loved Lulu and the kitchen going full blast, but today she needed the time to catch up on homework, behind because of the *Antiname*. Furthermore, she was, officially, still recovering from an illness. Yet, here she was on the step-stool, ready to hand down dishes to nose-covered-with-perspiration Lulu now giving a frustrated head shake as the intercom buzzed again. Susie stopped, cup in hand, to learn what now? Lulu's face told a lot as the perspiration spread to her forehead and the usually pink tip of her nose turned white.

She hung up with a: "Don't blame me, ma'am, if your dinner's late. Them dishes have not been used since I don't know when. They may all need washing; there's no electronic dust catchers down here in the pantry."

Susie had already moved the stool and was reaching for the stack of green and silver plates she hated. Bought for the house visit of Charlotte's prospective in-laws, and seldom used since the wedding, the dishes held a look of coldness along with their shrill cry of: "We are new."

Lulu, reaching, took them from her hands, meanwhile muttering to herself in Polish. At such times she seemed to get comfort from her mother tongue. She was probably saying what Susan Schnitzer was thinking: Mr. Schnitzer hated things that didn't match; Mrs. Schnitzer had remembered that along with the fact the second best china had no bouillon cups. All this only meant somebody would have to wash dishes for seven people— and the breakfast pots and dishes still in the washer.

"Take down eight of everything," Lulu was commanding. "It's exactly the day I'm gonna break one a them good dishes from 'the old countree that you can't buy here,' or so he told me when they ordered them." She stared up at Susie, seeing things, as she often did when "The Fatherland" was mentioned; for Lulu had relatives in Poland, now and then visited by West Germans who ordered them to take good care of their homes, as they were coming back to claim their own some day.

Susie, mostly to cheer Lulu, did two kick-turns with the best and biggest platter on her head, and a silver-banded waterglass in either hand. Lulu, admiring her skill while pretending frantic worry for the dishes, was soon happy enough to sing Polish songs and, using a place-plate as a flipping handkerchief, did the mazurka back and forth to the dishwasher. The fun did not hinder the work.

Susie worked swiftly, efficiently, as she had learned during summers with her grandmother. If Driving Pete's granddaughter or great-granddaughter-in-law, her grandmother's mainstays as charwomen, didn't show up, and a cabin was being vacated with a reservation due that afternoon, Susan Marie Schnitzer cleaned the cabin with the help of a boy-of-all-work. Her grandmother always paid her, of course, working with her when other duties were not too pressing, but no matter who did the work, she expected, and got, a good job. And if her beautiful daughter, the present Mrs. Herman Schnitzer, had not started winning beauty contests in her early teens she might have been that way, too.

Still, her mother had learned enough of do-it-yourself for company—pardon me, "guests"—not to expect so much from Lulu. Mrs. Schnitzer had used to feed and entertain Mr. Schnitzer's business associates, and worse, the hoped-for buyers of his plastic, strangers whom she had never met.

Susie, though no more than seven or eight years old had for the "potlucks" been put to work in the kitchen. Charlotte would be chosen to lay the table so that she might stay unmussed, and ready to greet her father and his guests with the agreed-upon words, something like: "Oh, Daddy, it's you. Mother was going to meet you at the door. She must be tucking Brandon in or on the upstairs telephone." There had been one telephone in that house; during those years her father's business seemed to soak up more money than he could wring from it.

While Charlotte answered the door, her mother would be fighting for time and dinner in the kitchen; urging Brandon to finish his supper and get out of the way upstairs; giving Susie fiercely whispered directions on what to do and when—always out of sight for Susie and her scars—; meanwhile struggling to get off rubber gloves, take a quick look at the dinner, and lastly mend her face, before rushing out to greet her guests, unruffled and bright as a plastic orchid.

Susie had then been too little to understand why, when getting up those early "potlucks," her mother was over-generous with short words, sometimes slaps, and even scoldings for Brandon. She now knew that the getting of a big meal, "something good, nicely served, just family potluck, no frills" in that old Highland Park kitchen with poor lighting, neither Dispos-all nor dishwasher, had been an agony for her mother. The only child of a widow, when, as a college sophomore at nineteen, she had married, there'd been nothing much behind her except school and the culture of her beauty. Her first years of marriage had been spent with her husband in Germany, where, in the earlier occupation years servants, for a "quickie" captain's wife, had been plentiful and cheap.

The intercom was buzzing again. Lulu answered with a: *"Wie viel Uhr ist es?"* Her question as to the time was one of the few German phrases she knew, and as the Popsicle Queen had also learned it, Lulu now nodded to the answer, then said: "She Ibben comen straightforth soon. Ma'am, nervous I be got—da Henglish she be sliding up, nacht." She beckoned to Susie.

The woman now wanted an hors d'oeuvres tray: "—just something simple; only two or three little hot things with the usual cold collection." And trippity, trippity, trip; polish for the silver salts and coffee service; and Susie's face in the maid's mirror. "A bit of that liquid makup would be nice, dear." "That you gave me? Do you think it will hide my scars?" She then repeated word for word her mother's kitchen orders so as to be spared the shame of giving them directly to listening Lulu.

She went to her purse, took change; dropped it into a tin tea-box on top the "kitchen patio" refrigerator; and then selected a well-chilled bottle of beer which she took to Lulu. "I am playing Brave Officer in the Foreign Legion; the desert sun is beating down upon the gasping troops, but cigarettes and beer are yet available—and most especially to the general."

Lulu clicked her heels and saluted as with the other hand she offered Susie a freshly rinsed "super colossal" ripe olive. She then retired to the basement for a cigarette while Susie went to work on the silver (plated) coffee service. Trouble with polishing a big piece of silver was it had nothing for your mind; and with Lulu gone, that mind ran on to where it had already been many times—the very probable probability that Miss Mary Lou Weatherford would ask Miss Susan Schnitzer where she had been on the night of the football prom.

"Think of the troubles of other people, for a change. Ben, for example," she told herself. Thoughts of Ben made the prospect of meeting the Negro-counting mother worse than her worry over the daughter. Her IBM leaped to something nice—Lans and Ter; but instead of staying on the pleasant memories, it went off onto Ter's talk of Mr. Weatherford up to look over her father's business—no, it wasn't her father's business any more—and possibly to buy it for the oil company.

If so, it would be the end of Bismarck's real life. She had

heard, when she was little in that second unsoundproofed house, a lot of low worried talk about lack of money for the business; his wife's dowry and his savings were not going to be enough. Soon, Mr. Graybo and his wife had been brought in for a "family potluck." A sweet couple, older than her father, they brought gifts for everybody when they came visiting.

She had scarcely got over the notion that Mr. Graybo was a mere employee instead of a full partner, when they took in Mr. Nevins. Young and sharp, all business, no little gifts from him; but he had made the contacts, got the orders, and—.

The intercom. She answered. Would Susie please tell Lulu "—to be certain the homemade rolls are hot, but not too brown, when the meat is served." Then came the fourth or fifth directive concerning the Yorkshire pudding; it should go into the oven— and be certain the oven was at the right temperature—in about five minutes.

Kind of sad to think of how her mother had forgotten Yorkshire pudding when she'd grown up with it and roast of beef for Sunday dinner. Was this the first she had had since marriage? Marriage? An exchange of Yorkshire pudding and sphagetti at least once a week for *schnecken* and *küchen?*

Lulu was back, her nose its natural color. It stayed that way, for Susie told only of her mother's advice on the rolls.

Lulu rushed to the pantry warmer. "Golly, it's a good thing she reminded me; dough's thawed but I gotta butter 'em up and pinch 'em around a little." Lulu went to work "homemaking" the dough bought in a Detroit bakery and kept in the freezer until time to thaw a chunk for "homemade" rolls.

One of the many shining facets of the Schnitzers' "jewel of a cook" was that she could be trusted to take the station wagon and do the grocery-buying, including beer. This helped the "jewel" even more than the Schnitzers. She was able to buy and store much contraband—insto-mashed potatoes, ready-to-serve frozen foods, a great variety of doughs, and other time-savers. These, like the insto-gravies and soups, with a pinch of this, a dibble or a dribble of that, herbs, a stir here and a punch there, were transformed into the "real home-cooked food" so prized by Mr. Schnitzer. Cake mixes, like tinned soups, were, on his food lists, *verboten*—now. Most forbidden things Lulu bought not only speeded her work, but were in the monthly run less expensive. Susie sometimes wondered if the Popsicle Queen knew—or cared. Mr. Schnitzer was as happy with Lulu's "homemade" food as with Mrs. Schnitzer's "homemade" *küchen.*

Lulu had made no attempt to find a Yorkshire pudding mix, but had studied several recipes before choosing one. The batter was now waiting in a cloth-covered bowl, ready to go into the oven, not in so many minutes, but then the doorbell rang.

The pudding batter waited for over an hour, as did Mr. Schnitzer who, with his living-area bar open and ready for business, could be heard pacing and muttering.

Kitchen work finished, Susie in the pantry was struggling with a phrase in Virgil, when her glance happened upon the after-dinner coffee spoons laid out with the coffee service. Compared to the just-polished pieces, the spoons had a yellowish cast. She rubbed away by the pantry sink, and had the fourth spoon half finished when the door bell buzzed. Her father had ordered her, along with the rest of the Schnitzers, to greet the Weatherfords at the door; no need for Lulu's answering when it was a "plain family dinner." Susie rinsed her fingers with the spoon, then rushed into the kitchen to send Brandon scatting down the side hall, and ask of Lulu, "Do I look all right?"

Lulu, sliding into the oven the baking sheet of hors d'oeuvres to be served hot, looked around: "Pretty as a picture, chick."

Susie dashed. She was already late. She could, as she crossed the dining area, hear the voices, each taking its turn like threads in a working hand-loom; her father's the thickest thread, loud, "hearty": "Ram, now, our better halves have met, but what about the teen-agers? Susan? Where is Susan?"

"Here, father," she called, and hoped her dread and general distaste for the whole business didn't show. Lady Macbeth was standing straight and still in a charcoal wool dress that brought out everything she had—though not, as her grandmother would have said: "in a music-hall sort of way." The Blessed Damozel looking down from heaven, four rosebuds on her breast, the pale gold hair smooth as starched linen, and those sun-on-northern-sandy-beach eyes untouched by any sinful thought, immaculate and undefiled as the white doeskin glove with a hand in it waiting for Miss Schnitzer's hand.

Miss Schnitzer reached for it just as her IBM registered a restrained, trouble-filled gasp from her mother, a snort from her father, and a snicker from Brandon. The next instant she knew that all were looking at her. Why? She had gone to the powder room a long time ago where she had looked at her face; no worse than usual. Oh, Jove, I forgot to get back into that must-always-be-worn-to-church girdle and my nylons have unrolled and fallen down. Her glance hit her father's pale eyes, iron-cold in his pink-cheeked face; behind him her mother was making a successful grab for her poise.

Something was squeezing her hand, a white glove. She looked up to meet Lady Macbeth's neon bulbs come on full with no flickering: "Oh, Susie, how do you ever find time to help, an' make the grades you do?"

At least, she thought that was what she had heard; the voice was even more southery than at school; then, she was realizing she had never heard a real southern accent, not until another voice came on, smooth, a perfect dairy mix, almost too thick to get through the spigot. "Why bless her auld sweet heart; she has been wucken so hahd in th' kitchen she has fogotten to tahk off her apun."

Lady Macbeth's mother, the drouthy desert woman she had watched in the school drive, took her hand, one glance like a cacti prick falling on what Susie knew were silver-polish-blackened fingernails. She remembered she had forgotten to use rubber gloves when polishing the coffee spoons. "You will have to give Magout Lucille lessons. She's nevah wucked in the kitchen."

She was wondering who was Magooucille, when Bismarck, with a fist in his voice, commanded : "Go take off that apron—at once."

She looked around, then down as the word *apron* penetrated. The oversize, ugly plastic, "dirty-work" apron, streaked with polish splatterings, covered all of her except head and hands.

Lady Macbeth's father was smiling at her, the same smile he had given that day in the rain. She wanted to return it; tried; failed, she guessed, for most of her mind was on backing away as quickly as possible.

It seemed miles to the pantry door. Lulu waited behind it with half a lemon. She caught a handful of Susie's fingers and rubbed them into the lemon, as she whispered apologies and lamentations because she had looked only at Susie's face; in between she begged: "Where are they, chick?"

"They what?"

"Your shoes, darling. Your girdle is in the basement bath where you pulled it off, nylons and all. You've got to have some shoes.—Oh my broiling oysters and bacon." She shoved the lemon into Susie's hand and dashed kitchenwards.

Susie's radar soon led her to the flats where she had taken them off when getting onto the step-stool. She was debating a trip to the basement for the required Sunday heels, stockings, and girdle when Lulu rushed in to put the hors d'oeuvres tray into her hands. "Don't feel bad, chick. This day is that way. I've read somewhere that Einstein was this way—forgetful like you."

"He wore his shoes, but thank you for the compliment," she said.

Once beyond the pantry door, she froze. Her computer refused all further information until she found herself sitting between Brandon and Lady Macbeth on the green-and-silver sofa near the fake fireplace. She gradually grew aware she had been smiling the same ten-cent-store smile so long it was frozen on her face.

Lady Macbeth was listening to Brandon's too-loud opinions of the fall-out shelter as a patriotic must. "Let the dirty Reds know we are prepared and not afraid." He went on to tell of the "rigorous" weekends he and other members of his group were spending in a shelter.

This girl, Susie figured, was the kind who would be just dying to listen to such talk; but bless her little heart, though she asked many an eyelash-flickering question in a voice breathless with interest, each was a wrong question, much like those Susan

Schnitzer asked. What did they do for air when that outside was filled with fall-out; and wasn't it quite dreadful to live so close to —well, that kind of bathroom?

Brandon, already angry from hunger, and forced by her questions to reveal that the "rigorous training under simulated conditions of atomic war" had taken place in camp tents on a site furnished with electricity, running water, and firewood, fell at last into lip-stuck-out silence.

Susie dropped her hands to her sides to keep from pulling her thumb. The real torture would soon begin. Here came Lulu, unflustered and immaculate in a frilly maid's apron, acting as if in the kitchen were a cook and a cook's maid, so that she hadn't a thing on her mind but serving the dinner.

Seating accomplished at last, her father announced in the uranium-weighted voice he used at such times the imminence of grace. She knew at once her parents had used the wrong signal flags. Bismarck was crawling into the long grace needed when something was not yet done; furthermore, he was making no attempt to hide from God or his guests his hunger and annoyance at the lateness of the dinner.

She had a lot to say, too; so much, church had left her half finished. She clasped her hands. "Oh, Jove, the all powerful, Cloud of Probability, and Neptune, forgive my lapse in not sooner thanking you for saving the good *Antiname* and the rest of us when that ignorant pilot tried to run from a wave. And Sweet Mary, mother of the dead God and the Christ who has never lived in most of us, forgive, I beg you, my many lies, and my selfish prayer in church that you will strengthen my IBM for the coming brain-skinning by that would-be psychologist. Others, I believe, have harder things; Ben Holmes, strengthen him and weaken his enemies; and I pray you try to smooth the way a bit for Angus; he has, I'm sure, troubles at home as well as at school; the road he has taken seems rocky.

"I pray you help me through this evil water of dinner as you helped me in the family's church; another one of those *Christus Surburbanus restrictus* which I'm forced to go to. Sometimes I wonder if you are there. I thank—."

Bismarck was clearing his throat.

"I must stop now. Thank you for listening. *Au revoir*." She dropped her clasped hands, made a small cross on her knee, and looked at no one.

Her father's prayer had stopped Mrs. Negro-Counter, but not changed her course. She was again on How-to-keep-the-Negro-in-his-Place.

Susan Schnitzer must up with an umbrella over her mind to shield it from this rain of garbage. How? Politeness demanded she at least try to speak to Mr. Weatherford between her and her mother at the foot of the table. She turned to him, but found him so absorbed in looking straight ahead at nothing she decided not to disturb him. Possibly he was listening to his spouse and host clean up the "police action" in Vietnam with nuclear weapons and another million men.

Finished with the North Vietnamese, the two turned to the draft resisters, peace marchers, and other subversives in the U.S.A. Mrs. Weatherford was for concentration camps; but Mr. Schnitzer saw the whole lot as traitors. "Hanging's too good for them—and I include all these old women who mouth around about peace."

The stomach-chilling bouillon quivering under its lemon slice and green feather of parsley did not chill her father's wrath; quite the contrary. He got the message: there would be no hot, thick, low-cholesterol soup, made, with every milligram of fat skimmed, from the mess that resulted from a long boiling of meat and bones.

She had heard him complain of soupless company dinners, but had never heard anyone tell him the reason—eating his soup, he too plainly showed his love of it with many a slurp and smack. He refused to taste the bouillon, and crunched away instead on celery and olives.

Mr. Schnitzer looked no happier when Lulu began to serve the salads; fruit, and very prettily arranged, but a separate course which meant hot "real food" was still some minutes away from that gnawing stomach of his. Two cold things in succession made for something of a chill in the dining area. The place was never able to hold down enough heat from the "cathedral ceiling" to register more than sixty-two degrees at table-top—Susie had measured.

Salads in place, Lulu had yet to serve the two dressings. Mr. Weatherford was interested in neither. "You don't have to worry," her mother urged. "Both are made with safflower oil. Herman's cholesterol count stays way down with the use of it."

"Yes, so he's told me," Mr. Weatherford said. "But I'm not overweight, and don't need to worry. Thank you."

Susie also declined as she suppressed a gagging shiver. Mention of safflower oil made her think of her father's much-discussed disposal system; he ate safflower oil to keep his personal drain field unclogged with cholesterol; when the House of Usher's drain field clogged the septic tank overflowed its black slimy stuff into the basement.

She glanced sidewise at Mr. Weatherford.

He sat easy as a man in a crowded dining car, seated with strangers, but not minding—too much. He was now looking at the painting on the pantry wall. His glance safely away from her, she studied his thin, tanned, gray-templed face, then from under lowered lids considered his hands.

She was trying to decide of whose hands they reminded her —Beeto's or Dr. Hefler's—when quick as a fish he turned and caught her glance before it could get away. "What is that painting?" he whispered, leaning toward her, speaking so she alone could hear.

"An investment in the essence of my mother, or so the interior decorator who sold it her said."

He thanked her and returned to his survey of unrepresentational art. Time was passing, passing. The salad plates were going, roast beef and hot plates coming; and Mrs. Weatherford now on "pink politicians." Bismarck, who always stood to carve, was on his feet, smiling at the prospect of cutting into the roast. He must have enjoyed the family butchering of hogs and calves when he was a boy on that farm up around Petosky where he had worked and gone to school twenty-six hours daily with two more hours spent walking each way; or at least that was the sum she had got one day as she added together the duties and chores he had recounted to Brandon. He was picking up the carving tools as he said: "I will now finalize the roast beef."

Every listener was supposed to laugh at that or work hard on a good imitation. Her mother (good wife) was the only one who so much as smiled. Bismarck showed his annoyance by bringing the first slice off in silence. "Please, Cloud of Probability, keep him so mad he can't talk, and so spare us his dialect jokes."

Now, he was mad; not only at his guests, but at his wife, the cook, and most particularly the beef; a second slice had revealed its rareness. He didn't care for rare roasts, preferring *sauerbraten* with lots of thick gravy. He was going to serve jokes while the roast chilled. He let the electric carving knife saw the air while he stuck out his lips and bulged and rolled his eyes; his version of a Negro. Had he ever known a Negro? Had she? No. Yes. She had forgotten Ben, but since the boat ride he was just Ben.

Bismarck shot one quick glance at Mr. Weatherford. He would make this employee laugh or have a stroke trying. Susie stared at her mother until their glances met, then begged with her eyes, and gave a slight nod pantrywards. Her mother turned away. She knew what her daughter was asking. Susie dropped her glance; no use to try again. She had not honestly expected the luxury of getting away to help Lulu; not today. In permitting her daughter to help the overworked woman of all work, the Popsicle Queen would be admitting her input was not equal to the planned output. She was determined to make these people think there was a cook back there; or was she following Bismarck's instructions?

Ugly gutturals and soon the uglier word *nigger* rolled into her ears. She would not listen or pretend to enjoy it. She looked at Lulu behind Bismarck's chair; straight and dignified she was, waiting and waiting, forced to listen to the so-called jokes she didn't like.

Brandon was whinnying; he often tried to imitate the gestures and the so-called dialect of his father's jokes. Mrs. Weatherford gave big smiles; but Mrs. Schnitzer got out nothing more

259

than the small "Fill-her-up?" smile of a weary gas-station attendant; she should be joyful to find the roast beef not dried out and Mrs. Weatherford as yet unspattered.

And Mr. Weatherford? Carefully she turned enough to see his face; he was lifting it from a survey of her lap. "Oh, Jove, why do you let me pull my thumb?" Did it matter that he saw? This man's road was not her road. "What road does he walk?" she wondered. Ter's gossip might be true; this man could be a prospective buyer, not of plastic, but of the company. Subordinates always laughed at her father's jokes long and heartily, with much shaking of shoulders and wiping of eyes. He had caught her glance again, and lifted his brows, the way of asking a question at school; he didn't know that, of course. She smiled without planning to, leaned close to that beautiful tweed jacket, and whispered: "There'll be others." He wouldn't get it.

"Thank you," he said, not deigning to whisper.

She felt a blush. He had got it. She turned in the other direction. She thought she caught a glance from Mrs. Weatherford, but it was as if she stood in the bow looking out to sea when somewhere aft a school of porpoises leaped all in a row, but by the time she turned her head the leaping fish were buried in a wave, so that she could not with truth say she had seen porpoises. She forgot Mrs. Weatherford when her father began a second, too-familiar joke.

"Oh, Mary Mother, please lock the hatches of my mind. Let me take none of this cargo aboard. Please put the *Mare Aegaeum* on my private TV."

The prayer was answered. Place names were going well. She was on *Creta*, trying to see if *Gnosus* had two or three s's, when she felt a thin, strong hand separating her hand from the thumb it pulled. She turned to smile an embarrassed, "Thank you," then went back to the map. It and the hand holding hers made a wall that let in no joke.

Carving accomplished, dialect jokes finished—at least while Mr. Schnitzer took the sharper edges off his appetite—the dairy-mix machine came on again, now from the "Subversion in Public Education" spigot, Susie thought. She occupied herself with the battle to eat at least something so Lulu's feelings would not be hurt, and also with the helping hand. Thoughtful, it always released her when she had to help herself to something such as when the silver dish of horseradish in whipped cream came round.

She served herself in the middle of a church-offering silence brought on by Brandon. He had, under cover of Mrs. Weatherford's declamation, begun whispering; the end was now falling into the silence. "But, Mom, whatever that ice-cream looking stuff is, I don't want it. I'll wait for some good hot gravy."

The Popsicle Queen explained there would be no thick gravy, while the whole table of people listened, not wanting to, knowing such rudeness is for the lower classes, but nobody able to start a cover-up conversation. Unnoticing, Brandon went on and on, wondering why the meat wasn't done when dinner was so late, and why the catchup wasn't on the table. And through it all her mother sat and held onto her smile. Kind of pitiful.

Lulu came round with the Yorkshire pudding, perfect. Even Mr. Weatherford took several bites. This did not keep him from noticing when she had finished the main course and both hands were idle. He took one. She went to *Sicilia;* her grandfather's home land and Ter's adopted country. She tried to see the places she and her grandmother had visited three summers ago. Nice for a little while, but—. What had Mary Lou said, the first time she had spoken since coming to the table?

A sudden pain attacked her ankle bone; so sharp most of her body jerked—she thought. A muscle spasm from over-exposure to cold? No, not that for Susan Schnitzer. It took a full thirty seconds to know what had happened. Mr. Weatherford was looking at her; the smile wrinkles in his cheeks too straight. Had he seen her jump when his daughter kicked her shin?

The tweed jacket was again coming close. "My daughter has been explaining how in your school you salute the flag daily; also that she has no classes with a Negro; and her mother need not fear the wrong kind of mixing at school social functions. At the prom you and she stayed with your crowd."

She had drawn closer, breath held with listening. Her unprogrammed "Oh" of relief came out so quickly, he smiled as if he were pleased to have given her interesting news. "Oh, the dear sweet girl! You wonder how she knew I didn't want my absence known.—Or is she covering up for herself?" Had she spoken aloud? No. He was still waiting for her to say something. All other ears were tuned to his wife.

"I hope," she said aloud, "to get to know your daughter better. Such a sweet girl, and so beautiful."

He thanked her. Her relief at being rid of the worry over Mary Lou's giving the truth away did not stop the pain in her shin. It still hurt; she lifted her leg high enough to rub the region above the ankle bone without sticking her head under the table. It was at this moment Mrs. Negro-Counter smiled at her. "My ole honey-bun heah and young Dick Pryor—th' fourth I mean not th' thud—liked you mighty well; dancen with you a lot at th' Prom."

Her parents were staring at her, with nothing, for the first time in her memory, with nothing but pleasure—and surprise.

Another kick came; she tried to cover the grimace of pain with what she hoped was a smile, but as a further precaution shook hair across her face. Somebody ought to take the matter up with shoe manufacturers; rubber heels made especially for kicking, no bruises. Nice to know she had danced with Pryor; she had liked riding with him in Robert's car.

The conversation now seemed less ugly and less dangerous; nothing much but the trappity, trappity, trap of the drouthy desert woman. "Mistah Schnitzah" knew the Pryors, didn't he? Mistah Schnitzah nodded. He knew them all right. He read the papers. The Pryors, plus an assortment of in-laws and relatives, belonged to the politico-socio-business-old-money crowd that ran the world; or so Susie had gathered from stray remarks heard at school.

Mrs. Weatherford hadn't made up her mind about Richard Pryor III, father of the dancing boy. His politics? You couldn't exactly call a man like that a "pinko," but well—. She had heard him pop off against one of the "truest, bluest, most liberty-loving"—odd, how when the woman got going in high gear she lapsed into a northern accent—organizations in the country. She couldn't understand the Pryors, sending their son to public school. She'd heard their two older children had also gone to public school; for political reasons, she guessed.

She abruptly turned to Susie. "You certainly do all right, honey; nice boy friends, and the grades you make. But ah've been waiten to heah you talk some moah. An' you don't say a wohd."

Susie, trying to think up something to say, had only managed to shake hair from one eye and push out her nose, when the woman next wanted to know how a young girl had, "—away up heah in th' nawth got such a nice accent? Why, I'd declah you'd come from some place in England—in spite a yo looks."

Her father was giving her a pink-slip look. She straightened, shook back the curtain of hair and said: "I spent the first six years of my life with my grandmother. I talk much as she does."

She repeated the last sentence quite loudly. Nobody had heard it the first time. Nobody heard the second. Her father had jumped on top of the conversation: "We left her overlong with a British nanny while I was serving my country in Germany." He sailed smoothly away into the ugly "sea of subversion and outright Communism in the U.S. educational system that threatens to wreck our government by the youth of our land."

Scatter aluminum foil and jam the reception, Susie told herself; trouble was she'd heard that speech so many times, parts had somehow got through to stick like dirty mud in a clam. Wouldn't it be fun to say: "Excuse me just a minute, folks. I want to run up and get a beautiful book from my room; a volume of Mao Tse-Tung's poetry. You'll love it. I wish I could write of the pond as he writes of a mountain." She wondered if she dared offer Angus the loan of the book—or Ter?

She was thinking of Angus and Ter when the word *grades* got through. Her grades? No; the low grades of Detroit children; a big lie. She had made good grades in and around Detroit—too good. She ought to forget that time she had run home with a first-semester report card all gold stars and H's; the memory stuck like a washed-up gob of refuse oil because Brandon and her mother had accused her of boasting.

"Little one, is it wool you gather?"

She came to with a shiver. She wasn't back in that kitchen, frozen to death with words, staring through the gray winter twilight at the crooked catalpa by the kitchen window, but at her father's table where Mr. Ramsey B. Weatherford III had dutifully tasted his meringue filled with ice cream and ginger pear, and now sat waiting for her to speak. "I—I guess I gather wool while I walk my road."

"And where does your road go?"

She smiled. In this world you took your warmth where you could find it. That little girl running home with gold stars had wanted to warm her heart by one certain fire. Thank goodness she wasn't that child any more. She could even smile at the faraway little girl.

He thought the smile was for him; or at least his smile seemed to say so. She turned away to find out if the conversation were again getting dangerous. No. Mrs. Weatherford, still the disc jockey, was playing the same record—the all-pervasiveness of Communism.

She'd better listen. Lady Macbeth had made some kind of sound—a gasp or groan. She was not the kind of girl to let out unprogrammed sounds without good reason.

The girl sat so straight and stiff, she reminded you of somebody who sat the same—. That body was Susan Schnitzer; she sat that way when she was scared silly and overcompensating for the wanting-to-come cringe. Lady Macbeth was scared stiff. Why? True, her mother's anti-Communistic record was spinning faster, volume increased, but tune unchanged; whirling away on subversion. What had come before to make Lady Macbeth cringe?

"Don't try to find out. Don't listen; hearing will make you sick. Let me take you into that heaven you built with Driving Pete at the bottom of the sea where all the sand-castles built by little children and carried away by the tide wait with your grandfather, your great-grandfather the sea captain, the Nova Scotian fishermen, and other good people and beautiful things." Her TV was begging, tuning in the sight, and she wanted to furnish the sound with that Driving Pete song: "I have a castle at the bottom of the sea, tax free, tax free. And over it a hackmatack—."

"—just like the Minute Women of Texas. Only we work harder." Why couldn't she wall away that woman's words when she had made walls between her and other seas of words? "Don't neglect the little things."

Oh, the work she and other patriotic women had done, and were still doing—here. Only one example was the thousands of telephone calls to school boards—don't bother with school principals; they had no real influence. "If you can get a school board to fire one or two—" English, history, and civics teachers were the easiest to catch and to get fired, "the rest will fall into line."

"Eternal vigilance is the price of liberty." Now, what was Mr. Schnitzer doing about those Reds in California who had refused to testify? but had, in spite of the hard work of the overworked FBI, gone into other states and got jobs? The woman would have an orgasm in a moment.

How did a woman look in an orgasm, that is, a sexual one? The marriage manuals left here and there about the house by Charlotte before her marriage and after had never been clear. "Go back to the wanderings of Aeneas or your heaven under the sea," her IBM was begging.

"Do you, Mr. Schnitzer, know that your children are no doubt associating with the child of a hard-core Communist?" So what, lady? Mr. Schnitzer is always finding Reds. "—smart enough to have a telephone listed in his father-in-law's name."

The Popsicle Queen's mouth was set in that I-can-hold-it-forever smile. But her eyes—. Susie looked away. The eyes had made her wonder if her mother were remembering another accused—punished without trial.

She was neglecting Lady Macbeth; no, Mary Lou she must always be now after saving Susan Schnitzer's neck with that pretty tale. Straight she sat as the Queen of Holland on her throne, except no queen sat with a hand on either knee, hands clenched into fists, blue white against the dark dress. No, not entirely white; on the nearer one a pink stain seeped down. It made you think of cherry popsicle juice, or that she clenched a piece of melting frozen blood. And how and from where had she got the blood ice? And why should she clench her hands at all? She didn't have a grandmother sent over the river—after she'd been that grandmother's child six years.

"He's had four different jobs in four states. And now you, sir, have let him keep the job in your community more than a year. That's longer than in any other place, after the time it took to get him kicked out—."

She had managed to shut her ears. She had tried to pull her thumb, forgetting that long, thin hand. She pulled gently; no release. A little distraction; not enough. That poor, mistreated man chased out of every job he could get. Why didn't he try to emigrate to Canada where there was no UnCanadian Activities Committee?

She wished she were that fly buzzing around the long crack where two pieces of plywood had sprung apart; must be warm up there. Nice, no hunters of suspected Communists to chase the flies.—"And do you know how I found him? I had his wife's maiden name on file for—." Shut out the words. If you stood naked in a blizzard, numbness would at last come to kill the pain; but nothing could give numbness to the hurt of words. There were four flies now; no, five; five. Did the other children spit on the chased man's children? Could there be six? Six what? Six children vomiting up mud? No, only five. Five flies circling.

She almost cried out with the pain of it, sharper than the other kick, and no more expected: all the dangerous deals were past—prom night, Ben Holmes.

"No, Mama, Ah looked as you told me, but Ah can't go rummagen in that orchestra roll-book." The popsicle juice was pinker now; you could almost call it blood-red; blood and sweat, cold sweat. Better to pull your thumb than bloody your palms with the nails of your clenched hand.

"Susan." Her father in his best pink-slip voice. What ailed him? That shoe heel again; this time on her ankle bone. She'd vomit with the pain of it.

"She is just day-dreamen. But, honey, this is a ser'us mattah. What Ah asked you was do you know a girl in orchestra—Catharine or Mollie Catharine Ah think—McWhorter, Scots. She plays the flute; got a music scholarship to a school last summah. Her mothah works in a library; her older sister won a scholarship to one of those pinko eastern colleges for women; she has a youngah brothah. I learned all that through the yeahs of hahd work I've done on her fathah. He's a known Red; refused to testify an' all that. Just let me find out wheah he works; an wheah his girl is tryin to get into college. I'll make certain no more of this Communist's children go to college; one with a scholarship. Imagine."

Susie had forced herself to look into the woman's face and follow her word by word. She could find in the words no reason for that last kick; the hand warming her hand could not take all the pain away. Her "No, Mrs. Weatherford," was a truthful statement. She didn't know a Mollie Catharine McWhorter whose mother worked in a library, who played in the orchestra, and had a younger—.

That would be Katy. All of her was dead—except the part that wanted to shiver. There was a whiteness and a glittering in front of her. She was looking at a silver salt dish on the white tablecloth. That meant she wasn't looking at the woman. She'd have to. She couldn't. She shouldn't. The watching eyes would read the knowing in her face, and hear things in her voice. The table was so still, all waiting for this coward to speak. She lifted her head, and got out words: "I wouldn't know her name. Our conductor in orchestra speaks to us only by instrument and position."

Had they swallowed the lie? Old Harp spoke only in such fashion to some lowly one such as herself. Katy was his pride. Could this woman keep her from getting into college? She was opening her mouth for another question—but this one was for the ceiling. Everybody was looking at the beamed ceiling as Mr. Schnitzer said in a voice that would have chilled frozen mercury: "Ram, what—." The "are you looking at?" never came. Mr. Schnitzer had got a proper focus with his bifocals.

That did not keep Mr. Weatherford from answering most pleasantly: "Counting flies."

Mr. Schnitzer was for the first time taking a long hard look at his "solid oaken beams," or so the former owner and the real-estate man had called them. "Ooh, do you think that bottom plank will fall on us?" And Mary Lou made, for her, a most unladylike business of pushing back her chair.

"Plank?" Mr. Schnitzer cried as he lost both his oaken beam

267

and his ballast. He sprang up before the finger bowls came or his wife could begin a graceful-hostess rise.

The hand touching Little Pig Toe was warm and gentle as it guided her foot into the slipped-off, forgotten flat. Seconds later he was pulling back her chair. So they hadn't got Katy—yet. Mr. Weatherford and the flies had tangled the line. She could smile up at him. "Thank you for keeping one hand warm, and for remembering my flats. It would be something to go barefoot a second time."

"Your bare feet didn't hurt anyone—unless they got cold and hurt you. Helping you was a pleasure," he added with a nice smile.

She couldn't return his smile when she heard Mary Lou, the blood on her hands, not showing in her voice. "Fathah, Susie wants to show me her room."

Susie accepted the news in silence. She had wanted to dash for the powder room, closer, but hurriedly led the way to her quarters. No one outside the family and Lulu—you could call Ter part of the family—had ever seen her official bedroom; and so learned how complete the domination of her mother and sister. That didn't matter too much—now. She shook her head to Mary Lou's apology: "You don't mind, I hope?"

They had topped the grand stairway and turned toward the side hall when the girl wanted to know if they were out of sight. Susie nodded, and after a choked: "Excuse me, please," ran.

She got there in time; finished quickly; not much to vomit. Instead of food, she had swallowed words for dinner, and the words would not come. Or was it her greasy, cowardly self she was trying to be rid of?

She stepped out to find Lady Macbeth standing under the fan, cigarette in one hand, glass of water in the other. She handed the water to Susie, blew smoke fanward, and said nothing. She was someplace else. She didn't look around as Susie took one of Dr. Laughton's pills from the bottle in the medicine chest, and swallowed it with a good deal of gagging. He had told her to call him when she was nauseated enough to need one; but this time she would—. Would what?

Wash the vomit tears from her eyes and consider her guest.

She stood in her nylons, shoe heels hooked over one arm. "High heels kill me," she said when Susie came to stand by her. "Mama was furious because that boarding school didn't teach heels—or girdles either. But believe me, she is a full professor of girdles and heels—and a lot of other things." She took another puff. "I thank you for not saying anything about the prom. Will my cigarette get you in trouble?"

"No. That fan goes through the roof and takes care of everything, even flowers. I—well—you see, I should thank you, about the prom I mean." She shook her head to the extended package of cigarettes. "I've not started."

"I wouldn't, if I were you. They don't help—any more than ordinary tranquilizers."

"That pill I took wasn't exactly a tranquilizer. My doctor prescribes them for nausea, but he dishes them out like they were ten-carat diamonds."

Mary Loud nodded, but for the nod you had to make your own translation. She stood inhaling, exhaling, staring. There was nothing impolite in her stare. She wasn't seeing anything, that is anything in front of her. Susie, studying her without exactly meaning to, saw the faint blue under her eyes was not blue eye shadow but blue skin. She could tell the blue was real because the drawn face was so goose-pimpley, so pale the rouge circles were pink plates glued to either cheek. The lipstick was also pale, pale-girl pink; the same color her mother now bought for her; "the wet look," or something like that, she had said.

"Tranquilizers don't help. Cigarettes don't help. I have wondered—if those other things—would—." She began shivering; two petals fell from the same rose. She never noticed as she said: "I told them."

"Them?"

"Katy's people."

"Oh?—And I was wondering how to do it." Susie couldn't think of anything else to say. She did remember to turn on the wall heater. Come to think of it, she was freezing cold, too.

"It's all my fault," the other said, shivering harder. "I wanted to see what a big northern public school was like. I would write last spring to the principal's secretary for any school material she could send." She looked at the cigarette as if wondering what it was, remembered, took a long draw. "There was a lot of stuff with Katy's name; honor rolls in the school papers, music programs; but it was her picture when she won a music scholarship for the summer. Fool-like, I brought all that home—it had come to my school. Why didn't I leave it there? The Hound of Hell read it—and went into her files."

"But can't Katy's father have a trial?" Susie asked.

Lady Macbeth stared at nothing and shivered. "I don't know enough. Since he was first fired in California, Katy's father has fought to get into court; his lawyers, I mean. But as I get it, Mama's side doesn't want a trial. It's easier and more fun to torture him this way. She thinks most courts are 'pinko.' That's her word, not mine. She hates the Supreme Court.—Katy's father could take the California oath, but he wouldn't talk of past associations; Oh God, I'm using Mama's words again."

She didn't know it, but she was also making fists again, cigarette crumpling in one. "They've wrecked him, made his family almost starve. Oughtn't that to be enough? Young as he was when it happened, he was a full professor in a good university. He got other jobs—after long waits—each was a little lower, and usually shorter than the last. Sometimes he went a full year, sometimes a semester, before he was called in and told he wouldn't be needed any more.

"When he asked why, he'd get little excuses instead of real reasons. Nobody knows, I guess—except the hunters and the hounds—but Katy thinks the FBI or people from the outfits Mama belongs to would come round with his dossier and threaten publicity with an investigation. He had a great future as a biochemist. Now, he is nothing much but a technician in a big hospital. At least there they say they will let him know, and put up a fight when the hounds sniff him out. Some are old men who were friends of his dead father-in-law. He was a doctor."

She threw the crumpled cigarette into the toilet and lighted another—after two tries. Her hands were shaking.

Susie got from the closet her winter dress coat, and draped it around Mary Lou's shoulders. "My father's house is cold."

"It's not that kind of cold—exactly. But thank you." She was off again, staring at nothing.

"You could pull that round you and still not hurt the roses. They're so pretty."

Mary Lou looked at her. She scared you. That face showing through the make-up. "Pretty? That's what she says, Mama.—I thought—you might be different, and know without—. Skip it."

Susie hesitated, and glanced uneasily around.

"I locked the door," Mary Lou said, gathering up fallen petals.

Still, Susie spoke in quick whisperings. "Sad pretty, I mean; the way flowers at a funeral are pretty. Yours make me remember. That is all I can do. I don't even know the names of the black people killed in the riots up here while I was gone; and so many in the south so long ago when I was little; even the children bombed to death in church—I've forgotten most of their names."

Mary Lou was nodding. Her face still showed, but the light in her eyes was from different bulbs, new ones Susie had never seen. She looked almost happy without a smile. "I guess the names don't matter—too much; as long as somebody remembers. —It's worse on Sundays in that church; it suits Mama's religion, which is Anti-Communism. She just kind of uses God to push it along.—Somebody's knocking on your door."

Susie was already running.

She opened the door to Brandon, still wearing his good behavior. He gave her the society section of a Detroit Sunday paper, plus the information. "Mom thought you might like to look at this." He then told her that Margaret Lucille's parents were leaving in five minutes; at this he showed disappointment, strange for Brandon, as he practically never enjoyed guests.

Mary Lou was still staring, when Susie got back. "Look," Susie begged. "Here's a picture with Angus in it, and a story about *The Christian Family*. Poor Angus." She thought he might not want his defeat known to the world, and changed course. "You wonder if he enjoyed posing."

Mary Lou, after a moment's study of the picture, was shaking her head. "He's faked in," she said, in a voice you could have called relieved. "They've already had some kind of shot with his head on it; after they got the group picture without him, they had his head blown up or down to fit the others, put it in, then made this photograph. Kind of a rough job. Mama had a man could do better than that. He could fix pictures of some politician on Mama's Red list, show him shaking hands with anybody, a Communist from Russia or a Black-Power leader." She smiled. "But in spite of the high wages she paid him, he testified against her in court; told the truth, I mean; she nearly died. An old Indiana buddy treaten her that way."

"Indiana?"

Mary Lou nodded as she took one more quick puff. "Mama's home state—I think. Her people had to move a lot—so I've kind of gathered; the Depression. But don't blame her on the south." She was shivering again as she opened her purse, getting ready to put on a new face or mend the old.

Susie waited by the hall door until she came, wearing heels and a nicely mended face. Now, smelling faintly of something—possibly a hint of lavender and certainly not tobacco—Mary Lou was the gracious young lady, giving a gracious farewell. And her face didn't show at all, but her southern accent did.

Mr. Schnitzer's face showed. The Weatherfords had ruined his Sunday afternoon's golfing. Coming too late, leaving almost immediately after dinner meant no golfing partner for him in the little remaining daylight. His pale eyes reflected shock as well as anger at such behavior in a subordinate.

Susie knew she was in for it; she would get a good lecture from both parents on a lot of things. The second the anti-ensemble by the front door had broken up, Bismarck turned to her. "Susan, your behavior—."

Lulu, polite as always, was interrupting with the information that during dinner Susie had had two telephone calls from two different boys. The second boy had left his number. The Popsicle Queen was for answering at once; could be that "polite Terence." Susie balked. "How do I know he's not some awful general-course boy?"

Her father for the first time she could remember took her

side with a thundering: "She's right." He had heard a "sad story about this upper class girl who fell for a boy little better than a drop-out. You don't know who—."

Lulu was back. The young man was on the telephone again. His name was Dick Pryor.

Susie saw beams coming through the storm of her father's anger. A pity Pryor didn't send her as he did her parents.

He was as usual all politeness—and business. He apologized for calling while she was at dinner; then explained that because Robert was now too busy for the job, he, Pryor, had taken over the management of "The Humans." Did Susie think she could spare the time to help him and Katy hunt old labor songs and hymns Angus might use as they were or arrange into hair or labor songs? Angus had to spend so much time practicing church music—they were already working on *The Messiah*—he couldn't take time to do any song-hunting now.

Pryor was driving into Detroit with Katy to make a search in the main library; there was almost nothing in the little local library. Did Susie think she could come along this afternoon on such short notice? Copying words and music would be a lot of work; but Angus thought she knew more about such songs than anyone else around. She mustn't blame Angus; he had said she'd be too busy.

Everybody would, Pryor went on, appreciate her help, if she could spare the time—and her parents didn't mind. "But you know as well as I do there are parents who see any kind of protest from signs to sing-ins as unpatriotic. You could just say I asked you for a Sunday supper date." He suggested she call him back in fifteen minutes to let him know if she could come. "Tell your parents you'll be back no later than ten. I have to get cracking on homework."

"I want very much to come and help," she told him. "It would—." Do what? How could she face Katy immediately after that conversation at her own family's dinner table? Tomorrow had promised to be hard enough.

"You sound shook-up. If anything's wrong and you can't come, I'll take a rain check," Pryor was saying.

She had forgotten him. "Oh, no, no. I want to come, to get

away. You see—one of our dinner guests—dumped a lot of garbage over—the father of a girl I like very much, and—."

He groaned, said: "Ugh. I just remembered Mary Lou told me some time ago, her people were having dinner with your people.—Don't let that manure-spreader get you down. She doesn't know it, but he's going to get a trial."

13

Katy was already in the car when Pryor came for Susie. Smiling, acting natural, wasn't easy—unless you thought of Mary Lou. Her job of telling would have been a hard one. You wondered if she'd told Katy at school or gone to the home and told the parents. Wonder was as far as you could go. You couldn't ask questions.

Katy's happiness made her feel worse. The girl so seldom had time or money for any kind of fun; the trip into Detroit was, like that boat ride, something of a blast for her. She talked more than usual: music, both her own and possible songs for Angus, quite a bit about her brother in junior high, and the doings of her sister, a college sophomore.

Working in the library, finding songs she thought Angus might use, Susie began to feel less desolate. Pryor helped; he might be dull, but he was thoughtful; when she and Katy declined a full dinner, he treated them to a splendid high tea in a nice place not far from the library. There, they compared the songs each had copied. Both Pryor and Katy liked the ones she had found. Their praise and Pryor's gratitude were pleasant, but sweeter was the thought that Angus might be pleased with them.

He was, and told her so next morning at school when he met her by the bike rack she ordinarily used. They walked together into the building, but as usual when with him, she was stricken with what her grandmother would have called "a fit of the shys;" and couldn't do much of anything but smile.

Meeting Angus and the others here and there, mostly at lunch, were pleasant parts of a not-too-miserable world—except when she wondered on the future of Katy's father and his family. It was good to be officially well again, and free to take long bike rides after school.

Once past the ugliness between school and the outer edges of the super-highway cut, the country was little changed from last year. Hard, searing frosts to brown the fields and bring down the leaves had not yet come; trees and brush along those roads "unimproved" with weedkiller, were in their full autumn colors; while in the still yet green fields, dairy cows and cattle grazed with here and there a flock of sheep.

Even nicer about being able to get out into the country was the chance to accept The Primitive's invitation to come visiting. The big woman had heard of her illness from Iggy, and was happy to see her again. She offered Susie, with a word of caution on her safety, free run of her barns, woods, fields, swamps, and ponds, not forgetting her home. Susie came to know and love them all, from the sheep fold to the sugar bush with the great kitchen tying everything together. She particularly enjoyed the big, iron, wood-fired cookstove that as the fall weather sharpened The Primitive used more and more while the electric range sat cold and idle.

Better than mere seeing was the doing. She would never have believed a place inland could have so many interesting jobs —from getting down hay for hungry cattle to washing butter fresh from the churn. And as they talked together, she learned The Primitive's language; she now knew that Bender, the big, friendly black and tan dog, was a cur-dog, not a feist, the look and feel and taste of "strung okrie" and what a diddle was. She learned the glory of walking in the sugar bush late in the afternoon when the long, low rays of the setting sun added yet more gilding to the red and gold leaves over her head and around her feet.

Often she would linger while the blue of the sky changed to

gray-black; then it was watch for her starting-home signal—the evening star. She would rush away, though not forgetting to tell The Primitive good night. Sometimes she was milking in the barn, but often she was in the kitchen getting supper for her husband. He worked in a factory miles away and got home late.

One afternoon she met Iggy at The Primitive's; and on another afternoon, while biking over a little-used back road. It was on such another lonesome road she met, late one afternoon, Mary Lou astride a big horse Susie in time learned was a Tennessee Walker—a breed of which she had heard from Uncle Jeff. Seemed Mary Lou's mama insisted she keep up with her riding; she was still taking lessons in horsemanship along with everything else in the book from dancing to French conversation and beginning ski instruction. Mary Lou, as they went along together, complained the only time she had to herself was out on the back roads with Jeb—her mama's name for the rented horse.

Susie listened with sympathy. Her mother had put her through much the same mill for years. She couldn't think of any suggestions on how to get out from under, busy as her mind was trying to frame a question on Katy's father without bringing in Mary Lou's mother. She at last managed a: "Does anybody know if Katy's father has been given notice—or anything?"

Mary Lou smiled. "I think there may be good news, real good, one of these days. Mama's been too busy with church work to do much sleuth-hounding this week. Anyway she's cussen out the courts. Another man like Katy's papa got reinstated in his old job. He had never belonged to the Communist party; nobody has any proof that Mr. McWhorter ever did either. He just wouldn't say what they wanted him to say."

Mary Lou stared across a field to glowing squares of barn light. "Don't you get tired of lies and tales? You remember all that to-do about Negroes moven in? And you know how it started? This widow got rid of her big house in—Wellington Woods I think they call it—and bought a smaller one out here. Her chauffeur and his wife, the cook, came down to do some work before she moved. They were black; that started the tale."

Susie nodded. Mary Lou looked down the road. "Why, it's

277

almost dark. Papa is home by now, and they'll both be havin' kittens. They're always worried when I'm riden around on what they call lonesome country roads."

"There's nothing, nobody to hurt you here," Susie said.

"Try tellen Mama that. Since that bank robbery, when she's not worryen about holdups, it's rape."

What an insult to Ter! She opened her mouth; remembered she should not show overmuch interest in or knowledge of the robbery, and said: "I've never heard any more about that bank robbery. Makes you wonder if it wasn't just another big tale—like the Negro Invasion."

"Oh, but that robbery was real," Mary Lou said. "The other night Papa said he'd heard the FBI was still prowling around, keepen quiet to make it easier to catch the robbers an' get the money back. —I must get goen in a hurry. Bye now. See you tomorrow." She put Jeb into a trot and was gone.

Susie watched horse and rider disappear over the next low hill. Mr. Weatherford was a lovely man; but he had his bank robbery gossip wrong. Ter had of course returned the money. He had taken the trouble to get the gun back to her grandmother's place; returning the money was much more important—and easier. If Ter had been too sick to do it right away, that doting Lans would have done it for him. Her godfather was not the kind to keep stolen money around. You wondered now why Miss Susan Marie Schnitzer had let stolen money stay in her quarters one minute after she knew it was there.

She had, guided through the dark by her radar, taken a short cut and was now abreast of The House of Usher. —Her father would be roaring about electric bills; lights on in Charlotte's suite. That didn't mean she and her husband were home, but that somebody had been hunting Susie. Now, she didn't dare use the secret passage. And what had she done wrong that a parent should want to see her? Probably a telephone call from Robert had excited her mother—as a critical illness in her daughter never would.

Could be Pryor. If you wanted to think of the most embarrassing thing on earth, it would be to let good old Pryor learn what his Sunday afternoon and evening date with the ugly-duckling daughter had done to the Schnitzer household. Her parents and Brandon thought she'd spent the time boogalooing down Broadway with the heir to the Pryor position and money. She had made no effort to change their minds, nor had she mentioned Katy. Her answers to their many questions were—well, it wasn't nice to pat yourself on the back—just enough to make them kind of happy, warming themselves with visions of the future of their daughter; but nothing they could quote that might get back to Pryor.

She figured it was because of him, and not Robert, a ukase had come down: henceforth, she was to use Charlotte's telephone, and if the school Handbook of Students was not yet finished, she could have her name listed with Charlotte's number. Sounded fine to be only another piece of fakery; a telephone in somebody else's room was a lot different from having one all your own. When Uncle Jeff or Angie or some other contraband friend or relative rang her up, she never felt as secure talking in Charlotte's living room as in the soundproof pantry.

A bigger extra dividend from that first "date" with Robert was the side-door key. She never knew if her father had forgotten to ask for it—unlikely—or had a little trap set waiting for her to return it—more likely—or if he had decided that since boys were at long last asking her for dates, she was worth an outside key. In any case she did not ask.

She now went in by the side entrance, slipped up the back stairs to her room, and was downstairs again, clean and neat for dinner, before anyone saw her. Then, it was, of all people, her father, smiling yet as he gave her his nightly inspection; nothing wrong, not even a shadow of lint on her dark wool dress. Smiling still more, he gave her the news that Robert had telephoned twice, and would call again at eight. "And what is going on here?"

The old fool tried to make his voice match that roguish look on his fat face. Be nice to say: "Robert needs an able seaman; one willing to keep shut at the risk of his life, but willing to steer when the captain passes out." Bismarck looked so funny in his new role of doting father, she managed a big bright smile with words to match: "Oh, Father, nothing's going on. Robert's just another boy. Kind of nice, though."

Her mother had come up, and so had Brandon. She was for the first time in her life, she guessed, doing something that really pleased her family. If she said, "No" to trips on the *Antiname,* it would be the end of Robert and his dates. That would break her parents' hearts. Why spoil all that joy by letting them know she was more seaman than girl friend? —She couldn't tell; she'd promised Robert, not in words, but just by keeping shut. Still, all those beams were sickening. Brandon of late was polite and respectful as she had never seen him—and for the same reason as her parents' smiles—she was having "dates" with a surgeon's son from The Village, plus one date from an even bigger wheel —that is, in their measuring system. It hurt. Whatever she herself accomplished in grades, skiing, or swimming—unless she could win a beauty contest—would neither please nor impress anybody in the House of Usher. Wrong; she had forgotten Lulu.

It was loathsome. Bismarck had this unbendable rule that during a meal nobody—except himself—should leave the table for a telephone call. He must have had a few pre-dinner highballs along with his usual beers, for as Lulu served the soup, he told her that if: "—Susie's young man should call again during the meal—," she had his permission to leave the table; thus, Lulu should let her know.

Lulu let her know during Bismarck's post-dessert pontification on the "socialistic tendencies" of a certain governor who "ought to know better."

Robert. He had been thinking of her, he said.

"Naturally," she answered, "or you wouldn't have telephoned."

She wouldn't be so cross, he said, if she could see all "—the charts and things, mostly borrowed, I've rounded up." Would she go boating again with him this Saturday? He would let her be captain—most of the time—and obey her in navigational matters.

"I'd rather you'd be captain—if you can get some sense into your head."

He hesitated, then asked if she ever read a Detroit daily. She told him she almost never did, and waited again. He seemed to be having trouble with his voice or his words or both, but he eventually managed to get it out. Did she remember in the marine-supply place, that old man, Mr. Bales, worrying over a cabin cruiser reported in distress? Well, it had gone down in that little gale last Saturday—within sight of the Canadian shore. He stopped again.

She shivered, waited, and asked at last: "The people?"

"Six; two were little kids; one they've not found." He got his voice in hand, and began to beg again. She would come with him, wouldn't she? He wanted to learn how to handle the boat. Time was short.

She agreed on the last. She had no time to spare; she ought to be at work this minute—English.

Oh, he would help her; he had had the same man last year, and saved all his theme carbons. She could use some of these and get by with a few changes here and there.

"They wouldn't help," she told him. "I have to come up with an autobiography. You don't know my life."

"I know enough. That autobiography you have to do in junior English is nothing but an exercise in making up college entrance applications that want your life history. The main thing in a college application is to give yourself proper packaging; also your life would depend on the college you're applying to; a life for MIT for example, would need to be quite different from one for Radcliffe, say. I could certainly give you the proper image just for English."

That so-certain voice stopped at last. "*Et vous aussi,*" she said.

"You know I don't understand French. Does that mean something like, 'And you too, Brutus'?"

"If you want to think so; but add a Madison Avenue accent." She stared at the wall of the telephone nook, "—soundproof plastic in a simulated wood design." The *Antiname* was real wood; such beautiful creaks she had made. She ought to give Robert a good, firm, lasting "No" to this boating business. —Certainly she would back out Saturday if the weather were threatening; but on a still day up on Huron or down in Erie, she could think about the autobiography, and go over the part she'd do tonight. "Miss Schnitzer, will you mention in this piece all the lies you tell yourself? And how can you make it clear to this would-be sailor it's the boat you've flipped over, not him, but—."

"Susie, are you still there?"

"Thinking," she told him, and knew he knew she would come.

Upstairs in her study, she finished next day's homework as quickly as possible so as to have the rest of the evening for that autobiography.

Yet, once settled for writing, she could only stare at the blank sheet of paper; and there was nothing, nothing but the paper staring back at her. She walked about her quarters. It wasn't words that eluded her. She could put down a lot of words, but they would be—without the rest—mostly lies. Suppose she told that English teacher—she could think of him only as "Mr. Twitty"—the truth? He would fling the paper back with red writing: "I asked for a factual account of your life, not fiction."

Anyway, she was too big a coward to write of her real life with her grandmother, the sea, the woods, Lans in those early years, and all the others now forbidden, the nice times in hospital, the horrible time when she first saw all those scars. Funny, she hadn't thought much about her scars lately. Oh, she was careful still; but mostly from habit, like always taking a back seat in class where nobody could see the back of her neck. Why had she quit worrying over scars? Was it because they were actually almost invisible now, or because Ter had wiped them away with words?

Ter? In writing that autobiography she mustn't so much as remember him. Her life was, as for all students, kept on file. Teachers had free run of the records; worse, so had the two un-uniformed policemen wandering around the building and grounds. Last year it had taken her several weeks to figure them out; unlisted on the staff or maintenance rolls, never mentioned by the Establishment, the police—regular members of the town squad—were spoken of only in whispers by the more knowing and daring of the boys. Suppose one of these school cops should read the truth about her life? That would be more disastrous than having that would-be psychologist pick holes in her brain.

Write it, and forget all the bad things, she told herself. You can't forget; not the worst of all, the last real night with your grandmother. That was the night the bulldozer came to smash out your life—or at least it thought it had. The thing had come during Lans's party of celebration for her escape from the blood-hungry young. She remembered how all had looked at each other, wondering, when the sound of those quick, impatient taps on the back door cut through the party talk and laughter.

The Popsicle Queen and her husband had come to tell Susie's grandmother what to do.

That night, she, for the first time, secretly disobeyed her grandmother. Put to bed and told to stay there, she sneaked back to listen from the stairs. She heard the Popsicle Queen, not frozen then, weep and carry on as she begged the grandmother to get back to Canada; the pleadings of Angie and Joe that her grandmother stay and fight the charges against her, and their begging to be allowed to take Susie at least during this time of trouble; Uncle Jeff, quiet, holding out for lawyers; Lans, wanting both her and lawyers until things were settled and she could go on living with her grandmother. All the voices for her grandmother and herself were at times drowned in blasts of anger from Bismarck. He was determined to have her grandmother quietly deported with "no scandal" and for "that you don't need a lawyer."

She heard it at last, quiet after Bismarck's roaring, her grandmother's voice, no tears, no shiverings: "And suppose I do go to prison here? I will not be the first, for the same reasons. I will still have my self-respect."

Beeto, man-size and a junior in high school, had also been sent from the room. He'd found her eavesdropping on the stairs, and carried her back to bed. She couldn't speak, not then, not even to Beeto; the chokes were too tight.

She wasn't holding Beeto's hand but pulling her own thumb as she stood on the strip of clear plastic the Popsicle Queen had laid as a walkway over the precious wall-to-wall in Susie's official bedroom.

She was wasting time, getting nowhere on her life for English. Might as well work on her image for that psycho; she'd give him what he wanted—the teen-ager alienated under the scars—and a lot of other things. Twice in last spring's interviews he had brought up her scars. She had never told him the truth. Nobody would believe the truth.

She settled herself over a volume on psychology, the third Iggy had loaned her. She at first found it heavy going, and had often to stop and look up a word in the handbook of psychological terms she had bought last year. Gradually, meanings began to get through enough to interest her. "Why, I'm beginning to learn a little of what I'll need to know when I get to be a researching pediatrician," she told herself. Sometime later she glanced at her watch; past one. She sprang up. She'd be late for school if she didn't get to bed.

The automatic alarm in her head brought her wide awake with minutes to spare before getting ready for school. Time enough to linger in bed listening to the gentle footsteps of the slow rain. Daylight saving was still on, which meant she could have the fun of biking to school through rainy dark—if she could persuade Lulu not to take her in the station wagon because of the weather.

Lulu?

She sprang out of bed. As usual since her "illness" Lulu would be waiting with a breakfast Susie did not want—but always ate at least some of—and a packed lunch kit which she didn't want either, but carried. She figured there were not too many Lulus in the world; when you were lucky enough to find one, a little consideration for her feelings was the least you could do.

She won a friendly battle without, she thought, hurting Lulu's feelings, though rain-hatted, rubber-booted, and coated she had to go. She fooled along so, enjoying the rain and the foggy, gray-black world in which most ugliness was hidden, she was almost late. The "School-Is-Beginning" gong came on before she was completely settled in homeroom, binder half unzipped.

She had planned to re-read for possible errors her report for English on *Typee*, but instead of the book report, found herself staring at a sheet of paper, blank save for half a sentence—the distance she had traveled on that autobiography. Now, how had she let it slip in? If she didn't catch herself she'd be back with the troubled, sorrowful child of last night. She'd be worrying about her scars again, forever looking round her for any glance that struck her face, then sliding away to hide the pity or the wonder or the disgust in the eyes.

Nobody was looking at her. No one had commented with their eyes on her scars in a long time. Come to think of it, gym, when it meant swimming, was the only thing she dreaded—now. Though one of the best of the girl swimmers, she always managed to be very early and into the pool before anybody was hanging around the locker room; or almost late when the others were already in the water. She insisted on wearing her own cap with its extra coverage front and back, and though she could do nothing about the ugly, ill-fitting school bathing suits that were a must, she made it a rule never to linger in one outside the water.

"What if," she asked herself, "you were one of those children you've seen in hospital; the ones with malignancies of bones or blood? How many have lost another arm or leg—or died? You and your precious scars."

The lecture and others like it dimmed the scars. They came back around a week later, the same bright red snakes across her forehead and neck as when newly made. It was in advanced swimming as she was going latish into the showers, she heard from out the huddle of swim suits the words she had expected for years. True, she had when little heard the words a thousand times, louder then, shaking the sky because unspoken, for things said with the eyes are loudest of all; though this voice was overly loud:

"Yes, Susie Schnitzer has scars—scars on her head and her face and—." The disgusted voice paused while its owner thought up the full catalogue of Susan Schnitzer's scars. "And they're on the backs of her hands, her arms, and her knees. —And I would say she is doing very well for herself, taking that wealthy surgeon's son on The Hill away from his Detroit love, and—."

Somebody gave a "Sh-sh-sh. I'd stay out of that dirty gossip."

285

There was a shrug in the other voice. "Gossip? It was one of those secrets everybody knew—except I'll bet Susan Schnitzer didn't know when she took him away from—you know who. I'll bet his parents are tickled to death to have him going steady—do you know I saw them, just the two of them, in his car Saturday morning headed in the direction of Detroit—with a girl like Susan Schnitzer. Wotta change. Her scars didn't keep her from catching that handsome guy; and are his people loaded. Some say his dad married his second wife for her money but he's not doing too bad himself. He charged fifteen hundred dollars for an 'exploratory' on mother, when all she wanted, or needed, from our family doctor was something for stomach pains she gets after a few highballs."

A whiny girl's voice came on, angry, weepy: "Scars? Do you call those little old white lines she has scars? Why, they're even kind of cute; and when she had her picture in the paper they didn't show at all. Furthermore she's got none where they matter, her body. What does Susan Schnitzer know about scars?"

Susie knew she eavesdropped, but couldn't help herself. She had long since stiffened. Now, to hear that fool crying over her poor self. She ought to have a little taste of Susan Schnitzer's hatred of the silent pity mixed with the curiosity in the screaming eyes; all those shiverings before strangers, of dread at each new door, of anyone taller close enough to look down on the top of her head. And now to hear this—. She was wading into the huddle as somebody said: "Susie, Vicki here is belittling your scars. Thinks she's the only girl with one."

Vicki? Vicki? That would be that crumby Vicki Maxwell in homeroom; a spoiled and lazy brat to whom she had no memory of speaking. Absent a great deal; late a lot when she got there at all, but never greeted with anything but a smile from Miss Mothering in homeroom. Usually, the girl somehow managed to make it to eight-point honor roll; and a mama's pet, too; driven even on fair days. And why was she blubbering, and whatever was she doing in Advanced Swim Class?

The girls had made way for Susie. Vicki, bleary-eyed and sniffling, studied her face as if she had been an animal in a zoo. Finished, she let out a yelping, sobbing: "O-o-o-h. And you call those cute little lines I can hardly see scars? Look at mine."

Susie looked at the face. Aside from the bleary eyes, it was perfect, pretty, with a little brown mole on one temple to make an interesting beauty spot. Her glance swept lower; she then saw the red welt rising above the bathing suit to the top of the breast bone. Only one thing made a scar like that—open-heart surgery. She had seen children in hospital.

This good-for-nothing girl was, or had been, a cardiac. The scar was ugly, a welt, red like most newly-made surgical scars. Pity, determination to hide the pity, for who wanted to be pitied, made her voice harsher than she had meant it to be. And the girl was something of a fool, carrying on over a surgeon's scar that had healed a heart—possibly. "You call that little thing something to cry over? Why, even now while still new it's nothing, nothing at all. You—you should have seen mine. My scalp torn all to pieces—and my forehead—and one shoulder; some on my back, my knees. Why I was practically shredded alive. I doubt if I can ever wear a low-cut evening gown."

"But you can get into a swimsuit this very minute, Susan Schnitzer."

That was Miss Perry, firm, a favorite teacher. The poor woman was always getting odds and ends of girls in this class, sent here usually because of a schedule conflict. The extra ones could seldom do more than paddle around at the shallow end of the pool; but with the rest of the class past their life-saving badges, there was always somebody capable of overseeing the ignorant newcomers.

Miss Perry's patience was certainly being tried today; when Susie returned, Vicki was just handing in her class card along with a perfect gale of hiccoughs and sobs as she told of a conference last week between her doctors and her parents. They had decided she must exercise, and said she should begin with swimming.

Miss Perry was nodding, trying, Susie guessed, not to show she was listening to something she already knew. She had probably had to have a conference with somebody or bodies over Vicki. She downed a shrug to ask: "Are we so awful as to make you cry?"

287

Vicki's sobs accelerated into high gear weeping. Two girls said: "It's her scar." Another added: "She didn't know until now how much it would show above a bathing suit."

Miss Perry for the first time appeared to notice the scar. She dismissed it with a quick head shake. "Sorry, I can't cry with you. I watched the news this morning; another friendly Vietnamese village napalmed by mistake."

Susie smiled at the woman; the first teacher in Eden Hills High she had heard mention the war; nor had it been mentioned by Memorial Assembly speakers. Nobody could have known from the orations whether the dead students had been killed in the Revolution or fighting Indians; all had, "—given their lives to bring peace and freedom to the world." Ugh.

Miss Perry deserved a good deed, loathsome as it might prove to be. She stepped up. "Could I please help the new girl today? I might—might even help her over her scar alienation crisis."

Miss Perry gave what from a teacher in a different school might have been a groan—everyone knew that teachers lucky enough to get into Eden Hills School System never had cause for groaning. "I wouldn't know about the scar alienation crisis," she said, her voice dry as her hair. Last summer she'd been a camp director out west or down in Mexico or someplace where her hair had suffered. "Oh, thank you." She smiled at Susie; the fact that someone was actually volunteering to get the whining fool out of her hair had been slow in getting through. "You know what to do with a beginner; start with floating—that is, if she's not too afraid of the water. Remember, nothing past the second white line."

Susie thanked her, then dashed for Vicki, still weeping.

It took only a couple of minutes to learn the girl had had plenty of water, that is, for a "delicate invalid child." Already accomplished in the not-too-common art of simultaneously whispering and floating, her tongue got more exercise than her body. She had liked best the tide pools around Bar Harbor; but: "You know, they were too cold for a heart patient like me." A cottage near Nag's Head on the Outer Banks had been better for her in the late summer; usually through Christmas vacation they had gone to Miami; and about March, or whenever her sniffles got bad, her mother took her to Bermuda. But (sobbing), wherever she'd had to go for her health, she'd always worn the "grooviest little bikinis."

"Really," Susie whispered when she could get in a word: "I'm not belittling your scars, emotional shock, or alienation or—."

"Lost identity," Vicki interrupted.

"Thanks. But that scar just isn't big enough to send your ego into a skid. What if it were on your face and other places where it always showed? —Like mine?" She went deep as she could in the shallow water where she thought how nice it would be to be little again, believing water enough—swimming in the sea, rain on her face, snow—would wash those scars away.

She had to come up for air. Vicki was waiting, eyes pouncing on her face, taking it apart, scar by scar. Susie gritted her teeth and let her look. She gave at last a sorrowful nod: "But yours are so little, so pale, so thin." She continued to study Susie's face as she talked. "And anyway I imagine yours were accidental. Nobody just took you and scarred you up. They could have made a cut across my stomach; where the scar wouldn't show with a low dress or a strapless bathing suit. Why, I might even have been able to keep my bikinis."

"After the surgeon had cut through I don't know how many nerves, blood vessels, and muscles so the scar would be on your abdomen?" Susie thought of things overheard in the hospital. "What if your surgery hadn't been a success?"

Vicki was annoyed. "The idiots knew it would be, or they wouldn't have tried it." Self-pity ran out of her like grease from broiling bacon, as she told how much better life was before surgery than now. Her mother was getting downright mean; why, she even insisted—now—that she do her own research, type her papers, help keep her room straight; and would Susie believe it, take the bus now and then, instead of being driven. "—And on top of all that, this scar, and the money my father had to pay above Blue Cross just to make a surgeon wealthy."

"Please," Susie hissed. "I was only about six and a half when I jumped through two windows—a regular plus a storm—and if

289

the surgeon and the pediatrician had not been the best men on earth—healing my mind as well as my body—I would today be the personification of sick-sick repulsiveness. So, please, do not denigrate the medical profession to me."

"Oooh. You know, Susie, you should write for TV. Such a vocabulary. And that jumping through two windows would be good on TV. Who was chasing you?" Vicki was so impressed she had for a microinstant forgotten her precious self.

Susie glanced warily at Miss Perry to find her busy with the five poor divers. "Nobody was chasing me. My father thought I thought he was—and that I was running from him. —I mean I think that's what he thought. He was calling me for lunch but I wasn't hungry and I hated sitting still so long at table for Saturday lunches—when he was there. It made him furious when I couldn't eat—people commented on my thinness.

"That Saturday he was in a very bad humor, storm-window Saturday in an old-fashioned house with no thermopanes, just glass storms in frames. And the boy who was to help hadn't come. But I loved it—screens off, nothing for a little while between you and the outdoors." She heard the rushing whispers poured out for Vicki's greedy listening. She must stop. This story was the true one, the same she had struggled through under the nurses' pitying eyes, and the doctors', and her grandmother's, only to have her words hit walls of unbelief; all had been certain the child was lying to save her father.

"She's not looking. Go on; why it's good as a TV serial." Vicki was so carried away, she forgot to put sobs into her voice.

Susie tried not to listen to her own tongue; it had gone crazy. "I played leaping from a boat smashing up and saving a drowning baby; and then with the windows and myself I played, 'Let's go in and out the windows.' And so I heard my father call, angry; and I thought: 'I will have one more good jump, run around the house, leap into the dining room, and be sitting at table when he comes.' And so I ran into the room where he had just put up the storms so clean I never noticed they were there. —I jumped."

"Oh, oh, go on."

Vicki had forgotten to whisper. Miss Perry had interrupted

her comments on a group dive to send a nasty look in her direction. "She's floating," Susie said.

"Good," Miss Perry said without taking her glance from Vicki. "Try keeping still—with all that breath you can swim the Detroit River; but first try a stroke."

They were for a few minutes silent; and it was plain that Vicki at some time or other had paddled in the sea or the family pool. Swimming wasn't the word for it, not energetic enough for a dog-paddle, but she somehow moved with a wriggle here and a flap there. Pity, the lazy thing didn't want to work at her swimming; instead, talk, talk; she forgot to sob, but remembered to whisper as she told of the whole new wardrobe she was getting because of her scar. Finished with clothes, she made herself comfortable in the shallowest water; and, chin on hand, elbow on the bottom of the pool, legs floating, studied Susie. "You know, I think I agree with my girl friend. Your face is interesting. Piquant, I think is the word."

Susie said nothing. She thought of Ter; he had said the same thing—about her face. He had also said: "It slid away." And what had that meant?

Vicki was giving a sorrowful head shake. "And your scars; they don't show at all."

"You should have seen them after my first round with surgery—there had to be a good many, of course—my own parents couldn't bear to look at me."

"Naturally, they couldn't bear to look at you, especially your father. He must have a simply terrific guilt complex because he made it possible for a little innocent child to run through a window. And, anyway, I'll bet they wanted you to be a boy, the way mine did me. —Or you may have been an accident. Away back then before the pill and the IUD no birth control method was more than ninety per cent perfect, and there—. Golly, what a mean look she's giving me. I'd better try a stroke."

Vicki flapped a few feet. Miss Perry got busy with another group of divers; and Vicki again settled herself in shallow water to come up with questions; among them: "Didn't the neighbors and a lot of other people think your father was guilty?"

Susie wished she could get away to the deep end of the pool

—or keep the door to her own private quarters shut. She had never before discussed her scars with anyone. And she ought not to whisper in Miss Perry's class, but—. "Things wouldn't have looked so awful if my father had not been in a very bad humor; the neighbors must have heard him yelling around. They may have seen him when he ran around the house to look at me. Unfortunately he was still carrying a yardstick he'd been using —on the windows, not me. —Out there on the ground I was too shook up to know how badly messed up I was. I just knew I had broken his windows. I think I screamed: 'I didn't mean to break your windows.' And then—."

Vicki had interrupted with a, "Wow. And all the neighbors were certain he had pitched you through that window. I'll bet your folks moved out of that neighborhood—quick."

"You'd better try a stroke. Stay put and watch now." Susie started away in slow demonstration. Vicki caught her ankle.

"Stay with me. Why didn't I try to make that teacher think I am afraid of the water? I don't want her to find out I can even try a stroke. I don't want to be forced to overdo. —They moved, I'm sure. What else did your father do?"

"The same thing I suppose anybody else would do; rushed me to the closest hospital. —My blood ruined the car."

"Wow. I'll bet a lot of people in that hospital had a lot of ideas. There are always stories in the newspapers that tell how doctors find children beaten half to death by their parents and the parents claim accidents. You wonder what your parents told them?"

Susie didn't wonder. She knew. While she had lain in the back of the car, enough consciousness returned to let a good deal of her father's loud talk get through along with her mother's repeated: "They'll never believe it." Pity she couldn't tell that part; such a clumsy lie, it was almost funny. But suppose gossipy Vicki spread the story and it got back to her parents?

Miss Perry was looking at her with nothing but sympathy as Vicki repeated her question. Now she was glancing at the clock; seconds later, she had stopped the class to ask for another volunteer to take care of Vicki. "I let the time slip by, and Susie has lost over half the period."

A tall blonde with a firm jaw stepped up, and, leaving Vicki in a pout, Susie swam away. Miss Perry, wonderful woman, had saved her from that last question.

She had, on reaching emergency, been conscious enough to hear her father's bellow: "I must have immediate help for my child. A big black dog scared her so she jumped through a window. I'm afraid she's bleeding to death." He'd sounded more angry than scared, she thought. Dogs frightened both Charlotte and Brandon; something must have happened to them.

The next several days were foggy—Intensive Care, surgery, more days in I.C., more surgery; and all around no yelling, no teasing from Brandon; low, kind voices that made her think of her grandmother.

Then, at last a bed in a room all to herself and her bandages with the surgeon—Dr. Hefler—and Dr. Laughton, along with other doctors and nurses in and out. They had asked no questions; they had had no need; the lawn had been her sea; grass clippings had mingled with the blood on her shredded knees. One day Dr. Hefler had brought her a small stuffed black dog; she loved it as she loved all dogs. Dr. Hefler had only smiled. Later, when she felt better, she told him, as she had told her nurse, what had happened. And because her father's part of the story was plainly untrue, nobody had ever believed the first part. All had been certain she was lying to save her father, who had chased her through the windows.

Nobody believing until here came this little idiot Vicki to believe and understand the first part. Perhaps truth was only for idiots and children. Vicki was a bit of both. Here she was on the high dive going into her second jackknife, Miss Perry and the whole class watching; and she hadn't thought of her scars. Could it be Vicki was right? Did her scars scarcely show now?

She surfaced to a clapping of hands and Miss Perry's: "Splendid, Susie. That was perfect."

She was biking home, and in spite of heavy traffic with cars honking at her, feeling scarless and happy, when she remembered the other thing overheard as she went into swimming—the business of her having taken Robert away from some female in

Detroit. Gossip or fact? You'd think if it were true, she'd have heard some mention of the girl in the car with the boys or at lunch. Robert, in spite of talking a lot, kept his secrets. His real mother was apparently one of them. Last Saturday on the *Antiname*, she'd hoped he'd at least mention her, but he had not.

She had also hoped he would say something about the red blanket and the black slip she'd rescued from the hold on that first trip, and had not seen since. She wondered if he'd put them back in the hold. She'd never know. He now kept the hatches locked—and she had never seen the keys. Robert had apparently decided that the hold and its contents were nobody's business but his.

Furthermore, she was now reasonably certain the slip did not belong to the second Mrs. Hedrick. She had never seen the woman, but her mother did in Garden Club. Susie had, without direct questioning, got out of her, "No, you couldn't call her tall. She's not dumpy, but on the short side, straight—and always beautifully dressed in expensively simple clothes."

In the first place such a slinky-hipped, big-busted slip as she had found would not fit Robert's step-mother; and in the second place, fit or no, she wouldn't wear such a piece of junk. Also, had the woman worn the same cheap, loud perfume as flooded the slip, her mother would have commented on it.

The slip, she guessed, would always be a mystery as were many things about Robert. Yesterday he had interrupted her pleasant after-school tea with Lulu and Brandon to telephone about another boat ride on Friday afternoon, a half-holiday for pupils because of Teacher-Conferences-on-Pupil-Evaluation. She'd told him she needed that afternoon for shopping in Detroit. He had said he couldn't go boating Saturday; so why couldn't she shop then; Science Club hadn't started yet; she could have all day. She couldn't very well explain what she meant when she said "shopping." Now that she was old enough to go alone and buy her clothing, "shopping" consisted chiefly in going to Angie's, or being picked up at some inconspicuous place by Angie or Joe or some of the help. The Montreal couturière who had made most of Susie's clothing since her first summer at the "Camp for Exceptional Children," when because of her scars she needed the covered-up look, sent everything to Angie.

The couturière was a most conscientious woman, insistent on proper styling as well as up-to-date measurements, preferably taken by herself, though she would accept them by mail. Fit and workmanship were perfect. Proud of her work and of being a Quebeçoise, she would not sew in Made-in-U.S.A. labels. Most of this along with tryings-on had to be done at Angie's any time when Angie was home.

The other part of the deal had to be done when banks were open. Her mother had, when Susie was small, known of the Canadian wardrobe that was such a help in getting ready for school. She had paid for it, and been grateful for the shopping, only one of many services afforded by that wonderful camp, "so good for Susie."

However, as Susie grew older, the Schnitzers wealthier, her mother insisted Susie begin to learn to buy her own clothing. Susie continued with her old dressmaker, easier and pleasanter, and she liked her things better than any she could find in shops. This created a money problem. Her grandmother insisted on paying all expenses while Susie was with her. Her mother gave her clothing money. She could not spend this for fear of arousing suspicion. Her grandmother expected her to put the Schnitzer clothing money into the same Windsor bank into which went all fees paid by Mr. Schnitzer to the "Camp for Exceptional Children." She had heard him comment on its cheapness, less than two thousand dollars for a whole summer with "a lot of travel" and Christmas and Easter vacations "thrown in" if parents wished. Cheap the camp might be, but after all these years, its fees plus clothing allowances were getting to be quite a pile.

Schnitzer clothing money had rolled in; she had bought nothing since coming home; brought nothing from Angie's except what she could carry under her *rebozo* the night of the party; and her mother was nagging about her need for new clothes. Instead of getting money from here to there and clothes from there to here she was going out again on the *Antiname*.

A still bigger problem was her savings account in a Detroit

bank. When she had first come to live in her father's house, she could never use the money given for school lunches. The business of buying the food, then trying to eat with a horde of gobbling, shoving children, many gawping at her scars, had gagged her. Lunch money, whether for "that place down the street," or in the schools with lunch programs, had accumulated. Extra money, when you had to share Charlotte's room as in those early years, had been too dangerous to keep around. She had opened a savings account with a Detroit bank—after making certain the bank was not used by her father.

She could not tell her grandmother of this account; she would worry because her Susie ate no lunch. Her father would blast her for not eating lunch, her secret ways, then cut off her lunch allowance and possibly demand the return of the saved money. Not all of it had come from him; already this year there was the Lans money, plus the record and cab money given by her mother. All that waiting to be dribbled into the bank so as not to arouse suspicion. No, not all; a good deal ought to go to worthy causes such as The Salvation Army, Bon Secours in Montreal, and some movements her father would call leftist.

There was also Katy wearing pretty much the same beat-up clothing as last year, handed down from her sister, Susie suspected. How did one go about giving a girl like Katy money—or clothes?

The extra clothing and accessories showered on her by her grandmother, Beeto, Uncle Jeff and Aunt Margaret, but most especially Angie, who traveled a good deal in search of decorating ideas for Joe's model homes, created a problem worse than that of extra money. She was always beating her brains to answer her mother's and Charlotte's questions: "However did you manage to buy that gorgeous sweater? Anyone would think it a real hand-knit imported from Sweden." It was, a gift from Angie. "Such darling boots; amazing what imitations Americans make; vinyl, I believe you said—and they look exactly like hand-sewn Italian suede." They were. And how would she explain those white leather boots from Spain Angie was holding for her? Possibly she should pretend to run over her clothing allowance. She never had, much to the amazement of her parents, and the annoyance of Charlotte, who could never keep within her own.

Oh, no! She had let her radar bring her to the House of Usher when she had planned a bike ride into the country. Now, she did not even remember what must have been a nice ride from school. She'd ruined it by chewing over Robert and her other problems.

They had compromised. He would, without taking time for lunch Friday, drive her straight to Hudson's. There she could shop for an hour while he lunched. Hudson's was a big store with a lot of entrances and exits, she could nip in one side, out the other, get to her bank close by, and be back with time enough left from the hour to buy something—if she could think of anything she needed.

She ought to have given Robert a good firm "No" on boating. At least she must think of some nice way to make him understand it wasn't Robert Hedrick III—or was he a IV?—she was wild about, but the *Antiname*. She wished she liked Robert as well; she might if he were as honest as the old boat.

The "No" never came. The *Antiname* had grown to be a part of her life, a secret she could share with no one save Robert. Times, it hurt like a pebble in your shoe, forgotten until you move your foot a certain way. It hurt when she called Beeto each Saturday immediately after Science Club, in order that the credit card he paid for would not show Detroit, where she was going. The pebble hurt when she called her grandmother on Friday afternoons, or declined the invitations of Angie and Joe for a Saturday's sail or a day-long visit. She had been hard-put to manage two dinners with them—after a quick visit to the bank that on Fridays kept late afternoon hours. She had also "shopped," and was gradually getting home the clothing that waited at Angie's.

She was, she figured, paying a high price for the *Antiname*. The lies she had to tell were the biggest part, but she also missed the forbidden relatives and friends. The disgusting thing was that this fall was the safest time she had ever had for long visits with them. She had the perfect excuse for spending a lot of time in Detroit.

Her mother was not only wanting her to buy at least one "date dress" with accessories and heels, but had also loaned her two credit cards: one for a large, good department store; the other for an exclusive, horrendously expensive boutique in

Grosse Pointe. She had had no time to pretend to use either.

Safer yet, there seemed little chance of the Popsicle Queen's taking time to shop with her as she had used to do with Charlotte. She was too busy. She had always been busy, but never with such a "tight schedule" as this year. Susie had never heard it discussed, but words dropped here and there, along with early memories, indicated that her mother had worked in Bismarck's office during the first struggling years of his business. If so, it was one of those family secrets, as carefully kept as the history of her grandmother. Now, the idea of his wife's "working" would doubtless give Bismarck a stroke, but Susie wondered at times if her mother didn't average at least a sixteen-hour day—when you counted everything. She had once heard her discuss household chores with about-to-be-married Charlotte.

First, when a woman had only one full-time servant, a laundress, and a heavy-cleaning woman, there were a good many odd jobs of housewifery left for her to do. Along with this, keeping accounts, the linen closets, odds and ends of mending, chauffeuring children, shopping for household staples other than groceries, conferences with the gardener and maintenance men, food and menu conferences with Lulu; all these took up much of her mornings.

Still, there had to be time left for beauty care, both at home and in hair, face, and body shops. Lately, one whole day each week had gone to a full tune-up at an exclusive place, some lately-found club a friend had recommended; like a woman's club, her mother said, where one had exercises, beauty treatments, a proper lunch followed by a food lecture; and in the afternoon, swimming, biking, and games. She planned to go there for several days while "your father" was in Wyoming to hunt mule deer.

Beauty care, shopping for Brandon's clothes as well as her own, plus activities connected with a country club of sorts, church, and a few other organizations were old stuff to her mother. Eden Hills, with its uncommonly large variety of clubs, had sent her still further down that joining road. First had come generous donations plus lowly work—washing dishes behind the scenes at church suppers, keeping display tables tidy during a flower show of the Garden Club—but soon she was getting on committees; this fall she was head of several.

The community specialized in art and uplift organizations. Art was a kind of religion of which one talked in a low, serious voice and ranged through flower arrangement and "potting" to morning musicales. Her mother was no ninny when it came to music—but much to Bismarck's disgust she was no good at understanding football. She seemed to be doing all right in uplift, represented in Eden Hills by an organization for everything from beautification of the streets to improvement of unsatisfactory organs and areas of the human body—feeble brains through gout-damaged big toes. Her mother became a Heart Volunteer, meeting biweekly for lunch and an afternoon of work.

Another afternoon, and sometimes two, went to her art— pottery; for this she took classes, bought clay and glazes, went wild with "creativity" as she messed around in "the loveliest butcher's smock." Susie had never seen any of her "pieces"; odd, how she and Mr. Twitty used the same word for very different articles—a clay shape, a theme, a book report—or that autobiography she was still trying to write.

There were in the outline questions concerning her parents. She supposed she'd have to put them down as a "popular" couple, or "people beloved by many," or some such. This was the puzzling thing about the Schnitzers; they entertained a good deal, both at home and the club; seldom was one of their invitations rejected; stranger still, they were invited out a great deal over and above the usual get-togethers with business associates, buyers, and poker or bridge partners. They had not yet made it into The Village; but if clothes and late hours meant anything, they were rising in the social world.

She supposed her mother was the attraction; she had good looks, good manners, mostly listened instead of talked, and seemed to have a fair amount of sense. Whatever the reason, her evenings out with Mr. Schnitzer had increased until it seemed Susie and Brandon had an early dinner alone together more than half the time.

Early dinners made for long evenings, and even when she lingered with Lulu in the kitchen, the time upstairs was long. In spite of five subjects, preparation for the psychologist, and her struggles with the autobiography, she had more free time than in other years. This was the first time since coming to live with her parents that she was not being badgered until forced to join things or take lessons. She had not even heard anything further of her need for pistol-target practice. She could thank her dates with the *Antiname* for that and that one "date" with and several telephone calls from Pryor. Her father was not above asking about him now and then; be fun to tell him that Pryor was not only manager of the kind of "group" her father hated, but was also something of a folknik, with an especial interest in the working men's songs she had learned from Driving Pete.

Homework finished, she often took time to put down a just-remembered song. There was also time to "think on things"; plan a new sailboat, study maps for next summer's buying trip with her grandmother, work on a "poem" or the rearrangement of a hymn for Angus. At such times she tried to occupy her hands with chores—doing her nails, sewing on labels, mending, or rolling up her hair with its unfashionable determination to curl too much.

Other nights she would fill her record player in the sound-proof study, lock all doors against Brandon, then go up to the attic, lift the insulation enough to hear, and settle herself to study or chores. Yet often she would find herself not working in the cone of light from her study lamp, but watching a candle flame, and, along with the music from below, listening to the wind or the rain.

The wind, the rain, and certain songs by Pete Seeger and Jacques Labrecque filled her with sorrow and a longing that made her want to run away. Some nights she did sneak out by her secret passage, bike to the closest telephone booth, and there call Angie and Joe, Jeff and Margaret, just for the sounds of voices she loved, the real smiles felt through the telephone wires.

Trouble was that coming home after a warm, happy conversation, she was not certain whether the wetness on her cheeks was rain or tears. If tears, why? She had told no lies—except they took for granted her evening calls were made from home. They'd have fits if they knew she was biking around alone in the dark. She would clutch a sea urchin or a sand dollar in her pocket and hurry back to the attic.

There, after the telephone conversation, she sometimes felt better, but often worse. "Things are better than they used to be," she would whisper to herself. "Time is passing, passing." This didn't always help the gnawing inside you; for what, you didn't know. Your eyes begged for long looks where hill or rock or sea met sky; but there was never much of anything here save a sunset from Charlotte's windows, close over the next low hill, and usually more smog than sunset.

Her ears remembered and begged for the sound of surf, the wind in the big spruce in front of her grandmother's summer house, the rain by the windows, and voices—voices more than anything. Her grandmother's lonesome-sounding and far away over the telephone wires didn't help her now; if she could hear someone say *about* or *house* as the station master said such words, or hear some French, or—.

She was being silly; now by her secret drawer, fondling dried rockweed. She quickly put shells and seaweed away, then locked the drawer, meanwhile lecturing Susan Schnitzer on her babyish ways: "What if you had real troubles like Katy or Ben or Angus? Lady Macbeth with all that TLC and togetherness doesn't have it easy. Everybody has troubles—except Robert; and that's because he walks The Establishment Road, and his father's road—at least everybody thinks so. More and more she was suspicious that he was taking the boat out unknown to and without permission from his father. She wondered, too, on Vicki's gossip; though she now and then was given charge of the girl during swimming lessons, Vicki, constantly overflowing with gossip, TV serials, clothes, and boys, had never again mentioned Robert's ex-girl friend—if there had been one.

Nicer to think of Angus and Driving Pete. They went together when you thought of certain songs; and you wished Angus could have Driving Pete's heaven. At least she could put him in that heaven under the sea she and Driving Pete had built together, where all things endured forever, sunrise on a gull's wing or a baby's laughter. "Just the laughter?" she had asked the old man. "I would hate to take Aunt Angeline's [she had in those early years called her Aunt instead of Angie] whole baby. She is so very fond of him."

"Just the laughter," Driving Pete had said in his own nice accent—a mixture of Nova Scotian English and lumberjack French. "Or the beeping of the sandpipers or the curl in a wave. They'll stay forever in our heaven."

And so would Angus, along with a lot of other people and things. You never knew. She might tomorrow find something good enough to put in heaven.

Nothing much out of the ordinary happened at school next day or the next. The *Purple Sunflower* came out as usual on a Thursday, and in it was Robert's second anti-miniskirt article. She didn't read it, and wondered if he'd take off next on overly-long hair for boys. Angus still had his. And why shouldn't he keep it? It wasn't long, not even dangling over his coat collar.

She learned of the thing good enough for heaven Friday morning on the way to school, when Iggy called to her out of the early morning dark. He was jubilant. Had Susie heard the good news? Mr. Soames's law firm had kept The Primitive out of jail, and her fines were not too heavy. Their roads separated before he could give her all the details, but there were enough to make her happy.

School out, Susie biked to The Primitive's to offer congratulations. She found the big woman so surrounded by others of the anti-weedkiller crowd, and bugged by telephoned congratulations, she had been unable to start the evening's barn chores. Her cattle and sheep got little food from pasture now, and must be fed. Susie had learned from helping on other evenings how this was done. The Primitive gave a pleased nod when she asked permission.

She enjoyed giving hay to hungry sheep and cattle, as she loved the big, hip-roofed barn. Going into it, she always felt she was entering a favorite church. Now at twilight before the lights went on, you could imagine the top hayloft high under the roof was a nave hidden in the shadows.

A few feet past the hall doors, high and wide enough for a loaded wagon, she stopped the better to smell and listen. The place at first was silent at your coming as a deserted church so that the smells came first—hay, corn, oats, chopped feed, silage —with over all these the odor she could not exactly place: that of the barn, she thought, wood, clay floor of the first story below her, old mortar of the stone foundation; she didn't know.

She did know all at once that somebody had been at work; she heard the rustle of hay, cattle feeding, and the old horse craunching corn; then softly from a haymow came the song:

I looked over Eden, and what did I see;
Comen for to shorten my hair?
A band of barbers comen after me.
Comen for to shorten my hair.
Spare my hair, kind barber, comen for to shorten my hair.

She smiled. Angus was singing; and using her arrangement of the chorus. He went on with another verse, but stopped when he swung himself down on the hay-lift and found her.

She wished she could think of the right things to say. You never had to worry over conversation with Robert; talk flowed from him as from Vicki. Angus was different.

Still, they had a fair conversation while together they fed the sheep, the rest of the cattle, and the chickens that were already going to bed. She told him how much she liked his singing. He thanked her for the work she had done on the song. They talked of The Primitive's not having to go to jail, and Angus told of the party of celebration Mr. Soames was giving for her and the lawyer who had pleaded the case. He didn't suppose she could go any more than he—church choir practice. And anyway, he guessed it was mostly for people over twenty-one who could drink.

Their talking so lengthened the chores, it was full dark before Susie knew it. Angus suggested he run with her as she biked; that way he could finish his track practice for the day. He was a grand runner, she decided before she was half way home, speeding through the dark as he directed. There wasn't much opportunity for talk, or anything but traveling. Still, it was nice; he ran up the drive and told her good-bye only when she had wheeled her bike into the gardening center.

Things were nice in the House of Usher, too, except her lateness in getting home had worried Lulu. She was apologizing for not having telephoned when here came her mother, so joyful she had forgotten her fear of wrinkles and was smiling all over the place. First, she wanted to know who was the "tall handsome young man" who had escorted Susie home.

Susie told her he was Mrs. Weatherford's favorite minister's son.

Her mother looked pleased, but another boy friend for Susie was not the only cause of her joy. Lulu told it first, then Brandon. One of her mother's pottery "pieces" had not only won the class prize; but it had also been seen by the chairman of their church floral decoration committee; the woman had asked for the use of it in the Service of Thanksgiving.

Susie was listening, interested, not pretending, to her mother's description of the "piece," when Bismarck got home to vaporize all that joy. Times, it seemed, he wanted her mother to have her mind only on his component parts and troubles, with a little spared for Brandon and beauty care. Who wanted to hear about pots when he had just learned "that old hillbilly" had been tried and "got off with a slap on the wrist?" He was in a blue-nosed fury. She had been found guilty, not of threatening the life of a man or attempted manslaughter, but only of illegal use of firearms, interfering with public work, holding up traffic, and a few other little things. Most of her fines had been suspended; she had only to pay for the nicked tire, time lost by men and machinery, court costs, and a few fines. The only drop of soothing syrup he could find was that; "Inadequate as her fines were, the old Red might still have to take in washing to pay for everything." He'd bet her lawyer had charged a pretty penny.

Susie put on a long face; and said she doubted the costs, whatever they were, would bother the woman. She'd heard the court had allowed her around half a million for the sixty or seventy acres of land taken by the superhighway; part of it of course was damage payment for cutting her farm in two.

Her father roared like a sea lion: Susie listened to too much gossip; that old hilly land wasn't worth anything like that much, unless of course some fool wanted to subdivide, and—.

Susie figured he had remembered one of two things, or both. She had heard his roars when he and her mother were discussing buying the House of Usher and its two acres. "But fifteen thousand an acre; I could buy a whole farm for that." The second thing he might be remembering was that "hilly land" brought a higher price from prospective owners of "custom built executive" homes than flat. He made a quick tack away from where he thought the wind was, and said with some contentment "the old thing" had got just about enough out of the Road Commission to pay off what she must owe for the place.

Susie gave a yet more sorrowful head shake: she had learned from "the boys" the woman had bought the land years and years ago, either during or just after World War II. She'd lost a relative in an accident; a lawyer—she'd better not say Mr. Soames and risk giving Bismarck a stroke—had read or heard of the accident, and got for her several thousand dollars in damages. Her children and her husband, some kind of skilled factory worker, had not wanted to go back to their old home in the south. So she bought land up here; she had wanted a place with "little hills if I can't have big hills," they said she had said.

She'd somehow heard—keep Mr. Soames out of it—of that old place up the road. The original brick house had been gutted by fire; nobody then thought of subdivisions coming close; in fact there were not any at all away back then; and so the woman had bought the place for almost nothing. She, her husband, and children had used brick from the old house to build another, and—.

Her father, unable to bear more, was stalking off for beer. Her mother had been listening with that "peace without negotiations" look. Susie wished she had kept her mouth shut. What she had told him was true. He believed her, or he wouldn't let it bug him so. Now, he'd be in a vile humor all evening, with dinner one long lecture on his favorite evil of the moment—subversion among college students who "made demonstrations." Her mother was gone, description of her pottery unfinished. She'd be the one to suffer. Tomorrow, instead of her father's voice, Susan Schnitzer would be hearing the voices of the *Antiname* and of Erie.

Next afternoon on the *Antiname* all voices were muted in a

windless, gray world. Few pleasure craft were out, and the up lanes were empty of salties. The closing of the Seaway was only around a month away, and the salties were all hurrying down to the sea.

She felt safe enough—now—on a calm day such as this with Robert alone in the wheelhouse. When you compared the Robert of that first trip to the Robert of now, he showed something like a thousand per cent improvement. He had learned enough to know he knew almost nothing of boats and water.

She ought to get to work on that autobiography, but now as usual she was wasting time by watching Erie; always different; today, a heaving mass of gray iron, water remembering a recent storm. Susie had always scorned the lakes; that is, as much as she could scorn any body of water; she had thought of them only as something a boat inland must navigate on its way to the sea. By now she had seen and felt a good many Eries and several Hurons, though none that really grabbed her as on that first ride —the one with Ben. She wished he would come again, but he never did, nor did Angus or Katy.

Together they could have watched the water. You couldn't do that with Robert. He never saw the changing face of Erie, or noticed wind or sun or cloud, or duck or Canada goose, heard whistling reeds, or marveled at the many shades of gray on Zug alone—save as hindrances or helps in navigation. His one thought was getting the boat from here to there.

He did not even see the *Antiname*. A long time ago somebody had put a lot of love and hope along with money into the boat. You could see that from the detail of the wheel and the few original fittings left. Robert worked among those old dead dreams and never wondered on the other owners. He was business all the way. Ben, in his face, his voice, his care not to capsize the old thing had shown he had a lot of the sailor in him. Her grandmother, relatives, in-laws, and many of her Nova Scotian friends had this same love of and respect for boats and water.

Over and beyond these were the men who made their livings or their starvings by the sea, the fishermen and sailors. Many all mixed up, like a working sea captain her grandmother knew, declaring he hated the North Atlantic, the cruelty of it, the treachery, shaking his fist at it, cursing the day he had wedded it; at last he had taken a "good job" on land with an export company—in less than six months so eager was he for the sea he had shipped as a first mate, unwilling to wait for a captaincy to come up.

Others were like Driving Pete. His young years spent inland as a lumberjack, he had come late to the sea; his sorrows were that all his working life had not been spent at sea, and he was now too old for anything but short-voyage fishing boats. The sea had taken her great-grandmother's husband and her one son-in-law. Yet she wanted to die within sight and sound of it.

Robert had neither the love nor the compulsion. All he wanted was to get there. And where was there? You couldn't tell from the shoals of charts, of which she caught only glimpses: the lower Seaway, the St. Lawrence River and portions of The Gulf, Belle Isle Passage, and what, after one quick, stolen look, she had taken for a strip of Greenland's southern coast. She never knew. Robert's first act after entering the pilot-house was to unlock the long chest, deposit more charts, and relock. A Canada goose flew up with a honking. She had not known it was there for puzzling over Robert.

She'd better get to work on that autobiography. She'd need to make a good grade on it, or end up with a B– or a C. She had never fallen so low; that didn't mean she couldn't. Still, all tests had brought A's. She had nothing to fear from the first-marking-period exam coming soon. She had also done all right on most of the biweekly book reports. Her other "pieces" had brought only low grades and frustration. Even Ter's work plus her own on the pond had brought nothing more than a B–, with a lot of red pencil: "The artist is not a scientist. Art has nothing to do with politics." So, such phrases as "man-wounded pond" and all those notes giving botanical names were red-ringed out.

She was studying the outline by which all were to write autobiographies when Robert rang the bell that called her to the wheelhouse. He wanted her to tend the wheel while he ran down the anchor. Finished, she returned to her studies in the small forward cabin. A short time later, Robert came with a portable typewriter in one hand and a great sheaf of what looked to be college applications under the other arm. His first question was a puzzler: "Susie, do you think that beginning sometime around late January—the exact time isn't set up yet— you can manage two longish evening dates a week for several weeks?"

She didn't know; she might be too busy.

"We could find a place where you could study. And don't look so grouchy. I'm doing exactly what you told me to do on our first trip together; signing up for night classes in boat-handling. I'll have to do it under our usual date cover. Dates, in the eyes of the old man, are normal; in fact he expects them; and so they're the best security measure possible. Thank God, you're not the type to get me in the soup by spilling the beans all over. —You understand, our evenings will be long. I'll have to go to Detroit, or maybe Ann Arbor. I'm not running the risk of finding some- body I know in the same class here in Eden Hills."

"It's time for tea," she said, and left for the galley. Setting up the tea tray, she tried to put the just-given information into her computer, but the computer kept rejecting it with a: "Why doesn't he want his old man to know? Most fathers would be happy to have a grown son able to manage the family boat."

There were no answers. Another mystery was his constant stocking of food, tinned and dried stuff that would keep. Cans, small sacks of sugar, flour, and salt, boxes and envelopes of mixes, jars and bottles of imported, expensive condiments and *confitures* had long since overflowed the galley cupboards, mostly locked; and were now put in the hold, always locked. He had "picked up the stuff" at home, he said. He also "picked up" cooking utensils, cushions, buckets, tools, rugs, table cloths, and once she had glimpsed what she thought was a stack of bed linens. Times, she wondered if *pinched* were not a better word. Would he spend his own money for this real Souchong tea? The last she had bought for herself had cost more than three dollars for six ounces.

She shrugged. It was none of her business. —"Oh, but it is. If he *is* pinching stuff, even from his stepmother, you're going along with him by keeping quiet—and by using a lot of the things, including the tea you are about to put into the pot." That was her guardian angel. Or was it her conscience?

She returned to Robert with a Coke and a sandwich for him, and tea for herself. Instead of a thank-you, she got an annoyed question: "Don't tell me you're still messing around with that autobiography for English? I distinctly remember telling you I'd do it. In fact I've done a rough draft."

"You don't know my life," she told him.

He set down his drink with a thump. Of course he knew enough. He'd seen a lot of her both in school and out. Anyway, wasn't her life basically the same as that of millions of other high school juniors, all sweating over practice autobiographies? They'd sweat still harder on applications to "the life-and-ancestor-oriented colleges" when the real deal came up next fall. Writing was not her whole problem. She must learn what her "Mr. Twitty" wanted; the best way to do that was, as he had already suggested, to use his carbons from last year. He had sold several; but there were many she could still use—after he'd suggested certain changes.

"But—it seems—well—dishonest to—."

He cut her off. "Dishonest? With that man? He's never had a thought all his own—on writing or anything else. Scare him to death. He follows the trend." He picked up a college application. "Now, let's forget your problems in English. Leave them to me. I think our typewriters are a good enough match you won't even have to recopy. —I almost forgot. First chance you get, slip me a few of your themes. I need to read them, so as not to give you a brand new style."

"But—I'm not—."

This time he thumped his glass again. "Please, Susie, don't be difficult. Let me give you help so you can help me with a rush job on college applications—twenty-four I've agreed to do; the kind where the college wants your life, hobbies, and everything else. Read a few; they'll make your autobiography look like duck soup—and it will be—for me. Don't look so horrified. It's not the same as taking college boards for somebody else. Perfectly legit —the kids pay, of course. Your part will be no strain on the brain, just time and care on the purely factual questions. Mostly for eastern colleges; a lot would rather grab off what promises to be a neat businessman than take a chance on some sloppy kid that shows sign of being another Fermi."

"Fermi wasn't sloppy. No real scientist is," she said.

"Let's not quarrel," he said as he handed her an application to which was clipped a scrawled-over sheet of ring-binder paper. "The information you'll need for births, parents, and all that jazz is here. But be neat; the most important thing is not the facts, but the total image the application gives." A typewriter ready to go came down in front of her. "We'd better get to work."

She inserted the first questionnaire, set the typewriter spacings as he directed—and miscopied the first name. She couldn't do anything for the frozen gray ashes of loneliness choking her to death. She had never been so lonesome; not even at her father's table or in the crowd on the first day of a new school. He had settled himself with pen and paper so close behind her he could see, and cried: "Oh, Susie, put your mind on it."

She didn't answer. He was so close and yet so far away. So far it didn't seem worth the trouble to try and remind him she had not agreed to help him earn money by doing applications for kids who were either too lazy or too stupid to—. Her grandmother would use a stronger term than shady business. A piece of erasing tape came in front of her nose as Robert said: "Here you are. I think we're bugging each other. Suppose I go work on this image in the salon? Be careful now."

She remembered at last to take the erasing tape, but couldn't think what letter it was for, and sat fiddling with it until he had gone. She then shoved the typewriter aside, and went to stand by a porthole. She stared a long time at Erie without seeing anything. Yes, she had been as lonesome as this with Robert. The most lonesome part of the trip was yet to come; the sitting alone in some cheap drugstore or snack bar—while he telephoned, always from a booth.

She'd of course never ask, but was weary of wondering on the person at the other end of the line. Answering service or human being, whatever it was, it could really grab Robert. Some nights he returned quickly with a grouchy, disappointed: "Too tied up to talk." This meant his nose would be out of joint all the way home. Other times while she fidgeted under the speculative gaze of the waitress, he talked for half an hour or more, to come back so happy he tipped the waitress extra.

A thump followed by a metallic bang and a clatter caused her to look around. The typewriter had slid from the narrow table onto a chair; then typewriter and chair had gone over together. The typewriter appeared undamaged. Still, she felt guilty. She must have shoved it too near the edge of the narrow table, though part of the blame should go to Erie, unnoticed, she thought, for hours. Not only was a wind coming up, but the rollers from the old storm seemed bigger, faster.

No use to try "neat typing" in this weather. She picked up a sheet of calculus review questions: "Find the area between the curve $x(y - e^x)$ sinx and $2xy = 2\sin x + x^3$ the y − axis and $x + 1$." That ought to take her mind off Robert.

She had finished only nine of the twenty-eight questions when Robert rang. His bit of learning had bred in him a healthy caution; he didn't like the look of the weather; wind rising, water roughening; and anyway with the boat rolling so they couldn't get any work done on the applications.

Susie couldn't decide whether he was running from bad weather or to that telephone. In any case it was up anchor, and push the *Antiname* for all she was worth, though it was still a good while before the early November twilight would thicken into darkness; and going up the Detroit River, wind and water were fairly quiet; nor did she see so much as a small-craft warning.

It was not the weather pushing Robert, but the pull of the telephone, she knew, as soon as he had rushed into the slip with such speed he struck a piling. His rush continued through the mooring, the locking of the boat, and along the dock, both loaded with school books, applications, his typewriter, and the usual picnic gear. Susie's arms were aching by the time they reached his car. Robert, stowing stuff in the trunk, glanced around the almost-empty parking lot and the deserted marina. Few were going out at all now in early November, and this time of day was too late for leaving, too early for coming in.

"Come to think of it, I ought to make a telephone call," he

said. "Might as well do it at that pay station. Only take a minute. You wait here."

He was already rushing off, carrying the keys, and the car doors still locked. Susie ran after, demanding the keys. Waiting by a locked car would be worse than waiting in a snack bar.

Tonight was different from his other telephoning nights. Gone only a moment, he was back, gay as an old clunker with a paint job and tune-up. Throughway traffic was heavy and slow, but all his impatient haste was gone. His happiness overflowed onto her; he apologized for the dimwit job he had asked her to do with the applications, but she was about the only person he knew who could be trusted not to tell things.

She didn't bother to ask exactly what he meant by that. He fell into a happy humming that lasted most of the time until he was pulling up at the Schnitzer side entrance. There, with an awkwardness strange for smooth Robert, he asked her to wait a minute.

More advice on applications, she was thinking as he cleared his throat in preparation; or could be he was going to mention his mother. She wished he would.

She heard his words, but they were so slow in penetrating, he added, peeved: "But I thought you'd like to go. Give you a chance to do some real research."

She still couldn't believe it. She was being asked for a date, her first real one; and not anything to flip over, only a study date in Detroit for which they would leave "immediately after school," and get home "latish; for we'll stay until the library closes."

She couldn't very well do research on the one topic bugging her—her life. She'd think of something. But don't tell him that. And don't leap like a little uneducated herring when it sees a baited hook for the first time. She managed a thoughtful frown with the question: "What night did you say?"

Friday, and he'd pick her up that morning for school so there would be no bother with her bike.

She soon gathered from his pleased look, and, though nobody was watching, his helping her to the door, that she had accepted. Door closed between them, she continued to stand by it, smiling, thinking she had done Robert wrong to be so suspicious of his "picked up" supplies, his locks, his telephone calls. He hadn't since the night of the party tried to pry into her secrets, so why should she want to nose into his?

She roused to the sound of feet on the side stairs; the Popsicle Queen.

She was plainly surprised to see Susie home so early, but asked no questions. She had bad news for Susie; Pryor had telephoned twice, eager to speak with her; but the last time he had explained that if she were not in by six, it would be too late for calling him; he would be gone. It was clear her mother felt Pryor a better catch than Robert as she mourned and wished she had known how to reach Susie. If only she could have come a bit earlier.

Susie felt somewhat the same way. She had probably missed another song-hunting trip into Detroit. She debated cheering the Popsicle Queen with the news of her Friday-night date—she didn't have to know it was only for study—with Robert, but decided to wait until later in the week. Her mother would either drag her off Monday after school or go alone to come up with a "nice date dress"; there wasn't time for anything but some off-the-rack outfit that would have to be altered in a great whirl of fittings. She'd also have to wear the thing to school Friday, or get Robert to bring her home, to dress.

Upstairs, door locked, she danced in her room to music coming only from her head, the Susie version of The Jumping Bean. Or would you call it Dance of the Bubbles in Your Heart? There was of course no such dance; possibly a little like one she had seen somewhere—Fiesta Night in San Luis Potosí or in the streets of Mexico City, or during the Winter Carnival in Quebec City, or could be only something seen on a residential street in east Montreal some long-ago spring when she and her grandmother had taken their walk at twilight among old streets near their anchorage where children and young brought out by the fine June weather had played and danced through the long twilight. She sprang high enough to touch the ceiling with the tips of her fingers, came down wondering why she was so silly-happy—a study date with Robert couldn't be the whole reason.

Monday morning Pryor brought back the frozen gray ashes. He came, as if he had been watching for her, while she was locking her bike into the rack at school. He insisted on finishing the job; and as they walked together to the door, he told her how sorry he was he had been unable to reach her Saturday. He had given a little wig-in for Angus; Mary Lou, now with her own car, had sneaked in after picking up Katy; a few others, mostly boys, had been able to make it; but all had missed her. He apologized for not having been able to plan his little blast in advance; but Angus had not received his ultimatum from The Establishment until Thursday after school; hair off by Monday morning or he would be expelled—no hearing, no appeal; no nothing; made you boil. The most Pryor could do was to talk to the wig-makers, who had already agreed to come at some future date. The only time the two could get together was on Saturday afternoon—and he hadn't been able to arrange that until Saturday morning after she was already gone.

"I wish I'd been home," she told him, and meant it. "But that wouldn't have brought back Angus's hair."

"Cheer up," he told her. "Next year, he'll be in some college, I hope, where hair like his won't cause so much as a second look."

The bell rang. He hurried away, but she took her time. It no longer seemed to matter whether she was tardy or not. The big hurt was seeing Angus pushed around; added to this was the lesser one of having missed the only party outside of school to which she had ever been invited.

She forgot that hurt when at lunch she saw Angus. His head had been shaved, she decided; no clippers could get that close. Worse, that bald head would get him into further trouble with The Establishment, for it was more noticeable than the supposedly long hair. He saw her troubled sorrow and whispered: "You ought to see that wig; better than my hair; those two experts from Detroit did a bang-up job."

"But I'll never see you wear it," she mourned.

"If you want to hear me ruin my voice and see me act the fool, we'll arrange it. Don't feel bad about my hair. I'm lucky in a way—it will grow back. I was only one of several criminals

315

called in: three cases of cigarettes-found-in-locker—nice how in a public school they can search without a search warrant—; two cases of sideburns; a sinner who had felt social studies was the proper place for discussing birth control; another sinner who had been trying to get signatures for a ban-the-bomb petition; and a poor clod in *huaraches* without socks, so innocent he didn't know what he had done wrong. We told him."

He smiled. She smiled and hoped he didn't know how close she was to tears.

Next day during Assembly she didn't smile, and she certainly didn't want to cry. Part of the time she felt as if she would vomit, but mostly she wanted to hurl the contents of her binder piece by piece toward the stage where the Assistant-Principal-in-Charge-of-Discipline was urging the student body to read *The Purple Sunflower*. The last issue had been unusually good, and most particularly the article on "Good Taste in Dress" by an outstanding senior, Robert Thomas Hedrick. Such lies! He was making the students believe the whole anti-miniskirt deal had come from Robert and other school-paper staff members.

The business bugged her so all day, she kept both the sand dollar and the sea urchin within quick reach. Worse than the thought that a high-ranking staff member of the school told lies were the uneasy wonderings on Robert. Could he have suggested the articles and be the real pilot instead of The Establishment? Either way he was an awful toady; worse than a toady, up there sitting on the lid with the administrative staff. The teachers, except a few, didn't count; they couldn't open their mouths to bleat any more than the pupils.

During the rest of the week, her computer stocked several questions and comments for the Friday date with Robert.

She used none of them. First, she was rather grateful to Robert for getting her out of dinner at The House of Usher. Her father had been in an unusually miserable humor all week; roaring out his angers over the recent elections, the bills, the mistreatment of Chicago police—and Brandon. Brandon's sin was that he wanted to quit "the group" so as to have more time for "the doings at school." Several times Susie had had to bite her tongue to keep from speaking out for her brother. He was, for the first time in his life, liking school well enough to try to learn. Several aftenoons he had shown her with a pride and joy he tried to hide, a C–plus or a B; grades practically unheard-of for Brandon. And now her father was blaming "indoctrination by that fancy school" for his declining interest in "the group." She'd have to dream up some way of making Bismarck see the light; to cross him directly by taking Brandon's side would only make things worse.

In the car with Robert, she wished Brandon could get out from under as she was now. She quit thinking of Brandon, and gave herself up to an enjoyment of the ride. The rainy twilight was coming down before they reached the outskirts of Detroit, but it was cozy in the car with the windshield wipers clicking away, muted like the sounds of traffic, by the voices of the rain; and behind, in front, and beside them a moving river of lights— red tail-lights, yellow oncoming signal-lights winking, the brightness softened by the rain, yet glittering, and the wet pavements reflecting the glitter.

And Robert was happy, too. He began humming, and soon was singing: "I can't think for thinken of you."

His singing couldn't compare with that of Angus or Ben, but the song was nice in the rain. She wished she could quit wondering who was "you;" her IBM laughed when her head hinted around it could be herself. Lost in her warm world, she never noticed where they were until this happy Robert was saying with a kind of mumble, as if he didn't enjoy the saying: "Now, don't worry, I'll be back before the library closes. Don't fool around by yourself—Detroit isn't Eden Hills. Have your dinner early and at nine forty-five stand behind those glass outer doors and watch for me. 'Bye now."

She stood stone still and watched the car crawl back into the line of traffic. All the jewels were gone from the lights. The friendly rain was only soot-blackened water, cold on your ankles, and colder as it caught you on the back of the neck. She turned away, and as in childhood lifted her face to search out the stone faces that ringed the library. She stared, searching, rain falling on her face, until from two steps higher a voice asked, that of a man, well bred to understand one should not frighten girls by coming too close: "May I help you, little girl?"

"The faces," she answered, not turning her head. "I can't find them."

"They are still there," he said, a hint of anger in his voice, "but washed so clean by some modern method, you can scarcely see them or read their names. They haven't changed places; they're still on the Woodward side. It's the library that's changed. Now, most people enter as you are, from Cass."

She said: "Oh. —I forgot. —I've been here many times— since—since they washed the faces." She tried to see the man's face, but could not as he was two steps above her, and now holding the umbrella over her. "Thank you," she said, and went on up the steps.

The umbrella stayed above her until she reached an outer glass door, and the man said: "Remember—always—the faces are still there."

"I won't forget again," she said.

"I'm sure you won't," the man said, going down the steps.

Automation took her into the library, then deserted her. She stood and stared and wondered why she was there. She must not be silly again as she had been outside, hunting stone faces through the rain; she'd learned the faces and their names as a child; she was old now with Caesar and his wars behind her, a bit of Virgil; she had both seen and read much of Shakespeare. Why was she fishing in her purse? The sand dollar couldn't help her now.

She had found what she hunted—a quarter. She looked around to learn the reason why she wanted that particular coin. The soft click of metal a few feet away told her she wanted the coin for a locker in the check corner where she would as usual leave her wraps and anything else she didn't need.

She found an empty locker, came away with key, notebook, purse, and pens; punched the board for Literature, English; and guided her legs to the indicated room. There, it took her only a little while to remember she was to begin research on the term paper every *in* university or college preparatory junior had to write for English before the end of the second semester. She had thought a paper on American labor ballads would be an interesting thing to write—if The Powers were agreeable to the subject. It had seemed wiser to do some research on ballads in general, beginning with those from Britain. She gave an annoyed headshake. She should have gone first to the card file.

She copied titles, letters, numbers; but once among the books, her IBM started acting up again, unable at times to do anything but send her walking up and down aisles to stare at the backs of books, not reminding her she was to find numbers to match the slips she held. She kept trying to get back to that child who would have laughed at such a hurt as this. Children always expected too much—everything from ownerless ponds to assuming friendly boys were boyfriends. She wasn't a child any more.

"Oh, make my bed soon, mother/ Oh make it deep and wide." Be nice to be a young man with a mother to make your bed. Robert was a young man, but his mother didn't make his bed—. "IBM, stay with the ballads; take my mind off Robert; you can't bring him back when he's away on his road. And don't let me think of that nice little dinner I thought we'd have together. I'll cry if you do."

That didn't help too much. Robert had in the car this morning been so sweet, so kind, giving Susan Marie Schnitzer her life ready for handing in; and a carbon in case she wanted to read it. She had not handed it in; nor had she read it. He had thanked her, effusively, you might say, for the applications she had typed.

That was this morning.

It was evening now. Remember that. Remember she was sitting by a library table with a stack of books in front of her. She lost herself in ballads, gulping ballads, swallowing the notes, long explanations that told their histories. They were so old, so very old, old as death and misplaced love and broken hearts. They were like old trees with widely wandering roots. And some of the roots were dead; no man today would ever die of a broken heart for another Barbara Allen; on the other hand young men still went to war, got drowned in winter seas as did Sir Patrick Spens, and some girls had mean mothers.

She wished she could do a ballad of her grandfather, a little man from a faraway country in a strange land, with at first only one true friend—the sea. And this "little Sancho of a man—." Who had called him that, Jeff? A little man who never feared the wildest seas, he had died on his boat within sight of harbor lights; but the sea had not killed him. There was time tonight, lots of time to try a ballad for him. And how should the rhyme scheme and the metre go? Iambics? And the refrain?

She looked up to see a sad-faced, cream-colored Negro girl at the end of the table. How was it to be a cream-colored Negro; here on earth? That would make a nice ballad, the building of my heaven at the bottom of the sea. She and Driving Pete had spent half a day arranging a spot for their whale family. Some day she would write to Gordie Howe to tell him that in spite of playing on the wrong side, her heaven had a place for him.

She had practiced ballad refrains; one for her grandfather; one each for Angus, Ben, and the girl at the end of the table; and gone back to work, copying a refrain; "From Noraway to Noraway," when over her shoulder came a dampish head and a disgruntled voice: "Susie, don't you realize what time it is? Hurry. I'm double-parked out front, and I've already spent ten minutes hunting you."

Robert dashed away. She couldn't very well dash after. She had to arrange her notes, go to the washroom, collect her things from the locker, and put on her coat.

The library was closing, but even so she had to wait for Robert. Fearful of a ticket for overlong standing, he had moved out of the line of cars waiting in the entrance drive, and unable to crowd in again, had to drive around the block three times; or so he told her with a good deal of exasperation.

Susie forgot to apologize for the trouble she had caused him; the car occupied her mind. First, it was overly warm and smelled as if it had just given a long ride to some skimpily dressed cigarette-smoking passenger. Secondly, there was another smell; strong, or at least more noticeable, when she first entered the car. Familiar, but where and when the cheap perfume? If she sat with it long enough, she wouldn't be able to place it, ever. She gave a long audible sniff. Robert, careful driver though he was, gave her a quick sidewise glance at the sound of the sniff.

He sniffed. Wouldn't help him any. He'd been with that perfume all evening, and couldn't smell it now. At a particularly well lighted intersection she studied the seat next to Robert. Two hairs, so tiny she could not have told their exact color, were pale as bits of spider web on the dark-blue upholstery. She put on one glove, pressed until the hairs stuck on a finger. She examined them at the next bright light. Somebody had worn a fur coat for which a good many poor little rabbits had died; pardon me, *lapin.*

Robert was looking at her again. This didn't keep her from investigating the always-empty ashtray. It was half filled with butts from one smoker; unless he had two females who used the same shade of lipstick to mark the same brand of cigarettes in the same way. She had never seen on anyone such hot, red-purple lipstick; it matched the perfume; and the perfume matched— matched that slinky black slip she'd found in the hold of the *Antiname.*

And that slip belonged to—. No, she wouldn't believe it. Yes, she'd—. The ashtray was flipped shut with such violence it let out a cloud of ashy dust. "Why do you want to look at that dirty mess?" Robert asked his voice angry as his closing of the ashtray.

"I find it interesting," she said.

He shrugged. "Sorry, but you'll have to get along without it. I'll clean it, and keep it that way—until my mother rides with me again. She smokes too much. —What's the matter?"

She wondered if she'd groaned, sobbed, or just let out with an "Oh, no."

"You surely know," he went on, picking up his words and putting them down carefully as bare feet on jagged rocks, "my parents, like a lot of other parents, are divorced. —I like to see my mother as often as possible."

Dr. Laughton couldn't be wrong. His mother was a great woman, now working as a doctor in Vietnam. She wouldn't smoke, not that much; or wear that kind of lipstick, or use that perfume. She could be wrong of course, but Robert had just told her a big black lie. Vicki had her gossip wrong. Robert Thomas Hedrick had not given up his Detroit girl friend. She, Susan Marie Schnitzer, had made it possible for him to keep her. Ugh.

15

Home, she had come straight to her quarters without seeing anyone. She remembered that much. But now, whatever was she doing, hands flying amid the tearing and crumpling sounds of paper? She looked around at the mess: shreds of typed sheets all over her feet, the floor, the desk. Robert Thomas Hedrick's— don't forget the IV—autobiography of Susan Marie Schnitzer. The author wasn't worth this stupid tantrum.

She began to pick up the paper. A pity she wasn't a maiden in a ballad; broken-hearted she would now be, melting with love instead of anger. That would be pleasanter. She could forgive Robert's use of her as a shield to hide his real love. She had used him; true, she had paid him for her grandmother's party; but dating him had made life easier at home, and the *Antiname* had been fun. It was his loathsome lie. Not all the gold in the Bank of England could pay for that. Did he think she was dumb enough to swallow such a tale? The nerve of him to have a doctor, any kind of physician, using that hot lipstick and sticky perfume. And didn't everybody know his mother was in Vietnam? Or did they? She'd never heard the first Mrs. Hedrick mentioned, not even by Vicki.

Vicki? No, she wouldn't know the answers to the red-lip-sticked girl. Was she the same love his father had sent him to

Europe to forget? And was he planning to skip out with boat and girl? All those charts and food staples meant something. He couldn't go now; the Seaway would be frozen before that slow boat could get down to Montreal.

She dropped a handful of paper into the wastebasket; Susan Schnitzer was nothing better than an old Greek freighter trapped in the Seaway ice. She had let Robert do that to her. Now she was going to let him ruin what had promised to be a fine weekend: Bismarck was gone shooting, not to get home before Monday week; the Popsicle Queen was leaving tomorrow morning for that week's tuneup she'd been looking forward to; Brandon, save now and then for questions concerning that 'Commie girl' Mrs. Weatherford had talked about, was in an unusually good humor; and Lulu as always was Lulu.

The nicest thing was looking forward to Saturday week. She was spending that day with Angie and Joe; they had a wonderful surprise for her, Angie had said when she telephoned. In the meantime she'd better get to work on that autobiography.

The Guidance Sheet with its "You should answer these questions," and the "Suggestions" that were musts, also wanted "Pleasant Experiences." Tonight she'd write of those. She'd pretend the background was the camp she had visited several times, from which her mother's letters and her own were forwarded.

Sometime later, she roused to discomfort, both in her arms and her stomach. Odd, she was in her usual position for writing —stomach downward on the cot, legs waving. She looked at the pages she had covered. They had taken her surfing and shell hunting along her grandmother's beach, picnicking on the rocks, sailing, and now she was on a "camp excursion" to Ottawa.

Her right hand and arm had written themselves into a cramp, while the left suffered from being leaned upon too long. But what ailed her stomach? She had given it no indigestible matter. She was careful that way, as Dr. Laughton directed. What had she had for dinner? Dinner? This time Robert had not offered even his usual Dutch treat at a snack bar with little to serve but calories.

She looked at her watch, almost two o'clock; the stomach

would quiet down; it never wanted breakfast. And where had the time gone?

During the weekend she often asked herself that question after biking, visiting The Primitive, but most often after a long stint on the autobiography. Attitudes they wanted on a lot of people and things; dreaming up proper ones had not been too difficult.

Monday morning as she biked to school she sang the gayest French Canadian songs she knew. Save for typing and retyping, cutting here and there, the autobiography was finished. Moreover, she had answered all questions—after a fashion.

The song stopped when she turned into a school drive. She felt as if everybody would be looking at her, whispering, laughing because they knew Robert Hedrick had made a fool of Susan Schnitzer. She straightened, put on a smile, and biked more rapidly. This young lady was not as brave as the child with the scars. She ought this minute to be in homeroom going over the day's Virgil, neglected for the autobiography.

She was settled in homeroom and just getting into Latin, when in came Vicki. First, a whine for poor Vicki: she'd had to come early to school this morning or ride that "awful bus"; her mother wouldn't bring her any more; all she could get was a ride with her father on his way to work; and when he left early as today, she had to come early. Imagine? She then got going. "I saw you Friday and waved. But you didn't see me for you were too tied up with Robert."

"Oh? —Sorry."

"I don't blame you. You know, it's like I told my mother: poor me, here I was being taken to the dentist, big deal, and you on your way to Detroit with your fantastic boy friend. Mother was interested to see the girl—she knows the Hedricks—who'd taken Robert away from that awful woman."

Susie thought she'd let out a short breath of relief; if Vicki didn't know the real deal between her and Robert, nobody did. She must show interest. "Was she so awful, the Detroit girl?"

"Sh–sh." Vicki looked around the room, as yet almost empty. "Girl? She's up, way up in her twenties—they say. But it's the kind of thing you don't talk about; you know, not when people like the Hedricks are mixed in. But from what I heard, *awful* is a weak word; 'experienced with men' is more like it—and not with just a lot of divorces. Lots of people get divorced, like Robert's parents. But, you know, nobody talks about that either.

"Don't you think it's funny that nobody around here's ever seen his real mother—a Swede, or Norwegian, or—." She shrugged. "She used to live in Detroit; she's not there now—I think. You never hear her mentioned."

The girl was primed. Why not pump her, Susie decided; much easier than getting water out of Driving Pete's hand-pump. "I suppose everybody saw the girl friend."

"Wow. You *are* an innocent. She was the kind of creature people out here wouldn't have in their homes." She drew closer, and went on in a barely audible whisper: "You surely know what a kept woman is? Robert's girl friend—ex, now, thanks to you—is kept in a Detroit apartment by a rich old geezer from around here. Don't you ever tell a soul." She shrugged. "You know I learned it not exactly by accident.

"My parents had dinner guests. I wasn't so much as allowed to eat with them, but when the men were still sitting around the table with brandy, and the women in the living room or powder room, I heard Father laughing his head off—I was listening in the pantry. One man was telling about how this high school boy, Robert Hedrick, was visiting a rich old geezer's woman, you know, for immoral purposes, while the old fool—he pays all her bills—was home with his family.

"Don't look so shocked. You know, you are an awful innocent. Why, they all do it, the old men; why that old geezer is fifty if he's a day. My father isn't that old, but I've wondered if he doesn't have a mistress, he's gone so much. He can almost never come with us when Mother takes me someplace for my health, claims he has to work."

"I don't wonder on my father," Susie said, so angry she forgot to whisper. "I know he doesn't have a—."

"Sh–sh–sh. There're kids all around. Your father's 'a highly moral, conscientious, patriotic, family man'; that's exactly what

Mrs. Weatherford said of him. And she's a perfect judge of character."

"Oh?" She remembered to come up with a belated "Thank you." She ought to write that down, make a nice line in that have-to bit on her father for the autobiography. "That girl," she said, still pumping, "must have something."

Vicki smiled on her as if she were a little child. "It isn't so much what she has, but how, you know, free she is with it. Somebody saw her with Robert; slinky type, I heard, with huge breasts. And do you know before she got to be a model of sorts, she was a go-go dancer. And don't tell me you don't know what that is."

Susie didn't. The "School-Is-Beginning" gong had come on. Miss Mothering was sending her "Now it is time to stop talking," glance around the room. "Oh, golly," Vicki said in her normal voice, "you know I've not told you what I planned to at all. I hope you have me in swimming."

Susie hoped not. Vicki had already ruined study time, and she had heard enough to scatter her wits like sand in a northeaster.

She had her wits well collected by orchestra. And a good thing. Old Harp was cross as a harpooned whale. Veterans' Day was Tuesday week. That meant orchestra must have that patriotic music, not chosen by Old Harp, perfect. It also meant time wasted in practicing flag salute from the orchestra-pit position. On stage would be Big Wheels with at least one oration from a *very* big one. And would anybody notice Angus with his non-salute? At least he would be less conspicuous than if the orchestra were onstage.

She couldn't do anything about that worry. He looked happy when he smiled at her, as did Ben, Katy, and Mary Lou. She didn't try to check on Robert's well-being. She dreaded the sight of him at lunch.

The meal was unexpectedly pleasant. Robert wasn't there. He had told Angus he would be having a conference on his next miniskirt article. Nobody wasted time on talk of him. Katy's father made the big news. Not only was his case going at long last to court with a definite date in January, but he was also getting an opportunity to do what he wanted to again. A Canadian university had, for the next academic year, offered him an associate professorship in teaching with an opportunity to do some research. Everyone was happy, but Mary Lou looked happiest of all.

Next day she was sorry she had to miss lunch. Coming out of chemistry, she remembered the piece of dreary business she should have seen to days before, and now could wait no longer —flu shots. She had promised to call Dr. Laughton's nurse last week to learn when she should come in. She must ring her up during lunch.

Dr. Laughton answered. He was asking: "And how is my future doctor?" before Susie could finish giving her name.

"Fine," she told him; and explained Miss Armstrong had asked her to call about flu shots. She had not intended to bother him.

No bother, he told her. Miss Armstrong was taking an early lunch in order to do an errand for him. Susie could come around for her first flu shot any day after school. He'd like to see her, check on her weight; he didn't want it to go off this winter as usual. Oh, yes; he also wanted to tell her of a letter he had just received from Dr. Marta Thorborg.

He talked a moment or so of the letter; mostly it was, she thought, a description of the doctor's work. Dr. Laughton's friendly words were not gettting through; she could think only that he was talking of Robert's mother, still in Vietnam. She had lied to herself again with that hoping, in spite of the evidence in the car and Vicki's story, that Robert had told her the truth.

She wondered as she came away if she had given Dr. Laughton a nice good-bye or even a decent one. She glanced down to see one hand closed, carefully as if it held an egg; the sand dollar from her purse. Had she crushed it? No. She returned it to her purse, and gave herself a good lecture. She'd lived through worse; she would not let being lied to by someone you had at least half-way trusted bug her so. She only hoped she never saw or heard of Robert Hedrick again.

She managed neither to speak nor smile at him until

Wednesday afternoon as she crossed the court on the way to Latin. Empty as the place was, he looked around before whispering: "Be sure and get set for a boat ride Saturday week. I can't go this Saturday."

The old geezer must be out of town shooting ducks, like Bismarck. She tried to put surprise into her voice. "Boating? With no insurance? It goes off in early November for most pleasure craft. But it doesn't matter—that is, for me. I don't think —I can manage it." She couldn't talk any more, and hurried away.

"Susie, there's something else." He was keeping beside her, and no longer whispering. "The office gave me this for you. I was passing by and told them I would be seeing you. It's—."

"I know," she interrupted, as the business-size envelope came in front of her face. She was clutching her purse, feeling for the sand dollar, not reaching for the summons from the psychologist.

Robert shoved it between her purse and binder. "Don't let this business grab you so. Why, he's not even a psychologist. You know what the letters after his name mean? Just a master's in social work; wants to write something learned about a bunch of kids.

"Say?" He was whispering again after another look around. "You won't spill anything about—well, you know—. Don't look so blank. Our boat rides together. Teen-age attitudes and reactions are big things now; notice I put a lot in your autobiography. In case he queries you on your favorite amusements, for God's sake don't come up with something like: 'Boating on the lakes with Robert Hedrick.'"

"You're cursing," she said, and heedless of a possible black mark ran the rest of the way to Latin.

Robert whispered as he passed her chair: "Aren't you curious about the date? It's next Wednesday, near the end of the lunch hour, an office file clerk told me. He sent a copy to the school so you wouldn't get tangled with Attendance."

When he had gone, she drew a long shivering sigh; he had given her a week for worrying; well, seeing as how she had worried and studied all fall, another week wouldn't wreck her.

329

She was ready for him—except her clothing; that would require a bit of shopping. Plenty of time to do that; she might go Thursday after school—if Old Harp didn't order after school orchestra practice for Veterans' Day.

He did, and kept them so late, Susie had to do next day's homework after dinner, instead of before as usual.

She was in the attic working away on physics when a sound, strange to the attic, caused her to look around. She heard nothing, and marked the line of a red curve to another point on the graph paper. She again stopped. She'd heard the sound again; a whispered, "Susie." Lulu was in her room above the garage; and Brandon had long since gone to bed. She was imagining—.

"Susie?"

She sprang up. No imagining that. She looked in the direction of her ladder to see a whitish blur in the heavy shadow, low as if someone stood on a lower rung. She started for her flashlight by the bed, but stopped when the blur whispered: "Susie, I don't want to scare you to death like last time. It's your cousin Ter."

"Ter," she whispered, and rushed to the ladder.

"Ter it is," he said, climbing up. "Did you find it?"

"Find? What?"

He bent to reach her ear. "The money, of course. I told you it slid away. I've come to find it and get it back to the bank."

"You mean—you mean you've not given it back?"

"How could I? I only learned after Dad got here and I went to get the stuff that it had slid down. To where is what I have to find out—tonight."

"I didn't know what 'It slid away' meant. That means the FBI is still hunting, and—. I wish you'd written me." She was having trouble with her voice.

"Write you? That place isn't Montreal, or even here where you can sneak a letter into a box. There are no mailboxes; no delivery; everybody goes to the post office; the school takes down its sack of mail, brings one back. And as for telephoning you, that would have to be done through the school."

He had while talking walked past her to the cold air return, taken a flashlight, and was now studying the upper end of the pipe.

Susie wished she could see his face; the circle of light from the study lamp left most of him in heavy shadow. If she could see his eyes, his strangeness might go away. This tall man with nothing on his mind but the business ahead was no kin at all of the sick teen-ager, quarreling with her one minute, saying nice things the next. He turned away from the pipe.

"Susie, darling, don't you realize you're standing by your study light, and nothing on but your night clothes?"

She skittered out of the light in the direction of where she thought she'd left a bath robe. She felt better; he was the same old Ter. The too-big winter nightgown of heavy cotton covered her from neck to toes. He seemed even more familiar as he continued: "And please don't remind me of the FBI. I've lived all these weeks waiting for that polite tap on my door—or a call out of class; I think up there they'd come with the Mounties. And what if the FBI got to Dad? It would be the death of him. And kill me. So I've come the very first chance I've had to get that money back. Why oh why didn't I throw it down when I ran? The real kick was over."

"You mean—you mean you didn't tell him?"

"Go whining to him? 'Oh, Daddy dear, please get your darling little boy out of the fix he got himself in.' Tell him his only son had—. How could I? He has enough troubles."

"But you had to tell him something, give him some reason why you came here, and then had to burn your clothes."

"Look, Susie, there are many things one cannot discuss with well-brought-up young girls. The tale I told Dad is one. He believed it; I made it bad enough to get a whale of a talking to. And as for the clothes, the old boy was too shook up by my illness—and everything—to notice mere clothes. Mostly I told him I'd ruined them with mud and falling into your swimming pool—and a few other reasons why they should be burned. His big worry was that I wasn't dressed warmly enough. He bought me an overcoat, best he could find, first thing next morning."

He came closer. "Do you think that was fun? That night I prayed for Judas. And all those lies. Let's get to work and not talk about it."

"I know a lot about lies," she told him.

"You told a lot for me. And I'm not forgetting. I didn't mean to be cross. I've let this business throw me off. I'm scared we won't find the money. I don't have much time. And I have to be careful to keep my tales straight, especially to Joe and Angie. They telephoned, and begged me to come down for Remembrance Day—your Veterans' Day—vacation."

He stopped, gave a poor imitation of a shrug, then went on: "Upper-form boys with my standing—my guilty conscience hasn't let me do much of anything but study—get a long weekend, Friday afternoon to Tuesday early evening. I flew straight to Detroit, that is as straight as I could make it. Angie and Joe think I'm spending tomorrow with a friend in Toronto. —And so they'll be meeting me tomorrow when the plane I told them I'd be on comes in.

"Worse, they've promised me a big surprise for Saturday; something I've been wanting a long time, Joe said. I can't figure what it is. Dad and my sisters are flying in, but I knew about that."

"They've promised me a surprise, too, for Saturday, a great big one," Susie said. She gave a little skip. "The surprise is Uncle Lans and you."

Ter's, "It's you," coincided with her "you." Both laughed, and Ter said: "One lie less. We won't have to pretend any more we don't know each other. Now, we can write and send our letters through Angie." The Ter she knew was gone. The stranger was turning back to the pipe. "Do you have any idea where the lower end of this goes? That's where the money went."

"No. I've only checked the upper end; it goes into the main cold-air return. Air from the lower comes up so cold, I'm certain it's from—." She hesitated. "I shouldn't say certain, but I suspect it comes from the fall-out shelter."

"Ugh. I suppose I'll have to get into that hole. You dress, then meet me in the basement." He was already by the ladder.

"But Lulu might—." Wasted breath; he was gone, and would keep on going; she had left Little Atlas off duty because she had planned to go back to her study for a bit of typing on the autobiography. The thing to do was dress quickly, get down to the basement, and try to keep him quiet.

Quick as she was, his whisper came to her out of the tool room when a ray of light took her to the half-open door. "Right you were, Susie. It's in the fall-out shelter pipe. Or at least something's there. Getting it out will be simple—but a bit noisy I'm afraid. Talk about thrift. I couldn't find one electric outlet in the whole corridor, so instead of your soldering iron, we'll have to use the little blowtorch."

He was forgetting to whisper. She came in and closed the door; then silently took the small blowtorch he handed her. She could in the overhead light see him clearly now; yet he was as much the stranger as when he had stood in the shadow by the ladder. Wearing coveralls he must have brought with him, and Bismarck's carpenter's apron, lost in his search for a proper tool, he was nobody she had ever seen. He selected a small pair of pliers from the assortment on the wall. "I guess that'll do it," he said.

They went out together. He was still the gentleman, opening the door for her, closing it, turning off the light, then keeping his flashlight turned so as to make a path for her to the fall-out passage door. She tried not to hang back, not to shiver, but the long oval of the heavy steel door now, as usual, bugged her. Ter opened it, and as always it swung silently on the hidden hinges Bismarck kept in perfect working condition. Then you had to remember to pick up your feet and step over the high steel sill curved to an exact fit with the door.

The worst part was the light: fixed refrigerator-fashion to come on when the door was opened, one dim, unshaded yellow bulb far down the sloping cement corridor went on, but only for three or four minutes after the door was closed. Near the end of whatever time it was, the thin blue light by The Door, the door to the fall-out shelter went on, and stayed—she didn't know how long.

333

The steel corridor door swung shut behind them. "Makes you think of a door to the classified quarters of a battleship," Ter said.

"It is; as much like one as my father could have made. It locks on this side, for it's the Keep-Out-the-Unpatriotic-Neighbors-Who-Didn't-Build-Shelters barrier. They are expected to come begging shelter when the bomb falls. —Don't you want to lock it? There's a lever of a thing that works bars—or something."

"Unless you're certain you know exactly how to unlock it, I'd rather take a chance on being caught behind an unlocked door than one I had shut but couldn't open." The yellow light was on, and he walked ahead of her, flashlight working over the cold air return that, supported at intervals by heavy iron hangers affixed to the ceiling, ran the length of the sloping passage. He stopped about a third of the way down the corridor, and stood looking.

"Why," he said when she had come to stand beside him, "the welding job? Air ducts are supposed to fit into each section; and all do until we get here at the very one I have to take apart."

"I think," she told him, "it's because of the cutoffs. There's one somewhere close to the shelter door, and another inside. They're damper-like deals to be set in a closed position when the bomb falls; they then shut out any chance of outside air coming in—if the house goes."

He said "Ugh," and she said nothing. She had never been in the place except during Bismarck's guided tours of instruction in "What to do in atomic warfare or a riot." On these trips she had tried to see and hear as little as possible. She forgot her horror of the place in worry over the noise Ter was making as he gently tapped the pipe with a small nail. The sound was so low, he put an ear against the duct the better to listen; but small as the noise was it might, in the piping, travel to Lulu.

One hard arm came around her hips, the other about her waist. "You're not tall enough to get your ear against it, but I want you to listen, and see if you think something is in there."

He had hoisted her to his shoulder before she knew what was happening. The childlike position for a young lady—not even Beeto picked her up now as he had used to do—interfered

334

with her concentration. The first tap she had to have repeated before the clear sharp ring of metal on metal got through. He took two steps that carried her past an unwelded intersection. "Now, listen here, closely."

She listened. This time the ring was muffled with fewer vibrations. He tapped another spot several feet nearer the shelter door. Once more the ring was clear and bell-like. "There's something inside at the place where you tapped the second time," she said, and wished he would unclamp that arm around her knees so she could slide from his shoulder.

He had forgotten she was there. "It's the logical place," he said, turning the flashlight beam to the other end of the corridor. "The duct, I figure, comes down in a sharp drop between the side hall and the pantry; the package was traveling fast enough to get this far before the friction stopped it here where there's almost no slope."

He had returned to the place with the muffled sound and was examining it under the flashlight, brighter now in the pale blue light that had come on as the yellow went off. "I'll only have to unsolder and solder back one end; the other's crimped like it ought to be; only a little plier work. Nice, the support is far enough back I can tip it down—but you may have to hold the duct to keep the long end steady."

He swung her down, then, while she held the flashlight, he went to work with the pliers on the fitted and crimped end. Watching him, she decided that though he probably had never before done this kind of job, he was not unskillful with his hands. The work went quickly, and with the pliers he made less noise than she had feared.

Unsoldering the other end was a different matter. Small as the blowtorch was, the hiss of its blue flame seemed to fill the whole of the corridor with a roar that bounced from cement ceiling to cement floor and from cement wall to cement wall.

She wished she could go stand at the foot of the basement stairs to watch and listen—or at least turn around to see if the corridor door were opening—the yellow light came on only after it was opened wide. She dare not change her position. Arms above her head, both hands on the pipe, face toward Ter with the roaring, hissing blowtorch, she had to stand stone-still not to jiggle the pipe, free on one end and loose in an overly large hanger.

Her one attempt to see behind her had brought a hissed command from Ter: "Please, be still and no more jiggling. I'm not exactly skilled in this business. One good jiggle and I'll get off the solder and onto the pipe—then your father will be calling the FBI to investigate the hole."

There was nothing for it but to stand exactly so and try to pay no attention to her gone-crazy senses. Once, her legs felt a wave of air that could come only when the door was opened; another time she heard a tap-tapping, so clear she forgot and started to look around. She remembered in time and turned back to the only things she could see, blue flame licking into the solder with enough light left over to show a few inches of pipe on either side, and less distinctly Ter's hands on the blowtorch. His face was a silhouette above nothingness. This made the blowtorch seem alive, a roaring, hissing little monster, happy to work alone without help from a human.

There was nothing in the world but the slowly, slowly progressing torch, the noise, and the fear. She ought to be preparing her mind for the psychologist next Wednesday noon. Odd, now that the date was set, she worried about him less.

The blue lights had gone off. She stared into the blackness beyond Ter. She couldn't see the Real Door, the one to the crematory vault where beer and human flesh would vaporize together. Had poets written anything like: "Lines Composed in My Fall-Out Shelter" or "Musings on Will I Be Vapor or Dust," "Soliloquy—."

"Susie, now's the time to hold. The leverage on this long end could bring it down with a crash. I don't know what it'll do. I'm finishing." He stepped away, capped the blowtorch to leave them in complete darkness.

"Now, I am scared to look," he whispered. "What if we heard wrong and nothing's there. Or it's something you've let slide down."

"Then, we'll hunt some more," she whispered. He was enjoying the dark, the suspense, and the danger of being caught. He

would make a grand sailor, loving, not fearing, the fog and the
dark and the wind. She wished she could think of something
other than that awful padded bra her mother had given her last
year; the thing had disappeared—it always came damp from her
dryer—and suppose it was making the muffled sound; or some—.

Ter examined the unsoldered joint under the flashlight. Satisfied, he took the pipe in both hands, and after telling Susie to
loosen, but not let go, her hold, he gave a gentle push. "Free all
around," he said, still cool, remembering to whisper. "I think
there's clearance enough between that back joint and the ceiling
to let me swing this end down past the next joint. Watch it now;
don't let me pull that end out of the support. I'll try to give you
light."

She held, watched, and waited while he, flashlight clamped
between hand and metal, manipulated the duct: first, down past
the next joint; then straight out, and at last so far down he had to
bend to hold it. "Nothing's coming out. I'll hold. Will you take
the torch and look?"

There was a wobble in her legs. Still, she rushed to take the
flashlight from him. She looked, and forgot to stifle a whispered
"Oh" of disappointment. How could she ever tell him? She got
up, slowly as an old woman. "It's—just something I've—. I can't
see anything but pink and silver paper."

"Oh, boy. Pink and silver's it. I remember looking around
the attic for something to put the stuff in—and saw that fancy
sack."

They exchanged places while he took the torch and studied
the position of the sack. What he saw made him still happier.
"You'd think the thing would slide out; but that won't matter. It's
close enough to the upper end I can reach it with my fist. One
good shove and out she'll come. We'll have to change places
again."

Moments later, Ter was commanding: "Don't touch it without gloves;" and the pink and silver sack—tightly closed with
paper clips, her own—was falling on her feet.

Ter went to work at once on getting the pipe back exactly as
it had been. He'd brought fresh solder, just in case. And had it
ever been a nuisance. He hadn't wanted customs wondering why

337

he brought solder into the States, so he'd coiled it round his waist under his clothing. After a while the stuff had begun to bite into him. Useless misery; customs had looked at nothing.

The rewelding, or so it seemed to Susie, went on more slowly than the unwelding. The hissing roar of the blowtorch, the holding, the listening, the almost overpowering impulse to turn and look at the door, were all worse than on the first round; for over in the dark where she could not see, the pink and silver sack of stolen money waited for whoever wanted to walk in.

Finished at last, Ter worried that the new solder, brighter than the old, might call attention to itself. He wished for a strand of spider web to serve as camouflage; or a sprinkle of dust might do the trick.

Susie pointed out that in her father's pesticided household, a fragment of spider's web would be more quickly noticed than a missing length of pipe. Dust would be worse; this section, like other parts of the place in which he spent any time, had electronic dust-catchers. She felt darkening were better done by some chemical; warm sulphur water might do it, or one of those super-powerful cleaning compounds—if it didn't eat the metal away entirely. She'd manage something before her father got back.

Ter collected his tools. "I might try something in the morning."

So he was going to stay the night. What had she left in the attic he ought not to see?

She forgot that wonder when, safely upstairs again, she looked at her watch. It was impossible to believe less than two hours had gone by since a tall stranger had come into her attic. The stranger was gone; in his place was the old Ter; happy, hungry, talking between bites of the sandwiches she had made for him. And talk so good to hear; he had not even quarreled at the lack of wine.

First he wanted to know if her parents would, as usual let her spend all her winter holiday, after Christmas Day, at "The Camp for Exceptional Children."

Oh, yes, she told him. They were already making plans and reservations for themselves and Brandon; she thought they'd decided on a tourist place in Mexico. Her mother had suggested she go with them; but she had begged for "Camp" because of the skiing and other winter sports.

"We'll have fun skiing together—and one lie less for both of us. Remember, after tomorrow we know each other." He then went on to tell how his father and Beeto had been hoping she could go with them to this place in Switzerland; small, but very good in every way; and best of all not crowded—yet—with German and American tourists; French was the most common language. His sisters had not seen much of Europe and were going. It would be great fun to have her along; and fun for her too. She'd never had a skiing holiday in the Alps, had she?

Did she think she could manage the trip on the q.t.; only from her parents of course? Her grandmother—he called her Aunt Elspeth—would know. She might even go.

She sprang up, too happy and excited to sit still—almost two weeks of skiing with Ter, Beeto, and the others. Then what? Why must she tear a hole in this good thing; but their next meeting might be years away in Sicily, where he had told her he planned to go. "I hope," she said, "you don't have to give up skiing when you go to Sicily."

He looked unhappy. Sicily wasn't out, completely; but his studies of agriculture were—for a while. He had told no one of his plans, but both his "old man" and his school advisor had had to be in on his college applications. And had they ever thrown out the static when they saw all those agricultural schools—Canada, the States, Europe—and nothing else.

He was angry now, pacing her study. Horticulture or even farming, they had told him, might make an "interesting hobby of sorts" for him, but could not be his life work; no indeed. He had been called in by the headmaster himself. The old fool was really knocked out. He had supposed such an "outstanding student" would be applying to colleges of Oxford and Cambridge—with his record he might make at least one. Didn't "the young gentleman" remember that for the last two years he had carried off the top prizes in both Greek and Latin? He had also done "exceptionally well" in math and science. He had the potential to be a classical scholar or mathematician.

339

"Phooey. I had also consistently made the highest grades in botany, but nobody said anything about that. All I can do is hope I get a turndown from all the old moth-heaps they insisted I apply to. If I don't, I'll manage somehow to sneak in a beginning of what I want to do. I can certainly work in as electives a little more botany and chemistry.

Disgusted by his own future, he turned to hers. What would her college major be? He'd never thought of medicine as a profession for a woman; but since seeing her, he'd checked around and learned there were several women doctors, many married. He supposed they had found husbands not too babyish to object to a physician wife. He didn't mean the field was for just any girl who could get through medical school; but his illness had made him realize Susie had a real talent for medicine. "The world," he said, when he had found her glance, "including Sicily, needs good full time—wives. But it—and especially Sicily —has a bigger need for good doctors." —She'd need servants of course, but—he saw no reason why a good doctor couldn't make a good wife.

Surprise and pleasure at his complete change of opinion left her wordless. He'd had so much trouble hunting words it must have cost him a lot to say it. She smiled at him. Pleasure changed to wonder when she saw the strange look he wore. If it were anybody but Ter, you'd think him embarrassed; but he had never been; even when she'd barged into him in her nightgown, he'd made it clear the embarrassment should be for her.

He disappeared through the study door with a mumbled: "Excuse me, I must get on with this business."

He acted hot and bothered, but Ter was always cool. And cool he was, when he came back with his briefcase.

She watched as, after putting on gloves, he dumped, without touching, the five little stacks of money out of her sack into an ordinary brown one that looked as if it had never been used. He put the sack of money into a ready-prepared package to be mailed to Miss Emily Dexter. In case Susie had forgotten, she was the girl he had, according to the paper, frightened into a state of shock.

Mostly the package was a box of candy for the girl; the best

340

he could find in the short time he had had in Toronto. He hoped she wasn't dieting—she was thin as Susie—and could enjoy the candy. He planned to send her sometime a piece of "not something so expensive it will scare her" jewelry. He wondered if she'd like jade earrings. Customs and buying could make for security problems, but someday he'd manage it.

Flowers would have been more suitable this time, but there was no way to deliver them fresh with the money. The letter, fastened to the package with transparent tape, was also for Miss Dexter; an apology, he said, but nothing that could pay for the fright he had given her.

And had the letter ever been a job? He could not of course use his penmanship. He was also afraid to use his typewriter. He had taken a stencil and done everything in block letters with pen and ink and paper from the U.S.A. He didn't want any suspicions that a Canadian had committed the crime. Nor was Susie to worry about that return address; he had at school checked a map of Detroit; no such street; nor had any telephone book come up with a Pedro Janisykwitz.

He got up wanting to know if Lulu still kept her gram-and-ounce kitchen scales in the cupboard above the spice shelf. Susie insisted she go for them. He didn't want her waiting on him, he told her; so they both went.

"I've been lucky," he told her when they were back from weighing the package. "First, I managed to make connections in Toronto with one of the few planes that comes to your airport instead of Windsor; I found an out-of-the-way stamp machine, got my baggage and checked it, got here before you'd gone to bed, and now the thing is weighed. Now for the stamps."

He was fishing for the stamps in his briefcase when he happened to see his watch. He sprang up, reminding Susie she ought to get at least a little sleep before she left for school. He might not even go to bed. He wanted to get the package into the mail as early as possible—after a normal time. He'd like to hop on Susie's bike and go now, but at three o'clock in the morning a lone biker might attract attention in this jittery neighborhood.

"But how will you get out of the house?" Susie wondered as they went to the bathroom closet for bed linen. "I'll be in school where I can't watch the drive while you come out by the secret passage."

He'd manage; he would probably get Lulu to call a cab.

"Lulu? Call a cab—for you? Why, she'd call the cops instead. And you'd still have all that money." She wondered if he'd gone out of his wits.

He took the stack of linen from her. "Susie, you worry over me too much. I'll manage. I can sneak out when you leave for school, or whenever I'm certain Lulu's in the kitchen. I will come knocking on the back porch door and play a variation of the 'I'm lost' deal you arranged for Dad. Worry over yourself; find an excuse to give Lulu for not coming home after school until eight or so. You can bike to the shopping center drugstore right after school, can't you? We can have a few hours together before it's time for me to get back to the airport. —Say, do you work for the FBI or the CIA? You certainly have the outfit."

Susie, going toward the ladder, turned sharply about, but checked an impulse to grab the micro-mini transistor Ter had found on the writing shelf. In the excitement of his sudden coming, she'd forgotten to hide it.

"I'll bet it's another gift from Beeto? They're convenient in lecture courses, but most especially when you're studying modern languages. You use it in school; lots easier than taking notes?"

"A little last year—mostly in a miserable American history course that was all lecture. Beeto gave it to me when I was taping swamp and pond sounds; he thought I might hang it in a tree for bird calls or tree frogs. I couldn't do that with my big one."

He'd lost interest in the tiny piece of machinery, and was eager to know if she had any swamp tapes he could listen to. He'd been hunting through catalogues for swamp records; he wanted some to compare with those he had made last spring in two swamps near his school. He was so pleased when she told him she had three tapes and their portable recorder on which he could get a playback, he never seemed to notice when she dropped the recorder into a bathrobe pocket. She guessed he didn't even know this particular tape recorder was a secret from

342

everybody except Beeto; and she hoped he had forgotten giving it to her.

She left Ter lost in an early April taping of the swamp with her big recorder, and hurried to bed. Once there, the people and things from the bottom of the sea and the top of the sky would not come. The official bedroom was not keeping them away, but excitement—with a dash of worry. Would anybody notice Ter when he put the package into a mailbox? Would it go into an ordinary mailbox chute, or was it so big he'd have to take it to the self-service post office?

She'd written anonymous letters against weedkiller to newspapers; some had been published; but she had never thought of an anonymous package. There had never been a need for one.

Yes, there was. Katy. The girl needed clothing. Susie would pretend to be an older woman, a kind of Mrs. Good Soul who had heard Katy's flute; and so admired her musical ability she wanted to give her something; "—not because I think you need, or even want, this clothing, my dear, but as a token of appreciation."

She would get something nice—sweaters, a knitted outfit, a dress—Katy could use anything. And Susie could use the Lans money; so far she'd managed to trickle only a small percentage of it into the secret savings account.

16

"'Sing,' said the mother bird. 'We sing,' said the three.'" It was an old brown book her grandmother had studied in school; and now Beeto read to her from it. He had wanted to read the story of the mill that would not stop grinding salt; but she wanted to hear of the birds and as he usually obeyed her—then—he came back to the: "'Sing,' said the mother bird. 'We sing,' said the three.'"

He could not understand that as long as he read, the birds sat in a line and opened their mouths and sang, but when he stopped they skittered away as sandpipers will, ahead of the last foam-fringed wave; for the birds she then knew best were the least sandpipers running in rows and crying like kittens in a storm. You could call it singing.

And now it was her turn to sing. Unlike the sandpipers she could not run—only sit and sing. Slangy, but a good word for telling things you didn't want to tell. Singing made the telling easier, sound easier, that is. It was hard to sing when you didn't want to sing, like Angus—he'd had to sing at baby funerals when he was a little kid, scared to death of his parents. No, her case was different. She was afraid she would sing.

Thinking on Angus was nice. Why couldn't she think of him and other nice things and people instead of bugging herself with the misery ahead? Think of Ter: Friday afternoon when they'd walked and talked and forgotten to eat; and Saturday, when, with all the others, they'd had a time getting a minute alone together; not that she'd resented the others—but people you love can sometimes get in the way. Beeto, coming with Lans and his daughters, had claimed most of her time.

Ter's Monday-evening telephone call had been the nicest of all. They'd arranged the time so she could be waiting in the pantry. Had he ever been happy—and relieved. The package had got through; he'd heard the news on radio, seen on TV Miss Dexter holding letter and candy, and read the papers until he was sick of the deal, especially his letter, and the wailing of the police because there were no clues. And they thought him a sailor from a tramp-ship. Imagine. They'd have something to laugh over together during Christmas ski vacation.

Laugh? Not now. Not here in the Great Rotunda as she walked past the school's war dead. Bronze tablets behind glass, set to turn like the pages of a book, held lists and lists of names through only five wars and into the sixth; for Eden Hills High was rather young, not even going back to the Civil War. Nice to be dead and all done up in bronze; a lot of togetherness, that, and girls like Susan Marie Schnitzer walking by and kind of envying you. Your Big Agony was over; your road ended; no more waiting for Godot in the cold. The last two pages, the ones now open, held the Vietnam dead. The four names at the bottom were brighter than the others—the autumn's dead, privates. Nice, the school didn't put that general-course tag after the name as on the graduation lists. You wondered if they'd volunteered or been conscripted, and if a general-course boy minded dying any less than a college boy. Their mindings didn't matter; the old ones made the music; the young ones danced the tune.

Why was she going in the wrong direction to scrub her hands? She lifted her binder; the clutching hands came with it; she sniffed and caught the soap smell. She must have washed between her last class and lunch. Lunch? She didn't want any. She was frozen inside, unable to remember anything since leaving home in the thin November dark except the hurt of her bra and the cold that no amount of heat could take away.

"Susie." Somebody whispered down into her ear as a warm

345

hand pried one of her own from the binder. Robert. She tried to pull away, but as she did so, the smell of tea sifted through the cold. "Don't squeeze too hard," he said, and curved her dying fish of fingers over something hot. "It's tea in a paper cup. No bag that you hate. Angus brewed a flask for you in chemistry lab."

"Angus? Why didn't he bring it? He knows?"

"I brought it because I wanted to see you. Of course Angus knows. I told him about your big deal today."

She let Robert guide her through a lunchroom door. She automatically worked her way through the lunchroom bodies, sounding their usual noises. Where she went or what she did while waiting for that time marked on the psychologist's slip didn't matter. Oh, but it did. Angus, pulling out a chair for her between Katy and Mary Lou, was saying: "It's Robert needs a psychologist. A sudden change in personality is a danger signal."

"Thank you for the tea," she said. She remembered at last to sit down, and soon to look at the others. All were looking at her, faces covered with freshly-put-on happy smiles. The family watching the child rolled down the hall they could not walk— the one to major surgery. Worse. All of them, thanks to Robert, knew what was coming up for her, that some fool was trying to find out if she were sick-sick. She took a sip of tea to hide her face. Odd, she could still taste; and the tea tasted good.

Angus was watching her. "Look, you'd better pay now in case you don't come back; you don't want Robert's death laid on your soul: fifty cents for finding you and serving the tea; fifty more for guiding you to the chair the girls saved. One dollar even."

Then all were laughing so that even other students turned to look, for Susie was offering Robert a dollar bill. He tried to cover his annoyance with cool words. "I'm only doing my yearly good deed. That idiot—he's studying social work, not psychology, I tell you—he has an IQ I'm certain at least fifty points lower than yours. He can't pull anything out of you that you don't want pulled."

The others nodded. "Psychoanalyze him and have fun," Katy said.

346

"Pretend you're a hard-core kid—the kind my father has. Talk a blue streak and confuse him," Ben suggested.

"And don't let him use a tape recorder," Angus said. "There's been a court case of some kind—I just heard family talk. Enough to gather my old man's worried; he used a tape recorder to gather material for his book."

"Worried?" Robert asked. "Why? If he could get sued—with a hint of scandal on the side—think of the publicity he'd get because he's a minister. His book would really sell then. —I forgot; we're supposed to be comforting Susie." He turned to her. "You don't really need comfort, do you, Susie? Think of this brain-squeezing session as a preparation for life. A job interview with a lie-detector won't seem so rough."

Angus poured her a second cup of tea. "Robert, will you kindly shut up? Why bring up lie detectors?"

"Her guy won't use one because he can't get one. But Susie should have ear plugs; all this happy talk," Ben said.

"Peanuts help me—when Mama's about to try some brain washen." It was Mary Lou holding out a handful of unshelled peanuts.

Susie took the peanuts and thanked her as Robert nodded. "Good. Be chewing one as you walk in—healthy, happy little girl so unworried she almost forgot and had to finish her lunch on the run."

She thought hard on lemons, those half-peeled, juice-dripping lemons in the Ryksmuseum. It worked. "And here's something I hope you'll take for afterwards." Angus held out a small plastic sack with the handle of a plastic spoon showing above the rubber band that closed the top. "Ground up lemon sours," he explained. "They're a good thing to have when you're frazzled, and haven't eaten in a long time."

She had thanked him for the confection, and was finishing the tea when Robert got up. "Don't overdo the nonchalance. Your man doesn't go by school periods; he cuts your lunch time by almost half; thinks if you come to him hungry, you'll talk faster, give him lots of material for his paper. —And don't forget you have to visit Attendance first."

She had forgotten, but didn't say so. She fished the appointment paper from her binder, then carefully got up. Any quick movement, even a deep breath, made the bra cut into her ribs. She managed smiles for all save Robert. She didn't bother to look at his face. He took her hand as if to lead her. She pulled free. She wished he would go somewhere, anywhere away from Susan Schnitzer. She could not get away from him; he was Sir Galahad walking with her down the hall as if she didn't know the way. Nor did she need a body bumper; during lunch and class periods the halls were almost empty.

She walked on, slowly, slowly, until she stood with her face framed in one of the three holes in the glass panel that separated Attendance from its prey. She slid the appointment sheet, her class schedule card, and on top her ID card through a slot below the hole. A long pale hand picked up the sheet and cards. She then watched a machine hunting through punched cards hung on a turning circle of metal; while beside it something like a typewriter, seemingly worked only by the bouncing ball, clicked away all by itself, as it came up with its slips for the late ones, the absentees, both excused and unexcused, the hospitalized ones, and the poor souls caught playing hookey.

Attendance was the end of the assembly line; beyond Attendance were the offices of Registration and Counseling and the big Administration section that included the principal and his assistants, among them Discipline. She saw students going in and students coming out; some with both parents, some with only a worried looking mama, but most with nobody, nothing but red eyes and a slow walk.

One of the slowest was a girl who stopped a few feet back from Attendance; she made no attempt to get into line, but stared at the glass hole in a sad, uncertain way as if she felt possibly she ought to step up to Attendance—or someplace. Susie, afraid her face was showing and the girl would see it, turned back to the glass hole. She had been thinking: "What an outlandish way to dress." She was wearing an out-of-date sack dress, except it wasn't a sack—now; more like a closely fitted slip on a pillow with too many feathers in the lower front half. Worse was the widely spread, old fashioned blazer she wore over the dress as if to hide its tightness.

Susie listened to the typewriter do her hall-passage slip. It had finished the Schnitzer, and was clicking out Susan M, all in caps. Next an x under F, then on to homeroom number, class period, class, telephone, numbers on ID card, date, time to the second; all facts needed for a quick check if the inmate didn't show up for class. Her ID card already had most of the information, plus her picture, but Attendance wanted the other, just in case she looked exactly like some other girl, and was planning a break by means of stolen identification.

The hall-passage slip came through the slit with the three documents she had brought. "Shall I send a guide with you?"

She was startled as if the pale hands had spoken. "No, thank you," she said, and looked up. The owner of the voice was staring at the top of her head as if that spiral crown were in plain sight and she didn't like it too well.

"Next," this particular piece of Attendance Personnel was saying. Susie grabbed her four papers and stepped aside. In turning, she saw the girl again; this time her profile. She was too self-conscious. Attendance had not been seeing a spiral crown on her head, but looking past it to a baby. The girl was about to have one. The girl's parents and everybody else would know she had given way to that excitement a girl should hold in check, as directed in last year's Hygiene III.

Her binder was suddenly slippery under the cold sweat of her palms; she stopped, a sickness welling up inside her. What if that man strapped Susan Schnitzer into that seat with the electrical devices that didn't kill you, only skinned your brain and soul bare for all to see? The name? The name? Lie-detector, that was it. She'd read about this girl, seventeen, who had wanted a little summer job as a government file clerk. They'd put her into a lie-detector and asked about her sex life.

That man might learn what "camp" really was by doing that to her. He'd also find out she was abnormal. Here she was close to sixteen with no sex life. She had never had that excitement that carried you away. No boy had seemed interested in giving it to her.

"Susie, a little lateness is all right, shows confidence; but don't overdo it. And quit trying to watch that poor girl. She's being sent home because she's reached the danger stage in a pregnancy out of tune. You can't see her now, anyway. She's down by the corner waiting."

Susie hadn't realized she was by the battery of glass exit doors, staring through them at a lie-detector, not the girl. Robert wasn't worth the trouble of an explanation. Odd, a long time ago he had made her angry, hurt her feelings and her pride. He couldn't hurt her any more. Some day she'd tell Ter of Robert Hedrick, and how they would laugh together. And what had Robert said? "Waiting? Who for what?" she asked.

"That girl. Who knows what she's waiting for? She already has her future," he said. He took her hand. "I had you in such nice shape. Now, your hands are cold, and you are chittering like a pump working a dry well. Before he has finished with you, you'll tell all; even—." He glanced around. "At least get in shape so you won't spit out your experiences with—me and the boat on—."

"I was just thinking," she said, both hands again on her binder.

"Don't ever think, especially in school. Just swallow," he said. Walking very close to her, as if she were the only girl on earth, he took her up the proper stairs, turned into the proper hall, walked her past the library door, and then after a quick look around, stopped. He took another look around before whispering. "Today, because of my grades, free reading time in AP English is free time—so long as you don't go wandering through the halls or outside—so today I've arranged to work for the library carting books hither and yon, so I can be waiting around in this hall with a book cart ready for you to fall on."

She didn't care if her eagerness to be rid of him showed in her face. "I won't be falling, thank you. But if you want to help —." Her carefully-thought-out plan came back into her head. "Have a cookbook for home ec. kitchen on your cart." She turned away, and started down the long hall, the farther end given up to offices of the academic staff. Robert caught her shoulder. She neither stopped nor looked at him, but stared at the papers she held, wondering on which was the number of her door. She found the number on the hall-passage slip, and then she saw the matching door. She stiffened.

"Be a good soldier now," Robert was whispering. "Don't give me away. Remember your grandfather, whatever it was he did."

"Died," she said.

Robert caught her hand, lifted for knocking. "You don't knock," he whispered. "There is an inner sanctum behind an inside door; that's where you get the works. In the outer, waiting part, this door leads to, there'll be only sweat seats. Keep you-know-what hidden as well as your face, but let your religion show."

He was gone at last. She was opening The Door, all alone in the world, except her—. "Don't be frightened. Come right in. I am waiting. You are already late." The loud, make-them-feel-your-empathy voice was coming through the second door, open into the inner sanctum. There he sat, the shiny milk-tank-truck of a man, playing at being a big shot too busy to go out for lunch; just finishing, she gathered from the crumbs, crumpled paper, and other debris.

She remembered her lines. "I apologize for being late. I didn't realize at lunch, time was going so fast. A bunch of us were laughing and talking." She had stopped in the doorway to give quick glances around the small room, while listening to her voice. Miserable: choked, squeaky with the beginnings of a shake; it would have to do better than this. Her smile, too, she guessed was pitiful. Had he noticed, or was it that he had overdone the empathy and couldn't let up?

He was saying: "Now, now, you must not be frightened. We are only trying to help you, Susie."

She was frightened—afraid she'd lose the tea and peanuts. Her name on his fat, loose lips had lingered too long in a rounded protrusion. She dropped her glance to the desk, studied it, then made a great business of turning her head to look about the room. She got her smile in better shape, she hoped, before asking: "Where are the others? Or do you mean yourself and tape recorder?"

"Please, Susie." He shuffled the papers on the desk so as to show its emptiness, then pulled out the drawers. "Look, will you. Why would I want to use a tape recorder? You teen-agers believe every stupid tale you hear. Come on, look."

She watched him move the swivel chair and himself with it away from the desk. He wanted her to go between him and the desk—so she wouldn't get a close look at all of his front.

She took three quick steps around the desk; she could now begin to squeeze her body between his chair and the wall, the squeeze so tight the chair moved forward. There was behind him nothing in or on the bare wall but one window. He had ducked his head, hunched his shoulders as if expecting blows; but soon recovered enough to swivel in her direction and sit, head craned to see her face. She smiled and, disregarding the opened drawers, sent a running glance down his shirt front. "I can get a better perspective back here," she told him, and after another microinstant of shirt study went back to the front of the desk.

Red tinged his well padded cheeks, and there was no ooze of empathy as he said: "Anything to get you over your fright so you can relax."

"I am relaxed, thank you," she told him as she tilted her head for a study of his shirt front from another angle. He should wear a girdle as did her father; there was such a hideous bulge of shirt and trouser, both ill fitting, kooky, especially the shirt, a pity the too-wide tie couldn't cover more of it. And why was the tie so wide—so long? So it would catch his falling food and so save the shirt, plainly laundered by a wife, not too good at the business. Did he quarrel at his wife for being a poor laundress the way Bismarck used to do in the old days when all money was going into the business?

She'd better get going on her own business. He was looking at her over the rim of a paper cup he drained with a loud sip. She felt sweat slide down an armpit. Her mind again slid away; this time to wonder if she should take off the new cashmere cardigan she wore over a matching slipover. No, the oozing sweat might show on a bared elbow. Anyway, this sweat didn't come from too much clothing in an overheated U.S.A. schoolroom; more like water from a weeping cake of ice.

Both empathy and smile were back as he asked: "Satisfied? Now, suppose you have this nice surprise I've bought especially for you, an ice cold beverage all teen-agers enjoy. Sit down and drink and relax."

She looked at the ceiling, spoke to the ceiling as she said: "Thank you." Her glance swooped down in time to catch him leaning far back in the chair in order to stick that stomach ceilingward. He straightened and sent his stomach forward as she bent her head above the desk and mumbled: "I don't have the habit."

The tie flapped around as he opened the bottle and shoved it toward her, and said: "Drink it and relax so that you will be able to sit down while I evaluate some of your responses to my interrogations in our in-depth interview of last spring."

She turned around as far as she could in order to pretend she was looking for someone behind her; yet not so far, but from the corner of an eye she could see that mountain of gray shirt try to follow—in case she said something. That big tie undoubtedly caught his spilled food, but its main function was to cover. "Don't be foolish," he said. "I am the only person in the room."

"What am I?" She'd whirled back so swiftly, the tie flapped again as he tried to put his stomach in line with her voice. Sweat was now running down between her breasts, the clammy cold-ness dripping onto the scorching pains of that too-tight bra.

"Susan, you are a very difficult subject." His speech was forgetting its training, such as it was. "Now, won't you please sit down." He was getting loud.

She turned all the way around to get her binder from the chair behind her. She said: "Excuse me," in a barely audible voice. She wanted to be able to hear the squeak of his chair as he swung it around to follow her voice. The squeak came. She unzipped the binder and took from it a fresh handkerchief, explaining: "I need to get the peanut salt off my fingers."

"Sweaty?" he asked, smiling as he leaned back in the chair to make his stomach point toward her mouth.

She listened to her IBM: "Don't let him scare you. He's trying to make it through some ersatz higher-degree mill outside the State of Michigan. Some place that will let him walk on the

353

beach and call it swimming. Mostly he took courses in sweat, coffee, and pep pills, the same as Charlotte's husband." She watched his hands now fiddling with that too-big tie. He gave her another sarcastic smile as he asked: "What is it? You keep watching me."

"I apologize," she said. "I lately read a book on hands, and was wondering if they are as revealing as the book said." She waited while he rummaged over the desk for pen and paper, then made a note. "According to the author, lower-class white-collar men with blue-collar fathers, you know, only one generation from the pick and shovel, take great pride in soft white hands—such as yours. Contrariwise, the upper-class man who doesn't have to care and does what he pleases—whether it's digging in his garden or climbing mountains—often has hard, rough hands."

He had taken no more notes. His hands had hidden their pretty selves under the desk. She finished with men and went onto the hands of the middle class wife who "has a time, because there's no money for a maid, keeping her hands in tune with those of her white-collar husband."

He began to look restless. She'd better be thinking up a name for this book in case he asked. No, he wouldn't. He was reaching into a coat pocket. He wanted to change the subject.

She saw what he brought out; batted her eyes; she was surely seeing what wasn't there. Staying up most of the night, no breakfast or lunch, not much dinner, could that make you have visions? The hand holding out the opened package of cigarettes was no vision; it was almost grazing her chin. She remembered Ben's talk. Anger took her fear away. One day at lunch Ben had told of how his father had heard that now and then a teacher or counselor got close to the Detroit wild ones by offering a cigarette during conference. If the hard-core type took it, the acceptance was a sign of trust in the giver not to squeal on him. She shook her head to the cigarette. Pity the ADC mothers to have such a cruddy fool turned loose on them. "You're using the right technique on the wrong subject," she told him, and thought her voice sounded as it should, nothing in it but word sounds.

He continued to try. "A cigarette might help you relax."

She no longer dared risk her tongue, and could only shake her head as he held the cigarettes under her nose. The picture of a fool tourist trying to feed a bear somewhere in Canada rolled across her TV screen as he insisted: "Don't worry, I won't tell."

It was like trying to bring in her sailboat against an offshore wind on a strong ebb tide. The wind was her rising anger. The ebb tide? Her what? Strength? She didn't have any. If she lost her temper she'd be sunk. And how he would love a "manifestation of lack of self-control as shown by inability to control anger." He would take pages of notes. He was watching her, ball-point poised. If only he'd stand up instead of sitting with his too-big shirt dripped down in folds; gray oxford cloth with all those little holes—convenient.

He watched her, smiling his narrow-eyed smile. She knew that smile, her father's pink-slip smile. No, it was a thousand-year smile; a thousand years could not wipe out the memory. She had lived through that smile—several times. She would function through this.

She smiled, but could not manage the deep breath she tried; the bra cut into her ribs so cruelly she stopped half way and wondered if the moisture she felt under the bottom of the bra were cold sweat or warm blood. Her rib cage was past any feeling but pain.

She grew aware she was pulling her thumb. He was watching the "manifestation of tension" he had commented on the last time. Let him watch. He couldn't see the cold sweat sliding down betweeen her breasts, dripping from her armpits, damp between her thighs. It would go running down, then oozing up and over her shoes as did the incoming tide when she walked across her great-grandmother's back meadow around the hill from the sea. You never saw nor felt it, only the oozing around your feet. You moved on; if the tide were high it could be nasty out there in the flats, worse than nasty. Here, she couldn't move on. The tide must come—suppose it was deeper than she was tall? She had forgotten she could swim.

"Now then," he was saying, empathy back, "will you please sit down and act natural. I am only trying to help you."

She wished for a deep breath, one long deep breath. She

couldn't manage it. She tried to smile, but could only put on the postage stamp kind, the tiny smile of a tired mail clerk during the Christmas rush. "Mary, Mother of my heaven under the sea, help me, please. Let me turn once more, and if he tries to follow with his stomach,—. Will I do it even then? Strengthen, I beg You this quaky coward."

"I'll pull up a chair," she said. Turning quickly around, she heard the squeak of his chair as he moved closer. She whirled back in time to find the pale hands busied with his tie as he looked down at the mound of shirt bosom. The balding head jerked up as she leaned across the desk. She held in the tongue that wanted to lick her dry lips; all so dry the three of them would rustle and click as did the dried catalpa pods above a stretch of road on the way to school. "Tongue rustled lips." That would make a good line in the story due next Monday in English.

"When are you going to sit down?" Mr. Milk-Tank-Truck had let his empathy get away. He was frowning at her, head lifted as she wanted it to be.

She swiftly bent far over the desk, thumb and fingers reaching in a wide, down dropping arc. She was more than half certain, yet dreading, recoiling from the soft man-flesh; so flabby fat it was swallowing her fingers. No, only little Peter Playman; dear Thumbkin, Lickpot, and Longman were grabbing hardness under the gray cloth, shaping the flat oblong of hardness. Everything was sliding away; the chair was tipping backward; she must not hang on and tear his shirt; would that be vandalism or assault and—. His head had struck the window-sill. She in following the tipped chair was sprawled stomach down across the desk with her feet off the floor.

She righted herself with a quick slide, then smiled on her work. Her sweaty fingers had made a fair impression of the tape recorder hidden under his shirt. She stepped back and, from behind the curtain of her hair, watched the man's clumsy attempts to right himself. He made slow work of it, for in trying not to tip over, he had flung up one leg as a counterweight, only to have it fall on the desk top as he tipped still further. And so he lay, struggling in the narrow space to get a leg off the desk and onto the floor. A pity the window-sill had been so close; without it, he would have upended backward onto the floor, legs treading air.

He at last got his component parts arranged in a more conventional manner, and after a little more time was able to speak in spite of breath trouble. "Any more of this, Susan Schnitzer, and I will call the principal."

"He wouldn't come." She nodded toward the intercom on its wall cradle. "That will connect you with an operator. Tell her you have a pupil you can't handle, and she'll connect you with the office of the Assistant Principal in Charge of Discipline—or you could ask for help from the school police. I would find the business an interesting experience; my first as a problem in discipline." The tide would come no higher. He was keeping quiet—except for his breathing.

She had heard no quakes in her voice; might as well finish. She put both palms on the desk and leaned above him. "Cooperation with people who tell me untruths is not my line. Last time you told us when we met as a group you were a psychologist. You are not. You are trying to get a degree in social work so you can oversee the poor." He had opened his mouth to speak, but had to content himself with a head-shake as she went on: "Last time you took recordings of everything, even—even when you had me bark like a dog, so that you might better check my reactions after what you called the 'unfortunate incident with a dog.' That time you denied you were making a tape. You were. I let you get by with it.

"I shouldn't have, for your own sake. Surely you know the rules of this school. You must also be familiar with the Yaegar Case. The child's parents sued in New York; the idiot who did the secret recordings took it to the Supreme Court—and lost again."

Susan Schnitzer, in spite of being "Outstanding Girl Student," wasn't much, but times you had to admire her various pieces of apparatus. Here she was frozen solid inside, thawing a little ice water on the outside, but her IBM and TV sound track were functioning in perfect synchronization. She knew nothing of school rules, if any, on tape recorders. She had never heard of the Yaegar Case until it popped onto her screen. Neither had the would-be psycho-social worker; but ignorance did not keep him from believing. Poor man, he was going to try the bear-feeding act again. This time with gum. He waved it under her nose with one hand while he held up the other for silence.

She shook her head to the gum.

He helped himself to two sticks and contemplated her as he unwrapped and gave them a few mashing-together chews. The chewing appeared to help him. He got back into his dignity, and was holding empathy firmly in both hands as he said: "I only want to try to help you with some evaluation and clarification of specific items in our previous interviews and written responses of last spring."

"I am helping you," she told him. "I am material for your paper. I will cooperate to the best of my ability when you take that transistor tape recorder out of your shirt. Otherwise, you may call whoever you want—Discipline, the police—or both; for I will not answer one of your questions. I can't help it if he finds me in hysterics. Then my doctor will want to ask questions; to him I am not a fit subject for interrogation by a would-be social worker with juvenile delinquents."

His gum chewing stopped when she shivered and gave a big urp. He sat a moment longer, chin tucked in like Napoleon, but Napoleon after Waterloo. He abruptly swiveled the chair until his back was to her. His moving elbows told he was unbuttoning his shirt. He then twisted sideways to unhook some kind of belt. He turned back with the tape recorder in one hand while he opened a desk drawer with the other.

She grabbed the recorder. Her attack so sudden, she had it before he knew what was happening.

He, for the first time got to his feet. "Don't you understand that in all my research the methodology invariably consists in giving the informant a number. Why, I did not even remember your name."

She nodded. "I noticed that; instead, you called me by a name used only by my family and intimate friends—the first three times when you forgot to remember you didn't know my name." She stopped to study the tape recorder. If this was the one he had used last time, she need not worry. Poor fidelity, for it was one of the cheapest as well as oldest of models. She flipped up her binder to form a screen, and under cover of it took out the tiny roll of tape. He could not see what she was doing, but started around the desk, begging more than commanding: "Don't wreck it. Remember vandalism of school property is against the law."

She smiled and stepped to the other end of the desk. She could keep him running round and round grabbing for his tape recorder the rest of the afternoon. No, only about five minutes; he hadn't the wind or legs for more than that; and smart man, he knew it. She laid the recorder without its tape gently on the desk. "You should get out of the habit of telling untruths. In the first place the school uses much more expensive and up-to-date models; and in the second place Administration would not let you use it on me—while you pretended to take notes—without the written consent of my parents."

He had already grabbed the tape recorder, and, without looking, shoved it into his desk. He gave no sign he'd heard her last speech.

She sat down so cozy-close her breasts were over the desk top. In spite of the two sweaters, a woolen skirt, opaque tights and other proper underthings, she had constantly to be on guard not to let a shiver show. Her feet were clammy wet, and the slip felt like frost-covered tin against her thigh; if she sat long enough the wetness would creep through to show on the back of her skirt. Her stomach was still trying to ride up into her throat. She had won only a minor victory. The real battles—not to show the torture, not to give anything away—were still ahead, as was the finding out how much he had learned from last spring's brain probes.

He had done a fair job of pulling himself together, chewing his gum more slowly as he studied her with something of her father's, "Is this spoilage or pickle I taste in the herring?" look. Might as well get started. "You say you want me to cooperate. I thought I gave you a great deal of time and material last spring, but—now—I'm willing to try again."

She smiled at the memory of last spring. Her ink blots had

been patterned after those the books showed for an intelligent but fairly normal teen-ager with average imagination. Her dreams had been beauties—also patterned after the right ones. "Don't dwell on your triumphs," she told herself. The thing to do was get him on her abnormalities; find out what he thought these were, but let him stay on her past only long enough to find out what he knew—and his suspicions. "You do have my sympathy in trying to do a big research paper. I have some idea of what a job that can be. I will help to the best of my abilities for I know abnormal children like me furnish your material."

He bit, asking: "Abnormal?"

"If I were not, you wouldn't have me here so much." The rest of the answer kept her going for several minutes. She gave him back his words from last spring plus words from the books and some of her own. "I am, as you know, in the ninety-nine-plus quartile in intelligence, achievement, and some aptitudes; and with these handicaps no girl can be normal; for as you pointed out my striving for grades is possibly but a seeking of compensation for lack of popularity."

She then went into one of his favorite subjects of last spring —scar alienation, its problems; "—for as you explained last time the main drive of the normal girl is hunting and holding a mate." Trippity, trip, trip. She heard the words and thanked that good old TV system; shook up it was, but still working. Trouble, though, was coming up in the audio mechanism. Strange, how a body could be so sweat-wet all below, but above so dry the head had to think of lemons to keep the tongue from rattling. A pity she couldn't make like a hard-core juvenile as Ben had suggested; she wished she could learn from one, a real hard one with lots of core. Three times he had tried to interrupt; if she could keep going, he would learn nothing, nothing at all. Now, her overheated tongue would have to let him ask questions. She gave what she hoped appeared to be a polite pause instead of lack of saliva.

"Susan, your use of the word *abnormal* I question. Many of us have little nervous habits and idiosyncrasies."

She managed what she hoped was a look of sympathetic horror, and sighed as much as the new bra would allow. "Don't tell me they've changed texts on you? Not again? I was repeating —and I have an almost photogenic—excuse me, I mean photographic—memory, what you said last spring; for then you certainly found me abnormal with a great many quiddities." She wondered if she'd wrongly used the last word; she'd heard it for the first time from Ter during the weekend. She'd better give it a quick cover. "I suppose you evaluated me by the text you were then using."

"Text?" he asked, then immediately added: "Skip it."

She wouldn't skip it. Her tongue was moist again. She went into another long account of a nonexistent book dealing with the "many changes in psychological attitudes toward the rearing of children." She managed, before he could ask for author and title, to get going on a book Iggy had loaned her, a work concerned chiefly with up-to-the-minute interpretations of Freud. The old interpretations she had never known; the new she did not understand too well. Yet, she had picked up enough phrases and ideas to keep her going until her tongue again went dry.

She stopped with the thought she'd made a mess of things. Her talking had only given him time to collect himself. Time was sliding by, but not exactly like a jet come in without its landing gear. "Susan?" He had all his empathy back, thick as refuse oil on Lake St. Clair. "Would you mind giving me your ideas on right and wrong?"

"Notatawl. I suppose you want a chapter on teen-age morals. Main thing is never break the big rules."

"Big rules?"

"Yes. Such as don't salute the flag in the wrong way; go to church at least twice on Sunday; never say or write or do anything that might hurt the Principal's Recommendation. Dress properly and avoid clothing frowned on by the school, such as micro-miniskirts; and don't get mixed up in things."

"What things?"

She flipped more hair over her face; she didn't trust it to stay zipped. She wondered if her voice sounded all right; there ought to be some kind of transistor earring you could wear at a time like this to tell you exactly what your voice was doing as it said such greasy things: "I mean all those batty causes. You hear of them now and then even out here; but not of course in the school paper. Stay away from peaceniks, beatniks, bomb-banners, and —." She stopped. Would he swallow such a nasty word? She'd never heard it from anyone except Brandon, who'd picked it up from one of his "group" leaders. "—niggerniks" she brought out at last, and was at once ashamed of having dirtied her tongue. She waited, hoping he would criticize her for using the word.

He said nothing. There was no censure in his face. Instead, he smiled and nodded, eager for more of the same. She sailed into another sea, Robert's; keep out of the troubled waters of controversial matters that might interfere with the future. Her future would, of course, or so she hoped, be mainly husband and children, but like a lot of modern women she might work for a while.

"And what kind of job would you like to work at, Susie?" His voice was tender as overdone broccoli.

"I would like to work on the IBM machines for God in heaven, if I get there, and am good enough in math and science."

His mouth had come open but no words were coming out. The censure that had not come for the dirty word was now strong in his face, and at last in his voice: "Don't be flippant."

"Flippant?" She leaned across the table and gave him a look of childhood belief betrayed; and was so choked with shock and surprise she could scarcely whisper: "How does it feel not to believe in God?" She registered horror as she sent a long glance ceilingward, and whispered: "Does anyone know—here? I can't believe an anti-religionist would be permitted in this school."

He looked as if he would like to go off and have a good cry. He jerked the package of cigarettes out of his pocket, without, she thought, knowing he had done so, for his fist was so clenched over the package, he cumpled it as he said: "How dare you? How dare you accuse me of not believing in God?"

She let horror grow in silence while he remembered what he was holding, and after several angry tries with a reluctant lighter was able to puff smoke into her face. She pushed back her chair. "You scare me," she told him. "Talking as if you were an agnostic —or worse, politically speaking, I mean. —I've heard Communists don't believe in God." He strangled on cigarette smoke—or something. Didn't the idiot know it was against all rules for anybody, even the principal, to smoke outside the staff lounges? Sail on. Sail on.

"As I see it, what with the population explosion and the U.S.A. more religious than it has ever been, God will have to use an IBM; he will have a punched card for each of us just like here in school. And if the punched cards get through the Big Selector—you're all right." She'd better take in this particular sail or try a quick tack; she wasn't getting any place; her wind and sea, save for too many, too quick puffs on the cigarette, had gone into a dead calm, as he looked through a sheaf of papers which she thought was her dossier.

"I mean, Susan," he said, empathy gone, and after a time of silence "what do you plan to do here on earth? Your record seems to indicate you are college material."

She covered her awareness of his planned insult by the use of *seems* with a lot of words. Yes, she hoped to go to college, and as for work: "I would rather like to serve my country and my Christ with work in that nerve-gas plant down in Indiana. The unnoticeable death gases are, I understand, not yet perfect. There is also need for a stickier napalm. Germ warfare would also be helpful—and interesting." No more of this kind of talk or she'd be vomiting.

He nodded, solemn as that old brick-faced gynecologist her mother had made her see when her menses began. "All the rest of your life." That is, the rest that counted; she had known that, but the pain was unexpected. "Pain? Menstrual pains are largely manifestations of a craving for attention and sympathy; a normal process, no reason for pain."

"And you had no pain during your mensus, sir? Normal process? So is death, sir." She remembered that because she had not said it. This man also knew all the answers. She looked at him. Still hunting through her dossier, he had finished the cigarette, and was comforting himself with a candy bar. She heard the opening of the outer door. That would mean another on the sweat-seat. Sometime, a million years ago, she had heard buzzers, and after a while, feet, hesitant, then silence.

She listened to this second set of feet, hoping. They came on so slowly, they might be coming to the inner door. That could mean her time was up and she was free, free. She realized she was listening to silence. The feet meant only another was now on the sweat-seat.

She was cold again, freezing cold, and alone, so alone. She stared through the window at the sky, and tried to think of a poem with a gray, gray sky, but instead thought of Erie as it had been last time, cold iron gray with reeds whistling in the wind and the salties gone from the up-lanes. She had seen one flock of wild geese go over, a high gray string against the gray sky. They had made her lonesome with wishings she could follow—except they were going in the wrong direction. Now, Erie would always seem as it had been on that last day, for she would never again be with Robert on the *Antiname*.

She thought she saw fine snowflakes away out there in the grayness. She hoped Ter's world was having snow; he would go skiing in the twilight after his classes were finished. "Think of Ter and that fantastic Christmas vacation, you'll be having together soon." She tried, but—.

"Susie, what are you thinking of?"

She wondered if she jumped. "Euclid, sir."

He was puzzled, happy-puzzled, another abnormality. "Euclid?"

"Yes, sir, I think of him when I look at the sky. He would be surprised and sad, at least for a little while, don't you think, when he learned the space age had outmoded his geometry; you imagine he looked upon it as absolute truth. Or did he? And is there such a thing as absolute truth?" She leaned forward, hoping. Her question might start him going for a while. Then, she saw that finger on her dossier and knew it was no good. He wouldn't jump in and bite off a chunk as Angus and Katy had the other day at lunch, and Iggy one morning on the way to school.

"Susie, I am wondering if your absent-mindedness has improved. What, for example, is my name?" And when she floundered, he continued after cleaning a tooth with his tongue:

"Don't you think it odd not to remember the name of a psychologist who has given you hours and hours of time?"

"I remember the letters after your name. They did not indicate psychology, but social work." He pretended not to have heard. She tried to think. Would it be too rude to tell him she thought of him as Mr. Weevil or Mr. Milk-Tank-Truck? If she could forget the cold and the loneliness, and the pain of the bra cutting into her like the barbed wire grown into the trees of The Primitive's old fence rows, she could fend off direct questions. "There are so many of you, I forget," she said at last.

He was the gull sighting a picnic basket. "You mean you have had many psychologists?"

She studied him through hair and half-shuttered eyes. His name had come to her, but so had words. "No, I think you are the first—if you want to call yourself a psychologist. I mean all of you, so many have been needed, so very many. You don't of course know the obstetrician who delivered you, but soon you are remembering pediatricians. Next, there are relatives outside the family, family help, baby sitters, Sunday-school teachers; ministers and assistant ministers. They came; they went; for, as you pointed out last time, my parents have moved a great deal. A new neighborhood brought a whole new set of most. There were nurses and physicians in and out of hospital—you were most curious about that last time—teeth men with their nurses and technicians; now and then an eye man just for checking; librarians, music and dancing teachers." You must mention camp but be careful; don't pull your thumb. "There were people at camp, beauty shop people, librarians, ski, swimming, dance, music, horseback-riding teachers. Their faces mostly I remember.

"All these are few compared to the people who have worked on me in school. This one semester, for example, I have five different teachers in five academics; there are three others for orchestra, physical education, and driver education, plus counselors, girls' and academic. Most will change at semester's end, except homeroom. I forgot homeroom, and I'm certain I forgot others. But at least that's enough to show you why I don't remember the names of all the workers who gave me a dab of paint here or a screw-turn there, or went over the body finish as I came down the assembly line."

She couldn't keep it up. Somewhere far away a bell buzzed. This room was like a coffin; bells, clocks, and schedules didn't matter any more. If she could be back out there, warm and alive, with students coming and going, she wouldn't even mind the bumping bodies.

"Oh, Mary Mother, take me away from this room. It is cold here and lonely. Forgive me the lies I tell, and that ugly word I used back there, I beg You. You understand I must have the proper image for this man so he will quit bothering me. Just now I told him the truth; he seemed to think I was trying to be cute. But he smacks his lips over the lies I tell. We have not yet tackled the big one. Make him, I beg You, swallow it—if he makes me tell it. Au revoir."

And here it came. "But are you certain I am the first psychologist? This camp for exceptional children you have attended each summer since the unfortunate dog episode, didn't it have any form of mental therapy; no psychologist?"

She was suddenly weak and tired; so tired she sagged forward, no longer needing all that starch, or whatever it was had held her up. This Grand Inquisitor, in spite of all the time spent over her in Torture Chamber, had only the old Official Schnitzer Version. This was a joint creation of the Popsicle Queen and a student-teacher in third grade where she had been placed after her first stay of almost a year in the "Camp for Exceptional Children." She had at first thought the woman was taking an interest in her because of kindness. Why else would she ask so many questions, visit her mother, then send her a thick letter, well sealed?

Her mother had read the letter and said nothing. That night at dinner she learned her father had read the letter and was greatly pleased by it. She also learned it was not a letter, but a case history, only one of twelve the woman was doing on "subjects chosen from Susan's class." She had at dinner given no sign of understanding, or even of hearing. Case histories she had thought were only for doctors and hospitals—and were kept secret.

366

She had never again spoken to that "kind teacher"; not a difficult feat; case history finished, the woman had lost interest in her. She ought to hunt her up and thank her for her lies and her pretending; her case history, school property, was apparently freely open to any curious body like this man. He had read—and learned nothing.

She'd better sit a moment longer with bowed head and hair over her face. This way she could hide her jubilation. "Thank you, Mother Mary, for saving my big secret. I know You care for neither bribes nor gifts, but pray smile upon the gilded candles, big ones, I will buy and burn in Bon Secours the first time I get to Montreal."

All that useless worry. She ought to have had more faith in the "conspirators," above all Margaret, Jeff's wife, whom no Schnitzer had ever met—as Jeff's wife. She it was who had "managed things" when, after the first hospitalization for the scars, Susan Marie Schnitzer had, on the suggestion of her surgeon and the consent of her parents, been sent to a "therapeutic institution" where children, recovering from illness and shock, but not mentally ill, did very well indeed. Susan had thrived so, Brandon had been on the waiting list for years.

Now, behind the curtain of her hair, she smiled at the warm memories of the hospital where "camp" had really begun. There, her friends and relatives—except her grandmother—could, after the first few days, visit her when the Schnitzers, who came usually only in the early evenings, were not there. Beeto, running in at odd hours, had brought messages from her grandmother over the river in Windsor. Angie and Joe and Jeff had come daily with gifts and messages and pleasant talk.

The only absent friend was Margaret. Then one day Susie had heard this voice in the hall; Margaret's voice—except it belonged to a Dr. Anderson. And was she ever slinging the big words around: nurse so respectful; her mother so respectful to this Head of the Committee of Acceptance. The head of the committee was polite, but uncertain the camp could handle the child. She would have to talk with him first. "A girl? Pardon me." The first interview should be with the child alone. Aunt Margaret had come sailing in with her Ph.D. sticking out all over, a brief-case under her arm, and all got up in a tailored suit.

What did Mr. Weevil want now? His voice was interrupting her pleasant thoughts. He was looking annoyed. He was annoyed. Good.

"Susan, I am too busy to repeat questions to a student who didn't hear because she is daydreaming. I wish to learn how you came through what many children find a most traumatic experience; that is the sudden and complete separation from a stable early environment that included a strong interpersonal relationship."

You pitied criminals in prison, but at least before they were sentenced when somebody questioned them, they had had lawyers—most of the time. And once in prison did they have to answer questions about attitudes as she was going to have to do now—pages and pages of attitude questions on that written deal: had she ever wanted to slap her mother; run away from home; did she enjoy being with her brother; did she envy him because he was a boy; her feelings about masturbation, ugh—.

"Susan?" He repeated the question.

Her confidence was so great, she straightened, shook back her hair the better to look at him before answering: "I'm afraid I don't know what you mean. My only traumatic experience, insofar as I know, was getting scarred."

He reminded her he was referring to her separation from her grandmother, with whom she had spent the first six years of her life.

She made big eyes of puzzlement. She had loved her grandmother, but as soon as she was old enough to understand, she had known of and wanted to live with her "real family." Trippity, trippity, tra-la-la-la-lee; Baby Goat getting over the bridge and still uneaten.

Don't be so happy, Little Goat. You're not all the way over the bridge. Your sex life, and a lot on attitudes which are nobody's business but your own, may still be the ogres waiting to chew you up. The Big Ogre was looking at her. He wanted to know why she had written she pitied her mother. She smiled. She was ready for that one. "My mother is so very fond of children and loves us all so, I've always felt she wanted a larger family. But," she added with a gentle sigh, "she has always had rather—delicate health."

He made a note on her dossier, and eyes on moving finger, was silent until the finger stopped. He now wanted to know why she had given such a "flippant answer to the serious question of: 'What do you think of Red probes?'" Her answer had been: "I would prefer blue, but in the U.S.A. Red is the sign for danger or heat."

She again made large puzzled eyes. "What else could I say about the handle of an electrician's tool? Or did you mean the probe used by a dentist or a surgeon?" No one must know she had first seen the two words in a newspaper caption on the morning of the day Bismarck had come to take her. She had wondered what the big letters said, and after a moment had been able to whisper the words: "RED PROBE REVEALS." She had gone on to the smaller type below, and there found her grandmother's name, Susan Elspeth Ramsey Minnardi. Angie saw her with the paper, and something in her face had told Susie she wasn't supposed to read it.

Mr. Weevil was shaking his head over her. "Surely in your current reading—*Time, Life*, and the daily papers, you must have read of Red probes—searches for Communists and Communist sympathizers?"

She shook her head. "That sounds like a slangy and disrespectful way of describing such a serious matter."

He was hunting another wrong attitude; no, only pretending; he had the question ready in that garbage can he called a brain. "Did it bother you when your mother changed her maiden name? And did you—as I suggested last time—learn why?"

She did the confidential bit of leaning forward and gazing at him. She managed a smile. "Mother thought it was funny and wondered where you'd found such an idea to exploit. I had a kindergarten teacher who must have been of Italian background; she misspelled my mother's maiden name. I guess it was the way I pronounced it—whatever the reason, she made it Minnardi instead of Maynard." She shrugged. "It was that way on my record for years but nobody noticed it."

She bowed her head, only partly to hide her smiles. "Thank

you, Queen of My Heaven, but don't you think such a miserable job deserves an E? That's flunk in this school—I'm unfamiliar with the marking system in heaven. If he had spent half as much time as he has ruined for me, searching Detroit papers around the date I supposedly left that 'interpersonal relationship' he could have learned. Pardon all the interruptions."

"You will, I suppose, never give up daydreaming. I have asked you twice to shake my hand."

He was standing, hand extended. The deal was over, over—except she didn't want to take his hand, or let him see the sweat-wet back of her skirt. "I hope all my abnormalities have given you a lot of material for your paper," she said.

"Abnormalities?" Empathy was thick as Uncle Jeff's eggnog. "You are one of the most normal, healthy-minded American teen-agers I have ever met. Considering all the factors that have made for your alienation, it is truly amazing. I may even use your reactions as a norm."

She downed a shiver, smothered an "Ugh" of disgust and said: "Oh, thank you, sir. Sometimes I think I am getting better. I remember your name now—Olen. You are definitely not Scandanavian; so tell me, before you changed it, was it something like Olenynokuff or Olyniawitzyski; or was there a witszerf on the end?"

His face said he would like to wring her neck, but his voice said only he would like to be rid of her in a hurry, while his words said: "Others are waiting so there is no time for personal questions. However, I can assure you I have my father's name."

She stifled an unladylike "Oh, yeah?" He had lied, her mother lied with the non-Italian name—and Susan Schnitzer had lied. It would be nice to ask the name of his paternal grandfather; a pity it was late and she weak and tired; cold because everything she wore was so sweat-wet, she listened for a dripping sound as she arose. She couldn't see his face too well for the black spots floating round and round. She stood a moment, careful to keep her back away from his glance; otherwise he might learn what all this perfect normalcy had cost in sweat—and blood, from the way her rib cage felt.

She managed to put on her "Oh-I-am-so-ignorant-but-sotrusting" little-girl look, as she gazed at the ceiling, and whispered in his direction: "Have you any idea where they keep theirs? Administration has to know what goes on in conferences, and also save the expense of transcribing notes. So, you know, this room is—." She moved her lips to form a "bugged."

He sent his glance over every part of the ceiling as he repeated "theirs?" in a shook up voice.

She went to the door with no fear of a look at her back from him. In the outer room a long-legged, greasy-haired, pimply-faced, general-course atom of humanity, chewing gum as he sprawled on the sweat-seat, was too busy dreading to do more than stare briefly at her face. A long blonde sat so that her knees held up her elbows; her elbows her hands; her hands her chin; and unaware of what she was doing to her make-up and her hairdo—a high pile now sliding toward her nose—she was tearing and chewing her fingernails as if working over a tough pizza.

She saw them well because she walked to the hall door with a sidewise backing, like a sick crab, she thought, in need of an osteologist. She had suddenly to struggle against wild, unseemly laughter; she had made A in biology last year, yet she called an osteologist for a sick crab. She was in the hall. That particular door was shut behind her—forever. The deal was over, over, over. She was normal, normal, a normal American girl, loving the right things, hating the right things. Climb to the top of the school clock tower, and make a splatter on the fake stones below.

She began a slow inching along the wall; several hard head-shakes changed the peacock tails back to black spots. She wasn't going into hysterical blindness before she could get off this bra; she remembered now the light above his desk had been bright, very bright.

The hall was empty. She dashed for an Exit door a few steps ahead. Past the door, she ran up a flight of stairs that ended near the home ec. wing. Practically empty most of the time, she would there find a wash room, closet, or preferably the model kitchen, where she could in privacy relieve herself of this mutilating bra. You couldn't blame the pain on the bra, but that transistor tape recorder under the holes she had cut into the front. She had planned to shop for a bigger bra, but all her time had gone to Ter. She'd lived through the pain; and this time she would know exactly what she had said. In those other sessions with the man last year she'd put the little tape recorder in her binder, but afraid to leave it on her desk, she had held it on her knees; reception had been so poor she never knew—.

Oh, yes, she did know now. She knew he hadn't learned any of her secrets. He hadn't learned.

She paused a moment at the head of the stairs. She'd had the feeling she was supposed to meet somebody or do something. She rushed on; it didn't matter; anything important she would have remembered. In spite of the pain it was good to move again and know that Susan Schnitzer still belonged to Susan Schnitzer.

A NOTE ABOUT THE AUTHOR

Harriette Simpson Arnow was born in Wayne County, Kentucky, and received her education at Berea College, and the University of Louisville. She taught for four years in public schools, but gave up teaching to devote more time to writing. She moved to Cincinnati, where in between working on short stories and her first novel she held odd jobs until her marriage in 1939. She and her husband bought a farm in the Cumberland National Forest, and for five years lived as writers and farmers. They moved to Detroit during the Second World War, and have since lived in Ann Arbor, Michigan.

Her first novel, *Mountain Path*, was published in 1936, and is still available in paperback. It is set in her native mountains, as is *Hunter's Horn*, which was published in 1949 with considerable success. Her third novel, *The Dollmaker*, published in 1954, became a bestseller. She has also done two works of social history, *Seedtime on the Cumberland* (1960), and *The Flowering of the Cumberland* (1963). Her books have received several awards, among them a prize from The Friends of American Writers for a novel published in 1954, and in 1961 an Award of Merit from the Association for State and Local Historians for a social history done in 1960.

A NOTE ON THE TYPE

The text of this book was set in Caledonia, a Linotype face designed by W. A. Dwiggins. It belongs to the family of printing types called "modern face" by printers— a term used to mark the change in style of type-letters that occurred about 1800. Caledonia borders on the general design of Scotch Modern, but is more freely drawn than that letter.

The book was composed, printed and bound by Kingsport Press, Inc., Kingsport, Tennessee. Typography and binding design by Anthea Lingeman.